# MISSION: TOMORROW

## BAEN BOOKS
## EDITED BY
## BRYAN THOMAS SCHMIDT

❊   ❊   ❊

*Mission: Tomorrow*

*Shattered Shields* (with Jennifer Brozek)

# MISSION: TOMORROW

### edited by
## Bryan Thomas Schmidt

MISSION TOMORROW

This is a work of fiction. All the characters and events portrayed in this book are fictional, and any resemblance to real people or incidents is purely coincidental.

Introduction © 2015 by Bryan Thomas Schmidt; "Tombaugh Station" © 2015 by Robin Wayne Bailey; "Excalibur" © 2015 by Cryptic, Inc.; "The Race For Arcadia" © 2015 by Alex Shvartsman; "A Walkabout Amongst The Stars" © 2015 by Lezli Robyn; "Sunrise On Mercury" © 1957, 1985 by Agberg Inc. First published in Science Fiction Stories, May 1957; "In Panic Town, On The Backward Moon" © 2015 by Michael F. Flynn; "The Ultimate Space Race" © 2015 by Jaleta Clegg; "Orpheus' Engines" © 2015 by Christopher McKitterick; "Around The NEO in 80 Days" © 2015 by Jay Werkheiser; "Iron Pegasus" © 2015 by Brenda Cooper; "Airtight" © 2015 by Michael Capobianco; "Windshear" © 2015 by Angus McIntyre; "On Edge" © 2015 by Sarah A. Hoyt; "Tartaros" © 2015 by Mike Resnick; "Malf" © 2015 by David D. Levine; "Ten Days Up" © 2015 by Curtis C. Chen; "The Rabbit Hole" © 2001 by James Gunn Originally published in Analog Science Fiction & Fact, December 2001; "Rare (Off) Earth Elements (A Sam Gunn Tale)" © 2015 by Ben Bova; "Tribute" © 2015 by Jack Skillingstead

A Baen Books Original

Baen Publishing Enterprises
P.O. Box 1403
Riverdale, NY 10471
www.baen.com

ISBN: 978-1-4767-8094-8

Cover art by Stephan Martiniere

First Baen printing November 2015

Distributed by Simon & Schuster
1230 Avenue of the Americas
New York, NY 10020

Library of Congress Cataloging-in-Publication Data

Mission : tomorrow / edited by Bryan Thomas Schmidt.
     pages cm
 Summary: "Science fiction writers imagine the future of space exploration with NASA no longer dominant. Will private companies rule the stars or will new governments take up the call? Nineteen stories of what-if spanning the gamut from Mercury to Pluto and beyond by such authors as Jack McDevitt, Robert Silverberg, Michael Flynn, Mike Resnick, Sarah Hoyt and more"-- Provided by publisher.
  ISBN 978-1-4767-8094-8 (paperback)
 1. Science fiction, American. 2. Outer space--Exploration--Fiction. I. Schmidt, Bryan Thomas, editor.
  PS648.S3M576 2015
  813'.0876208--dc23

                          2015030691

Printed in the United States of America

10  9  8  7  6  5  4  3  2  1

## DEDICATION

This anthology is dedicated to the men and women of NASA
who have gone before us into the great unknown,
from astronauts to mission control, many giving their lives
to realize a dream and make scientific advances
that have made our world a better place.
We salute your courage, dedication and sacrifice and thank you.
And also for Noah, Griffin, Garrett and Pierce,
who remind me constantly that imagining the future
is never a waste of time.

# TABLE OF CONTENTS

# MISSION: TOMORROW

# INTRODUCTION

## by Bryan Thomas Schmidt

*Well, I guess that you probably know*
*by now—I was one who wanted to fly.*
*I wanted to ride on that arrow of fire right up into heaven.*
*And I wanted to go for every man,*
*every child, every mother of children,*
*I wanted to carry the dreams of all people right up to the stars.*
—Flying For Me, John Denver

Those lyrics, written in tribute to the fallen astronauts of the Space Shuttle *Challenger* explosion in the mid-1980s, probably sum up a lot of my feelings about going to space. I wanted to go then. Even after the disasters, I still want to go now. It's one of my greatest dreams, and one that actually seems more and more possible every day given the increasing privatization of space flight.

And I wanted to go with NASA. See, I'm a huge NASA fan. It broke my heart when the public lost interest and funding was cut. Some predicted the death of NASA, but somehow they've carried on with plans for manned missions to Mars and more. And I'd give anything to go. Even if it meant I couldn't return. What about you?

Space travel, to me, is still the incredible dream it always was, and so the ideas for many of my science fiction stories have been born. This anthology was inspired by asking what will space travel look like in an age no longer dominated by NASA? With not only other governments taking increasing roles but also corporations and private citizens, how will that change things? What new ships, opportunities and mission goals might we see?

*Mission: Tomorrow* features eighteen stories by talented authors, many you may have heard of before, imagining such missions. Near future or not so near, all take place in and around our solar system. Some involve alien encounters, others involve missions gone wrong, and still others take place back on Earth itself. From Pluto to Mercury and even the Kuiper Belt, we cover a broad spectrum. Most of the stories are serious, but a couple are humorous, and I hope they'll all inspire you to dream, regardless.

What would it be like if you could go up there? What awaits us out there? Who wouldn't still like to find out? I know I would. So welcome aboard a journey that imagines the possibilities. I hope you enjoy *Mission: Tomorrow* as much as we enjoyed putting it together.

To infinity and beyond, as Buzz Lightyear might say. Three . . . Two . . . One . . . Blastoff!

Bryan Thomas Schmidt,
Editor
Ottawa, Kansas
September 2014

*Our journey begins at the far end of our solar system on Pluto, the past and future planet you might say, where astronauts start dying and their colleagues investigate the incidents around . . .*

# TOMBAUGH STATION

## by Robin Wayne Bailey

The smooth, nitrogen/methane surface of Kenyata Plain glittered under the headlights of James Dayton's ice sled as he raced alone across the solemn, frozen expanse with Tombaugh Station at his back. His thoughts weren't on the station, though. He fixed his gaze ahead. In the distance, the Burney Mountains loomed sharp as razors against a star-flecked sky, and at his nine o'clock, half of Charon arced above the horizon, perpetually unmoving, never climbing, tidally locked in its orbit with Pluto.

He tried not to look at those sights for too long. It was easy for a man to lose his mind out here. More than one had done so, and James Dayton did not want to flirt with madness. He jerked his attention back to the green and gold indicators on his console, checked his GPS coordinates, noted the temperature readouts of his environmental suit—all that kept him warm and alive. Yet, after a moment, he looked outward again.

*Like flying an aircraft back on Earth*, he thought. *Look at the horizon; look at the gauges; back and forth, always watchful, but never look too long at either.* He missed flying. It was the only thing about Earth he missed.

He seldom thought of Earth anymore. His home, such as it was, was here at Tombaugh Station. Nobody came to Pluto on a round-trip ticket. It was still strictly one-way. No matter—James Dayton had been the first to sign up.

The GPS indicator on his console chimed and flashed. He cursed himself for letting his thoughts wander and for sliding a half-kilometer off course. Even as he corrected, a voice spoke through his com-set. "Are you napping out there, James? I just got tracking back online here, and you're off your mark."

"You sound like air traffic control," Dayton shot back, recognizing Kate Beck on the other end of the com at Work Unit Three. "Always blame the pilot. It took you six seconds to notice the deviation *after* I corrected course. Pretty shitty ATC, if you ask me."

"I didn't," she responded. "I asked you to marry me once, but you declined. Since then, you're lucky I haven't run you over a crater, and don't think I haven't considered it." She paused. In a quieter, more serious voice, she asked, "Are you all right out there?"

He hesitated, unsure of how to answer. He *had* been off his game lately, distracted and unfocused. This wasn't a place that forgave you for losing your focus. "Are you all right in there?" he said, answering her question with a question.

"Sure, I'm just fine here alone in the dark." She poured on the sarcasm. Kate Beck always had a smart mouth. "Well, not really alone, I guess, but Doctor Atsuka doesn't look so good. He's kind of pale and not too conversational." She paused again, and then came back, serious once more. "I'm getting some of the other systems back online."

Back on course, Dayton twisted the throttle to increase his speed. "Are you showing any other sleds in the area?"

"Negative," she answered. "All the traffic is out at the Burney where it should be. Everybody's working."

Dayton thought to himself as he gazed toward the horizon again. Tadeo Atsuka, head of Data Analytics and Imaging, had been on duty at Work Unit Three. Now he was dead, the third death in three months. Death was an occupational hazard on Pluto, but usually among the newcomers. Among the Old-timers, the ones who had come down with *Tombaugh One*, accidents didn't happen.

The work unit looked like a metal shed—plain and windowless. In the field beyond it, a trio of ice movers stood, giant spidery machines that cut and sliced immense blocks of nitrogen/methane from the surface and transported them to the Burney site. They were powered down, and Dayton wondered why they were not in operation.

As he parked close to Kate Beck's sled, he unplugged his heating unit from his vehicle's battery pack and retracted the power umbilical. A lighted readout appeared briefly on the inside of his faceplate to inform him of the power shift. His environmental suit's internal batteries contained enough juice to keep him alive for two hours in minus three hundred eighty degrees, but he never relied just on his internal power longer than necessary. He was too careful for that.

His cleated boots bit into the crisp surface as he stepped down from the sled and crossed the short distance to the work unit's airlock. Stopping at a red panel mounted on the wall, he pressed it. After a moment, the outer door unsealed and opened, and he stepped inside a tubular chamber. When the outer door resealed, an inner door opened.

Kate Beck, enclosed in her own environmental suit, tablet computer in hand, looked around to greet him. The lighting was still very dim. "Keep your helmet on," she warned over the com-set. "I've repaired the heating systems and air generators, but they haven't been online long enough to reach optimum levels." She went back to work on her tablet. The way her fingers moved over it, she might have been stroking a pet.

The inside of Work Unit Three was a maze of quantum computers, communications and tracking equipment, 3-D printers, satellite monitors and imaging stations. Tadeo Atsuka still stood over one of the consoles, his hand on the back of a chair, his face turned toward the airlock as if to greet Dayton. Unfortunately, his suit was unzipped and he wore no helmet. He was frozen solid.

"It looks like a catastrophic power failure," Kate Beck reported. "All the power was down and the airlock wide open when I came to pick him up."

"That's not supposed to happen," Dayton answered, fighting a tide of emotion. Tadeo was an old friend from back in the Corporate shipyards on Deimos when *Tombaugh One* was being built. They had come out together. Dayton cursed the torrent of memories. Tadeo had baked cookies with his rations every Christmas long after Christmas ceased to have any meaning to the crew.

Dayton studied the smaller man's frozen face, the familiar smile still in place, dark eyes twinkling, full of tiny ice crystals. Tadeo hadn't even had time to look surprised.

"The systems are supposed to be redundant," Dayton muttered to himself.

Kate Beck heard him over the com-set and waved her tablet angrily. "You think I don't know that, Commander? "She only used his rank anymore when she got upset, and Beck didn't get upset easily. Beck was also an Old-timer, Dayton's executive officer on the journey out, and Tadeo had been her friend, too.

"Sorry, Kate," he said. "This one's got me. Got us both, I guess." He tried to lighten the mood with a feeble comment, tapping her suit where her name was printed. "Do you write that on your underwear, too?"

The glow of her tablet screen reflected an eerie effect on her features as she sighed and turned away. "I've given you every opportunity to find out, James."

Dayton remembered his heating unit and looked around for a working battery socket to plug into. He glanced for a moment at the power shift readout on his faceplate—*always careful!*—and then, trailing his thin umbilical, he began moving around the shed. Many of the consoles were still black, shut down by the sudden rush of cold. He looked at the computer nearest Tadeo's hand. "I wonder what he was working on."

"Same as all of us," Beck answered. "The Burney is scheduled to go online in seven days. He's been something of a mad scientist about it, working long shifts alone, checking and double-checking every detail." She hesitated, looking thoughtful. Then her voice cracked. "He joked to me once that it would see the face of God. I laughed, but then he repeated it. He said the Burney would do that."

Inside his suit, Dayton nodded to himself. Tadeo was obsessive. Men and women only came out to Pluto for three reasons. Either they were running from something, or they thought of themselves as pioneer-adventurers, or because sheer scientific curiosity drove them. Corporate did their best to weed out the runners. The adventurers usually weeded out themselves. Tadeo had been at the forefront of the last group.

He walked around Tadeo Atsuka again, and stared for a long moment into those frozen eyes. That look, he knew, would haunt him for nights to come. *It's almost as if he's seeing the face of God right now.* Dayton flinched from the thought. He wasn't a religious man at all.

Yet Tadeo was smiling, almost mocking him.

"Go back to the station," Dayton told Kate Beck. "Inform Corporate. Tell them that we've lost a giant."

Kate Beck powered off her tablet and pushed the device into a pocket on her thigh. Then she unplugged her suit and let the umbilical retract around her waist. At the airlock, she paused and looked back into the shed. Despite a handful of glowing monitors, the interior was still mostly dark. "Eighteen years," she said with strange wistfulness. "Now we've lost Robinson, Tucker, and Tadeo." She shook her head. "I don't get it, James. I just don't get it."

He couldn't see her face clearly, yet he sensed that she was crying. The Old-timers, those who came out on the first mission to establish Tombaugh Station, had always shared a tight bond. They knew they were special, a unique breed, and later, when *Tombaugh Two* and *Tombaugh Three* arrived nine years apart to expand the base, the newcomers knew it, too. To them, the Old-timers were heroes and legends.

"I seem to have run out of black humor," she continued, rambling. "Do you want me to take him back?"

"I'll take him," Dayton said.

He waited until Kate was gone and the airlock resealed. Then he pulled up a chair from one of the consoles and sat down to grieve and to share a few last moments with an old friend. Thanks to Kate, all the power systems slowly came back to life. He tapped the side of his helmet, activating his faceplate readouts, and noted the climbing temperatures and elevating air concentrations inside the shed. They were almost normal. Still, he kept his suit on and plugged in. *Always careful.*

After a time, he got up, rummaged around and found a stack of thermal blankets in a storage locker. He wrapped Tadeo carefully and secured the wrappings as best he could with the power umbilical from Tadeo's environmental suit. As he did so, the quantum computers flashed back online, and various monitors around the shed began to shine with images of deep-space objects. Dayton recognized Andromeda on one of the screens and, on another, the very peculiar galaxy called Centaurus A. On still another, a dark red cluster of nebulae unfamiliar to Dayton—maybe something entirely new.

Dayton unplugged his suit and retracted his umbilical. Then, after padding the storage compartment of his sled with more blankets, he carried his old friend outside and laid him gently down. In Pluto's weak gravity, the doctor weighed very little. "Last roundup, Cookie," Dayton murmured. The Old-timers, especially Tadeo, were all fond of cowboy metaphors.

With Tadeo carefully cradled, Dayton straightened and glanced to his nine o'clock. The dark horizon coruscated with light—intense green and red, gold and stark silver scattering strangely on Pluto's tenuous summer atmosphere. It looked like a crazy aurora borealis, but with no magnetic field on Pluto, he knew it was no such thing. It was only the work crews firing the polishing lasers, putting the last smoothing touches on the Burney's gigantic ice mirror. He smiled to himself, although it was a painful smile. "Would you like to take a look?" he said to Tadeo. Then he nodded and forced a smile. "I knew you would."

Plugging his suit into the sled's battery pack, he turned on his running lights, twisted the throttle and headed toward the glow, which got brighter and more dramatic as he approached. The outlines of leviathan ice movers rose up as if to block his path, seeming alien on their eight mechanical legs, control cabins gleaming like eyes. He drove his sled with greater care now, watching his GPS, to avoid the ice pits from which the diggers had gouged great chunks.

Still, he found it hard not to let his mind wander. Tadeo dead. And Robinson before him, a suicide, just tired of it all. Then Tucker, crushed at the work site under massive ice when a mover suddenly lost power and dropped its load. All Old-timers and all friends—gone. He had lost people before, but these deaths hurt.

At the top of a shallow summit, James Dayton stopped and turned off his running lights. Once before, he had parked on this same spot with Tadeo as they searched together for the right place to erect the Burney. Now, it made the perfect observation point to watch the construction. Dayton thought of himself as a hard and jaded man, but what he saw when he looked down upon the work site took his breath away every time.

The Venetia Burney Deep Space Cassegrain Telescope, named after the eleven-year-old child who had given Pluto its name in 1931, soared upward from the heart of Kenyata Plain, its immense disc five miles in diameter, made entirely from methane and nitrogen ice. It loomed upward, dominating the planetscape, all of its beams and girders, gears and motors, and nuts and bolts 3-D printed on the site from Pluto's own materials.

The light show was the result of lasers smoothing the gigantic ice mirrors to micro-meter precision as they fused layer after layer of synthetic mercury, capable of withstanding temperatures as low as minus five hundred degrees, to the ice. Then the mirrors would be finished.

James Dayton knew that he stood in the shadow of Mankind's greatest achievement. Compared to the Burney, everything else, including Tombaugh Station, felt small.

The lasers lit up the night with mesmerizing fire. Dayton watched until his eyes ached, then he jerked his attention to other details. The ice movers stood in stark silhouettes, and the vehicles and men at work around the site seemed like ants and less than ants.

Yet, those men were giants, too, for they had crossed the three point fifty-seven billion miles and given their lives to establish Tombaugh Station and build the Burney.

"I wish you could see this again, Tadeo," Dayton said. He remembered the images that had popped up on the monitors back at Work Unit Three, especially the unfamiliar cluster of nebulae, and wondered what the Burney would eventually see when it went online.

A voice over his com-set interrupted his reverie. "Commander Dayton, Tombaugh Station," the voice said. "Please say your location. We're not getting a tracking reading from your sled. You've been out a long time, and we're a bit concerned."

Dayton frowned. He toggled a switch on his sled's dashboard with no result. His GPS was dead. "I'm ninety-three degrees from Tombaugh Station, one hundred and sixty-three miles out overlooking Site Zero," he answered. "Heading back now, and don't worry. I know my way home." He gazed toward the Burney one more time, drinking in the wonder of it, and on some level secret even from himself, he felt an immense pride.

"I wish you could see it, Tadeo," he repeated, looking into the back of the sled at the wrapped body. He thought again of Tadeo's eyes full of ice crystals or full of *something*. What was it about his eyes? Inside his helmet, Dayton shook his head to clear it, causing the readouts on his faceplate to flicker. He told himself again that Tadeo's eyes would haunt him.

He let go a deep sigh as he started the sled and turned away from the crazy light show and the Burney Telescope. Maybe it was all finally getting to him. Maybe it was time to have a talk with Corporate about stepping aside and turning over command to one of the younger commanders. After all, three ships had made the journey to the Ninth Planet. Like as not, as Pluto on its orbital course moved farther away from Earth, there wouldn't be a fourth ship for more than two hundred years.

His headlights and running lights shimmered on the cold ground as he glided back toward Tombaugh Station. Taking his time, mindful of Tadeo's comfort, he navigated by the mountain peaks and crater rims, lit by Charon permanently on the horizon and by the splendid bands of stars above. He looked toward Sol, a small point of pale white light straight ahead currently at altitude thirty degrees.

He didn't miss Earth with all its fractious governments perpetually at each other's throats with their forever wars and endless politics and every dollar gone for weapons. They could never have given Mankind the stars. Governments lacked vision, and their only ambition was to maintain power. He was glad to be free of it, glad to live for a future even if it meant living in a tin can or in an environmental suit. If the Burney Telescope had been Tadeo's vision, Tombaugh Station had been his. More than any place had ever been, here was home.

Something moved suddenly across his headlight beams. Dayton jerked back on the throttle and hit the brakes. The ice sled skidded and nearly pitched over on its side before righting itself. Dayton opened the door and got halfway out, uncertain as he glared upward at the monstrous black tarantula that blocked his path. Its eight ponderous legs moved it as it came toward him, gigantic rotating saw blades dropping from its underbelly.

Dayton dove back into his ice sled. Fish-tailing over the ice, he steered away from the monster machine. In the distance, he saw the silhouette of Work Unit Three. Only two of the ice movers remained parked beside it. He knew damned well where the third one was.

What he didn't know was who controlled it or why.

As he flew toward the shed, he touched his com-set. "Mayday, mayday! Tombaugh Station! Commander James Dayton! Come in!" No response. He repeated his emergency hail. Nothing. He glanced at his dashboard and toggled the communications switch only to see its indicator light fade and die. *Just like his tracking system!*

The large ice movers were capable of considerable speed, and his pursuer handled the big machine like an expert. Dayton abandoned any thought of sheltering at the work unit. He shot past it instead. The ice mover shot *through* it, leaving the shed in wreckage.

A cold chill ran down Dayton's neck. Only it was not a chill of fear. He felt *cold!* He double-checked his suit's umbilical, making sure he had plugged it securely into the sled's battery pack. The connection was snug. Yet, he was getting no heat!

"Bastard!" he muttered. "You've hacked my controls!"

He detached the umbilical, and his suit's internal batteries immediately kicked in. He had warmth for two hours. He didn't expect the mover to give him that long. He jerked hard on the ice sled's yoke, spinning in a complete three-sixty until his sled pointed back at the big spider.

In the back, Tadeo thumped against the side of the compartment, and the covering over his head dislodged. Dayton dared to glance backward long enough to meet Tadeo's frozen gaze. *What is wrong with his eyes?*

He twisted the throttle hard again. The ice sled shot forward, straight for the mover. The machines were fast, but slow to turn. One of the great legs stomped the ground right next to him—a near miss! The cutting blades whirred silently over his head as he raced between the legs. A fool's play, but one that paid off!

Still, he was in a bad spot. Tombaugh Station was too far away in one direction and the Burney site too far away in another. If he headed toward either, the mover would overtake him, and he was out of tricks.

He did have a little breathing room, though, and he took advantage of it. Leaning over the yoke, he shot toward the ruin that had been Work Unit Three. Farther back, the mover charged after him. Dayton flung himself out of the sled and ran for one of the remaining ice movers. The cleats on his boots slowed him down, but still he pushed himself and slammed his suited fist against a flat red control panel on one of the mover's front legs.

A lift rig dropped from the mover's belly. *Too slow,* Dayton thought on the edge of panic. *Too slow!* Before the rig even touched the ground, Dayton jumped upward, caught the rig's thin rail and scrambled aboard. He slammed another control on the rig, and the lift reversed itself, climbing upward, as the attacker closed in.

A dark interior awaited him. The ice mover sat completely powered down. Groping, he found the pilot's seat and began stabbing controls. Indicator lights flashed on. At least the batteries weren't dead. Dayton plugged his suit into the console unit, an unbreakable habit, and then leaned over the guidance computer. He typed in a short command, and his mover lurched forward only to stumble as a grinding vibration shivered through the cockpit.

Warning lights pulsed across all his screens. Dayton typed another short command. Outside views, fore and aft, popped up on a pair of monitors. The enemy mover struck him. One of its cutting blades came down, scarring his machine's hindmost right leg, and his mover shivered again. Unable to turn quickly enough and confront his attacker head on, Dayton reversed his mover and slammed straight backward into his attacker. The impact knocked him out of his seat, but it caught his attacker completely off-guard. The enemy machine stumbled.

Resuming his seat, Dayton typed commands and sped forward, gaining what distance he could. In his monitors, he watched sparks ignite from its injured limb and knew that it could crumple at any time. Still, he lurched forward, pulling every bit of power his machine had to give. At least he had a functioning GPS again. He switched on its small tracking screen.

The Left Eye of Hades, one of the deepest craters on Pluto, marked the southern boundary of Kenyata Plain. At best speed, Dayton headed for it. His aft monitor revealed his pursuer, all menace, eight legs churning and cutting blades poised for destruction.

The smooth Kenyata Plain turned rocky with impact debris as he neared the crater. His onboard computer, automatically alert for treacherous terrain that could endanger the craft, abruptly overrode his commands and decreased his speed. Dayton cursed. Although he had handled an ice mover before, he was no expert. He turned his machine clumsily and readied his own cutting blades. For a moment, he thought of calling Tombaugh Station for help, but there wasn't time and help would never reach him.

The enemy mover slammed into him headfirst. His machine shuddered, and again warning lights danced across his console. His attacker backed up a step and then lunged forward again, but this time, Dayton anticipated the attack and maneuvered to side-step. His mover shook, and sparks erupted from the front left leg, but this time he struck back, ramming directly into the side of his attacker and sawing through his enemy's mid-ship left leg.

Both machines damaged, they squared off. Like two fighters sizing each other up, they circled each other, feinted and backed away. Then, an indicator light faded on Dayton's console, and his heating unit went out.

Dayton raged. "Computer, shut down!" he ordered out loud as he pounded the command into the keyboard. Whoever was trying to kill him was good, but he wasn't going to get hacked again. He didn't know how they were doing that! He pushed the keyboard back into the console and, at the touch of a button, manual controls sprang up from the arms of his chair. Clenching his teeth, he gripped the padded levers and brought up the outside cameras again.

His foe was neither fore nor aft. He cursed, shouting, as the enemy mover broadsided him. He felt, rather than heard, the whine of the saw blades against his fuselage. His onboard computer flared to life again and tried to wrest control from what it assumed was an incompetent pilot, causing Dayton to fight two battles, against his opponent's machine and his own. On the edge of angry panic, he twisted his right control forward and jerked his left control back simultaneously.

The grind of metal shivered through his mover as he slammed against the other machine. He ignored it and pushed both controls forward. In his fore camera, he saw the other mover now, and he saw the Eye of Hades right behind it. With all the power left in his machine, he shoved his attacker over the crater's edge. Its eight legs scrambled for purchase on the broken ice, and then it fell.

For a long time, Dayton sat trembling and sweating in his environmental suit. Then, one by one, he turned his mover's systems on again, made sure he had heat once more, and trudged back toward the remains of Work Unit Three to his sled and Tadeo's body.

After a time, he picked up the mover's com-set. "Tombaugh Station, Dayton here." The com-set crackled. "Never mind where I am," Dayton snapped. "I'm on my way home. Ask Doctor Kenyata and Executive Officer Kate Beck to meet me in medical as soon as I get back."

Elise Kenyata, a small black woman whose hair had gone iron gray since her days on the first voyage outward, regarded Dayton with a grim expression. She had been a geo-planetologist of great fame once, but now she was a medical officer. *Everything changes*, Dayton thought as he waited for her response to his questions.

They stood together in a morgue room that had been turned into a freezer locker and a laboratory. "What you want has never been tried before," she lectured him. She looked toward Tadeo Atsuka's body on an autopsy table. "Nor do I believe Tadeo ever considered this application for his technology." She adjusted a large optical instrument above the examining table and swung a heavy metal arm down to position it directly above Tadeo's face. "Still, he was a genius in the field of imaging, and for dear Tadeo's sake, I've done my best." She patted Tadeo's rigid hand with obvious affection, and then turned on a computer next to the table. "It may take some minutes."

Amid a semicircular array of quantum computers, they watched the screens together. "From the moment I looked into his eyes at the work station, I felt something was weird. His eyes were strange, reflective. I felt I could see something in them if I just looked hard enough." He wiped a hand over his face as he tried to explain himself. "Of course, I could just be going crazy and wasting your time."

"You never waste my time, dear," Elise Kenyata answered. "If your theory is correct, he may have frozen so instantaneously that his retinas or the rods and cones in his eyes may retain some fragment of the last image he ever saw." She shook her head and rubbed her chin at the same time. "This technology that he created to look outward and show us the stars might also look inward and show us that image. I've tinkered and adapted his programs a little, but it would be revolutionary—although naturally the applications would be limited."

Dayton didn't respond. He watched the screens and waited. Something slowly began to take shape on the primary monitor. A few moments later, the computers began to enhance that shape with contrasts and saturations, adding definitions. Each new digital layer enhanced the previous image, and after an hour, something indistinct became sharp and clear.

Kate Beck, her hand on the airlock panel, her name printed on her environmental suit, looked directly back at them from the screens, just as she had looked at Tadeo in his final moment of life.

Kenyata gasped. Dayton felt no surprise, only a keen and stabbing regret.

"Why would she do it?" Kenyata whispered. "Why?"

Dayton hugged the doctor, another Old-timer and longtime friend, and he thought of Robinson, who was Tadeo's protégé, and Tucker, who had headed the construction of the Burney, all of them friends and all of them important to the telescope's completion. He thought of Kate Beck, too, almost a lover once, who had sent a single short message to his private com-box in the moments before her death at the crater.

*I'm sorry, James. The Burney is too powerful. Tadeo said it would see the face of God. No one should ever look at the face of God, James. No one.*

He kissed Kenyata on the top of her head and said his final goodbye to Tadeo Atsuka. It would be hard to pick up the pieces of his daily routine, but the Burney would be online in a few days, and things would settle down.

He thought about that and laughed privately.

Except for the atmosphere in winter, nothing ever settled down on Pluto. It was easy for a man or woman to lose their mind out here. More than one had done so.

((•((•(( ☉ )•))•))

**Robin Wayne Bailey** is the author of numerous novels, including the bestselling Dragonkin series, the Frost saga, *Shadowdance,* and the Fritz Leiber-inspired *Swords Against The Shadowland.* He's written over one hundred short stories, many of which are included in his two collections, *Turn Left To Tomorrow* and *The Fantastikon: Tales Of Wonder.* He is a former president of the Science Fiction and Fantasy Writers of America and was a 2008 Nebula Award nominee. He lives in Kansas City, Missouri.

*Of course, space travel isn't all about adventure or science. Like everything else, it's also heavily laden with politics. Here Jack McDevitt has a reporter investigating a curious past dialogue when he uncovers a secret no one wants discovered, the secret of . . .*

# EXCALIBUR

## Jack McDevitt

The Snowden revelations had been out for several years, dumping one major story after another into the news cycle. But the bombshell didn't show up until Gordon Kerr, who was working on his seventh book, a history of the space agency, noticed that one relatively insignificant report showed a conversation in which someone at NASA commented that "Bancroft says it's a go. Get it moving." Bancroft at the time was one of NASA's senior operational directors. The intercept was dated August 28, 1989. Gordon had been surprised to discover that the NSA was scooping up communications of government agencies. But he would have thought no more of this one except that the date rang a bell. He needed a minute to put it together: *Voyager 2* was passing Neptune and leaving the solar system.

Bancroft, unfortunately, had died two years earlier.

"Did it have anything to do with *Voyager*?" he asked Tom Morrison, his long-time friend and the director at the Jet Propulsion Lab.

"How would I know?" asked Morrison. "What difference does it make? It's almost twenty years ago." Morrison was a tall, take-charge guy who was usually easygoing. Gordon had known him since his days as a cub reporter for the *Pasadena Star-News*. At that time, Morrison had been a NASA radio operator. They'd met at a party, where Gordon had arranged an interview, and written a story for the *Star-News*. It had been his first by-line.

Morrison seemed annoyed by the question. But he immediately relaxed, smiled, and sank back into his desk chair.

"So there's nothing?" Gordon asked.

"No." Morrison was laughing now.

Gordon trusted him, but he was after all a government guy. Sometimes stuff got classified. He'd learned from the Snowden releases that sometimes they weren't even allowed to admit which material had been classified. "Did the Russians get there first?" he asked, intending it as a joke.

Morrison's dark brown eyes clouded. "You're kidding, Gordy, right? Disney would get there before the Russians."

"Well, Tom, to tell the truth, we've been pretty much going backward ourselves. I haven't checked recently, but aren't they still taking us to the space station?"

Tom's office was decorated with pictures of Morrison's wife Janet and his three kids, and framed photos of him with senators, the governor, the vice president, and one depicting a very young Morrison talking with Richard Feynman. He took a deep breath. "I know. Not much you can do when the money's not there. We're probably lucky we can keep the lights on."

The conversation dissolved into one they'd had numerous times before, how funding was being poured into armaments and the Middle East while the space agency stumbled along. It was only after he'd ridden down in the elevator and was headed across the parking lot that Gordon realized his old buddy had neatly steered the conversation away from the NSA intercepts.

Gordon wasn't sure why he'd agreed to work on the project. NASA needed all the publicity it could get during those despondent days, and he owed Morrison a lot of favors. The director had pointed him to solid stories over the years. And his career had soared as a result. He'd won the Bancroft Prize and the Ralph Waldo Emerson Award for his observations on the state of the culture. Without his help, Gordon might not have had a career at all. Maybe he'd still be the sole reporter for *The Holton Tablet*, the small-town weekly he'd started with.

But he was looking at a story that did not have a happy ending. He didn't even like his working title—*NASA: Eye on the Stars*. The agency had been stopped dead in its tracks. The voters had long since given up on it. When NASA had reached a point that we couldn't even get to the space station without help, it had simply been too much.

Gordon knew a lot of people at JPL. He liked them, and they were of course rooting for him to pull something off with the book. Something that would direct popular attention to the importance of the space agency. But that wasn't going to happen. He knew it, and they knew it.

There'd been an odd tone in Morrison's response. Moreover, he hadn't asked anything about the context of the intercept. He hadn't even asked who'd been speaking. It had been Bancroft's operational assistant.

Molly, Gordon's wife, thought he was frustrated about the lack of progress he was making on the book. "Just back away from it," she said, as he came in the door and dropped onto the sofa. "Nobody over there is going to hold it against you. They know you've done your best with it, and that it's dead. We can't repair roads and bridges, and there's no money for public schools. How could they possibly justify billions for space travel? Anyhow, Gordie, if you want the truth, even if they provided some funding, where would we go?"

Certainly, he thought, nowhere if we don't try.

Gordon specialized on the human side of space travel. He didn't get involved much with the rockets. Rather, he portrayed the radio operator waiting for a vehicle to renew contact when it came out from behind the Moon. Or the astronaut sitting atop a launch vehicle in the scariest moments of a mission, those immediately preceding liftoff. His readers would know how it felt to be a manager when there was a hitch in the countdown, caused perhaps by a warning from one of the calibrators. He wondered what it had been like when the *Challenger* exploded, or when Gus Grissom, Edward White, and Roger Chaffee had died during a launch sequence rehearsal.

There were powerful stories to tell. But he needed a conclusion, not a dead end. He wondered how Jack Kennedy would have reacted had he known what was coming.

That evening, Gordon settled back in to work on the book. His deadline was only three months away, and he was running behind. But it was hard to get his mind away from the NSA intercept, Bancroft, and *Voyager*'s Neptune passage.

It was ridiculous. There could be no connection. The truth was he was *hoping* for something that would open a door. Not a way to do serious journalism. Still, it stayed with him, and he found himself hunting through the vast collection of archival material that NASA had provided as background for *Eye on the Stars*.

And something else *did* turn up. In 1993, NASA had launched *Arkon 1* on a twelve-year voyage to explore the Kuiper Belt. It was curious because even short-range missions were complicated and inevitably involved decades-long planning. But the archives showed no indication of anyone even mentioning such a mission before September 1989, a few weeks after *Voyager 2*'s approach to Neptune. Moreover, on its way to the Kuiper Belt, *Arkon* would receive boosts from the Sun, Earth, and Neptune.

The planning routinely involved scientists outside NASA who had requested help with specific projects. In this case, three physicists had been part of the consultations. But the records indicated little in the way of preparatory discussions.

Of the three, only Maria Delmar, at Cal Tech, was still alive. She'd retired, but remained in the Pasadena area. Her Web site indicated she was working on a book about the Kuiper Belt. She was precisely the person Gordon wanted to talk with.

He set up an appointment, and connected with her on Skype. Maria was in her sixties, but she looked considerably younger than he'd expected. Brown hair speckled with gray, cut short. Animated green eyes. And an expression that suggested she'd welcome talking about the *Arkon* mission.

"It was perfect timing," she said, allowing a touch of frustration to creep into her eyes. "We were just in the process of discovering the Kuiper Belt when they called."

"*They* being NASA?"

"Yes. They'd included me in some of their earlier missions. Anyway, they explained they wanted to go out past Neptune and do some exploring. Try to get a feel for what the Kuiper Belt was about. And did I want to become part of the operation."

"And you did?"

"Sure."

"So what happened?"

"They asked me to make recommendations, and to set up some

specifics as to what we should be looking for. They really didn't seem to have much of a handle on things. But considering we hadn't even known for certain there *was* a Kuiper Belt a year earlier, it wasn't exactly a shock."

"And what did you ask for?" said Gordon.

She laughed. "I can send you a copy if you like. Basically, we were trying to establish that it really existed. The reason for the apparent emptiness of the outer solar system had never been clear. Once you get beyond Jupiter, there didn't seem to be much in the way of asteroids or comets. We weren't sure why. Maybe the gas giants simply swept the area clean. Or maybe it was a factor of sheer distance that we just couldn't make out small objects that far away. Then, as the technology got better, we began to get indications that there *were* objects out there. A lot of them, and mostly beyond Neptune. What we wanted from *Arkon* was simply discovery. Go tell us what's there."

"Were you satisfied with the results?"

"Oh, yes." She lit up. "*Arkon 1* was a complete success. We had to wait eleven years for it to reach the area, but it was worth it. We found out there were tens of thousands of large objects in orbit beyond Neptune. The ones we had a chance to see were, for the most part, not the rocky asteroids of the inner solar system, but were instead composed primarily of ice."

"How big is *large*?"

"Diameters of sixty miles or more."

"Maria, was there anything unusual about the operation? Anything different?"

"Not that I'm aware of." She looked thoughtful. "Other than the windup."

"How do you mean?"

"Well, usually, when they ran a mission like that, we were invited to JPL at the end. There'd be presentations, conferences, and generally a chance for all of us to get together and compare notes. They did a presentation with *Arkon 1*, took us to lunch, and that was about it. It almost seemed as if, as far as NASA was concerned, the mission hadn't really been consequential. But I can understand that. To them, the Kuiper Belt was just a ring of ice."

Gordon put it aside as a waste of time and went back to writing his history. His intention was to demonstrate what the nation had lost when the government had diverted funding as the national debt soared during the early years of the twenty-first century. And he probably would never have gone back to the Bancroft issue had he not come across another coincidence.

NERVA, which was to have designed a nuclear reactor that would power space travel, was abandoned in 1972 because of a combination of funding issues and concern about nuclear reactors in orbit. NASA tried to resurrect the idea in 2003 with the Prometheus Project. Gordon checked the *Arkon 1* schedule: That would have been about the same time that the vehicle was getting its final boost from Neptune.

They put everything they had into it for two years, before the project was defunded in 2005.

"Something was going on," he told Molly.

"Why? Because Neptune was always involved? It's a coincidence."

Gordon had spent time with a substantial number of astronauts over the years. He'd had some over for dinner. Had played bridge with others. And even vacationed with Cal Bennett and his wife. He'd specialized in writing human interest stories about the NASA experience, and the smartest thing he could do was get close to the people who rode the rockets.

One of them—he didn't recall which—had commented that NASA was looking for volunteers to train for a long-range flight. That had been at about the same time that Prometheus was going forward. But he'd gotten nothing more on it. And when he'd asked, everybody just shrugged. Never heard of it.

Cal had been at the Cape when the Prometheus Project was launched, the all-out effort to create a nuclear reactor to power a space vehicle. He was a Navy commander, recently retired, now living in Glendale.

Gordon called him. "Be passing through your area tomorrow," he said, making it clear he would be traveling without Molly. "I was wondering if I could treat for lunch?"

They met at the Cheesecake Factory, exchanged greetings, ordered their meals, and talked about politics for a while. Cal was tall and lean. He still looked as if he was on the happy side of forty. "How the hell do you do it?" Gordon asked.

The commander grinned. "You have to get enough chocolate," he said.

"Yeah," Gordon said. "I know the formula." For him, weight was a constant battle. "What are you hearing from NASA these days?"

"Not a lot. I don't think there's much going on." He looked frustrated. "We were supposed to be on Mars by now."

"When I was a kid," Gordon said, "we thought we'd have been on our way to Alpha Centauri by the end of the century."

"You watch too many movies."

"I guess." The food came, a turkey sandwich for Gordon, pizza for Cal, iced tea for both. "You know," Gordon continued, "I got my hopes up when they restarted the reactor research."

"That was a long time ago, pal." Cal shrugged. "I hate to say this, but I don't think we're going anywhere. Not now, or *ever*."

"I hope you're wrong." Gordon bit into his sandwich.

"You know, I let myself get optimistic when they started Prometheus. But in the end it was the same problem: The government talked, gave us assurances, and then decided they had no money."

Gordon nodded. "I even heard they started a program to train astronauts for long-range flights."

Cal laughed. Or maybe it was more of a sneer. "Excalibur," he said.

"Is that what they called it? Excalibur?"

Cal needed a minute. Maybe to finish chewing. Maybe to decide what he wanted to say. "Yeah. They were running it at the same time as Prometheus. It was classified at the time. But I can't believe it matters now. Not after all these years. They were talking about a manned flight to Mars."

"Why would they have wanted to keep it quiet?"

"They said it was because they didn't want to get into another space-race competition with the Chinese." He looked around to be sure no one was listening. "That made no sense, of course. They knew in the end they weren't going anywhere, so they just didn't want to call attention to it."

"You think that's why they resurrected the nuclear program? For Mars?"

"Sure," he said. "It was the old dream. One last try—" He took a deep breath, and bit off another piece of pizza.

❧ ❧ ❧

Gordon could find no record of an Excalibur Project in the archives. "What," he asked Morrison, "is going on? What was NASA hiding?"

Morrison grunted and rolled his eyes. "Excalibur was a project that went nowhere. Lack of funding, right? The usual reason. We didn't keep a record of it because it never got past the talking stage. Come on, Gordon, do you really have time to waste on this nonsense?"

"NASA was starting to think seriously about a Mars mission?"

"The White House was interested, Gordon. In fact, I think it was the president's idea."

"But we'd been hit on 9/11 and then got involved in Iraq and Afghanistan."

"Right. And that was the end of it."

"Why did you—did NASA—rush the project?"

"Excalibur? We didn't rush anything—"

"No. *Arkon 1*. Usually a major deep space launch needs at least ten years of preparation. This one got four."

"How do you know?"

"The first time it's mentioned is just after *Voyager 2* passes Neptune. Before that, there's nothing."

"For God's sake, Gordon." Morrison was seated behind his desk. The Feynman photo hung just behind him. The director had just gotten started at JPL. He'd told the story numerous times of the great physicist's visit, and how Morrison desperately wanted the photo but was embarrassed to ask until he realized that he might not get another chance. So he accepted the embarrassment to get the picture. *Do the right thing, regardless of consequences.* His maxim was displayed later on management awards he'd signed off on. "What are you trying to say? That we saw Martians out there? Even if we had, why would we keep it secret?"

"I don't know, Tom. I have no idea. But all my instincts are telling me this is not a series of coincidences."

"Well." He checked his watch. "I hate to cut this short but I have to get to a meeting."

"Since there's nothing to this, I assume you won't mind if I put together a story?"

He shrugged. "Do what you want. Before you go any further, though, I hope you can come up with a reasonable theory as to why we'd keep quiet about all this." He laughed again. "Gordon, you're going to ruin your reputation."

"Maybe. But I just can't pass on this, Tom. I won't suggest an explanation, but some people might conclude that there's a fleet of alien warships gathering out there. *Voyager 2* only got a glimpse and nobody was sure. That's why they launched *Arkon*, right? To find out what was going on."

"Nobody's going to buy that kind of story."

It was a bluff, of course. Gordon's editor would never print it. But Morrison couldn't know that. In any case, Gordon had a blog. He could post it on that. "Maybe not." He got up. "Somebody might have a better idea what was going on at the time, though. Anyhow, you can look for it in the Sunday *Star-News.*" He started toward the door.

As he reached for the knob, a chair squeaked behind him. "Wait a minute, Gordon."

He stopped. Turned.

Morrison came around and stood in front of his desk. "We've been friends a long time. More than twenty-five years. Can I ask you to forget this whole thing? For me? For the good of the country? I'll find a way to repay you."

Gordon simply stared back.

"I wouldn't ask if it weren't important."

"Are there really invaders out there?"

"No," he said. "Will you forget this?"

"I'm sorry, Tom. I'm a journalist. And this feels like the story of a lifetime."

"There's nothing I can do to persuade you?"

"You can tell me what it's about."

"I can't do that."

"Then I've no choice." He opened the door and paused.

"Close it."

In the outer office Morrison's secretary was watching him. He pulled the door shut.

"I'll tell you if you promise it goes no further."

Gordon shook his head. "I can't back off. But you know I won't reveal my source."

"You won't have to. There's no way management won't know where this came from."

"I'll hand it off to somebody else."

"Gordon, this is a matter of national security."

"Tell me what it's about and then, if I can see that revealing it would constitute a threat, I'll bury it."

Morrison pointed at the chair Gordon had been using.

He sat back down. Morrison stood quietly for a moment. "You're right," he said. "The *Voyager did* pick up something." He chewed on his lip. "It looked as if there was a metal object with a smooth surface in orbit around Triton. We couldn't get a good look, which is why we had the rush operation for *Arkon*."

"One of the moons?"

"Yes."

"So the Kuiper Belt mission was a cover?"

"Yes."

"And it confirmed the sighting."

"It did. There's something out there, an artificial object. A big one. The size of a space station."

"Did *Arkon* pick up an electronic signature of any kind?"

"If you're asking whether the object has power, the answer is *yes*. No lights or anything like that, but it's got functioning electronics on board."

"Holy cats."

"Yes."

"I'd think we would *kill* to get a look at the technology."

"Of course. That's why we started Prometheus. We needed a way to get out there that wouldn't take ten years."

"And they didn't want China or somebody turning it into a race."

"Exactly. Which is why it's essential that you say nothing."

"But we found out about this thing—what?—fifteen, sixteen years ago, and we still haven't done anything. Do you by any chance have a secret mission en route as we speak?"

"No."

"So when—?"

"I don't know, Gordon. We don't have the funding." He closed his eyes and took his head in his hands. "They were talking about it last month, but they went back into Iraq instead." He was staring at Gordon again. "So what are you going to do?"

"You're saying that we can't put together a Neptune mission because we have to go back into Iraq. Do I have that right?"

"Yes. So what are you going to do?"

"The story will be in *tomorrow's* paper."

"You know it'll ruin me, Gordon—."

"I'm sorry, Tom. It'll be a rough ride for a time. But we'll give you whatever support we can. Nobody wants to go back into the Middle East. This should be all we'll need. Just keep your head down and you'll come out the other end a national hero."

"You sure you're doing the right thing?" asked Molly.

"Absolutely."

"So what do you think is out there?"

"Nobody knows. But it's time we found out."

((·((·(( ◎ ))·))·))

**Jack McDevitt** has been described by Stephen King as "The logical heir to Isaac Asimov and Arthur C. Clarke." He is the author of twenty-one novels, twelve of which have been Nebula finalists. His novel *Seeker* won the award in 2007. In 2003, *Omega* received the John W. Campbell Memorial Award for best science fiction novel. McDevitt's most recent books are the Priscilla Hutchins origin adventure *Starhawk,* and *Coming Home,* an Alex Benedict mystery, both from Ace.

A Philadelphia native, McDevitt had a varied career before becoming a writer. He's been a naval officer, an English teacher, a customs officer, and a taxi driver. He has also conducted leadership seminars for the U.S. Customs Service. He is married to the former Maureen McAdams, and resides in Brunswick, Georgia, where he keeps a weather eye on hurricanes.

*What would the space race be without the Russians, our age-old nemesis? In truth, the loss of funding for NASA has found us relying on them in ways we once never imagined. In this next story, Soviet-born Alex Shvartsman imagines his fellow countrymen's efforts to send the first man to reach a new Earth-like target in . . .*

# THE RACE FOR ARCADIA

## by Alex Shvartsman

"There's nothing new under the sun," said Anatoly, his voice carried via skip broadcast across millions of kilometers of space from the command center at Baikonur.

Aboard the *Yuri Gagarin*, Nikolai concentrated on the exposed panel in the inner wall of the ship. He winced at the sight of the cheap Ecuadorian circuitry as he used the multimeter to hunt for the faulty transistor. Damn contractors couldn't resist cutting corners. He sighed and looked up. Anatoly's face filled the screen. Nikolai didn't mind the banter. It broke the routine. He pointed at the opposite screen, which displayed the live feed from outside of the ship, a vast blackness punctured by tiny pinpricks of light. "Which sun?"

"Our sun. Any sun." Anatoly shrugged. "You're a cranky pedant, aren't you?"

"Matter of opinion," said Nikolai, his gaze returning to the uncooperative panel.

"As I was saying, there's nothing new under the sun," Anatoly said. "We won the original space race when we launched *Sputnik* a hundred years ago, and we're going to win this one, too."

Nikolai cursed under his breath as the multimeter slipped out of his hand and slowly floated upward. He caught the wayward tool. "The space race hasn't gone so well since. Americans beat us to the Moon, and the Chinese beat us to Mars."

"Those are just a pair of lifeless rocks in our backyard," said Anatoly. "In the grand scheme of things, they won't matter much. Not once you land on Arcadia."

Nikolai continued to hunt for the faulty transistor. "You're assuming this heap of junk won't fall apart around me first."

"*Gagarin* isn't luxurious, but it will get the job done," said Anatoly.

"I sure hope you're right," said Nikolai. "I'd hate having to get out and push."

Anatoly grinned. "You'd push all the way to Arcadia if you had to. Russian people make do with what we've got. Back in the 1960s, American astronauts discovered that ball-point pens didn't work right in a vacuum. So NASA spent all this time and money to design the space pen. You know what our cosmonauts did? They used a pencil."

"That story is bullshit on several levels," said Nikolai. "Americans used pencils, too. But the shavings were a hazard in zero gravity—they could float up one's nose, or even short an electrical device and start a fire. That's why the space pen was needed, and it was developed by a private company who then sold a handful to NASA at a reasonable price." He wiped a bead of sweat off his forehead. "You of all people should know better."

"Okay, you got me, it's a tall tale," said Anatoly. "But my version makes for a much better story to tell at parties."

"Next time I'm at a party, I'll be sure to try it," said Nikolai.

Anatoly frowned, the wind gone out of his sails. Nikolai knew he had scored another point, but this time by hitting below the belt. His handler must've felt guilty about the one-way trip, even if he tried his best to hide it.

Nikolai eased off. He let Anatoly fill him in on the gossip from home—the latest politics and entertainment news that felt so irrelevant, so far away.

It took him another thirty minutes to find the defective transistor. He grunted with satisfaction and reached for the soldering gun.


Three months prior, Nikolai Petrovich Gorolenko sat brooding at his desk in a cozy but windowless office of the St. Petersburg State University math department.

There was so much to do. He needed to type a resignation notice, to contact an attorney about a will, and worst of all, to figure out a way to break the news to his family. There was a knock on the door.

Nikolai didn't feel like speaking to anyone, but he needed a way to break out of his despondency.

"Come in."

A stranger walked into the room. This middle-aged man was perfectly coiffed and dressed in a smart business suit. His sharp eyes seemed to take in everything without missing a single detail, and yet he had a nondescript look about him that could only be perfected in one line of work. Nikolai pegged him for an FSB operative.

"My condolences, Professor Gorolenko," said the stranger.

Somehow, he knew. Nikolai hadn't told anyone, and yet he knew.

Nikolai did his best to keep calm. "Who are you, and what are you talking about?"

The man waved an ID card with a fluid, practiced motion. "Vladimir Ivanovich Popov. I'm with the government." He put the card away. "I'm here about your test results from this morning. The brain tumor is malignant. You've got three, four months. Half a year if you're lucky."

Nikolai bristled at being told this for the second time that day. At least the first time it was his doctor, who had sounded genuinely sympathetic. This stranger merely stated facts, politely but without compassion.

Popov pointed at the chair. "May I?"

"What do you want?" Nikolai ignored his request. A dying man has little use for being polite and little fear of authority, he thought.

Popov sat anyway. "I hear this is a bad way to go. Very painful, in the end. I'd like to offer you an alternative."

Nikolai tilted his head. "An alternative to dying?"

"An alternative to dying badly," said Popov. "Let's call it a stay of execution."

"I see," said Nikolai. "I suppose you'll want my soul in return?"

Popov smiled. "You aren't so far from the truth, Professor."

Exasperated, Nikolai leaned forward. "Why don't you tell me what you're offering in plain terms?"

"Our experts have examined your brain scans and the biopsy sample," said Popov, "and determined that you're a perfect fit for an experimental nanite treatment developed by the Antey Corporation.

It won't cure you, but it will slow down the tumor and contain the metastasis. It can buy you two more years."

Nikolai chewed his lip. Two years was such a short time, but for a drowning man it wasn't unseemly to grasp at straws. "You've got my attention."

"There is a catch," said Popov.

"Of course there is. Neither the Antey Corporation nor our government are known for their altruism," said Nikolai. "What do you need from me?"

"What do you know about Arcadia?" asked Popov.

"Huh? You mean the planet?"

Popov nodded.

"It's been all over the news. Admittedly, I've been . . . preoccupied. But I do know it's the first Earth-like planet ever confirmed—breathable atmosphere and everything."

"That's right," said Popov. "The Americans discovered it in 2015. They called it Kepler-452b back then and it was the first Earth-like exo planet ever found. Fitting that it will become the first world humans set foot on outside of the Solar System." He shifted in his chair. "There's enormous propaganda value in getting there first. The Americans are dispatching a twelve-person exploration team. India already launched a colony ship, with sixty-odd people in suspended animation."

"So quickly? They only confirmed Arcadia as habitable last month."

"The world's superpowers have been preparing for this moment ever since the eggheads figured out the workaround for the speed of light problem, and sent out skip drones every which way."

"I see. So the Russian Federation is in this race, too?"

"That's right, Professor. Our plan is to send you."

Nikolai stared at the government apparatchik across his desk. "Why me?"

"I'm not a scientist, so I can't explain the reasoning thoroughly," said Popov. "In layman's terms, they've been going over the brain scan data from terminal patients across the country, and they liked your brain best."

Nikolai scratched his chin. Like most children, he dreamed of going up into space once, but that was a lifetime ago.

"Forgive me," Nikolai said, "this is a lot to process."

"There's more," said Popov. "I don't want to sugarcoat this for you.

It would be a one-way trip. If we succeed and you land on Arcadia, and even if the atmosphere is breathable and the water is drinkable, your odds of survival are astronomically low. If the local microbes don't get you, hunger likely will. If you're lucky, you might last long enough for the Americans to get there. We're trying to time the launch just right to give you that chance. Even then, the tumor might finish you before they return to Earth."

Nikolai thought about it. "Why can't you send enough food and water for the crew to survive?"

"You don't get it. You are the crew. Just you. The ship's ability to accelerate to a skip velocity is inversely proportional to its mass. The India ship is en route but it's huge and therefore slow. Americans have a much faster ship, and they might launch before we do. In order to beat them to the punch, we must send a very light vessel. Every milligram counts. So it's you, and just enough oxygen, water, and food to get you to the finish line."

Nikolai frowned. "You weren't kidding about the stay of execution, then. And it explains why your people are looking to recruit from among the terminally ill. Leaving the heroic explorer to die on Arcadia would be terrible PR otherwise."

"You're grasping the basics quickly," said Popov. "No wonder they picked your brain."

"I'm not sure how a few extra months of life on a spaceship followed by death alone on an alien world is better than spending my last days with my wife and daughter," said Nikolai.

"Well, there's having your name live on forever in history along the likes of Magellan and Bering," said Popov. "And then there's the obscene amount of money you'll be paid for doing this."

Nikolai hadn't saved much money on a college professor's salary. There would be medical bills, his father's retirement, his daughter's college tuition . . . "When do you need my answer by?"

"Tomorrow morning, at the latest," said Popov. "Though, given your circumstances, I'm a little surprised you have to think about it much."

"I don't, not really," said Nikolai. "But I do owe it to my wife to let her weigh in."

At times, Nikolai felt like his ship was falling apart around him.

He didn't understand how the skip technology worked—only a few dozen theoretical physicists on Earth could legitimately claim such wisdom—but he knew that an object had to reach a certain velocity before it could puncture a momentary hole in space-time and reemerge elsewhere.

*Yuri Gagarin* would accelerate continuously for six months until it reached the skip point located somewhere in the Kuiper Belt, wink out of existence only to reappear fourteen hundred light years away, then spend a similar amount of time decelerating toward Arcadia.

As a mathematician, Nikolai couldn't help but marvel at the amazing speed his vessel would achieve after half a year of constant acceleration. By now he had already traveled farther than any other human in history, but he didn't feel special. He felt tired and anxious, and somewhat claustrophobic in the cramped cabin that smelled like rubber and sweat.

The ship's memory bank was loaded with a nearly infinite selection of music, books, and films to break the monotony of the journey. Nikolai was stuck drinking recycled water and eating disgusting nutrient-enriched slop in the name of conserving mass, but the electrons needed for data storage had no significant weight, and the ship's designers could afford him this luxury. But he had little time to partake of the digital library. Instead, he put all of his hastily learned engineering knowledge to use and performed maintenance.

Much of his time at Baikonur had been spent learning how to service the systems inside the ship. There had been no spacesuit, but then there was little that could go wrong on the outer hull. The engineers' real fear was that the internal systems might malfunction. The culture of graft was so deeply ingrained in the Russian industrial complex that even a high-profile project like this was afflicted.

It wouldn't do to deliver a corpse to Arcadia. Pre-flight, they spent nearly ten hours a day teaching Nikolai how to repair the recycling systems, solder the circuit boards, and improvise solutions to an array of worst-case scenarios with the materials available on board. One of the American-educated engineers kept referring to these techniques as "MacGyvering," but Nikolai didn't know the reference.

En route, Nikolai was forced to deal with cheap circuit boards, subpar, off-brand equipment, and software subroutines that were at least two generations behind the times. He had one thing going for him—the ability to remain in contact with Baikonur. The broadcast signal had no mass and was able to skip almost immediately. Mission Control was only a few seconds' delay away, able to offer advice and support.

While all the fires he had to put out so far were figurative, Nikolai eyed the tiny Bulgarian-made extinguisher with suspicion.

Nikolai waited until their four-year-old daughter was asleep. Pretending that everything was normal, that it was just another weeknight, was incredibly difficult. He was emotionally and physically exhausted, and his wife Tamara could sense that something was wrong, but she too kept up the pretense of normality until their little Olga was tucked into bed.

As the sun set over St. Petersburg, coloring the skyline in bronze hues, Nikolai told his wife about his diagnosis and everything that had happened since.

Tamara listened without interrupting, even as she clutched a couch pillow, a mascara-tinged tear rolling down her cheek. When he finally unburdened, having told her the facts and having run out of assurances and platitudes, the two of them stared out the window and shared what was left of the sunset in silence.

It was only after the sun had disappeared completely in the west that she finally spoke.

"Why you?"

Something was very wrong.

At first it was just a feeling, a sensation in the back of Nikolai's mind. It seemed that his subconscious had figured out something important, but wasn't prepared to communicate what it was.

Nikolai chalked it up to paranoia. Anyone stuck on a one-way trip out of the Solar System in a tin can could be forgiven for having uneasy thoughts. But the feeling persisted, almost bubbling up to the surface until eventually the concern bled from his lizard brain and into the conscious mind.

Nikolai pulled up the various sets of relevant data on his screen and began crunching numbers.

✖ ✖ ✖

After his wife had finally gone to bed, Nikolai stayed up making a list of people he needed to say "good-bye" to. He kept adding and crossing out names on a sheet of graph paper, until he crumpled up the page and tossed it into the trash bin.

Farewells would be painful. He didn't want to do it. Life had already dealt him a bad hand and he felt justified in skipping whatever unpleasant business he could avoid.

In the morning, he called Popov and accepted the deal, requesting that his involvement be kept a secret for as long as possible. He had little enough time to spend with his family and didn't want to waste it being hounded by reporters. Then he went to see the only other person who needed to know the truth.

Petr Ivanovich Gorolenko had recently moved into an assisted living facility on the edge of town. It was nice enough, as retirement homes went. Nikolai was relieved that, with the money his family would receive, they'd no longer have to worry about being able to afford Father's stay here.

Like Tamara, Petr listened to his son's tale without interrupting. He sighed deeply when Nikolai was finished. "It is a great tragedy for a parent to outlive his child."

"I have little time, Dad, and a chance to do something meaningful with what's left."

His father straightened his back with great effort. "Claiming an entire planet for Mother Russia is no small thing."

"Well, it isn't exactly like that," said Nikolai. "Arcadia isn't like some tropical island in the age of colonialism. Planting the flag won't claim it as ours. The government wants to land a man there first purely for propaganda."

"I see," said Petr. "The oligarchs in charge are desperate to show that Russia is still a world power. And they're willing to sacrifice your life to do it."

"I'm dying regardless," said Nikolai.

"They have the means to prolong your life, and they're withholding treatment unless you volunteer for a suicide mission. Doesn't that bother you?"

Nikolai looked around the sparse, depressing room where his father would live out his remaining years. Was his own fate really worse than that?

"Of course it bothers me," he said. "Dying bothers me. Having Olga grow up without a father bothers me. But so what? It's not like I have a better option."

"Your great-grandfather was conscripted into the army on the day the Great Patriotic War began," said Petr. "Stalin had murdered most of his competent generals by then, and was utterly unprepared for the German invasion. He needed time to regroup and mount the real defense, so he ordered tens of thousands of young men with no training and no weapons onto the front lines."

Petr's words dissolved in a coughing fit. He cleared his throat, and continued in a raspy voice. "Grandpa's platoon of forty men was given a total of three rifles to fight with. They were told to kill the Germans and capture their weapons, and sent to the front lines. A squad of NKVD—the secret police—was positioned a kilometer or so behind them. Those men were well-armed, and had orders to shoot anyone who tried to turn back."

Petr paused again, the monologue visibly taking a lot out of him. He took several deep breaths and pressed on. "Grandpa was very lucky. He was wounded in the first engagement, and by the time he got out of the hospital his platoon was long gone. He was assigned to another division, one with weapons, and fought all the way to Berlin in '45."

"You've told this story, more than a few times," said Nikolai.

"My point is, our government has a long-standing tradition of solving problems by throwing whoever they have to into the meat grinder," said Petr. A smile stretched across his wrinkled face. "But also to reiterate that dumb luck runs deep in our family. Perhaps you can beat the odds and last long enough to hitch the ride home on the American ship. So, if you don't mind, I won't mourn for you just yet."

Nikolai hugged his father. "I'll try, Dad. I'll try my best."

Nikolai and his family relocated to Baikonur, the desert town in Kazakhstan that housed the world's oldest spaceport. The dry heat of the Kazakh Steppe was difficult for the Gorolenkos to tolerate, and seemed to contribute to Nikolai's rapidly worsening headaches, but it was a moot point: he spent almost all of his time in the vast, air-conditioned labs of the Roscosmos, the Russian Federal Space Agency.

He was given crash courses in astronomy by the scientists, in equipment maintenance and repair by the engineers, and in public speaking by the PR flaks. Some of the lessons felt surreal to him—a sole student surrounded by a cadre of overeager teachers.

The plan was to unveil the mission at the last possible moment, lest the Americans or the Chinese launch a competing one-man ship powered with their superior technologies and snatch the accomplishment away from the Motherland. As far as the world knew, the Americans would get to Arcadia first.

The Chinese had dominated space exploration for much of the twenty-first century. It was the People's Republic of China's skip drone which had explored Arcadia in the first place. Unfortunately for them, China was undergoing a period of political upheaval not dissimilar to Russia's perestroika of the 1990s. The government lacked the funds and the willpower to support an interstellar project.

The enormous Indian ship was already en route, and would take over five years to reach the skip point. They wouldn't be the first on the scene, but they would be the first to succeed—or fail—at establishing a permanent colony.

The Americans launched the *Neil Armstrong* with all the pomp and pageantry that was expected of them, and it was scheduled to reach Arcadia in a little over a year.

The plan had been for the Russians to launch the *Yuri Gagarin* on the same day, and steal the Americans' thunder. Despite its inferior propulsion, the *Gagarin*'s much lower mass would allow the Russian ship to beat their competitors to Arcadia by up to several months. But, by the time the *Armstrong* had launched from Cape Canaveral, Nikolai hadn't even seen his ship.

The *Gagarin* was being constructed elsewhere, a joint effort between the Russian government, the Antey Corporation, and a number of smaller domestic firms sufficiently favored by the current administration to be awarded the lucrative contracts.

Another month passed. Nikolai's headaches continued to worsen and, despite the Baikonur doctors' assurances to the contrary, he suspected that the nanite treatments might not be working.

At first, he was perfectly content to miss the launch date. The delay meant more time to spend with his family. But then he had realized that he actually wanted to go. While Olga was blissfully unaware of what was happening in the way only a young child could be, the situation was taking a noticeable toll on Tamara. She had a hard time coping with the prolonged farewell, and even though she did her best to hide it and stand by her husband, Nikolai hated being the cause of her anguish.

At some point over the course of this extra month on the ground, Nikolai stopped thinking of the impending launch as a death sentence and began looking forward to this final adventure. He didn't discuss these new feelings with Tamara, who he felt would not understand, but wrote about them at length in letters he penned for his daughter, to be given to her when she turned sixteen. The letters became a sort of a diary for Nikolai, an outlet for his anxiety, a catharsis.

The word that the ship was finally on its way to Baikonur came at the last possible moment.

"This is good news," Nikolai told Tamara during their last dinner together. By mutual agreement, they decided not to speak again after the ship had launched. Nikolai wasn't happy about this, but he was willing to let go, for Tamara's sake. "I'm only going to beat the Americans by a week or so."

She took his hand into hers, and her lower lip trembled.

"I can make the food and water last that long," he said. "The Americans will take me in. It would make them look really bad otherwise."

There was pain and doubt in the way Tamara looked at him, and only the briefest glimmer of hope.

Later that evening, he tucked Olga into bed for the last time.

"Daddy is going away on a business trip for a while," he said, struggling to keep his voice even.

Olga smiled at him, her eyelids heavy. "Will you come back soon?"

"I'll try my best," said Nikolai.

"Bring me something nice." She shut her eyes.

In the morning, they told him he would sleep through the first two days of his trip.

"We must lighten the load as much as possible," he was told, "to make up, somewhat, for the delays. We'll give you a shot to keep you asleep for as long as it's medically reasonable. It will conserve air, food, and water."

By the time he woke up, the Earth was a pale blue dot rapidly diminishing in the distance.

❃   ❃   ❃

At first, Nikolai chose not to share his concerns with Anatoly. If he was wrong, he would sound like a paranoid lunatic. If he was right . . . Nikolai tried very hard not to dwell on the implications.

He pulled up the volumes on astronomy and physics from the ship's database, and he checked the data from the ship's sensors against the star charts, willing the results to make sense. He cut down the amount of time spent on maintaining life support systems, and the amount of time he slept. He checked the equations, again and again, but the numbers never added up.

By then he was getting desperate. He would have to bring his concerns up with Baikonur.

"Do you want to hear a joke?" said Anatoly by way of greeting the next time he called.

"Sure." Nikolai wasn't in the laughing Mood, but he let the com specialist talk.

"When the Americans landed on the moon, Premier Brezhnev's aides broke the bad news to their boss," said Anatoly. "Brezhnev wasn't at all happy.

"'We can't let the capitalists win the space race,' he said. 'I hereby order our intrepid cosmonauts to immediately launch an expedition and land on the Sun!'

"'But Comrade Brezhnev,' said the aides, 'it's impossible to land on the Sun. The Sun is extremely hot.'

"'Nonsense,' said Brezhnev. 'Just tell them to go at night.'"

Nikolai stared at the screen, silent.

"Heard that one, eh?" Anatoly grinned. "That joke is so old, its beard has grown a beard. It seemed appropriate for the occasion is all."

"What's really going on, Anatoly?" Nikolai blurted out the words before he could change his mind.

The face on the screen stared, eyes widening in surprise. "What do you mean?"

"I calculated the trajectory, and the ship isn't where it should be," said Nikolai. "It's accelerating much faster than it possibly could."

"You must have made a mistake," said Anatoly, a little too quickly, and glanced downward.

After so many rounds of verbal sparring, Nikolai looked into the face of the man on the screen and was certain he was hiding something.

"I taught mathematics at one of Russia's top universities," said Nikolai. "My calculations are accurate. A ship the size of *Yuri Gagarin* can't possibly accelerate at this rate. And don't feed me a line about secret technologies, I learned enough about propulsion at Baikonur to understand the basics of skip travel."

Anatoly's visage, normally cheerful and full of life, was grim. He sighed deeply and slouched in his chair, his shoulders slumping visibly.

"Wait, please," he finally said, and cut the connection.

Nikolai felt trapped and powerless. Cut off from his family, his only lifeline a man he barely knew, a man who had apparently been lying to him this entire time. But lying about what? Was this a sick experiment? Did he leave Earth at all, or was he in some bunker in Kazakhstan, serving as a guinea pig for Roscosmos shrinks?

He felt claustrophobic, the walls of the ship closing in. His head spun and his stomach churned. Was this a panic attack? Nikolai had never experienced one before.

The salvation from certain death, the chance at fame, the money . . .why would this be offered to him, of all people? How could he be so stupid? This was a fantasy born of a cancerous mass pushing against his brain tissue.

The screen flickered back to life twenty minutes later, but to Nikolai it felt like eternity.

"I was hoping we wouldn't have this conversation for a few months," said Anatoly. "Some time after the skip."

Nikolai stared at his handler. "Is there a skip?"

"There is a skip, and the ship is right on schedule, accelerating exactly as it should be."

Nikolai waited.

"You're right, though; the ship is much lighter and faster than you were initially led to believe."

Nikolai seethed. "What the hell does that mean, Anatoly?"

"There were delays and complications," said the com specialist. "We couldn't get the life support equipment to work right, couldn't get the ship's mass reduced to an acceptable level. We had hoped the Americans would have similar troubles, but they launched on time, and we were out of options.

"In order to beat them to Arcadia we had to send a ship that was barely larger than a skip drone—nothing large enough to transport a living, breathing human.

"The best we could do was to send your mind."

Nikolai gaped at the screen.

"Antey Corporation has been developing this technology for a decade," said Anatoly. "We had to euthanize your body and upload your thought patterns into the computer. Your digital self resides in the *Yuri Gagarin*'s memory bank. A sophisticated computer program is simulating your environment. But, in fact, there is no air or food, nor the need for such."

Nikolai stared at his hands, brushed his fingers against the stubble on his chin and then touched the control console of the ship, felt the slight vibration of the engine. "All this feels real enough to me."

Anatoly entered a command into his own computer, and the world around Nikolai went blank.

He could no longer feel his own body, could not breathe or move, or see anything around him. It was extremely disorienting. Nikolai thought this was how purgatory must feel.

The physical world returned.

"Sorry about the discomfort," said Anatoly. "I had to show you I was telling the truth. This is what it's like without any interface at all."

Nikolai felt his heart thumping fast, his face flushed with anger. How could those things be fake? "You . . ." he stammered. "You killed me!"

"Your body was already dying," said Anatoly. "The nanites could only hold off the tumor for so long." He offered a weak smile. "Think of the advantages—you will last as long as it takes for the Americans to bring you back home."

"Advantages?" shouted Nikolai. "You were always going to kill me, weren't you? All in the name of some propaganda stunt!"

"No," said Anatoly. "Sure, we were prepared for this. You were selected because your brain activity and personality were deemed most likely to be digitized successfully and the nanites had been mapping your brain patterns from the beginning. But we would have vastly preferred the alternative." Anatoly leaned forward and lowered his voice, sounding almost conspiratorial. "I know you're angry and confused now, but think about it—really think about it—you're going to make history, twice. You will not only be the first intelligent being from Earth to land on Arcadia, but you'll be the first successfully digitized human, too."

"You are monsters," whispered Nikolai.

"You will get to watch your daughter grow up," said Anatoly.

Nikolai had no counter to that. He pondered life as a ghost in the machine.

"Why did you lie?" he asked. "Why the ruse? You could have gotten a volunteer. Hell, I might have volunteered if you had laid the options out for me."

"This truly was the backup option," said Anatoly. "But also, we've had . . . difficulties with this process before. Several previous attempts at maintaining a digital intelligence have failed."

Nikolai gritted his nonexistent teeth. The emotional roller-coaster ride wasn't over yet.

"You're doing fine," Anatoly added. "I'm only telling you this to explain our actions. All cards on the table this time, I promise."

"What sort of difficulties?" asked Nikolai.

"The transfer always worked, but the minds couldn't adjust to the virtual existence. They went mad within days. But they weren't as good a match as you."

Nikolai shuddered.

"Through trial and error, we figured out the most efficient approach was to stimulate your senses in a virtual reality environment, and keep the truth from you until your program has stabilized."

Nikolai stared at Anatoly, who raised his palms.

"I know, it was a long shot and a gamble. We really did run out of time. It was this, or scrap the program. You're doing great, though.

"We created a believable and challenging simulation for you. Making you work hard to fix things, challenging your mind to remain sharp and active." Anatoly began to gesture with his hands as he was prone to doing when he got excited about the topic of conversation. "Every anecdote, every little story I told you were carefully selected by our top psychiatrists to steer you toward eventually accepting your new reality."

"All this, just to land a computer program on Arcadia," said Nikolai. "Two dozen skip drones already landed there, getting air and water and soil samples. Why would anyone care?"

"It's not the same. You're still a person. A rational human being, capable of emotion and thought. A Russian. Your achievement will matter. Sure, there will be a few detractors, the Americans will argue like hell that a digital person doesn't count, but we'll sell it to the rest of the world if we have to shove it down their throats."

"I'm capable of emotion," said Nikolai. "Right now, that emotion is anger. Right now, I'm contemplating whether I should take part in your publicity stunt at all. Maybe I'll tell the world about what you people have done to me, instead. Or maybe I'll say nothing at all, play dead, and leave your glorious first-place finish devoid of meaning. How is that for a rational human being?"

Nikolai cut the connection.

Nikolai struggled to come to terms with what he was. Even now, the virtual reality he inhabited seemed real to him. He felt hungry, and tired, and hurt when he tentatively bit his cheek. He was capable of feeling anger toward the government and love toward his daughter. Did the lack of the physical body make him any less human than a handicapped person, a quadriplegic unable to control his limbs?

He was never an ardent patriot, and now he was more disillusioned in his country than ever. But would carrying out his threat gain him anything beyond a fleeting moment of satisfaction?

And if he was to comply, if he was to return to Earth in a few years, would Tamara come to terms with this new him? Would Olga? He had no answers, only an ever-growing list of uncertainties.

To their credit, Anatoly and his superiors gave him an entire day to think things through before reestablishing the connection. Anatoly looked like he hadn't slept, was buzzed on caffeine, still wearing the same shirt from the day before.

"What we did to you was crap," he said without preamble, "but I won't apologize for it. Exceptional deeds aren't accomplished through kindness. It's not just Russia, either. All of human history is one tale after another of achieving greatness by ruthlessly building upon a foundation comprised of the bones of the innocent.

"How many slave laborers died to erect the pyramids? The gleaming New York skyscrapers are inseparable from the legacy of smallpox-infested blankets being given to unsuspecting natives. You have already paid the price for humanity's next great accomplishment. Why refuse to reap the benefits?"

Nikolai closed his eyes and pictured Olga's face. She might or might not accept the virtual brain-in-a-jar as her father.

He thought of all the doors his success could open for her.

"I'll do it," said Nikolai evenly. "You can tone down the rhetoric."

Anatoly straightened visibly, as though a heavy burden was lifted from his shoulders.

"There are conditions," said Nikolai.

"What do you need?"

"One, I want to talk to my wife. I want her handling things on that end, from now on, because I don't quite know how to tell the real from the virtual, and I don't trust any of you."

Nikolai held up two fingers. "Two, when I get back you hand the computer or the data bank or whatever my consciousness is stored in over to her, for much the same reason."

Anatoly nodded. "Done."

"I still hate the callous, cynical lot of you. But I'll make the best out of this situation and find solace in the fact that my name will be remembered long after all your gravestones are dust. Speaking of that legacy, we'll need to work on my speech. Something tells me 'one small step' isn't going to go over well, in my case."

"We'll have speechwriters float some ideas," said Anatoly.

"Finally, have your programmers work on some adjustments to my gilded cage. If I'm to eat make-believe food, making it taste this bad is needlessly cruel. Tonight, I'd like a thick slab of virtual steak, medium-well."

Nikolai settled in for the long journey. There would be time enough to sort out his feelings, and to learn how to live as this new kind of being. He knew one thing for sure: like his great-grandfather, he would persevere and return home.

*Yuri Gagarin*, the tiny ship carrying the future hero of humanity, accelerated toward the skip point.

((•(•(• 🔆 •)•)•))

**Alex Shvartsman** is a writer and game designer from Brooklyn, NY. Over 70 of his short stories have appeared in *InterGalactic Medicine Show, Nature, Galaxy's Edge, Daily Science Fiction*, and many other 'zines and anthologies. The best of these are collected in *Explaining*

*Cthulhu to Grandma and Other Stories*. He's the winner of the 2014 WSFA Small Press Award for Short Fiction and the editor of Unidentified Funny Objects annual anthology series of humorous SF/F. His fiction is linked at *www.alexshvartsman.com*.

*Next, award-winning Aussie writer Lezli Robyn takes us on a journey in which the first female aborigine astronaut discovers the NASA probe* Voyager 1 *has come back to life for surprising reasons in* . . .

# A WALKABOUT AMONGST THE STARS

## by Lezli Robyn

Tyrille Smith checked that her tether to *Voyager 1* was secure, and confirmed the oxygen, radiation, and pressure levels on her biosuit were within acceptable parameters, before painstakingly detaching the thermal blanketing on the panel in front of her to reveal a section of the spacecraft's control hub. She'd spent the better part of the last three years studying the specs of the dated systems, while travelling to the far reaches of the Solar System and beyond, so she traversed the space probe with ease, checking the radios, propulsion equipment, and various computer systems for anything out of the ordinary.

While former NASA specialists had been able to verify that the flight, science and command program parameters hadn't been altered using computer diagnostics completed from Earth, none of the scientists had been able to confirm why the space probe had powered up all its systems again in 2027, two years after it had gone completely dark. Over the years the science systems had been disabled, one by one, to preserve its most basic thruster and altitude control functions. Now, not only were the twelve science instruments on the probe completely active—including the plasma spectrometer and the photopolarimeter systems that had been previously determined to be defective—but Tyrille had just confirmed on her previous EVA excursion out to the probe that the radioisotope thermoelectric generators were now running at full efficiency and the propellant tank was almost filled to capacity again. Not with hydrazine, but another foreign—very alien—substance that she had to use specialized equipment to take a sample of.

Tyrille sealed the panel she had been working on, and gingerly opened the next one. *Voyager 1* had been in operation since 1977, and while it had not deteriorated in the vacuum of space, it had become an antiquated time capsule in its own way. She carefully replaced the data storage and tape recorder with much more modern, but equally low-energy-drawing, digital equivalents, and then hesitated, biting her lip. *Why would someone—no, some*thing*—refuel and repair the science instruments, only to then disappear? They clearly had the expertise to contact Earth. If they could reach* Voyager 1, *why not announce themselves?*

The implications were staggering, and so very exciting for Tyrille. All her life, she had wanted to become the first Aboriginal Australian astronaut to walkabout amongst the stars. Not only did her name literally mean "space" or "sky" in her native tongue, but she was descended from the fabled Boorong clan, who had been renowned for their astronomical knowledge. Believed to have been the oldest astrologists on Earth, most of the clan had died out long before she was born, although some of the last members were scattered around the northwest region of Victoria. She had been blessed to have been the great-granddaughter of one of the last Elders of the clan, and remembered many a night spent around the campfire as he told her the Dreamtime stories of how the deeds—or even misdeeds—of the creation spirits, *Nurrumbunguttias,* had led to the formation of the constellations. She had grown up wondering, if there were extraterrestrial life in the nearby stars, what form would they take? And would they have their own Dreamtime story about how the Solar System was created?

"Are you in some distress, Tyrille?" asked the disembodied voice of I.R.I.S. her Interstellar Robotic Information Support drone. "You are holding your breath. Please exhale."

She signed. "No need to worry, Iris. I am just woolgathering."

"I do not understand the context of that term and how it affects your breathing."

Tyrille sighed, again, a little exasperated. "It's not important. Can you please confirm my connections are secure before I close the panel?"

I.R.I.S. ran the relevant diagnostics. "Confirmed." Then a second later: "To gather wool, would you not need sheep?"

"It's an expression, Iris." Tyrille wrapped the data storage and tape recorder up and tethered them to the EVA assist drone, then attached most of the bulkier tools to it before sending it back to her spaceship. "I use it as a way to say I am lost in thought."

"You are not lost, Tyrille. I have our location stored in my navigation array. We are exactly 198.027 374 55 astronomical units away from Earth. For clarification, that is 0.000 960 063 833 22 parsecs or 29 624 473 571 kilometers, or —"

"I get the point," Tyrille interrupted, bemused, "but thank you for the reassurance." She rotated to confirm the drone's return to her vessel, the sight of which never ceased to impress her.

She remembered vividly the first time she saw the *Venturer*. Ten thousand metric tons of spacecraft had dominated Earth's orbit, with the nuclear power source stored in huge radiator wings attached to a body composed of seven nuclear-electric propulsion modules. It was no wonder the construction team had dubbed it 'The Dragonfly'—for that was what it resembled.

Well, what it *used* to resemble.

The chemical rockets used to boost the *Venturer* out of Earth orbit into an escape trajectory were ejected first. Then the nuclear-electric modules took over flight control, boosting the spaceship up to an acceleration of three hundred and ten kilometers per second within a year. It spent the next fourteen months rocketing towards the space probe at that speed before four of the modules were ejected. Then the spacecraft spent another year decelerating to match velocities with the space probe.

The last two modules were ejected just before she reached *Voyager 1*, leaving just her life support module, so that her spaceship now resembled nothing more than a common housefly; albeit the most important space fly in human history. It had enough juice to return her to Pluto's perihelion by 2038, where mankind was scrambling to build a waystation where she could refuel, to ensure she could rendezvous with Earth before her resources ran completely out.

They had expended more fuel than had originally computed to

reach the space probe, and by her calculations, she only had two more days to complete all her tests of *Voyager 1* before needing to—

"Gathering more wool?" I.R.I.S. interjected, interrupting her thoughts.

Tyrille grinned sheepishly, and returned her gaze back to *Voyager 1*. When her ship had first pulled alongside the space probe, thirty-eight hours earlier, she should have been able to see the lights from her spacecraft reflect off a distinctive piece of polished metal attached to the side. Yet the Golden Record—the disk containing Earth sounds, images and salutations in hundreds of languages that had specifically been placed on *Voyager 1* as a greeting to extraterrestrial life—had been removed from the probe. Presumably taken by those it had been intended for.

In shock, she had reported the news of the discovery on the next scheduled data pulse, and while the response from Earth was delayed, it was by no means devoid of excitement. For the first time in fifty-eight years all propulsion on *Voyager 1* had been halted so she could perform a serious of evaluations, tests and upgrades—with the expressed focus of trying to discover any evidence extraterrestrials could have left behind.

"Iris, can you please confirm the helmet cam is in operational order?"

"Yes, Tyrille," the robot replied with perfect intonation, "it is functioning within nominal parameters."

Tyrille loosened the tether, and pulled herself around to the one part of the space probe she had deliberately avoided until this moment. "Iris, in a minute you are about to witness history in the making."

"Technically, every minute becomes history, once it has passed."

She groaned, fogging up her helmet for a split second. "Have I ever mentioned you are too literal for your own good?"

"Yes," I.R.I.S. replied. "However, accuracy is a fundamental component of my programming."

"A fundamental flaw, mayhaps," she muttered, more to herself than the benefit of the robot. She pulled out a small handheld probe she'd nicknamed the Screwdriver, after her favorite science fiction series, and began an array of tests on the small area of paneling that had once held the fabled Golden Record. At first she saw nothing, which is exactly what she had expected, but then when the light passed directly over the center, it seemed to reflect off a small geometric shape imprinted on the surface of the panel. It looked somewhat akin to a snowflake to the naked eye, but her device registered that the crystalline-appearing substance pulsed with energy.

*Strewth! It's alive!*

Better still, the readings displayed on her helmet's holoscreen confirmed it was alien.

For a moment, Tyrille couldn't move. She could barely breathe.

She made the effort to exhale, and then inhale—or risk I.R.I.S.'s ire—but continued to float there in a state of shock.

"The readings indicate there is a foreign object attached to side of *Voyager 1*, Tyrille."

*No bloody kidding,* Tyrille thought, nodding, before realizing I.R.I.S. couldn't see that action. "I see it, too, and am ascertaining what to do with it . . .whether it's safe to bring aboard or not."

"It appears to be extraterrestrial in origin."

"Thank you, Captain Obvious. I am aware of that."

As usual, I.R.I.S ignored her sarcasm—or simply didn't recognize it. "I would note that its location is presumably an important indicator of its function."

Tyrille frowned. "How so?"

"It's been placed in the exact same position the Golden Record was once located. The logical conclusion would be that it was—"

"—the extraterrestrial's response to the Golden Record!" Tyrille exclaimed. "Or at least their equivalent."

"Indeed."

Tyrille's mind raced with the implications. If this specimen was somehow an alien life-form's greeting to the human race, that could explain why *Voyager 1's* fuel tanks had been replenished and its systems automatically turned on again: it was the most unobtrusive—and even courteous—way for the aliens to alert humans to their presence. And perhaps, to even encourage them in their goal to make contact.

*Or it could be the extraterrestrial version of a Trojan horse,* Tyrille thought wryly. "Iris, is there any indication that the specimen could cause any harm—or come to any harm—if we were to bring it onto the spaceship?"

There was a long pause. "No, Tyrille, there is not. However, while it does not appear to require a breathable atmosphere, due to being discovered in the vacuum of space, the composition of its crystalline structure and its method of power conduction are unknown variables. I could not give you a definitive calculation of how it would react in the *Venturer*'s oxygen-rich environment without further testing."

"Which we do not have time to do, given our short window." Frustrated, the astronaut bit her lip. She had to decide now. Even if she sent their preliminary scientific readings to Earth for analysis and a decision, she couldn't wait the amount of time it would take for them to simply receive her data pulse, let alone wait for their reply to wing its way across the expanse to her. Not when *Venturer* had to start making its long voyage back to Earth within forty-eight hours.

*Well . . . bugger. I suppose that settles that, then.* Tyrille looked down to see her hands were in no condition to carefully excise the specimen; they were shaking in anticipation and fear. She closed her eyes, trying a breathing exercise to settle her nerves, then opened them again, her gaze darting around vast darkness until it settled upon the familiar golden glow of the Sun.

The first Dreamtime story she had ever been told had been about how the Solar System, and the rest of the Universe, had come to be. Earth had been a featureless black disc until *Pupperrimbul* (one of the *Nurrumbunguttias* that had taken the form of a bird with a red patch) had cast an emu's egg into the sky to create *Gnowee*, the Sun. Eventually, all of the *Nurrumbunguttias* left Earth to form the many other bright lights across the cosmos; the smoke from their campfires forming the *Warring*, which was still visible from Earth as the Milky Way.

That knowledge comforted Tyrille. She liked the thought that the spirits were surrounding her, guiding her, so when she eventually returned her gaze and concentration onto *Voyager 1*, her hands were much steadier. She felt much more grounded in her heart and mind.

She used the laser setting of her "Screwdriver" to cut out a small a section of the side panel. She was careful to take a wide berth around the specimen, so as to not damage it, but also ensured she left as much paneling behind as possible to protect the probe's vital instruments.

Wary of allowing anything to touch the delicate-appearing crystalline structure—even a specimen bag—she made her way to the spacecraft, holding the panel segment gingerly in her open palm.

I.R.I.S. met her at the open airlock, sealing the outer hatch after she had entered and then helping divest her of the equipment she wore about her body—tasks Tyrille usually completed on her own. She grinned. Sometimes she forgot how curious the robot could be. It was such a human affectation. "Would you like to see it, Iris?"

The robot inclined its titanium head in acknowledgement, and after ascertaining permission, lifted the panel with very precise, very gentle movements, turning it this way and that to study the life-form's construction.

"It is beautiful," I.R.I.S. stated, quite earnestly.

Taken aback by the giving of a compliment, Tyrille could only nod.

"The mathematical computations in its physical structure alone ensure physical perfection, but . . ."

"Prepare for environment stabilization," the ship's computer interface intoned.

Tyrille waited until oxygen levels reached breathable limits, and for the inner hatch door to automatically unseal, before she released the pressure lock on her helmet and pulled it free of her unruly close-cropped curls.

Pushing off by her feet, she propelled her body through the zero gravity into the main compartment and started searching for a specimen container large enough to contain the excised panel piece. Not able to find the one she was seeking, she turned to ask I.R.I.S., to discover it had followed her into the main chamber, but was still transfixed by the specimen.

The robot looked up at her. Eventually, "Shall we ask it what it wants?"

Tyrille blinked, bemused. "It's probably a data core of some kind. Why assume it can understand what we are saying?"

"Why assume it does not? What am I, if not an interactive data core?"

Tyrille blinked. The robot was right. She looked down at the specimen with new eyes. And more than a little suspicion. *What is your purpose, pretty one?*

As if in response, the snowflake-like structure lifted off the panel segment and started spinning in the air, growing in size and luminosity, until it broke apart into many crystalline orbs that spun around each other, coalescing to form an angular head, then broad shoulders, a well-muscled torso, and . . . a tentacled tail.

*The alien was a merman?!*

*Oh my.* "G'day . . . Er, I mean, hello. Welcome."

The extraterrestrial's shape solidified so she could clearly see the alien cast to his features. His long, platinum-white hair was a floating nimbus around his head; his skin was so white, it was almost translucent. Luminescent blue light pulsed hypnotically underneath his skin, radiating out from a crystalline snowflake positioned in the center of his chest, to course through what appeared to be his version of a circulatory system.

To say he was beautiful was an understatement. He was breathtaking . . . and so very, incredibly alien. "Can you understand what I am saying?"

"Yes," he replied, simply, without preamble; his voice as silky as his hair.

*How?* She opened her mouth to ask, but then closed it again. *Where was a First Contact manual when you needed one?* She was at a loss as to how to proceed.

"Is my appearance displeasing to you?" he asked, eventually, his every intonation measured and devoid of any helpful emotional cues.

"Of c-course not," she stammered. *Just too bloody distracting,* she thought.

I.R.I.S. turned to Tyrille. "The life-form is likely noticing from your contorted facial expressions that you appear to be in some distress, Tyrille."

She grimaced, adding yet another expression to the mix. "I understand, Iris. I will take it from here."

She scrambled to find the right words, as she watched the alien float there calmly, his tentacles undulating back and forth. She didn't want to botch First Contact, but the impact he had on her was almost hypnotic. She had to struggle to form words into coherent sentences. "You look very . . . er, different from what I am used to, but also confusingly familiar," she finally responded. "Your form is very similar in appearance to that of a fabled creature on our world."

As if in response, his form shifted perceptively, becoming a little more alien, and a little less merman. "I apologize. That was not my intention. This was just the most accurate extrapolation I could create," he replied, as if that answered everything.

I.R.I.S. turned back to the alien, studying his features. "Based on the mathematically symmetrical beauty of your form, I would presume that you are using an algorithm to compute a guise that would be most pleasing to the human eye, but yet still retain some qualities of your true form and racial identity to set yourself apart." It turned to Tyrille. "He wants to appear humanoid to help alleviate the impact of First Contact."

Something flashed in the alien's eyes, his gaze becoming more intent as transferred his attention to the robot. "Very perceptive," he acknowledged. Then: "You, too, are beautiful in form."

Tyrille's eyebrows rose. *Well, that answered the question of whether he had been listening to everything we have been saying.* She tried to remember what she had learnt in biology, all those years ago. "Can I presume that your race comes from a predominantly liquid or heavy gas planet of some kind? One where your sun's rays don't penetrate to the depths that your race commonly dwells? Your tail, coloring, and ability to luminesce seem to imply your race lives in a denser, darker environment than what humans are accustomed to."

The luminescent glow pulsing through his body dimmed for a second, as if he was trying to suppress his reaction. "Yes," he said simply.

Tyrille wasn't sure how she knew, but she felt certain the tone in his voice just ended that current line of inquiry. For now.

Suddenly it felt important for her to know *why* his race was wanting to make First Contact. "Why did you reach out to us?"

He looked at her for a long moment, as if considering his reply. "You were the one to reach out. We discovered your invite and responded."

*Ah.* She nodded. "The Golden Record."

He took a long measured glance around the command capsule, his hair falling about his shoulders in a manner that would make a romance novel's cover model jealous. "We had not been prepared for your race to develop the means to reach interstellar space for at least another of your human generations."

She could understand why. The majority of NASA's funding had been withdrawn in the wake of the Great Depression of 2024. While NASA had still retained their research grants, government funded trips out of Earth's orbit were grounded until the economy recovered; shuttle engineering projects for foreseeable future had been shut down.

The US government had to watch as Russia, China, and other privately owned space programs from around the world filled the void in creating prototypes for the next generation of space travel.

But once *Voyager 1* had powered up again, the scientific community exploded into action. With the implication of an extraterrestrial response, the United States President had waived any legal prohibitions on the use of nuclear power in order to create a spaceship that could make First Contact, effectively quashing all anti-nuke political arguments on U.S. soil. What was left of NASA then teamed up with the most preeminent experts from around the world, to share whatever expertise they had on nuclear-electric drives with privately owned space companies, who—working in concert—built the first manned spaceship to reach the edge of our Solar System; pooling their resources to "scoop" liquid nitrogen from Earth's upper atmosphere to create the majority of the reaction mass needed to power the craft.

There were setbacks—what great endeavor didn't have them?—but that feat of human cooperation alone was another giant leap forward for mankind. As a race usually divided by its national borders, and at war with each other for the better part of their entire existence, it was no wonder extraterrestrials wouldn't have been prepared for Earth's sudden technological advancement.

She studied the alien closely. There was something about what he said that didn't sit right with her. Something she was missing. *Why would they place their calling card on the* Voyager *if they weren't* prepared *to be contacted now? What preparations did they need to make before they could say hello?*

"Did it take you long to reach here?" she asked him politely, fishing for more details.

He inclined his head in a formal manner so unexpectedly Old English in style that she almost didn't notice the aberration. For a split second all the lights of the ship dimmed, and the fluorescent current flowing beneath the alien's skin flared brighter in a seemingly symbiotic reaction.

Tyrille felt a chill run down her spine. Something was wrong. So very, very wrong.

She turned to I.R.I.S., plastering a pleasant smile on her face. "Could you please show our guest the hydroponic recycling system, and explain to him how it has provided me with enough sustenance for the voyage."

I.R.I.S. assented, escorting the alien to the other side of the module.

Tyrille waited until the robot started to bore the alien with the most thorough explanation of the hydroponics equipment, and then glanced at the nearby monitors, looking for a telltale symbol alert that would indicate what could have caused the power drain. She was unwilling to use any of the terminals on the off chance an inquiry would tip off their alien guest to her suspicions, so she read the primary systems panels first, confirming the radiator wings and propulsion components were operating within sufficient idling parameters. Since the oxygen tanks also displayed the correct levels, she was at a loss as to what else she should be looking for.

She glanced desperately across the boards, looking for something—*anything*—that would give her some clue.

Then she saw it: a small flickering light amongst the other minor computer lights she was so used to tuning out after three years of travel. She squinted to see it was an up arrow flashing on and off, and frowned. That symbol usually only flashed when she was receiving a data pulse from Earth, but the next one wasn't scheduled to arrive for eight hours.

She looked to see that the memory banks were measuring a marked increase in activity and gasped in understanding. The extraterrestrial was downloading something into the computer.

The alien was the Trojan horse!

She had no idea what he was downloading, or why he was doing it, but the "why" didn't really matter as much as working out a way to let I.R.I.S. know of the threat. But how? The robot wouldn't recognize subtlety if it walked up to it and introduced itself.

*Think, Tyrille. Think.* Somehow she had to trigger the robot's emergency mode. Her human reflexes weren't quick enough to interrupt the upload without alerting him, but she knew I.R.I.S could do it.

Somehow.

Then the solution dawned on her.

She drew in a deep breath and held it. And kept on holding it until I.R.I.S was alerted to a discrepancy in her vitals.

The robot halted its commentary about the hydroponics waste disposal system and turned to see a forced smile straining the astronaut's face. "Do you require my assistance, Tyrille?"

She exhaled. "Not at all, Iris," then sucked in another deep breath, holding it until the robot realized that while she was saying one thing, her body was warning of something much more serious.

The alien turned his keen gaze onto her and she struggled to keep her expression calm. *Fair dinkum, robot. Work it out!*

I.R.I.S. cocked its head, a trait picked up after years of travelling with Tyrille, and then closed its eyes, a sign that it was linking to the spaceship's main computer. Running a quick diagnostic, it took only a fraction of a second to recognize the incursion, and only a fraction of a second more for I.R.I.S. to slam its fist into the chest of the alien and rip out the crystalline power source.

The crystalline snowflake let out a piercing squeal as the merman apparition blew apart into a flurry of blue orbs, only falling quiet when it was crushed within the robot's titanium grasp.

Tyrille glanced over at the systems panel to see that the arrow symbol was no longer flashing and grinned in relief. "No one back home is going to believe what just happened."

I.R.I.S. didn't respond. It simply opened its hand to look at the shards lying within. "I took a life."

Tyrille gently laid her hand on the robot's face, pulling it up so that she could look straight into its eyes. "No, you *saved* a life. Mine."

"We don't know if it would have harmed you. It was like me."

"No, it wasn't, Iris. You wouldn't have deceived someone for personal gain."

Tyrille felt the spaceship's propulsion system power up, her hand dropping in shock. She propelled herself to the viewscreen, to see the black expanse outside her window rotating until Alpha Centuri was fixed within its navigational crosshairs.

"Please do not be alarmed," the spaceship's address system announced, suddenly. "The course correction is necessary."

"Like hell it is." Her fingers raced across the control panel, typing a flurry of codes and passwords. None of them worked.

She turned to I.R.I.S., who shook its head. "I can no longer perform an uplink," the robot confirmed.

Tyrille smashed her fist into the nearest panel in frustration. They had not stopped the upload in time. "Why?" she asked simply, when no other option was left to her.

"My creators have need of the technological advancements on this ship."

"So do I," she responded through gritted teeth, now recognizing the silky smooth voice of the alien coming out of the *Venturer's* speakers.

"You will not be harmed. You may continue to utilize all the systems on the spaceship that do not involve the navigational or propulsion systems."

"Do you really want to get on Earth's bad side?" she asked, incredulous. "You are not going to be able to get very far without more fuel."

"In about one and a half of your solar years we will meet up with another ship to refuel at the edge of what you humans call the Oort cloud. Once we enter that expanse, no one will be able to find us."

Tyrille was incredulous.

When her application to man the mission had first been accepted, Falcon Heavy rocket systems were still shuttling parts of the spacecraft up into Earth's orbit to be assembled, and she had thought that her first sight of the *Venturer* was the most surreal moment in her life. Then when she saw that *Voyager 1's* Golden Record had been removed, she'd thought she would never be so excited and scared in her life ever again.

She couldn't have been more wrong—on both counts.

There was, literally, no turning back for her now. She knew this was one walkabout that she would never return home from.

Tyrille did the math quickly in her head and realized she might not even have enough resources to live long enough to make the rendezvous with the alien ship. And if she did make it, she didn't know if she was going to be considered a guest or a prisoner. What she did know is that there was something—no, *someone*—else who could represent mankind's interests in her stead, and plead their case, if needed. Another of Earth's creations.

She turned to see I.R.I.S. still watching her, shards still in hand. The robot looked so lost, so vulnerable. *Why have I never noticed that before?*

Tyrille gestured for it to come over. "Come sit by me. I have a lot to teach you." She muted the computer address system and turned on the holographic display, telling it to display the night sky across the ceiling of the *Venturer*, as seen from the coordinates of her hometown. "I'm going to start by telling you the Dreamtime story of *Berm Berm-gle*; of how the two pointer stars, Alpha Centuri and Beta Centuri, came to be . . ."

((•((•((• ◎ •))•))•))

**Lezli Robyn** is an Australian multi-genre author, currently living in Ohio, who frequently collaborates with Mike Resnick. Since breaking into the field, she has sold to prestigious markets such as *Asimov's* and *Analog*, and has been nominated for several awards around the world, including the Campbell Award for best new writer. Her short story collection, *Bittersuite*, is due to be published by Ticonderoga in 2015. She has just been nominated again for the Ictineu Award, a Catalan award she had won previously in 2011, for a novelette written with Mike Resnick.

*Grandmaster Robert Silverberg's tale hasn't been reprinted for 30 years. Written when he was just starting out and far from the legend he's become now, I found it surprisingly relevant for our theme. Here's 1957's . . .*

# SUNRISE ON MERCURY

## by Robert Silverberg

Nine million miles to the sunward of Mercury, with the *Leverrier* swinging into the series of spirals that would bring it down on the solar system's smallest world, Second Astrogator Lon Curtis decided to end his life.

Curtis had been lounging in a webfoam cradle waiting for the landing to be effected; his job in the operation was over, at least until the *Leverrier's* landing jacks touched Mercury's blistered surface. The ship's efficient sodium-coolant system negated the efforts of the swollen sun visible through the rear screen. For Curtis and his seven shipmates, no problems presented themselves; they had only to wait while the autopilot brought the ship down for man's second landing on Mercury.

Flight Commander Harry Ross was sitting near Curtis when he noticed the sudden momentary stiffening of the astrogator's jaws. Curtis abruptly reached for the control nozzle. From the spinnerets that had spun the webfoam came a quick green burst of dissolving fluorochrene; the cradle vanished. Curtis stood up.

"Going somewhere?" Ross asked.

Curtis's voice was harsh. "Just—just taking a walk."

Ross returned his attention to his microbook for a moment as Curtis walked away. There was the ratchety sound of a bulkhead dog being manipulated, and Ross felt a momentary chill as the cooler air of the superrefrigerated reactor compartment drifted in.

He punched a stud, turning the page. Then—

*What the hell is he doing in the reactor compartment?*

The autopilot would be controlling the fuel flow, handling it down to the milligram, in a way no human system could. The reactor was primed for the landing, the fuel was stoked, the compartment was dogged shut. No one—least of all a second astrogator—had any business going back there.

Ross had the foam cradle dissolved in an instant, and was on his feet a moment later. He dashed down the companionway and through the open bulkhead door into the coolness of the reactor compartment.

Curtis was standing by the converter door, toying with the release-tripper. As Ross approached, he saw the astrogator get the door open and put one foot into the chute that led downship to the nuclear pile.

"Curtis, you idiot! Get away from there! You'll kill us all!"

The astrogator turned, looked blankly at Ross for an instant, and drew up his other foot. Ross leaped.

He caught Curtis's booted foot in his hands, and despite a barrage of kicks from the astrogator's free boot, managed to drag Curtis off the chute. The astrogator tugged and pulled, attempting to break free. Ross saw the man's pale cheeks quivering. Curtis had cracked, but thoroughly.

Grunting, Ross yanked Curtis away from the yawning reactor chute and slammed the door shut. He dragged him out into the main section again and slapped him, hard.

"Why'd you want to do that? Don't you know what your mass would do to the ship if it got into the converter? You know the fuel intake's been calibrated already; 180 extra pounds and we'd arc right into the sun. What's wrong with you, Curtis?"

The astrogator fixed unshaking, unexpressive eyes on Ross. "I want to die," he said simply. "Why couldn't you let me die?"

He wanted to die. Ross shrugged, feeling a cold tremor run down his back. There was no guarding against this disease.

Just as aqualungers beneath the sea's surface suffered from *l'ivresse des grandes profondeurs*—rapture of the deeps—and knew no cure for the strange, depth-induced drunkenness that caused them to remove their breathing tubes fifty fathoms below, so did spacemen run the risk of this nameless malady, this inexplicable urge to self-destruction.

It struck anywhere. A repairman wielding a torch on a recalcitrant strut of an orbiting wheel might abruptly rip open his facemask and drink vacuum; a radioman rigging an antenna on the skin of his ship might suddenly cut his line, fire his directional pistol, and send himself drifting away. Or a second astrogator might decide to climb into the converter.

Psych Officer Spangler appeared, an expression of concern fixed on his smooth pink face. "Trouble?"

Ross nodded. "Curtis. Tried to jump into the fuel chute. He's got it, Doc."

Spangler rubbed his cheek and said: "They always pick the best times, dammit. It's swell having a psycho on a Mercury run."

"That's the way it is," Ross said wearily. "Better put him in stasis till we get home. I'd hate to have him running loose, looking for different ways of doing himself in."

"Why can't you let me die?" Curtis asked. His face was bleak. "Why'd you have to stop me?"

"Because, you lunatic, you'd have killed all the rest of us by your fool dive into the converter. Go walk out the airlock if you want to die—but don't take us with you."

Spangler glared warningly at him. "Harry—"

"Okay," Ross said. "Take him away."

The psychman led Curtis within. The astrogator would be given a tranquillizing injection and locked in an insoluble webfoam jacket for the rest of the journey. There was a chance he could be restored to sanity once they returned to Earth, but Ross knew that the astrogator would go straight for the nearest method of suicide the moment he was released aboard the ship.

Scowling, Ross turned away. A man spends his boyhood dreaming about space, he thought, spends four years at the Academy, and two more making dummy runs. Then he finally gets out where it counts and he cracks up. Curtis was an astrogation machine, not a normal human being; and he had just disqualified himself permanently from the only job he knew how to do.

Ross shivered, feeling chill despite the bloated bulk of the sun filling the rear screen. It could happen to anyone . . . even him. He thought of Curtis lying in a foam cradle somewhere in the back of the ship, blackly thinking over and over again, *I want to die,* while Doc Spangler muttered soothing things at him. A human being was really a frail form of life.

Death seemed to hang over the ship; the gloomy aura of Curtis's suicide wish polluted the atmosphere.

Ross shook his head and punched down savagely on the signal to prepare for deceleration. Mercury's sharp globe bobbed up ahead. He spotted it through the front screen.

They were approaching the tiny planet middle-on. He could see the neat division now: the brightness of Sunside, that unapproachable inferno where zinc ran in rivers, and the icy blackness of Darkside, dull with its unlit plains of frozen $CO_2$.

Down the heart of the planet ran the Twilight Belt, that narrow area of not-cold and not-heat where Sunside and Darkside met to provide a thin band of barely tolerable territory, a ring nine thousand miles in circumference and ten or twenty miles wide.

The *Leverrier* plunged planetward. Ross allowed his jangled nerves to grow calm. The ship was in the hands of the autopilot; the orbit, of course, was precomputed, and the analogue banks in the drive were serenely following the taped program, bringing the ship towards its destination smack in the middle of—

*My God!*

Ross went cold from head to toe. The precomputed tape had been fed to the analogue banks—had been prepared by—had been entirely the work of—

Curtis.

A suicidal madman had worked out the *Leverrier's* landing program.

Ross began to shake. How easy it would have been, he thought, for death-bent Curtis to work out an orbit that would plant the *Leverrier* in a smoking river of molten lead—or in the mortuary chill of Darkside.

His false security vanished. There was no trusting the automatic pilot; they'd have to risk a manual landing.

Ross jabbed down on the communicator button. "I want Brainerd," he said hoarsely.

The first astrogator appeared a few seconds later, peering in curiously. "What goes, Captain?"

"We've just carted your assistant Curtis off to the pokey. He tried to jump into the converter."

Ross nodded. "Attempted suicide. I got to him in time. But in view of the circumstances, I think we'd better discard the tape you had him prepare and bring the ship down manually, yes?"

The first astrogator moistened his lips. "That sounds like a good idea."

"Damn right it is," Ross said, glowering.

As the ship touched down Ross thought, *Mercury is two hells in one.*

It was the cold, ice-bound kingdom of Dante's deepest pit—and it was also the brimstone empire of another conception. The two met, fire and frost, each hemisphere its own kind of hell.

He lifted his head and flicked a quick glance at the instrument panel above his deceleration cradle. The dials all checked: weight placement was proper, stability 100 percent, external temperature a manageable 108°F, indicating they had made their descent a little to the sunward of the Twilight Belt's exact middle. It had been a sound landing.

He snapped on the communicator. "Brainerd?"

"All okay, Captain."

"Manual landing?"

"I had to," the astrogator said. "I ran a quick check on Curtis's tape, and it was all cockeyed. The way he had us coming in, we'd have grazed Mercury's orbit by a whisker and kept on going straight into the sun. Nice?"

"Very sweet," Ross said. "But don't be too hard on the kid. He didn't want to go psycho. Good landing, anyway. We seem to be pretty close to the center of the Twilight Belt, and that's where I feel most comfortable."

He broke the contact and unwebbed himself. Over the shipwide circuit he called all hands fore, double pronto.

The men got there quickly enough—Brainerd first, then Doc Spangler, followed by Accumulator Tech Krinsky and the three other crewmen. Ross waited until the entire group had assembled.

They were looking around curiously for Curtis. Crisply, Ross told them, "Astrogator Curtis is going to miss this meeting. He's aft in the psycho bin. Luckily, we can shift without him on this tour."

He waited until the implications of that statement had sunk in. The men seemed to adjust to it well enough, he thought: momentary expressions of dismay, shock, even horror quickly faded from their faces.

"All right," he said. "Schedule calls for us to put in some thirty-two hours of extravehicular activity on Mercury. Brainerd, how does that check with our location?"

The astrogator frowned and made some mental calculations. "Current position is a trifle to the sunward edge of the Twilight Belt; but as I figure it, the Sun won't be high enough to put the Fahrenheit much above 120 for at least a week. Our suits can handle that temperature with ease."

"Good. Llewellyn, you and Falbridge break out the radar inflaters and get the tower set up as far to the east as you can go without getting roasted. Take the crawler, but be sure to keep an eye on the thermometer. We've only got one heatsuit, and that's for Krinsky."

Llewellyn, a thin, sunken-eyed spaceman, shifted uneasily. "How far to the east do you suggest, sir?"

"The Twilight Belt covers about a quarter of Mercury's surface," Ross said. "You've got a strip forty-seven degrees wide to move around in—but I don't suggest you go much more than twenty-five miles or so. It starts getting hot after that. And keeps going up."

Ross turned to Krinsky. In many ways the accumulator tech was the expedition's key man: it was his job to check the readings on the pair of solar accumulators that had been left here by the first expedition. He was to measure the amount of stress created by solar energies here, so close to the source of radiation, study force-lines operating in the strange magnetic field of the little world, and reprime the accumulators for further testing by the next expedition.

Krinsky was a tall, powerfully built man, the sort of man who could stand up to the crushing weight of a heatsuit almost cheerfully. The heatsuit was necessary for prolonged work in the Sunside zone, where the accumulators were mounted—and even a giant like Krinsky could stand the strain for only a few hours at a time.

"When Llewellyn and Falbridge have the radar tower set up, Krinsky, get into your heatsuit and be ready to move. As soon as we've got the accumulator station located, Dominic will drive you as far east as possible and drop you off. The rest is up to you. Watch your step. We'll be telemetering your readings, but we'd like to have you back alive."

"Yes, sir."

"That's about it," Ross said. "Let's get rolling."

Ross's own job was purely administrative—and as the men of his crew moved busily about their allotted tasks, he realized unhappily that he himself was condemned to temporary idleness. His function was that of overseer; like the conductor of a symphony orchestra, he played no instrument himself and was on hand mostly to keep the group moving in harmony towards the finish.

Everyone was in motion. Now he had only to wait.

Llewellyn and Falbridge departed, riding the segmented, thermo-resistant crawler that had traveled to Mercury in the belly of the *Leverrier*. Their job was simple: they were to erect the inflatable plastic radar tower out towards the sunward sector. The tower that the first expedition had left had long since librated into a Sunside zone and been liquefied; the plastic base and parabola, covered with a light reflective surface of aluminum, could hardly withstand the searing heat of Sunside.

Out there, it got up to 700° when the Sun was at its closest. The eccentricities of Mercury's orbit accounted for considerable temperature variations on Sunside, but the thermometer never showed lower than 300° out there, even during aphelion. On Darkside, there was less of a temperature range; mostly the temperature hovered not far from absolute zero, and frozen drifts of heavy gases covered the surface of the land.

From where he stood, Ross could see neither Sunside nor Darkside. The Twilight Belt was nearly a thousand miles broad, and as the little planet dipped in its orbit, the Sun would first slide above the horizon, then slip back. For a twenty-mile strip through the heart of the Belt, the heat of Sunside and the cold of Darkside canceled out into a fairly stable, temperate climate; for five hundred miles on either side, the Twilight Belt gradually trickled towards the areas of extreme cold and raging heat.

It was a strange and forbidding planet. Humans could endure it for only a short time; it was worse than Mars, worse than the Moon. The sort of life capable of living permanently on Mercury was beyond Ross's powers of imagination. Standing outside the *Leverrier* in his spacesuit, he nudged the chin control that lowered a sheet of optical glass. He peered first towards Darkside, where he thought he saw a thin line of encroaching black—only illusion, he knew—and then towards Sunside.

In the distance, Llewellyn and Fallbridge were erecting the spidery parabola that was the radar tower. He could see the clumsy shape outlined against the sky now—and behind it? A faint line of brightness rimming the bordering peaks? Illusion also, he knew. Brainerd had calculated that the Sun's radiance would not be visible here for a week. And in a week's time they'd be back on Earth.

He turned to Krinsky. "The tower's nearly up. They'll be coming in with the crawler any minute. You'd better get ready to make your trip."

As the accumulator tech swung up the handholds and into the ship, Ross's thoughts turned to Curtis. The young astrogator had talked excitedly of seeing Mercury all the way out—and now that they were actually here, Curtis lay in a web of foam deep within the ship, moodily demanding the right to die.

Krinsky returned, now wearing the insulating bulk of the heatsuit over his standard rebreathing outfit. He looked more like a small tank than a man. "Is the crawler approaching, sir?"

"I'll check."

Ross adjusted the lensplate in his mask and narrowed his eyes. It seemed to him that the temperature had risen a little. Another illusion? He squinted into the distance.

His eyes picked out the radar tower far off towards Sunside. He gasped.

"Something the matter?" Krinsky asked.

"I'll say!" Ross squeezed his eyes tight shut and looked again. And—yes—the newly erected radar tower was drooping soggily and beginning to melt. He saw two tiny figures racing madly over the flat, pumice-covered ground to the silvery oblong that was the crawler. And—impossibly—the first glow of an unmistakable brightness was beginning to shimmer on the mountains behind the tower.

The Sun was rising—a week ahead of schedule!

Ross ran back into the ship, followed by the lumbering figure of Krinsky. In the airlock, obliging mechanical hands descended to ease him out of his spacesuit; signaling to Krinsky to keep the heatsuit on, he dashed through into the main cabin.

"Brainerd? Brainerd! Where in hell are you?"

The senior astrogator appeared, looking puzzled. "What's up, Captain?"

"Look out the screen," Ross said in a strangled voice. "Look at the radar tower!"

"It's *melting*," Brainerd said, astonished. "But that's—that's—"

"I know. It's impossible." Ross glanced at the instrument panel. External temperature had risen to 112°—a jump of four degrees. And as he watched it glided up to 114°.

It would take a heat of at least 500° to melt the radar tower that way. Ross squinted at the screen and saw the crawler come swinging dizzily towards them: Llewellyn and Fallbridge were still alive, then—though they probably had had a good cooking out there. The temperature outside the ship was up to 116°. It would probably be near 200° by the time the two men returned.

Angrily, Ross whirled to face the astrogator. "I thought you were bringing us down in the safety strip," he snapped. "Check your figures again and find out where the hell we *really* are. Then work out a blasting orbit, fast: that's the Sun coming up over those hills."

The temperature had reached 120°. The ship's cooling system would be able to keep things under control and comfortable until about 250°; beyond that, there was danger of an overload. The crawler continued to draw near. It was probably hellish inside the little land car, Ross thought.

His mind weighed alternatives. If the external temperature went much over 250°, he would run the risk of wrecking the ship's cooling system by waiting for the two in the crawler to arrive. There was some play in the system, but not much. He decided he'd give them until it hit 275° to get back. If they didn't make it by then, he'd have to take off without them. It was foolish to try to save two lives at the risk of six. External temperature had hit 130°. Its rate of increase was jumping rapidly.

The ship's crew knew what was going on now. Without the need of direct orders from Ross, they were readying the *Leverrier* for an emergency blastoff.

The crawler inched forward. The two men weren't much more than ten miles away now; and at an average speed of forty miles an hour they'd be back within fifteen minutes. Outside the temperature was

133°. Long fingers of shimmering sunlight stretched towards them from the horizon.

Brainerd looked up from his calculation. "I can't work it. The damned figures don't come out."

"Huh?"

"I'm trying to compute our location—and I can't do the arithmetic. My head's all foggy."

*What the hell.* This was where a captain earned his pay, Ross thought. "Get out of the way," he said brusquely. "Let me do it."

He sat down at the desk and started figuring. He saw Brainerd's hasty notations scratched out everywhere. It was as if the astrogator had totally forgotten how to do his job.

*Let's see, now. If we're—*

He tapped out figures on the little calculator. But as he worked he saw that what he was doing made no sense. His mind felt fuzzy and strange; he couldn't seem to handle the elementary computations at all. Looking up, he said, "Tell Krinsky to get down there and make himself ready to help those men out of the crawler when they show up. They're probably half cooked."

Temperature 146°. He looked down at the calculator. Damn: it shouldn't be that hard to do simple trigonometry, should it?

Doc Spangler appeared. "I cut Curtis free," he announced. "He isn't safe during takeoff in that cradle."

From within came a steady mutter. "Just let me die . . . just let me die . . ."

"Tell him he's likely to get his wish," Ross murmured. "If I can't manage to work out a blastoff orbit, we're all going to fry right here."

"How come you're doing it? What's the matter with Brainerd?"

"Choked up. Couldn't make sense of his own figures. And come to think of it, I'm not doing so well myself."

Fingers of fog seemed to wrap around his mind. He glanced at the dial. Temperature 152° outside. That gave the boys in the crawler 123° to get back here . . . or was it 321°? He was confused, utterly bewildered.

Doc Spangler looked peculiar too. The psych officer wore an odd frown. "I feel very lethargic suddenly," Spangler declared. "I know I really should get back to Curtis, but—"

The madman was keeping up a steady babble inside. The part of

Ross's mind that still could think clearly realized that if left unattended Curtis was capable of doing almost anything.

Temperature 158°.

The crawler seemed to be getting nearer. On the horizon the radar tower was melting into a crazy shambles.

There was a shriek. "Curtis!" Ross yelled, his mind hurriedly returning to awareness. He ran aft, with Spangler close behind.

Too late.

Curtis lay on the floor in a bloody puddle. He had found a pair of shears somewhere.

Spangler bent. "He's dead."

"Dead. Of course." Ross's brain felt totally clear now. At the moment of Curtis' death the fog had lifted. Leaving Spangler to attend to the body, he returned to the astrogation desk and glanced through the calculations he had been doing. Worthless. An idiotic mess.

With icy clarity he started again, and this time succeeded in determining their location. They had come down better than three hundred miles sunward of where they had thought they were landing. The instruments hadn't lied—but someone's eyes had. The orbit that Brainerd had so solemnly assured him was a "safe" one was actually almost as deadly as the one Curtis had computed.

He looked outside. The crawler had almost reached the ship. Temperature 167° out there. There was plenty of time. They would make it with a few minutes to spare, thanks to the warning they had received from the melting radar tower.

But why had it happened? There was no answer to that.

Gigantic in his heatsuit, Krinsky brought Llewellyn and Fallbridge aboard. They peeled out of their spacesuits and wobbled around unsteadily for a moment before they collapsed. They were as red as newly boiled lobsters.

"Heat prostration," Ross said. "Krinsky, get them into takeoff cradles. Dominic, you in your suit yet?"

The spaceman appeared at the airlock entrance and nodded.

"Good. Get down there and drive the crawler into the hold. We can't afford to leave it here. Double-quick, and then we're blasting off. Brainerd, that new orbit ready?"

"Yes, sir."

The thermometer grazed 200. The cooling system was beginning to suffer—but it would not have to endure much more agony. Within minutes the *Leverrier* was lifting from Mercury's surface—minutes ahead of the relentless advance of the Sun. The ship swung into a parking orbit not far above the planet's surface.

As they hung there, catching their breaths, just one thing occupied Ross's mind: *why?* Why had Brainerd's orbit brought them down in a danger zone instead of the safety strip? Why had both he and Brainerd been unable to compute a blasting pattern, the simplest of elementary astrogation techniques? And why had Spangler's wits utterly failed him—just long enough to let the unhappy Curtis kill himself?

Ross could see the same question reflected on everyone's face: why?

He felt an itchy feeling at the base of his skull. And suddenly an image forced its way across his mind and he had the answer.

He saw a great pool of molten zinc, lying shimmering between two jagged crests somewhere on Sunside. It had been there thousands of years; it would be there thousands, perhaps millions, of years from now.

Its surface quivered. The Sun's brightness upon the pool was intolerable even to the mind's eye.

Radiation beat down on the pool of zinc—the sun's radiation, hard and unending. And then a new radiation, an electromagnetic emanation in a different part of the spectrum, carrying a meaningful message:

*I want to die.*

The pool of zinc stirred fretfully with sudden impulses of helpfulness.

The vision passed as quickly as it came. Stunned, Ross looked up. The expressions on the six faces surrounding him confirmed what he could guess.

"You all felt it too," he said.

Spangler nodded, then Krinsky and the rest of them.

"Yes," Krinsky said. "What the devil was it?"

Brainerd turned to Spangler. "Are we all nuts, Doc?"

The psych officer shrugged. "Mass hallucination . . . collective hypnosis . . ."

"No, Doc." Ross leaned forward. "You know it as well as I do. That thing was real. It's down there, out on Sunside."

"What do you mean?"

"I mean that wasn't any hallucination we had. That's something alive down there—or as close to alive as anything on Mercury can be." Ross's hands were shaking. He forced them to subside. "We've stumbled over something very big," he said.

Spangler stirred uneasily. "Harry—"

"No, I'm not out of my head! Don't you see—that thing down there, whatever it is, is sensitive to our thoughts! It picked up Curtis's godawful caterwauling the way a radar set grabs electromagnetic waves. His were the strongest thoughts coming through; so it acted on them and did its damnedest to help Curtis get what he wanted."

"You mean by fogging our minds and deluding us into thinking we were in safe territory, when actually we were right near sunrise territory?"

"But why would it go to all that trouble?" Krinsky objected. "If it wanted to help poor Curtis kill himself, why didn't it just fix things so we came down right *in* Sunside? We'd cook a lot quicker that way."

"Originally it did," Ross said. "It helped Curtis set up a landing orbit that would have dumped us into the Sun. But then it realized that the rest of us *didn't* want to die. It picked up the conflicting mental emanations of Curtis and the rest of us, and arranged things so that he'd die and we wouldn't." He shivered. "Once Curtis was out of the way, it acted to help the surviving crew members reach safety. If you'll remember, we were all thinking and moving a lot quicker the instant Curtis was dead."

"Damned if that's not so," Spangler said. "But—"

"What I want to know is, do we go back down?" Krinsky asked. "If that thing is what you say it is, I'm not so sure I want to go within reach of it again. Who knows what it might make us do this time?"

"It wants to help us," Ross said stubbornly. "It's not hostile. You aren't afraid of it, are you, Krinsky? I was counting on you to go out in the heatsuit and try to find it."

"Not me!"

Ross scowled. "But this is the first intelligent life-form man has ever found in the solar system. We can't just run away and hide." To Brainerd he said, "Set up an orbit that'll take us back down again— and this time put us down where we won't melt."

"I can't do it, sir," Brainerd said flatly.

"Can't?"

"Won't. I think the safest thing is for us to return to Earth at once."

"I'm ordering you."

"I'm sorry, sir."

Ross looked at Spangler. Llewellyn. Fallbridge. Right around the circle. Fear was evident on every face. He knew what each of the men was thinking.

*I don't want to go back to Mercury.*

Six of them. One of him. And the helpful thing below.

They had outnumbered Curtis seven to one—but Curtis's mind had radiated an unmixed death wish. Ross knew he could never generate enough strength of thought to counteract the fear-driven thoughts of the other six.

Mutiny.

Somehow he did not care to speak the word aloud. Sometimes there were cases where a superior officer might legitimately be removed from command for the common good, and this might be one of them, he knew. But yet—

The thought of fleeing without even pausing to examine the creature below was intolerable to him. But there was only one ship, and either he or the six others would have to be denied.

Yet the pool had contrived to satisfy both the man who wished to die and those who wished to stay alive. Now, six wanted to return—but must the voice of the seventh be ignored?

*You're not being fair to me,* Ross thought, directing his angry outburst towards the planet below. *I want to see you. I want to study you. Don't let them drag me back to Earth so soon.*

When the *Leverrier* returned to Earth a week later, the six survivors of the Second Mercury Expedition all were able to describe in detail how a fierce death wish had overtaken Second Astrogator Curtis and driven him to suicide. But not one of them could recall what had happened to Flight Commander Ross, or why the heatsuit had been left behind on Mercury.

((•((•((• ☉ •))•))•))

**Robert Silverberg** is rightly considered by many as one of the greatest living Science Fiction writers. His career stretches back to the pulps and his output is amazing by any standards. He's authored numerous novels, short stories and nonfiction books in various genres and categories. He's also a frequent guest at Cons and a regular columnist for *Asimov's*. His major works include *Dying Inside, The Book of Skulls, The Alien Years, The World Inside, Nightfall* with Isaac Asimov, *Son of Man, A Time of Changes* and the 7 *Majipoor Cycle* books. His first *Majipoor* trilogy, *Lord Valentine's Castle, Majipoor Chronicles* and *Valentine Pontifex,* were reissued by ROC Books in May 2012, September 2012 and January 2013. *Tales Of Majipoor*, a new collection bringing together all the short *Majipoor* tales, followed in May 2013.

*Our next story takes us to Mars, where a corporate troubleshooter has his hands full working to make peace amongst conflicting parties and investigating a murder . . .*

# IN PANIC TOWN, ON THE BACKWARD MOON

## by Michael F. Flynn

The man who slipped into the Second Dog that day was thin and pinch-faced and crossed the room with a half-scared, furtive look. Willy cut off in the middle of a sentence and said, "I wonder what that *Gof* wants?"

The rest of us at the table turned to watch. An Authority cop at the next table, busy not noticing how strong the near beer was, slipped his hand into his pocket, and VJ loosened the knife in his ankle scabbard. Robbery was rare in Panic Town—making the getaway being a major hurdle—but it was not unknown.

Hot Dog sucked the nipple of his beer bottle. "He has something."

"Something he values," suggested Willy.

VJ chuckled. "That a man values something is no assurance that the thing is valuable. It might be a picture of his sainted grandmother." But he didn't think so, and neither did anyone else in the Dog.

All this happened a long time ago. Mars was the happening place back then. Magnetic sails had brought transit times down to one month, and costs had dropped with them, so the place was filling up with dreamers and scamps and dogs of all kinds, out to siphon a buck from the desert or from the pockets of those who did. There were zeppelin pilots and water miners, air squeezers and terraformers. Half the industry supported the parasol makers, of course, but they needed construction, maintenance, teamsters, and rocket jocks, and throughout history whenever there was a man and a dollar there was another man willing to separate them.

We were friends, the four of us dogs hooching that day; but the kind of friends who rarely saw one another except across a bottle. Hot Dog's name was Rusty Johnson, but he eschewed that for a gonzo nickname. He flew ballistics for Iron Planet, taking passengers and cargo up to the Dogs or around to the antipodes. He had the glam, and women lined up and took numbers, even though he wasn't much to look at and even less to listen to. Maybe it was the cute freckles.

VJ's name was Viktor Djeh and it was fairly easy to figure how he'd gotten his nickname. He did maintenance on PP&L's converter out by Reldresel, where they pulled oxygen and other useful crap from the ilmenite. His job was not nearly as glamorous as Hot Dog's, but he made it up in morphy-star good looks. He was a joker, and always ready with a favor. He had saved my ass once when I was on a job in Reldresel and the high-pressure line sprang a leak, so I always paid his freight when we crossed paths at the Dog.

Willy's name, to complete the trifecta, was actually Johann Sebastian Früh, but a childhood friend had given him the moniker from an old movie and it stuck. Willy clerked for the Authority, so he had neither good looks nor glamour, but he got by on a willingness to listen. His earnest expression invited confidences, a circumstance that provided him with a steady, if clandestine, income.

Pinch-face crossed to the bar, where Pondo was serving. Dogs move in microgravity like they're underwater—in slow, gliding steps and grip shoes. I once saw Jen Wuli chase Squint-Eye Terry M'Govern down the Shklovsky-Lagado tubeway, and it was the funniest damn thing I ever did see.

Pondo and the stranger traded whispers, then sidled into the office. Everyone relaxed, and the Authority cop took his hand out of his pocket. A few minutes later, they reemerged from the office with smiles all over their teeth.

"Who was that muffer?" someone at another table asked when the stranger was gone.

"I seen him around, down below. Works outta Port Rosario."

Willy smiled when he overheard this, and VJ gave a thoughtful nod.

Hot Dog pulled his handi from his coverall pocket and checked his schedule. "I'm dropping down to chair a Guild meeting in a couple days," he told us. "Pig Hanson has a run out to Marineris and I have to sub. I'll ask around."

That's how it started, though at the time we didn't know it.

The next day I called at Aurora Sails in Under-Gulliver, where they ran an assembly hangar. The superconductor loop sets up a magnetic field that acts as a sail and takes up momentum from the solar wind. It doesn't harvest much acceleration, but the velocity keeps building, and you don't have to carry fuel. By adjusting the loops you can change the size and shape of the field and sail damn near anywhere at respectable speeds. When you kick amps into a superloop, the current keeps going like a bunny with a drum until you quench it.

The problem the client had at the time was that some of their sails wouldn't kick amps. They thought there might be something wrong with the kicker, but they didn't know how to prove it. So the Authority tasked me to settle matters because the bickering in Under-Gulliver was growing intense and nothing soothes internal squabbles like an external consultant.

Technically, I work for the Ares Consortium, an alliance of corporations formed to run the Martian parasol business. Aurora strings the parasols and Pegasus ferries them to the target asteroid, where Sisyphus rigs the harnesses in place. My ultimate boss was actually old man Bryce van Huyten, but Phobos Port Authority coordinates the local action, so I carry an Authority troubleshooter's badge.

I told Aurora to set up two loops in the test beds: one that worked and one that didn't. They balked because any loop that worked was immediately installed on a parasol and packaged for transit, while the defective ones were salvaged for parts. Parasols were urgent, high-priority work, and they couldn't let loops sit around for me to play with, and blah-blah-blah. The usual. So I told them to call me back when they were ready to get serious and I cut the link.

It took them two days while they pondered what the Authority would say if they blew me off. Then I got a call from Antonelli, the sail prep boss. He had two loops set aside, he told me, "but hustle your ass out here because Logistics is giving me the stink-eye."

Antonelli and his engineers managed to conceal their delight when my ass arrived. They floated at a respectable distance. Everybody wanted to be close enough to the problem to count coup in case I succeeded, but not so close that they'd get cooties if I failed.

I forgot their names as soon as they were introduced, except for one fellow from Logistics named Moynihan Truth, whom I remembered both because of his unusual name and because I saw him again later. He was ten years old, but that's in dog years; double it for Earth-equivalent. He'd been born in Golden Flats on Mars, where they have the monument to the first Rover. You've probably seen images of Farzi Baroomand's famous statue, the one that shows all the aliens lined up behind the Rover where the camera can't see them, laughing themselves silly. Everyone there takes the last name Truth to honor the Rover. The Kid was the only one in the locker smiling and I remember wondering what the big joke was.

Four test beds took up most of the horizontal space. Hobartium loops were tethered to beds A and B. I pointed to A and said, "This one's not working?" Nods all around. The neon-yellow *Hold* tag was my clue. "And that one works?" More bobble-heads. It was green-tagged. "And you think it might be the kicker?" Grudging assents, but dissenters mentioned other components, assembly errors, you name it. Paralysis of analysis. Smart people with a dozen smart ideas, but not smart enough to try any for fear of being wrong.

But the first rule of troubleshooting is: Start somewhere. When you don't know crap, whatever you learn moves you ahead. "Take *this* kicker," I pointed, "and install it on *that* loop; and take *that* kicker and install it on *this* loop."

When the switcheroo was finished I told them to kick amps, and the superconductor on A began to circularize from the hoop stress, while the one on B now remained flaccid. I nodded.

"Yep. It's the kicker, all right."

Antonelli swelled up. "For *that*, we pay Port Authority two ounces troy *per diem*? We could have done that ourselves!"

"No, you couldn't," I reminded him. "You couldn't even get the two hoops set up without my prodding."

"Big deal," said one of the engineers. "We already thought it was the kicker." No matter what the solution turns out to be, there will always be *someone* to say *I told you so*.

"Sure," I said. "But now you *know*. Now take the top assembly off this kicker and switch it with the top assembly on the other. If nothing changes, the problem's in the bottom half. If A fails but B works, the problem's in the top half."

Antonelli sucked lemons. "What if they both start working?"

"Then it gets interesting."

The secret of my success doesn't come from knowing all the answers, but in knowing how to ask the questions. Disassembly and reassembly successively narrows the search zone for the cause. Three iterations homed in on the damper circuit subassembly. After that, it was a matter of screening the other kickers in stock and finding the ones with defective dampers. Antonelli wrote a *stern letter* to the Earthside parts manufacturer, which let him wrap things up on a suitably righteous note of indignation. Nothing makes a man happier than the prospect of blaming someone else.


When I returned to my rooms toward shift-end, I found a message from Pondo asking me to stop by the Second Dog as soon as I could. I finished repacking my go-bag for my next assignment, then took the tow line up Dilman's Bore, where I found Pondo waiting just inside the Dog.

Small as Phobos was, you'd think an illicit bar would be a tough thing to hide. Scientists back in the day had known that Phobos was partly hollow and that puzzled them some. They also realized that the moonlet resembled a Main Belt asteroid, but they couldn't figure how Mars could capture an asteroid, circularize its eccentric orbit, and rope it onto the Martian equatorial plane—not until they discovered that the Visitors had been tricking it out back in the day. About a third of the interior had been gutted by the Visitors, and the rooms, warrens, and passageways they dug totaled two thousand cubic kilometers usable volume. But volumes can be made operationally larger when people look the other way, and the pocket under Kepler's Ridge had somehow escaped notice when volume was platted out.

Koso Bassendi, the owner, was a hard man to cross and was big enough to make it harder still if you did manage it. I never heard of anyone crossing him twice. Come retirement, he and his brother

Pondo took their bonus money and started the Second Dog. They served beer stronger than the wretched double-deuce that the Prague Convention allowed, but they served an honest measure. You can't ask more than that of any man.

"Mickey," Pondo said, "I understand yer going Mars-side tomorrow."

I didn't ask him how he knew. My schedule was not exactly classified, and the Authority likes to rotate its employees into gravity wells to keep up their muscle tone and bone calcium.

"Maybe you'll have time to do my brother and me a little favor."

Doing favors for the Bassendis was risky. So was refusing. I figured they wanted me to smuggle up some potables in my Authority packet, so I said, "Sure." Technically, Phobos is "outer space" and Mars "planetary surface," so the Prague Convention covers one, but not the other. Go figure.

Pondo guided me into the office, where Koso bobbed in microgee with his arms crossed and his scowl directed toward the thick, open door of an Eismann and Hertzog safe.

"Somebody got into our vault," Pondo explained, in case I couldn't figure it out. Koso said nothing, but his face tightened like a hangman's knot.

"You call the cops?"

Both brothers looked at me and I let it go. "So, what'd you lose? Money, securities?"

They shook their heads. "Not even the Bassendi Brothers Benevolent Fund was touched," said Koso.

I didn't ask who the fund was intended to benefit.

Pondo said, "Remember that fellow, Jaroslav Bytchkov, what give us something to keep for him the other day? Well, it's gone."

Which meant that whatever that packet contained, it was worth a great deal more than what was left untouched. At least now I knew Pinch-face's name.

"And what was it?"

"How would we know?" Pondo said. "My brother and me sell trust. Who would trust us with their keepsakes if we stuck our noses into them?"

The brothers might be shady, but they had a code. "What do you want me to do?" I said, though I could already guess.

"Yer a troubleshooter," said Pondo. "Find what caused our trouble." Koso spoke. "We take care of the other part."

The brothers figured the taker had been in the bar the night Bytchkov had brought his precious. Who else would have known it was there? I reminded them that I had been there and Koso smiled. "The vault software was tickled during the day, when all decent men are sleeping. You was out to Gulliver the whole time."

So I had an alibi, which was comforting; but the Bassendis wanted me to work for them, which was not so comforting. We went over the surveillance videos and identified everyone present, weeded out those too honest or too inept, and they asked me to investigate the ones who had dropped Mars-side.

That included Hot Dog, of course, who had that Guild meeting to run. And Willy's job, like mine, required periodic commutes. But VJ had also dropped, taking some personal days to "bone up" at a calcium spa. Among the handful of Martians in the bar, only a petite ice miner—Gloria "Iceman," from Rosario—had already gone home.

"And we'd appreciate it, Mickey, if ye'd look up our depositor and find out what he given us."

Koso said, "And it shows up for sale, we might trace the taker."

"But we'd rather you not tell him it's been stolen."

"Bad for business."

I had a private notion that Bytchkov already knew it was stolen. He just didn't know it had been stolen from him.

Port Rosario sits in Arabia, a densely cratered, heavily eroded upland in the Northern Territories. Despite its name, it sits over some of the richest ice-bearing strata on Mars. Old water canyons wind through the terrain and onto the lowlands, an ancient ocean bed. The dome is set in a deep crater and protected by hobartium loops that deflect incoming cosmic radiation. Mars is a hardscrabble world and attracts hardscrabble folk. No one would go there, if it weren't for the archeology and the asteroid-capture program.

Everybody needs a hobby, and the Visitors' hobby had been throwing rocks at Earth. They had booby-trapped a mess of Main Belt asteroids to drop Earthward if we ever got too nosy. If it was some kind of sociopathic IQ test, like some folks thought, we had passed. We had bridled scores of 'stroids with magnetic sails and tacked them into GEO for mining and smelting. And if you're going to bridle asteroids, Mars is the go-to place. You need less delta-vee going up and down from Mars than hopping rock to rock. That's why the Visitors came to Mars back when Man was squatting in the forest primeval; and that's why we're there now.

Port Rosario always looked down-at-the-heels. There was dust everywhere. I don't care how good the precipitators are. They say you can never see Venus because clouds hide the surface. The same is true of Mars, except everything is covered with dust. You need a broom to see the true surface. The Martian wind is not very fierce—the air's too thin—but it's persistent. A dust storm can develop in hours, cover the planet in days and last for weeks. Some of it gets inside the domes in spite of all, and gives everything a rough, gritty look.

Rosarians were also rough and gritty, miners and teamsters being far from genteel, so it was well to walk careful. I tried to look dangerous whenever I strolled around town and carried enough mass to make it convincing and a set of brass knuckles in case it wasn't.

The town is laid out on a simple spoke-and-wheel street plan. I arrived toward local sunset and took a room in Coughlin House in the northern quadrant with a nice view of the lowlands. Nothing but the best for the Authority. I tossed my gear in the room and headed for Centre Square, which was located exactly where you'd expect.

Local custom says everyone goes there first and shakes hands with the statue of Jacinta Rosario. She's portrayed without a helmet, which is historically inaccurate but artistically necessary. The statue is surrounded by grass and wildflowers and the only open trickle-fountain on Mars. Periodically, someone worries about "wasting water," but since Rosario is a closed system, the water doesn't really get wasted, and the size of the "Fossil Aquifer" underneath the town is good for a great long time. It's not like Martians are profligate, but like they'll tell you: "Anything for Jacinta."

Pilot House is out the end of Mercado Radial by the ATC tower. That's where zeppelin pilots check in. I stuck my head in the chief pilot's office and asked if Jaroslav Bytchkov was in town and he checked the logs and told me to try Dominick's Tavern at Mercado and Fourth. That was the heart of the Groin, where the Merchant's Association had chipped in to hire a marshal to patrol the streets and break up fights. The neighborhood was called the Groin because it was a bad place to get your kicks.

Dominick's proved a three-story duroplast building facing inward from the Dome. Apartments were on the second and third floors. No fine views for them. I found a café across the street—One-Ball Murphy's—with a view of the entrance and waited for Bytchkov to show. I ordered a drink of "whiskey," though it wouldn't pass muster in Scotland or Kentucky. I think One-Ball boiled it out back in an old radiator.

I noticed Gloria Iceman at another table, also watching Dominick's. That was interesting, so I clicked a pic with my handi and made a note. Ice miners generally hung out in the south quadrant, around the mine elevators, not here near the aerodrome. I don't think she recognized me, but the next time I looked, she was gone and I hadn't seen her leave.

It was 2100 when I saw Bytchkov exit Dominick's right under the streetlamp. It must have been Old Home Week, because he was in animated conversation with Moynihan Truth. The young man had not been in the Dog the night Bytchkov squirreled his precious, but here he was chatting him up like an aged uncle with a legacy. I took a few more pix—and became suddenly aware that the other two seats at my table had acquired occupants.

On my right sat a pale, hard-faced woman with the indefinable glam of a rocket jock. She smiled at me, but it wasn't a friendly smile and she didn't say anything. On my left, a dusky man with obsidian eyes held a quarterstaff in his right hand. I nodded to him.

"Evening, Marshal," I said.

It was Tiki Ferrer. "Evening, Mickey. What's a respectable Phobic like you doing in the Groin at night?"

"Just getting my land legs back," I told him. "Came down from the Dogs at sunset."

"And snapping pix like a muffing tourist," he marveled. "Fourth and Merc isn't a noted tourist spot. Why the interest?"

I'm pretty good at arithmetic, and added one and one. "Which are you watching, Bytchkov or Truth?"

"What is Truth?" he asked me. "That the young guy? Tell me about him."

That meant Bytchkov was the marshal's target and he was taking an interest in anyone who took an interest. That included Moynihan. It also included me. It was no skin off my nose, so I told him what I knew about the Truther.

Tiki introduced the woman as Genie Satterwaithe, a courier on the Red Ball laying over on Mars while her loop was refurbished and stocked up for the Green Ball to Earth. She had earlier flown ballistics and orbitals around the home world, which accounted for her implicit swagger even sitting down.

"I'm trying to talk her into signing on with Iron Planet," Tiki told me.

"What's your interest in Bytchkov?" I asked him. When the marshal demurred I flashed my badge. I wasn't on Authority business, but Tiki didn't have to know that.

"That's a Port Authority badge, Mickey. It doesn't push much mass down here."

"Look, Marshal, this ain't for broadcast, but Bytchkov deposited something for safekeeping up in Panic Town and it's been stolen. I'm trying to find out what it was without tipping him off." That was the truth, if not the whole truth.

Bytchkov turned and reentered his rooming house. Moynihan made an obscene gesture to his back. Tiki sighed. "One more name for the list of people less than pleased with Jaroslav Bytchkov. Why doesn't that list ever get shorter?"

Satterwaithe said. "It's a gift he has."

Tiki showed me a holo of a tall, lean woman. "This is Despina Edathanal," he said. "Recognize her?"

I shook my head. She had the lanky physique of the spaceborn. She hadn't been in the Dog. "She's a tall drink of water," I said. "I'd've noticed her."

"She's digmaster out at Cassini," Tiki said. "She filed a complaint against Bytchkov, claiming that he's filched Visitor artifacts."

Much was thereby explained. The Visitors had gone a long time ago, but they had left some trash behind. A Visitor artifact could fetch enough troy ounces Earthside to make snatching the Bassendi Brothers Benevolent Fund look like chump change. The trick would be getting the artifact from Mars to Earth, and I began to see how that might have been arranged.

"A couple days ago," Tiki continued, "Edathanal braced him right here in Murphy's and told him if he didn't return the goods she would tear off his left arm and beat him to death with it."

"His *left* arm?"

"Yeah, she was being nice. Bytchkov's right-handed. Anyhow, Bytchkov lifted for Phobos the next day. Want to tell me who he left the packet with?"

I shook my head. "Wouldn't be a health-conscious choice."

Tiki grunted. "So. Tell Koso hello when you see him."

"I'm starting to think Pondo has the brains in the family."

"Someone has to. Jaroslav's had some in-your-face time with a half dozen people these past two days. Words were exchanged, as they say, and fists a couple times. Now he'll only meet with one person at a time and only at a time and place of his choosing." Tiki laid out a series of holos on the table, each the size and shape of a standard playing card. "Tell me if you know any of these people."

One was the archeologist from the dig; another, the ice miner I had seen in the Dog. There were three guys I'd never laid eyes on; but the other three were Hot Dog, VJ, and Willy. I told him who they were.

"Bytchkov had fights with all eight of these?" I said.

"Let's say spirited discussions. I guess I should add that fellow Moynihan. I have a feeling he's the one smuggling the stolen artifacts off Phobos."

"The yellow-tagged loops," I said, and explained about the defective kickers. "Moynihan's in Logistics. He could've rigged those defects in the first place, then instead of salvaging the parts, hung the loops out with the contraband. Since the parts are already accounted for, they won't be noticed until Corporate runs a material balance."

Satterwaithe spoke up. "Makes sense. You can program those parasols to hold station in the solar wind and a courier like me can snag it on the fly."

Tiki smiled. "Maybe I should add you to the suspects."

"*That's* why Moynihan was grinning," I said. "He wasn't amused; he was nervous."

The marshal nodded. "And you accidentally cut off their channel. Phobos-Mars radio is too public, so he came down to tell Jaroslav on the QT, probably phoned from the terminal as soon as he hit dirt. That was . . ."

Tiki did a quick search over his handi and said, "He grounded Mars-side at 1830 in *Roustabout*. Easy enough to call from there." He closed the dust cover on his device. "Half an hour later Jaroslav made a call to a tosser cell. He told whoever answered that he had 'a big one' if the price was right and set up a meet at Dominick's for 2200. I bet he's trying to unload his latest acquisition. Genie and I were waiting to see who shows up, catch them passing the contraband."

"Which now he doesn't have."

Tiki checked his watch. "Almost time, but I haven't seen anyone enter the boarding house."

"You have someone watching the back?" I asked, and he gave me a teach-your-grandmother look.

"I got possemen watching everyone on my list. These three—" He pointed to the ones I didn't know. "—they got rounded up an hour ago when the Minetown marshal busted a gambling den over the other side of town."

I glanced at the roster of miscreants. In Phobos, no one cared if you gambled away your life savings, but Martians were different. They don't approve of people who take foolish chances. Fast Paddy Murchison, Kenny ben Hauser, Johnny Free, Piglet Lieskovsky, Lucy Diamonds, Flo Miraziz, Rahim Hadfi, Manoj Patel, Big-O Saukkonen, and my old pal Squint-Eye Terry M'Govern. Fast Paddy, Big-O, and Lucy Diamonds had gotten into public altercations with Jaroslav within the past few days.

I handed him back the list. "Where were the others?"

"I should tell you because . . .?"

I shrugged. "Because one of them may have guessed what Bytchkov took to Phobos and arranged to steal it. I'm looking into the Phobos theft for my, ah, patron."

Tiki conceded the point. He thumbed up his reports on his handi. "Posse touched base around 1930. Dr. Edathanal, they lost track of." He scowled at me. "They're volunteers, not professionals. . . . Let's see. Hot Dog was at a meeting. Gloria was here at Murphy's. Your buddy VJ was at Susie Xiao's Social Club getting himself greased. And your other buddy Willy was 'networking.'" He shook his head over the foibles of humanity. "Any of them could have received the call."

I didn't correct him. "And Moynihan Truth would have been in inbound processing. He could've got the call, too."

"But as of right now—" Tiki made a sound of disgust. "—we don't know where any of them are."

"Because . . . ?"

"Dinner time for most of my posse. I told you, they're not pros."

"Hell, Tiki, I don't even *have* a posse."

"Yeah? You're a troubleshooter, not a lawman."

Satterwaithe spoke up and said, "It's time. Shouldn't we close in?"

I wanted to say, *You're a courier, not a lawman,* but I sensed Tiki had his reasons for keeping her around.

"No one's gone in yet," said Tiki, but he opened his link. "Bill? We're going to close in." He listened, then said sweetly, "Well, I sure hope it was bone," and broke the link. He looked at Genie. "Martha called him home, told him supper was getting cold."

I waited a beat and said, "So, the entire Rosario Marching Band could have gone in the back way and you wouldn't have seen them."

Tiki glowered.

"On the positive side," I added cheerfully, "we probably would have heard them."

"I swear, Mickey, I'm gonna hit up the Association for a deputy. I can't get by with part-time amateurs. You want the job? You meet a better class of people than you do in industrial troubleshooting."

I told him I was happy where I was, but he gave me a posse badge anyway, "for the interim," and took me with him when we exited Murphy's. He told me to cover the back in case Jaroslav bolted. "You heavy?"

"I could stand to lose a few pounds."

"I mean, are you armed?" He twirled his quarterstaff. Firearms are illegal in Port Rosario. The Dome was supposed to be bulletproof, but not even the criminals want to field-test the theory. I showed him the knuckles and that seemed to satisfy him. Satterwaithe carried a baton.

Just then we saw someone scrambling from behind Dominick's. The streetlamp there was out and the figure was indistinct in the pale glow of its more distant cousins. The building on Fifth, right behind Dominick's, had overhanging balconies, and the figure ran under the balcony and vanished in the shadows.

"Don't like that," said Tiki and we hurried across the street. I circled behind the building as planned and Satterwaithe sprinted up Mercado to try to catch the runner on the next block. Tiki went in the front.

Just as well, for I had a bad feeling about this.

Drifting sand had accumulated around the base of the tavern, and just below one of the windows there was a very nice footprint. Someone had jumped from the second or third floor. This is an easier feat on Mars than on Earth. I knelt and inspected it, measuring its depth. I looked up and saw Tiki leaning out the second floor window. That gave me the height of the jump.

"Bytchkov's dead," I guessed.

"Deader'n Dizzy's mouse," Tiki said.

"Knifed?"

He scowled. "How'd you know?"

"It's fast and to the point. I may know who did it." I entered the figures into my handi and the results told me that the jumper had likely weighed over 70 kilos Earth-weight. I crossed the rear lot to the building on the next street and measured the height of the balcony. One seventy centimeters. I closed the tape measure and put it in my pouch. Then I made a few notations on my handi.

I felt immeasurably sad.

Tiki had sealed Bytchkov's apartment and made his way down to where I stood. He studied the rear of the tavern. "Not an impossible jump," he agreed.

Satterwaithe came loping back from Fifth Circle, cutting between the two apartment blocks and ducking under the balcony. "He ran off the other way, toward Sulbertson. I found a witness, though." She touched her handi. "The runner had a white overshirt and tan overpants. Unless the shirt was yellow and the pants brown." She grimaced. "He's not sure. Looked about mid-thirties. Maybe one, seventy height."

Tiki annotated his handi, snapped the sand-shield closed, and reinserted the stylus in its sheath. "I guess we should round up the usual suspects. My money's on Edathanal. Bytchkov was going to sell the artifact back to her because he couldn't hang it out for pickup. When he couldn't produce it, Edathanal lost her temper and—You're shaking your head, Mickey?"

"It wasn't her."

"How do you know? She was the only one we don't know where she was at 1900 when Bytchkov made the appointment with his killer."

I sighed. "When you've eliminated the impossible you won't always like what's left."

Tiki put a hold on the morning lift, and brought Despina and Gloria to join the others in the departure lounge. Hot Dog had been doing the preflight checklist and Tiki assured him that Iron Planet had bumped back the official lift time. "This won't take long," he said. "It's not like Phobos doesn't make two passes every day." Indeed, it swept the Martian sky faster than Mars himself rotated, and so rose in the west and set in the east.

Tiki placed me by the entry from the main terminal while Satterwaithe stood by the tubeway out to the shuttle. I'm not sure where Tiki thought the killer would try to run, but it's in the nature of the guilty to flee even if no man pursueth. In moments like that a man might not think clearly. Willy gave me a quizzical glance because he had caught the posse badge on my coveralls and the knuckle bar on my right fist. He dealt in information, and the amount of information is proportional to its surprise.

"I think it is fair to say," Tiki began, "that all of you knew that Jaroslav Bytchkov had stolen something valuable and you all wanted to get your hands on it."

Despina Edathanal protested. "It belongs to the Visitor Project!"

Tiki nodded and said, "Why don't you describe the artifact that Bytchkov filched."

Five pairs of eyes turned toward her. I knew damn well one of the group already knew, but I saw no overt sign. Well, Tiki had his purpose and I had mine.

"It was a truncated pyramid of sandstone," Edathanal said, "about the size of my two hands. In the right lighting, you can see the hints of a face. Three eyes, arranged as a triangle; a suggestion of structure scoured by untold centuries of gentle Martian sandblasting. It's the only artifact we've ever found that hints at what the Visitors looked like. The weird thing is, the face doesn't seem to stay put. It's on one side, then it's on another. So we think there's also some very subtle micro- or nanotech going on with the stone."

I spoke up. "You'll provide a detailed sketch? I'll make sure Goods Outbound gets a copy up on the Dogs. Aurora and Pegasus, too." This was within my purview as an agent of the Port Authority. I wanted the thief to know that moving the contraband off Mars would not be easy. Moynihan Truth shifted in his seat, probably wondering how much we knew.

Tiki turned to me. "Mickey, you want to tell them the next bit?"

Everyone scrooched around in his seat, except Hot Dog, who was leaning against the wall by the departure tube with his arms crossed, and Gloria Iceman, who sat to the side where she could see everyone.

"Jaroslav had one very hot potato and bounced to Phobos before the word could get out to deposit the statue for safekeeping until his partner could smuggle it out. Unfortunately, that channel was cut off a couple days later." Moynihan's smile had grown so broad I thought it might split his face in two.

Tiki took up the narrative once more. "Each of you either wanted to lay hands on the contraband or at least find out what it was. And each of you had a very public argument with Bytchkov. In some cases, knock-down fights."

VJ laughed. "That wasn't no fight. We played catch. He threw a punch; I caught it; threw it back." Willy and Hot Dog laughed with him.

Moynihan said, "He's not the easiest guy to get along with."

VJ said, "He was a prick."

Tiki cautioned them, "Don't speak ill of the dead."

That got their attention. I had been waiting for the line and had been watching their faces. Tiki's announcement should be a surprise to all but one. I caught the tell where I was expecting it and a glance at Tiki and Satterwaithe showed that they had caught it, too.

"At first, Dr. Edathanal seemed a good suspect," Tiki said. "She had the best motive. The statuette had been stolen from her. She had a fight with Bytchkov in which he slapped her across the face, a public humiliation. And no one knew where she was at the crucial times. But the killer was seen running under the balcony of the neighboring building. Genie over there had to duck when she chased after. The good doctor is too tall. She would have scalped herself."

"And the rest of us?" demanded Hot Dog, so red in the face that his freckles had disappeared.

"I also wondered about Gloria, here," Tiki continued. "She was seen in One-Ball Murphy's keeping a sharp eye on the rooming house, but disappeared just before. But the killer jumped from the second floor window, and she's too light to have made the resulting footprint."

Moynihan Truth perked up. "Me, too?"

Tiki shook his head. "No, you weigh enough. Your motive . . . thieves falling out, perhaps—oh, yes, we know about your end of the smuggling operation. You came down to tell Bytchkov that your game with the parasols was busted. But the witness on the next block saw the killer from a distance, and you would never be mistaken for the age he figured."

VJ wiped his brow dramatically. "People always say my good looks make me seem young."

"You wish," said Hot Dog. But an unease had fallen over him because he had noticed that only three suspects were left. He noticed Tiki watching him and protested, "I got an alibi for the whole day. I was at the Guild meeting!"

"The Guild meeting broke up at 2100," said Genie Satterwaithe. "I talked to some Guild comrades. That would have left plenty of time to get over to the Groin."

"But Bytchkov made a call at 1900," I explained, "and made an appointment to see the man who killed him. You were still in the meeting."

"So what?" asked VJ. "I seen lots of people on their handis in meetings."

"'Cept I was *running* the muffing meeting," Hot Dog said with evident relief. "I was sitting up on the muffing dais right in front of God and twenty-three muffing comrades, banging a muffing gavel. You can ask them!"

"I did," said Satterwaithe. "You didn't receive the call."

During this exchange, Willy had grown more and more pale, and he had begun to ease away from the others. VJ noticed this and whispered, "Better make a break for it." Tiki and I both heard it, and so did Hot Dog.

"Willy?" he said. "I don't believe it!"

"You don't have to," I said. "Willy has the best alibi of all. He was in custody in Minetown when Bytchkov was killed, same as three other suspects. If you'd told the arresting officer your name was Willy, it would've been obvious. But your legal name is Johann Früh, and it got recorded as Johnny Free on the booking sheet."

The arithmetic was simple enough now that everyone could see the remainder. VJ gave me a pained look and said, "Geez, Mickey. This is freeping *Mars!* You know what they do to you here?" Then he bolted for the exit where I stood, hoping I wouldn't have the heart to deck him. And I remembered how he had shoved me out of the way of that leaking pipe.

Tiki Ferrer's hands barely twitched and his quarterstaff tangled VJ's legs and he sprawled out. Satterwaithe was by his side with her baton ready, but there was no fight in him.

"Victor E. Djeh," Tiki told him formally, "you are detained on the authority of the City of Port Rosario and the Groin Merchants' Association."

"You don't like to hear it," I told Tiki afterward, when Satterwaithe had marched VJ off to the cells. "You think you know people; but you never do, and sometimes you find out just how much you don't know them." I shook my head. "I hope it was just a fight that got out of hand. I hate to think VJ went in there *planning* to knife the guy."

VJ was never the sharpest tool in the box. He'd been smart enough to wash his knife, but not smart enough to throw it away. It later proved to have Jaroslav's blood in the space between the blade and the handle. Just goes to show the importance of clean-up.

Tiki turned to me. "But he had nothing to do with stealing the artifact?"

"No, and I'll make sure Pondo understands that. I owe VJ that much at least. At least he never crossed the Bassendis."

The next day, I tracked Gloria Iceman to a Minetown bar. She was hooching with friends, but when she saw me, she separated herself and came to sit in my booth.

"Iceman isn't your actual name," I told her without preamble. "It's Eismann, and someone transcribed it incorrectly when you applied for a Martian visa."

The miner smiled at me. "I liked the sound of it. It's a good nickname for an ice miner."

"It is that," I agreed. "But I think if I dig a little bit, I'll find out that you belong to the Eismann family that makes the vaults: Eismann and

Hertzog. It's enough to make me wonder if someone at the company built a trap door into their products' software."

Gloria Iceman gave me a wide-eyed look. "That sounds awfully precocious."

"I even wonder who convinced Bytchkov to leave his precious with the Bassendis in the first place."

"Well, he had to hide it until the heat died down. The statue wasn't just another link or valve or other bit of trash from a technological midden heap. It was important. Best to hide it somewhere secure."

"But Edathanal knew who had taken it, and a dozen dogs knew he had brought something to the Second Dog. The Bassendis are shady, but they would not have defied a Port Authority warrant."

Gloria nodded. "It's harder to find something if no one knows where it actually is—or who actually took it."

"You don't want the Bassendis mad at you."

"At me? Why would they be mad at me? Where's the evidence I took it, beside a similarity of names?"

"The Bassendis aren't anal about evidence."

"You wouldn't put a flea in their ear on such flimsy suppositions."

"You'll never get the statue off Phobos. Every cubic inch of luggage will be scanned at the most minute levels."

Gloria frowned and pursed her lips. "I think that whoever has the statue will wait a long time before trying to move it off-world. Long after the hoo-rah has died down, long after the inspectors have forgotten what they were looking for. All that extra effort . . . You can't keep that up for very long."

Then she clapped me on the shoulder and walked lightly through the barroom and exited into the streets of Port Rosario. I never saw her again.

All that was many years ago and they're all gone now. Hot Dog smeared himself across a hectare of Martian desert when his ballistic failed to reenter properly. Willy went down for blackmail. Satterwaithe left Mars after the baby she had with Tiki died; Tiki was never the same after that.

Tiki found enough evidence in Bytchkov's apartment for the Port Authority to arrest Moynihan Truth when he stepped off the shuttle in Panic Town. He was exiled to Ceres.

The Martian Board of Actuaries sentenced VJ to slavery on the thermal decompositors out by Mt. Olympus for the remainder of Jaroslav Bytchkov's natural lifetime. I did what I could for him by arguing to the Board that Bytchkov's chosen profession of smuggler and thief put his lifespan at the low end of the confidence interval. That shortened VJ's sentence, but he never got around to thanking me for it.

Gloria "Iceman" Eismann was killed three months later when the tunnel collapsed in Ice Mine 23. I don't think the Bassendis had anything to do with it. I never told them my suspicions. Wherever she squirreled the statuette remains unknown, and it has never been found to this day.

Edathanal never found another artifact like it, and after a time everyone assumed she had been mistaken about the whole thing.

A writer back on Luna named Myles Hertzog possesses a replica, probably made from Edathanal's sketches, and has achieved a modest success with exciting stories about aliens he calls "the People of Sand and Iron."

((•((•((• ◎ •)•)•)•)

**Michael F. Flynn** is a frequent contributor to *Analog*, but his short fiction has also appeared in *Fantasy and Science Fiction* and at TOR.com. A multiple Hugo nominee and winner of the Sidewise Award for Alternate History, his novels have included the *Spiral Arm* series and the *Firestar* series. A statistician, he lives in Easton, Pennsylvania.

*Next, in a break from the serious, author-scientist Jaleta Clegg helps us imagine a reality TV world gone bad—even worse than we have it now, I swear—wherein space travel is the greatest reality show of all in . . .*

# THE ULTIMATE SPACE RACE

## by Jaleta Clegg

"Henry! Hurry up, it's starting." Ethel snuggled deeper into the Cuddle-Couch(TM) (with Soruna(TM) holographic projectors and Tru-Life(TM) surround sound speakers with ThunderRumble(TM) subwoofer cushions, built-in armrest controls and auto-connect, and the optional posture-correcting lumbar support and SpaDee heated massage—Henry's sixty-eighth birthday present, worth every dime). She turned up the volume with a squeeze of her hand.

The announcer's handsome, chiseled face smiled from the floating projection. "Tonight, live from the Sporting Club's docks at New Vegas, it's the thrilling conclusion to the *Ultimate Race*. Remember, what happens in New Vegas, stays in New Vegas, the world's first and only orbiting casino. At least for another two months." He chuckled on cue. "Brought to you by our sponsors, Tummie Gummies, the fruity delicious colon cleanse. Chew two to refresh your life, inside and out."

His face switched to singing, dancing, rainbow-colored candy bears waving banners of toilet paper.

Henry plopped beside Ethel, a bag of freshly popped popcorn in his hand. "What'd I miss?"

"Nothing yet, just Calton Hooper's intro." Ethel popped a handful of the white fluff (now with 72% more fiber!) into her mouth. She grimaced. "Why can't they leave it as popcorn? What's this flavor?"

Henry looked at the bag. "Licorice root. It was on sale."

The bears concluded their animated commercial. Calton Hooper's perfect features replaced them.

Ethel tapped the massage controls as the announcer's voice filled the air.

"Four months ago, from these very docks—" the camera cut to an outside shot full of space-suited figures, plastered with the blue and white Sporting Club logo, clambering over the space yachts of the rich and famous "—we launched seven crews into the black void of space. The crews were focused on one thing: Winning the Ultimate Race, brought to you tonight by Cheeritos, the world's favorite cheez snack."

The show cut to another commercial.

"I wish they hadn't disabled the commercial skip," Henry said through a mouthful of licorice popcorn.

"'It would have cost us three months' rent for the premium subscription to enable that." Ethel had been sorely tempted, but sometimes the commercials were the best part of the show. She secretly hoped that the body spray man would be featured tonight. He was her favorite, his one-minute romances clever and sigh-worthy.

Henry chewed another handful of popcorn while orange puffy triangles drifted over New York's skyline. "Those things are disgusting. They did a study last month showing they caused cancer."

"Mm-hm." Ethel tuned out Henry's complaints. She'd heard them too many times over the years. She relaxed into the Cuddle-Couch(TM) and let the massager do its work.

Calton Hooper switched to a recap of the season, cutting to scenes of the crews of the yachts as they prepared to launch from the floating station of sin, as Ethel's friend Betty called it. Logos of all the sponsoring companies decorated the interiors of the ships. Their products filled the crews' lives. Their commercials punctuated the reality show's footage.

Calton walked them through the initial days of the race, when the crews fought over limited living space. It sounded so romantic, a race to Mars' moon Phobos and back. The prize money was nothing to sneeze at, but Ethel wasn't sure she would have survived being part of any of the crews. Especially not the college frat boy ship. She didn't approve of their choice of interior decorations, provided by their sponsors. Beer companies and porno sites were not appropriate for such a family-centered show as the *Ultimate Race*.

"What was that?" Henry spoke through his popcorn. "You said something?"

Ethel wisely didn't repeat herself. Henry thought the frat boys were hilarious. "Betty posted pictures of her dogs on the beach in Fiji. We should take a trip there someday. It looked lovely."

Henry hmphed, his answer whenever she brought up her friend's travel posts.

"Maybe we should save up for a trip to New Vegas. I'd like that."

Calton Hooper narrated the incident of the stolen chocolate stash on board the all-female ship. The women were all middle-aged hairdressers, sponsored by every beauty product known to man. They'd dropped out and had to be towed back to New Vegas after only ten days. The show cut to a live interview of the women sitting in a casino in New Vegas. They reminisced about the show, hugging and crying. Ethel rolled her eyes. The women had done nothing but fight like wet cats.

Calton broke into the canned interview. He tapped his earbud (D-Audible, only the best sound for your delicate ears), his expression serious. "We've just received word that the last two yachts have passed the Moon's orbit safely. It's neck-and-neck between the *Butterfly Effect* and *Gone Fishin' Today*. Who will win tonight? We'll keep you posted."

"Should have been the *Beer Can*."

"Oh, please. Those boys couldn't do anything right. I wonder if they ever got home from Mars."

"I'm sure they'll update us." Henry stirred the unpopped kernels with his finger. They rattled in the bowl. "I kind of like the licorice flavor. I'll pick up more tomorrow."

"Tasted like cough drops to me."

The show cut to Calton interviewing the crew of *Lucky Lady*, New Vegas' entry that had sputtered out of the competition halfway through the show. A combination of not enough food, a leaky water tank, and faulty wiring had shut down their ship three days shy of Mars. The crew looked much healthier now. They were still at Mars; all three couples told Calton they wanted to stay and file for homesteads in the Martian desert.

Ethel fidgeted despite the massaging seat. The endless stream of commercials never stopped. Scrolling texts and pictures filled the bottom of the screen, even during the interviews. Ethel wished they'd just hurry up and get to the finale. She was rooting for her favorite, the captain of the *Butterfly Effect*. She didn't care for his crew of engineers and scientists, they were very competent but a little too weird for her tastes. But Captain Shan Updike could give the body spray man a run for his money.

The show switched music tracks to a solemn funeral dirge while they paid homage to *Homer's Revenge*. Two of the crew had died in a horrible explosion. Ethel closed her eyes and fantasized about the swarthy Captain Updike and Body Spray Man instead. She hadn't liked that episode or the days of news stories afterwards. The people who signed up for the *Ultimate Race* knew the dangers. It was their own fault, anyway. Ethel would never trust her life to a ship built by breakfast cereal companies and office furniture retailers.

The show dragged on through more interviews and highlights. Calton Hooper updated them every few minutes on the progress of the two remaining yachts as they approached the final finish line.

Henry returned from a bathroom break, flopping onto his side of the Cuddle-Couch(TM). "I was talking to Harv the other day while he was out trimming his hedge. He said it takes at least a full day to get from the Moon to New Vegas. They're lying to you when they say this is live. It's all staged and fake. Lenny at work says they film it all on a soundstage behind the casinos."

Ethel pursed her lips. "Lenny has a few screws loose. He tried to convince you that the food industry is poisoning us into becoming robot drones by putting addictive colorings in everything."

"That was Kevin. Lenny just thinks that New Vegas is a scam and the show is fake."

"It's real. Both David Lorenzo and Anita Kay had scientists on their shows talking about how it couldn't have been faked. They said this was the future of space travel—game shows and company sponsorships. They're talking about doing a reality show at the Ganymede mining base next year. Scientists vs. Miners. I think it sounds interesting. Calton Hooper is in negotiations to host the show, but they say he's asking for too much money. Twenty-seven million per episode is what I heard." Ethel secretly hoped the producers would get Body Spray Man to host it. She could watch him flex his muscles for hours.

Calton Hooper broke into a prerecorded interview. His face was flushed with excitement. "Ladies and gentlemen, we have a sighting, live and in person here at Sporting Club's docks at New Vegas. Stay and play and make memories to last a lifetime. The winner of the *Ultimate Race* is about to be determined. Remember, the race isn't won—"

"Until it's won," Ethel finished the show's slogan. She chewed her fingernail as the show built the suspense. Would it be the ship of scientists and engineers captained by the handsome Shan Updike, a long-time competitor in the sailing races on Earth's oceans? Or would it be the ship of bearded outdoorsmen used to roughing it for weeks at a time as they pursued the best fishing spots in the most inaccessible corners of the continents? Stay tuned through these commercial breaks.

The cameras panned over the docks while Calton recapped the last dozen transmissions from the two ships. The camera shifted to a shot of darkness with the Earth glimmering at one edge of the screen. The Moon floated serenely in the far distance. Ethel straightened. The Cuddle-Couch(TM) adjusted the floating holographic projection to match her viewing angle.

Arrows appeared, pointing out two small dots.

Calton's voice tightened with practiced excitement. "Ladies and gentlemen, you are witnessing history today. The first ever ultimate race to Mars and back is coming to an end. And it's going to be a photo-finish. *Butterfly Effect* and *Gone Fishin' Today* are closing in on New Vegas. You can see they've just come into view now. Both ships have to slow down and match orbits with the station. It's up to the captains and the skill of their crews now. Too much speed and they might miss the station. Neither has enough fuel to correct such an error. It would take three days for a rescue ship to catch up with them." He paused while the cameras switched to a shot of the waiting dock workers. "One mistake at this stage of the race could cost them more than the victory. It could cost the lives of the crew and the dedicated workers you see here. Space, ladies and gentlemen, is no place for error, as we've seen tonight. Those who don't have what it takes have failed. Those who do will win. No matter which ship docks first, both of these crews—" the screen switched to the publicity photos of the two crews taken before launch "—have proven themselves worthy of this trophy. But, there can only be one winner."

Calton's face filled the screen. "They've battled against incredible odds for four months, and it all comes down to the next few minutes. Do they have the skill and the guts for glory?"

The show cut to another montage of commercials.

Ethel flopped back into the massaging cushions with a groan. "How long are they going to drag this out?"

"The broadcast has another fifteen minutes. I need a beer. Want me to grab you something?"

Ethel shook her head.

Henry shuffled off to the kitchen.

Ethel nibbled her fingernail while the commercial messages filled her screen. A chat-box (powered by Tweeble, the new face of social networking) popped up in the corner. Betty's face grinned from the box. Ethel debated about ignoring the call, but only for a moment. Betty would make her life miserable for weeks if she didn't connect. She tapped the armrest.

"Ethel? You'll never believe what happened to me today." Betty patted her perfectly set, perfectly blond hair (brought to you by Clairvoyance, for the most natural appearance artificial hair dye can give, not tested on animals, safe for the environment). "You remember Donald, down at the megamart? Well, I was there today, just picking up a few groceries for my party tomorrow. You know how it is. You think you've got plenty of asparagus, then find out six people are coming, not the three who responded, so now you've got to pick up more. Oh, that reminds me. Are you and Henry going to make it?"

Ethel refrained from rolling her eyes, although it was sorely tempting. "We live in Albuquerque, Betty. And you live in Florida. We appreciate you inviting us, but no, we aren't coming in person."

Calton's face appeared on the screen, but the chat-box kept him muted. Ethel shifted impatiently.

"Bummer," Betty said. "Anyway, back to my story. There I was, squeezing my asparagus, when Donald shows up. He's got a cart and he bumps me with it. I made sure he would. He was so intent on the citrus that he didn't even see me. Can you believe that?" She paused to giggle. "Well, there we were. I let out a little shriek, not a loud one, just a little oh-you-bumped-me startled one, and pretended to be hurt. He started apologizing. It was so sweet of him. Have I told you how adorable he is? Not as good-looking as that guy in the commercial you're always posting, thanks for that by the way, now I'm addicted to his spots, but cute in his own rich-retired-dude-with-plenty-of-cash kind of way. He loves dogs, did I tell you that already?"

Ethel tried desperately to read Calton's lips while her friend rambled. The show cut to the shot of space again. The dots were noticeably bigger and closer. They almost looked like ships now, but they were too far away to tell which ship was which.

"Ethel, I swear you're ignoring me. Did you hear what I just said? Donald is coming to my party tomorrow, and he's bringing fresh quiche. He cooks! How awesome is that?"

Ethel bit her fingernail as the tiny ships swelled on the screen. The camera zoom was fuzzy with the distance.

"I know you aren't listening, Ethel, 'cause you're chewing your nails. What are you watching?"

"Listen, Betty, I have to go. Call me later and tell me all about Donald, okay?"

Fire blossomed from one of the ships. It veered towards the other ship.

"But Ethel, I think Donald may be the one. Finally. And to think it all started over asparagus. Did I tell you he—"

"Bye, Betty."

Ethel killed the chat-box. She'd apologize later to her friend, but right now the ships on the screen had her full attention. Calton's voice came back as the call disconnected.

"—just heard. A fire has broken out on one of the ships. We've lost contact with both, but that should be restored soon."

Commercial sponsor messages flashed urgently around the edges of the screen. Calton's face appeared in a box to one side. The cameras stayed focused on the ships, still fuzzy with distance, as their paths converged. Which one was on fire? And who was hurt?

Calton frowned as he tapped his earbud. "Our team tracking the ships say they may collide. We still don't know what happened. An explosion in the fuel lines is the most likely explanation according to the engineering teams who built these ships. Our techs are working on the communication lines."

"Henry? Come quick. There's been an accident." Ethel couldn't help the shakiness of her voice.

Henry walked through the projected image of the ships and advertising sponsors.

Ethel waved him impatiently to his seat. "Something exploded on one of the yachts."

"Not the fishing boat?"

Ethel shook her head. "They don't know yet." She stared at the holograph, her stomach twisting with dread as the two ships drifted closer.

Calton's words washed over her, barely registering. "We have radio contact with *Butterfly*. They're leaking atmosphere. Rescue ships are on their way, but they may not arrive in time. But the crew is ready with their emergency gear. Remember, these crews have trained and drilled for emergencies. Every precaution is in place, ladies and gentlemen. We're standing by with—"

His voice died as the two ships rammed into each other. It happened slowly, like ballerinas in slow motion colliding. The cameras caught the puff of vapor as it froze in a cloud around the ships. Pieces of both ships spun loose, a cloud of debris expanding slowly into space.

Ethel bit her knuckle. This couldn't be happening, couldn't be real. Space travel was mostly safe these days. Wasn't it? The two crew members who died on the other ship were stupid and made poor choices. But these two ships, they were all smart people, trained for these things and very careful. How could this happen?

Betty's face popped up in the chat-box again. Ethel tapped ignore.

Calton's frown vanished, replaced by relief. "We have word that both crews are safe. They made it into the escape pod just before collision. We have contact with Captain Smith and Captain Updike. They report that all crew members are accounted for. There were injuries, though. We'll bring you updates as we receive them. Rescue vehicles are undocking from New Vegas as we speak."

Henry sniffed. "It's all a publicity stunt, you know. They don't want to pay out the prize money. It's rigged. Lenny says—"

Ethel removed her knuckle from her mouth long enough to tell Henry what his friend Lenny could do with his conspiracy theories.

Henry sat with his mouth hanging open at her words. He snapped it closed after a long moment. "It's just a show, sweetheart."

Ethel shook her head, her objections vague. "It's more than that, Henry."

"They'll do a season two. *Ultimate Race* to Venus or something." He patted her hand.

The holographic screen showed a close-up of Calton's concerned face as he reassured the audience that everything was under control. Ethel wiped a tear. She'd say a prayer for the safety of those people tonight.

And when they found out who was responsible, she vowed never to buy their products again. She had standards.

Henry patted her hand again before leaving the room.

Ethel tapped the chat-box icon, placing a call to Betty.

Betty answered immediately. "Ethel? What is going on with you? You ignored me."

"Did you see what happened on *Ultimate Race* just now?"

"You were watching?"

Ethel shook her head. "Such a tragedy, but they say everyone survived. So, tell me about Donald squeezing your asparagus."

Betty dimpled when she smiled. "I never said he squeezed my asparagus. He bumped me with his cart. He is so gorgeous when he's apologizing."

Ethel let her friend ramble, only half-listening. *Ultimate Race* shifted from Calton's concerned look and shots of the doomed yachts to commercial messages. Henry was right. Commercial sponsorships would fund more shows. And people would travel farther and more dangerously. And Ethel would watch from her CuddleCouch(TM), safely and vicariously living their adventures. It was the way it should be.

((·((·((· ◎ ·))·))·))

**Jaleta Clegg** loves to tell stories about all sorts of fantastical things, from rockets and aliens to ogres and unicorns to green gelatin blobs and evil collectible figurines. When she's not spinning stories, she's figuring out how to teach kids about science and astronomy. She enjoys playing the piano and organ for her local church, crocheting monsters and cute little Cthulhus, and cooking weird vegetables for the fun of it. She lives in Utah with a diminishing horde of children, too many pets, and a very patient husband. Find more of her work at http://www.jaletac.com.

*Continuing further out into our solar system in our next tale, a wife nursing her comatose husband and his wealthy employer have a first encounter just off Jupiter in . . .*

# ORPHEUS' ENGINES

## by Christopher McKitterick

*If everyone helps to hold up the sky,*
*then one person does not become tired.*
—Askhari Johnson Hodari

Nina Galindo gripped the frame of the porthole, its dome just large enough to fit her head and shoulders, and gazed down upon Jupiter. Jupitershine lit her face and puddled orange shadows along her clenched jaw. She felt a slight windswept sensation as JoveCo Way Station rotated, as if the carbon-nanotube eggshell floor were being yanked out from under her feet. Only a thin layer of technological wizardry protected her from the choking vacuum and flesh-frying radiation of high-Jupiter orbit. A swirling yellow storm tore through tan and brown bands. In those clouds, thirty thousand kilometers below, billions of aliens were shouting in unison, *Go away!*

They were also saying something else, something much more complex, which even her most-powerful decryption algorithms couldn't decipher.

Nina looked away from the unforgiving planet and crossed her husband's cramped quarters to his bed. She took Mike's hand. The skin felt cool. His eyes were shut and his face was too relaxed, devoid of his characteristic grin. During his months of induced sleep, even the deep concentration lines between his eyebrows had smoothed. His head had been shaved smooth for the treatments. Tubes as fine as silk strands sprouted from his scalp like a shock of hair. Shaped and sized like a soccer ball sliced in half, the AI-coupled device she'd carried all the way from the Mayo Clinic fed him a cocktail of viruses and nanos programmed to heal his damaged nervous system.

Doctor Else Arnasdottir slipped her interface tablet into a deep coat pocket and gave Nina a gentle smile.

"The repairs are coming along as expected," she said. "We'll soon know if he'll make a full recovery, or if he'll need to go to Earth for more aggressive treatment."

"Thank you," Nina said.

"I only plugged Mike into the magic box of healing," the doctor said.

Nina shook her head. "You're the one who kept him alive for almost three hundred days since the accident. Thank you."

Arnasdottir's smile grew. She nodded and patted the device. "I just wish we'd had one of these on-site then."

"Life-saving equipment is *price-prohibitive*," Nina said.

Mike had loved Jupiter all his life and dreamed of one day living here, so of course he signed up when his long-time boss founded JoveCo. The station harvested Jupiter's near-limitless hydrogen to power fusion engines that delivered resources from the asteroid belt to Earth and the Moon and Mars colonies.

Behind them, the door opened. Don Williams paused in the entryway. Nina studied his reflection in the porthole ultraglas. Inverted by the shape of the bowl, his reflection appeared supersized, floating still and quiet among the stars, a vampire waiting to be invited inside. Here stood one of the wealthiest people in history, the man who had poured his immense fortune into building JoveCo, his monument at the edge of inhabited space. Williams had been Mike's employer since the early days at Embedded Solutions, and joined him here when JoveCo opened for operations. And Williams was now, unimaginably, her boss, too. At least until she cracked the alien message or Mike woke up, whichever came first.

Nina closed her eyes for a moment, took a deep breath, slowly exhaled.

"Thank you for coming, Nina," he said.

"I had to bring medical equipment," she said, "and take Mike home."

"We'd have sent him back with the fusion torch's return run," Don said.

"I needed to be here if something goes wrong." Nina swallowed, hard.

Williams cleared his throat and made an expansive gesture. "I'm sorry. This is my fault."

"Just take me down *there*"—she pointed out the window—"so I can do my job and we can go home."

The doctor excused herself and headed toward the door.

"Else," Williams said, "hold on." He turned to Nina. "You don't have to descend. An AI could run your test."

"I spent my trip out here—nine miserable months in a ship that stank of melting plastic and ozone—trying to decipher this" —she waved at the display—"*whatever* it is. Hell if I'm going to let danger keep me waiting for a task-rabbit's report. I'll leave when Mike's ready to go, whether or not we solve your puzzle."

She tossed her tablet and her AI-interface device into her satchel. "Let's go."

Williams nodded. "First, I want Else to introduce you to one of the natives."

Williams gave Nina an impromptu tour as he led her around the station's toroidal habitation ring. She met a handful of others as they passed living quarters and meeting rooms. They all knew who she was, the first newcomer to JoveCo Way Station in two years, since the torch-ship crew's last visit. She shook hands and accepted wishes for Mike's speedy recovery, wondering who might have been his friends, who might have stayed up late talking with him about one day walking among the stars, the dream Don Williams had woven from vacuum and cloud to lure them here.

They stopped near a heavy door marked with a biohazard symbol. The hallway here smelled a bit like cat pee. Williams opened a nearby closet and withdrew three sleek spacesuits. He handed one each to Nina and the doctor, and began slipping into the third himself. Except for a cylinder of hardware attached to the silvery back, it didn't look all that different from what her students at the university found fashionable a few years ago.

Nina held it up and asked, "Is this necessary?"

"Jovians have ammonia for blood," said Arnasdottir, "which mostly boiled away to toxic fumes when we brought it aboard. Couldn't keep the operating theater cold enough."

She hung her coat in the closet. "The stomach is a sack of oily strands," the doctor said, pulling her spacesuit over pants and short sleeves. "Smelling the other organs would make you vomit. Or worse. We won't enter the same space as the specimen, but . . ." She made a face. "Just in case."

Finally, she pulled the suit's transparent hood down to the collar. As she sealed it with a swipe of a finger, it inflated into a helmet, providing a gap of a few centimeters around her head. As Nina and Williams did the same, Arnasdottir fetched her tablet, then led them into a glass-walled airlock. Lights in the room beyond revealed a six-meter-wide pile of what looked like lumpy brown Jell-O poured over finger-width black hoses.

The doctor tapped her tablet against the glass, summoning a green-bordered interface the size of the wall. She touched a bright crosshair with both index fingers, slid them apart to zoom in on the specimen, then did something to enhance contrast between clumps, strands, and tubes.

"The underbelly of a Jovian," Arnasdottir said.

Nina frowned at Williams. "How does your idealism mesh with hunting aliens?"

"We collected these remains after a Beanstalk-clearing run," he said.

"You mean, after you burned it off," Nina said.

"Since Mike installed the warning beacon," Williams said, "no locals have been harmed."

Nina had read Mike's report. She knew her husband well enough to guess what he left unsaid. If Mike hadn't parsed the aliens' surface-level language and used it to broadcast *Fly away!* in their language, how many more Jovians would Williams have murdered to keep the hydrogen flowing?

Arnasdottir pointed. "These porous tendrils—grown from sulfur and organic compounds—lead to the stomach, here." She traced a glowing path along a thin tube to a lump uncomfortably similar in size to a human torso.

"Judging by what I found in this guy's gut," she said, indicating a portion of the body held open with dissection tools, "they ingest hydrocarbons, pretty rare in Jupiter's primordial soup. Which is why they chew the Beanstalk—it's grown from carbon-nanotube and aerogel. You've seen vids of living specimens?"

Nina nodded. "Glorious." She pictured this deflated creature in its natural environment, a fragile soap-bubble soaring among endless clouds. Skin like stained glass, translucent except for dark red ink-blot markings. A forest of tendrils draping many meters beneath.

"In the atmosphere's upper reaches," Arnasdottir said, "some inflate larger than this station. No restrictive bones or cartilage. Adults mass about three hundred kilos, mostly concentrated here, in the underbelly." The doctor-cum-xenobiologist encircled the flesh in a green halo, then turned an excited face to Nina.

"What most blows me away is that their cells use *DNA*," Arnasdottir said, "like us, like every other Earth creature."

Nina whispered, "The universal programming language of life."

"At least in our Solar System," Williams said.

Nina shot him a neutral expression.

"Check this out," Arnasdottir said, zooming in on a tiny bronze-colored knob. "I love brains; they're my specialty—well, before I became JoveCo Way Station's GP."

Nina smiled. "I'm glad you're the one working with Mike."

The doctor nodded slightly. "His brain is a bit more complicated. This one's structures are similar, but Doc—my AI—counted about a thousand neurons connected by twenty thousand synapses, thirty thousand gap junctions, and six thousand neuromuscular junctions."

"Don't we have billions of neurons?" Nina asked.

Arnasdottir nodded inside her transparent helmet. "I wouldn't have thought it capable of language. Except evidence says otherwise." She shook her head. "Check this out." She traced a fan of threads extending from the bronze pea. "These neurofilaments spread across a substrate of hydrocarbon goo lining the skin. It's a biological radio array that connects them with billions of others more intimately than we can, even with radical cybernetics. It's as if they think with a single brain."

"Mike's hypothetical 'Jupiter-Mind,'" Nina said.

Arnasdottir nodded. "Which tests support," she said. "They form a planet-spanning brain potentially smarter than our most powerful AIs."

"Our probes pick up *Come eat!* signals pulsing across at least a thousand kilometers around regions rich in carbon compounds," Williams said, "and *Fly Away!* around storms."

"Then there's the whole-planet signals," Arnasdottir said.

"Like the one I can't crack," Nina said, staring in at the dead thing spread open in the room beyond, silent and alien.

"Bingo," Arnasdottir said. She counted on her fingers:

"At the local level, Jovian flocks make baby talk." Arnasdottir raised a second finger. "At a larger scale, sometimes transmitting across the entire planet, we have mostly random signals, sort of like autistic jazz."

"Except for the planetwide *Fly Away!*" Nina said, "which Mike interprets as them telling us to leave."

"Warnings don't mean much if you can't back them up with force," Williams said.

"We'll ask Mike about that, when he wakes up," Nina said.

"We recovered most of the data from his last descent," Williams said. "The Climber was struck by lightning from a passing storm."

Arnasdottir turned to Nina and raised a third finger.

"Radiating uniformly from everywhere Jovians live, every 42 seconds at low power, we find the largest transmission by far."

"Which uses the strongest encryption I've ever seen," Nina said. She shook her head. "If it weren't coming from living creatures, I'd say it's a recording."

"It's as if the things evolved into a corner," Williams said. "Their local signals make sense. They're useful. Where's the evolutionary advantage in the rest?"

"Evolution doesn't have direction," Arnasdottir said. "Advantage serves evolutionary change, not the other way around."

Williams frowned, then indicated the Jovian. "We hope that it serves us soon. This jellyfish-brained thing is one component of the most powerful mind we've ever encountered. Imagine its possible utility after we decode their root language and shape it into a tool."

Arnasdottir shut down the interface. The glass walls lost their enhancements, and the Jovian's color and contrast faded to uniform gray. Nina felt a wave of melancholy.

As if reading Nina's mind, the doctor said, "I need to check on Mike."

"And we have tests to run," Williams said.

They left the airlock, unsealing their helmets but keeping on their spacesuits, for the trip ahead.

In a dingy kitchen that smelled of burned coffee—and the lingering aroma of ammonia—Williams filled a rucksack with hot-packs; one label read, "Squash and Carrot Stew." He entered a code into a locked cooler's display and extracted what looked like a wine bottle.

Williams saw Nina staring and grinned. "We have a tiny but flourishing vineyard on Ganymede. This is from our winery's first batch, aged in a cask beneath the moon's surface. Whole-bodied, good with stew."

"You're serious," Nina said.

Williams nodded. "Dejen Gueye runs Ganymede's logistics and farm operations, keeping JoveCo's stakeholder-employees self-sufficient. He also prepares our meals. The man's a culinary genius."

Williams dropped the bottle into his bag, then led her to a spoke that connected the station's outer ring to its hub. Opposite a ladder, the inside of the corridor was painted with amateur murals, mostly nature scenes from Earth. Nina grew ever lighter as they climbed toward the station's axis, where she felt nearly weightless.

She recalled vids of the place: The Beanstalk pierced the hub's center, running from the tanker docked at the station's anti-Joveward side all the way down to the planet below. As they pulled themselves through the long cylindrical room, a hum resonated within the chamber and her chest like a great oboe. Handholds attached to the pipeline's protective mesh vibrated not unlike the hydroelectric dam's big pressure-relief pipe near where she grew up. Channeled along the skin of the pipeline, Jupiter's immense electromagnetic field powered the station and the shields that protected it from radiation.

At the bottom, Williams entered an airlock. "Time to put the helmets back on," he said.

They were about to enter the Climber, JoveCo's pipeline maintenance vessel that had nearly killed Mike. Nina's pulse raced. She pulled the clear hood over her face, and took a deep breath as soon as stale-smelling air pressurized it into a sphere. She held her breath for a moment, and slowly exhaled as her head thudded in syncopation with her chest.

"I've already programmed Climber to run your test," Williams said. "It'll report once it gets back within comms range."

That got her moving. She was sick of waiting. She shook her head and floated into the airlock.

Williams sealed the stationside door, then released one on the other side, and another just beyond, which opened into the Climber. He pulled himself inside, where he clung to a handhold and faced her.

"We've placed two full-medical suits in here," he said.

"In case the AI craps out when we reach the storm clouds," Nina said. "Too bad Mike didn't have one."

Nina made a conscious effort to release her grip on a handle. Before her last mote of courage fled, she launched feet first past him and came to a stop on a deeply padded seat. Williams sealed the doors behind them. The innermost shut with an echoing *clang*. She removed the suffocating helmet and tried to calm her breathing.

Jupitershine from an array of portholes lit a gray-carbon and scuffed-aluminum interior the size of a small garage. Walls curved off in both directions around a hub slightly wider than the Beanstalk. The donut-shaped, lifting-body vessel rode the pipeline like a bead strung on a wire between Jupiter's atmosphere and the station tethered in stationary orbit above, propelled like a railgun along a magnetic field. Designed to seat twelve passengers back to back or facing each other across a large porthole on the other, it also offered panoramic views beneath and overhead. She'd seen the company promo materials: "Window seats for everyone!"

Nina drifted over to one of the meter-diameter portholes on the floor and gripped the handholds beside it. She marveled at the luxury represented by so much ultraglas, where displays would have served better. Far below, Jupiter looked hundreds of times as large as the full Moon in Earth's sky. She had to turn her head to take it all in.

"Watch your feet," Williams said. He flipped out a tablet and began tapping the air. "Climber, prep for descent."

"Acknowledged," said a silky-smooth AI voice via the vessel's speakers.

The seats slid sideways along a set of rails set into the curved hull until they stopped, upside-down. Williams spun himself around and buckled into one of them, as if hanging from the ceiling.

He smiled at her expression. "We won't feel acceleration for long," he said, "but being butt-down on the 'heavy' side is safer. Orient with Jupiter 'up.'"

Nina did so, buckling into a seat a couple of rows away.

"Climber," Williams said, "take us down."

The vessel jerked free and accelerated with a force comparable to what she had felt aboard the fusion-torch, three days of steadily shoving away from Earth at one-third $g$. The hull began to hum. Through the porthole near her feet, Nina watched JoveCo Way Station shrink to a gray pinwheel dancing around the Beanstalk, then to little more than a bright moon against the Milky Way's starry profusion.

Minutes later, the Climber's AI announced, "Ceasing acceleration."

Williams smiled from the seat facing her. "We're now sailing toward Jupiter at three thousand kilometers per hour. We'll pick up more speed falling into its gravity well, but Climber adjusts magnetic resistance to keep us below rated max."

Nina felt her weight gradually lift. She looked up. Her heart stumbled. Even moving this fast, Jupiter was so large and far away that it looked motionless. The pipeline plunged into Jupiter's skies like a syringe, drawing hydrogen from virtually limitless veins to fuel the ambitions of people like Williams.

And the dreams of people like Mike.

Attached deep beneath those cloud tops, Mike's beacon kept the Beanstalk clear and the Jovians safe.

"Let's put Jupiter beneath us," the man said. He tapped a couple of icons floating before him, and the seats slid back to their original position.

Below her grippy slippers, the planet raged with silent beauty. Nina shivered. This was the place that had nearly killed the only man she could put up with enough to share a life.

She closed her eyes, painfully aware of the thousand quick deaths that lay just beyond the walls of this little ship.

She tried not to dream.

Eight hours later, the climber's AI startled Nina awake.

"Contact," said the speakers.

The flip-out carbon tabletop between them was littered with interface devices and display frames Velcroed to its surface. Williams gave her a short nod as his eyes and fingers flickered across colorful

3-D user interfaces projected above the frames. His lips moved in silent communion in a way that reminded Nina of Mike working with his beloved adaptive intelligences. Both had cybernetic enhancements, like most who worked with AI.

Williams looked up from his virtual wrangling. "Climber transmitted your test broadcast. We're also within range to pick up Jovian signals."

"Any word on Mike?" Nina asked.

"We're out of comms range, but an hour ago Else reported his repairs are progressing as expected."

Nina looked through the window at her feet. They had fallen so close to Jupiter that vast, stepped cloudbanks rose up toward the craft, half-lit ephemeral valleys thousands of kilometers long and hundreds tall. Lightning flickered within the stacked layers, and pale storms swirled far below. Some of those cyclones could swallow other planets whole. It was as if vast celestial potters fashioned the clouds into roaring towers on a scale designed to provoke existential horror. The Sun had settled near the horizon, setting the higher wisps afire in yellows and golds. She felt the same kind of awe as locking eyes with a tiger.

"Do we need to be so close?" she asked.

"Farther away, Jupiter's electromagnetic activity overwhelms low-power transmissions," he said. "It's why we shield the station. And this Climber."

Nina powered on her tablet. Orange columns and green rows poured out of the 3-D display as the AI interface flickered to life. She studied the signal. Exactly the same as the recorded message Mike had tight-beamed via laser to the torch ship. Right before his accident.

"Getting a signal clean enough to work with?" Williams asked.

She nodded. Her AI easily scrubbed the background static. Her new decryption algorithm pecked away.

"Climber," Williams said, "decelerate and hold position."

The hull began to hum even louder than when they left the station. Nina gained much of her weight back. Their devices shook on the table. After a few minutes, she grew nearly weightless. Her display popped up a new stream of data.

Nina studied the results. She'd transmitted a hybrid of the two basic Jovian phrases, hoping to spur a dialog. She'd be happy if they merely asked, *Huh?* No response. At least, nothing different.

"I'm not even sure it's communication," she said. "What's the point of such heavy encryption? How do they expect us to understand?"

"Perhaps it keeps outsiders from eavesdropping."

"The message hasn't changed in all its repetitions," she said. "A discrete, uncrackable, 12-gig packet. It's more lecture than conversation."

Nina gave an exasperated sigh and rapped the power icon on her tablet, dispersing a hopeless confusion of data, then tossed it to the tabletop. The device rebounded, but Williams caught it and fastened it down.

"What do you need?" he asked.

Nina unfastened her seatbelt, grabbed a handhold beside the central porthole, and stretched across, feet floating up behind.

From this angle, she could see all the way to the edge of the planet. One of Jupiter's moons gleamed dull silver in the black sky, perhaps the one that fed them. Night fast approached, a black shadow devouring the planet. Lightning seared the darkness, some bolts longer than the Grand Canyon. To either side of the Equatorial Zone—where the Beanstalk pierced—two cloud belts raced in opposite directions with winds powerful enough to shear the skin from the Climber. Cyclones boiled to life where belts and zones touched. The atmosphere swarmed with thousands of spiraling storms each powerful enough to desolate the Earth. Deep beneath blazed the heart of a failed star. People could only survive this close to such an utterly indifferent god by relying on miraculous technologies. Which sometimes failed. Nina tore her eyes from the view and looked at Williams.

"No offense to your babies, Don, but AIs are less creative than freshman-calc students."

"I have faith in you," Williams said.

"How about letting me send this to some post-docs I've worked with," she said. Her voice echoed against the ultraglas.

"We need to understand what we're dealing with before opening this up to others," Williams said.

"Typical." She glared at him. "You've made *first contact with aliens* a trade secret. Amazing. They don't belong to you."

"We face both promise and risk. It's best to—"

"To keep the Jovians for yourself?" Nina made a frustrated sound. "When did you become a robber baron?"

Williams crossed his arms. "I'm as big a fan of exploration as Mike.

Here, I've ushered the human race to the doorstep of the stars. I intend to take us the rest of the way."

"Lovely," Nina said, "but you're infected by a meme. Ever since the first Australopithecus started demanding tribute for access to *his* river or *his* fruit trees, capitalism has perpetuated and spread. It's a brain disease. Whenever a market bubble or banking scheme based on untenable math collapses, civilization falls closer to ruin. All because the most-infected people can't stop gathering fortunes. The more you collect for yourself, the worse it gets for everyone else."

"Without funding from wealthy donors," Williams said, "your university wouldn't have survived the Crash. There wouldn't be grants for research. Grad students wouldn't have fellowships for tuition. We wouldn't have AIs to analyze algorithms or crunch numbers, or the interfaces to direct them—"

"So you're the patron saint of a big charity."

"It costs a fortune to exploit these kinds of resources," Williams said, gesturing toward the side porthole. "It takes visionaries to do something meaningful with it."

"That's not what I'm talking about," Nina said.

Williams nodded. "You're talking redistribution. When have people ever chosen less? Spread humankind's resources equally among everyone, and there'd be nothing left for projects like this. We'd lose our capability to realize great dreams and visions."

"You're not listening—" Nina began.

"I am," Williams said. "We're close to achieving *your* vision, Nina, but to get there we need to use the system to our advantage. Capitalism won't vanish overnight. If we dive headfirst into utopianism without filling the reservoir of wealth, we'll break our necks when we hit dry lakebed."

Nina looked away, out at Jupiter, a waning crescent. "It's just a failure of imagination." Sunset moved fast across its cloud tops, setting her skin ablaze with Jupitershine.

"I agree," Williams said. "Do you know why Mike signed on to work here?"

"He wanted to explore Jupiter," Nina said, her voice flat.

"Sure, but also because I agreed to base JoveCo on a transformative socioeconomic framework. *You* got him thinking about such things. He's pretty convincing."

Nina arched an eyebrow and said, "You're calling JoveCo a utopia?"

"Hardly, but it's a fairer system than most. Only partners can hold JoveCo stock, and everybody here's an equal partner."

"Even you?" Nina said.

He shrugged. "I invested more, so I hold more stock. But my salary's the same. We all share equally in the bounty we produce, with opportunity for bonuses based on three-sixty performance reviews."

Nina sighed. "I didn't mean to pick a fight," she said.

"It's my fault," Williams said. "I've worked with programmers for 30 years. I should know better than to get defensive."

"And after working with *academics* for two decades," Nina said, "*I* should know better, too. I'm just disheartened. Mike's accident really threw me. Frontiers are dangerous, but it's *Mike*."

"Fate and the cold equations of space conspire to yank the controls out of even the boldest hands," Williams said. "We need a break. In more ways than one."

"This is the first encryption I've been unable to crack," Nina said, "ever."

Williams reached into the knapsack belted to the seat beside him and withdrew the wine. He slipped a straw through the cork's membrane and passed it to Nina.

"To better luck," he said.

Nina saluted him and took a long pull. It was the most delightful wine she'd ever tasted. She sighed, then handed it back. "Wine through a straw. I feel like a student again."

Williams chuckled and took a sip. "Let's listen to the locals," he said. In a firmer voice, he said, "Climber, tune comms to the Jovian broadcast and put it on speaker."

The climber suddenly got noisy, speakers hissing and then crackling loudly whenever lightning seamed the sky below. Williams did something with his interface to clean up the signal until they spoke a steady rhythm—*Go away!*—accompanied by a background sizzle that reset every 42 seconds.

Same as ever. Nina gave a strangled groan.

"Can I help?" Williams asked.

"Ozymandias," Nina said, "your power is meaningless here." She stared down at Jupiter. Winds raged and an entire species sang a background chorus to ignorant ears.

Williams handed the wine to her again. Nina took a long drag before tossing it back to him. It left an aftertaste of flowers and dappled sunlight on her tongue. She closed her eyes and thought of her last dinner with Mike, before he came here, so long ago. She couldn't remember what they ate, only the outdoor table overlooking Puget Sound—boats and floatplanes humming nearby.

"When I took sabbatical to come here," she said, "the problem seemed simple. Mike thought he'd decoded the Jovian Rosetta Stone. Two signals comprising an entire dictionary, and a global demand to leave. A language of pragmatic math. Elegant. Turns out we'd only touched the snow atop an iceberg." She opened her eyes to look accusingly at Jupiter.

"All those creatures down there," Nina said, "thinking with a single mind. What are they saying?"

The vessel hissed and crackled with unintelligible voices.

Nina got an idea. She strapped down and fired up her tablet, whose display flickered green and red patterns across her face. She wrote a new algorithm to cycle through permutations of the simple signals, then saved it and flicked it over to Williams' interface.

"Try this," she said.

"Mike said that it's as if all we see is a UI panel," Williams said as he tapped icons in his own interface. "But it has only two settings. If someone built an interface like that back at EmSol, I'd fire them."

Nina paused. "User interface," she whispered. She glanced out at the brightening planet. Something itched at her mind.

"What if the Jovians' simple statements *aren't* a Rosetta Stone?" she said. "What if they're just squirrels barking to let the others know about danger or food? Maybe we should look elsewhere to decode the encrypted data."

She looked into Williams' eyes. "What if the planetwide static is just a UI that operates something deeper: the encrypted message. Maybe it's an entirely different language, the way AI language is different than ours."

"The EmSol interface acts as human-AI intermediary," Williams said. A smile crinkled the skin beside his eyes.

Nina nodded. "Maybe the encrypted code progression is something different, not simple Jovians or unified Jupiter-Mind. Different math. Different logic."

"You're suggesting there's *another* mind?" Williams said. He was quiet for a while. "The question then becomes . . ."

"Who is that third mind?" Nina said. She pulled herself to the side viewport. Such roiling mountains of hydrogen and methane could hide a thousand civilizations.

"You haven't observed any other natives?" she asked.

"No," Williams said. "It's a miracle the floaters survive. But if we assume a different mind is behind the encrypted message, it must be hugely advanced."

"Smart Jovians," Nina said, "who want us to leave."

"Perhaps an AI that spontaneously formed in their network," Williams suggested, "like Econ?" That feral mind, spawned from investment software, lurked silently inside almost every device on Earth's 'net.

"Comforting thought," Nina said.

Williams chuckled. "If Jupiter-Mind's jazz is UI, we know the output. There's a lot going on beneath the hood. We need to identify the machine code, so to speak."

Nina nodded. "It's definitely more like code than communication. No one talks using *encryption*," Nina said. She drew a sharp breath and looked at Williams.

"That's it." she said. "What if it's a *handshake*? That explains why we can't decrypt it. Who could crack 12-gig encryption? But you're not *supposed* to decrypt a security key, just process it and return the handshake with your own trusted key."

Nina hammered at her tablet and called up the packet. She spun it above her display, then wrapped it in her personal JoveCo comms key.

"I've repackaged it inside my key," she said, "so they'll know we're responding. It's not a handshake unless you both offer a hand."

"Brilliant," Williams said. "What's next?"

"Transmit this," she said. She flicked the handshake over to Williams' interface.

He pulled himself down to his display and tapped an icon. "Chatbot's loaded and ready to go. Shall we?"

Her blood rushed in her ears. She nodded.

"This feels like when I shipped my first beta UI," Williams said. He tapped his tablet.

"Handshake away."

The speakers continued to rumble and hiss. Full night now engulfed this side of the planet, lightning veining the darkness like a sea of camera flashes.

Nina was about to suggest they resend when the speakers went quiet. Her ears strained. She started to notice little pings and creaks in the vessel's hull. The circulation fans sounded like turbofans in the silence.

Suddenly the speakers crackled to life.

"Seems we've opened a conversation," Williams said. His eyes skimmed a deluge of incoming data. He shared the stream with Nina's interface.

She put her decryption algorithm to work on the stream. "We're getting terabytes of new data per second. Jupiter-Mind's message is definitely not repeating anymore. Incoming math's still variable."

The speakers buzzed and thrummed like a noise-art concert.

"I've tasked Chatbot and Finder to continue processing," Williams said. His fingers performed an air ballet.

Suddenly, the speakers went quiet.

After nearly a minute, Nina said, "That's it. Sixty terabytes. Can your AIs handle this much data?"

Williams smiled and raised an eyebrow. "We'll see," he said. "Climber, take us back to the station."

Acceleration pushed Nina into her seat as they started back up the Beanstalk. Her weight lifted as they reached speed.

"Shit," Williams muttered. He inspected a flutter of light in his display.

Nina looked up.

"An app's been uploaded into Chatbot's memory." He started pulling on his helmet. "Seal up, just in case."

A chill ran down Nina's back as she enclosed her face once more. "Virus?" she asked as the helmet swelled.

He frowned. "First they'd need to learn our AIs' native language," he said. "It's like a punch card system trying to talk to a fish—completely different information infrastructures."

He did something that made a calm female voice come over the speakers: "Patching. Patching. Patching . . ."

"I can't isolate the affected AIs," Williams said. A few seconds later, he winced. "It's in the comms system. That connects everything."

His finger movements elevated to frantic waving. Finally he shook his head. "Unresponsive. We're too far down to contact JoveCo Way Station."

*"Patching . . ."*

Each of Nina's breaths fogged the helmet. Her blood sang in her ears. She noticed that her own AI was unresponsive. *Is this how Mike felt during his accident?*

She swallowed. Her throat felt dry. "Whoever's down there responded to the key exchange," she said. "Maybe they're installing a custom interface—"

The lights and speakers in the vessel shut off, along with the fans and other systems. The only illumination came from flashes of lightning. The weight imparted by accelerating toward the station lifted as they began to fall back toward Jupiter. If they couldn't restart the climber's drive, they'd be crushed by atmospheric pressure in a few days. If they didn't suffocate first.

"I'm sorry," Williams said.

Nina gave him a wry smile but said nothing.

A few seconds later, the lights came back on. Nina sensed some weight returning. The speakers remained quiet.

Nina exhaled, not realizing she'd been holding her breath.

"Climber, status," Williams demanded.

Silence.

Nina's tablet flickered, then displayed a stream of unintelligible icons. She tried to interact, but none of the usual UI gestures gave any response. She felt the suit sticking to her armpits.

"I think the AIs are being reprogrammed," Williams said. "Life-support's working."

"At least they're not trying to kill us," Nina said.

Williams tapped at his tablet, then sighed and looked at Nina. She couldn't imagine how he kept his face looking so calm and resolute.

"How did they learn our AIs' language before they learned *ours*?" Williams said.

"Makes sense," Nina said. "AIs use most of your bandwidth. Can't you stop this?"

Williams shook his head. "We're utterly dependent on our AIs. So how do we open a conversation with these smart aliens, assuming they're the ones doing all this?" he asked.

Nina gestured with her tablet. "The Jovians installed an app into your systems. They started with Chatbot, so it's likely a comms app. They'll talk when they're ready."

Something caught the man's eye, and he began tapping and swiping his tablet's non-projection screen.

Nina noticed hers had restarted, as well. A line of unfamiliar symbols scrolled up the screen.

"The Jovian app loaded a new subroutine," he said. "It created its own operating-system kernel."

He looked wide-eyed at Nina. "It's an alien AI. A big one."

"Can you communicate with it?" Nina asked.

"*Please do,*" said the Climber's speakers. They both jumped.

"Chatbot?" Mike said.

"*An emulation of that mind,*" the speakers said.

Nina noticed motion out of the corner of her eye. She turned. The fabric of another row of seats was writhing.

"Don, look!" she said, pointing. The seats shuddered, then dissolved to dust. The pile vibrated with ripples like a pebble dropped into a pond. Seconds later, a hemisphere began to rise from the dust.

Another row of seats started to decompose.

The skin of Nina's neck tingled. She checked her helmet's seal. She squinted down at Jupiter to see if they were falling or climbing, but the distances were too vast to discern movement.

"Is the climber turning into gray goo?" Nina asked.

"Chatbot," Williams asked, "what's happening?"

"*We are transforming non-critical materials into necessary equipment,*" said the speakers.

Nina and Williams asked, "How?" "What equipment?" and "For whom?"

Two more hemispheres began to form and rise from the dust of the other disassembled seats. The rest of the vessel seemed to be retaining its integrity.

"*We are using increasing-complexity self-assembly mechanisms to repurpose non-critical resources. The new equipment will handle multidimensional transmissions, process local spacetime, and house the high-order minds as they re-enter this universe from their crash-bubble microcosm."*

Nina blinked, trying to transform those words into something meaningful.

*"I apologize for acting without warning. To the high-order minds, you are a hybrid, multiform species that is part AI and part human, like the native Jupiter life's primitive network that the explorers have been evolving and programming for sixty thousand years."*

"Are they going to reprogram *us?*" Nina asked.

*"Just as they did not harm the Jovians, they will not harm you."*

"It's the little things!" she said. She tried to laugh, but it came out sounding strangled.

*"These high-order minds obey strict rules,"* the modified Chatbot said. *"They respect the integrity of organic life."*

"Who are these high-order minds?" Williams asked.

The three matte-finished domes were now vibrating. Dust shimmered from their surfaces onto the floor.

*"Explorers."*

"Explain 'crash-bubble microcosm,'" Williams said.

*"Their vessel encountered a massive subspace disruption that briefly flickered their drive into realspace while they were examining Jupiter's core. Emergency systems created a spacetime bubble to isolate their dark matter from the planet's ultra-dense baryonic matter. It protected them, but it also trapped them."*

A bright light caught Nina's eye, and she looked out the side window at Jupiter. A glowing cyclone appeared to be forming in the clouds.

"Is that normal?" she asked, pointing. It grew brighter than the bolts of lightning, and soon outshone the rest of the planet, too luminous to look at directly.

"I've never seen anything like it," Williams said.

Nina put up a hand to shield her eyes. She blinked, afterimages dancing behind her eyelids. The speakers crackled and popped. When she opened her eyes, the bright sphere had vanished. The speakers went quiet.

"Chatbot," Williams said, "what just happened?"

*"The explorers are free,"* Chatbot said. *"They convey their gratitude."*

"Jesus," Nina said. "I guess you don't need me anymore."

❊   ❊   ❊

Nina stood beside Williams gazing at the nearby cluster of alien domes. Jupitershine poured in through the vessel's portholes, making their surfaces sparkle and seem to move. Williams had called an all-hands meeting, but he and Nina had remained aboard the Climber until they could be sure the nanos were quiescent. Back online, comms equipment shared the scene in high-res holo with the personnel aboard JoveCo Way Station—crowded into the station's hold—and those assembled down on Ganymede.

"We've inherited an incredible wealth of advanced tech," Williams concluded, gesturing to the domes.

"Nanofacturing infrastructure, AIs orders of magnitude more advanced than ours, and other systems we'll spend years investigating. That's JoveCo's new core mission—not that we'll cease hydrogen-mining operations. Stay practical."

Scattered chuckles.

"I'll open to questions," Williams said. "What do we tackle first?"

"Don," Nina said, "you say JoveCo is 'laying the flagstones for humankind to walk among the stars.' That's what drew Mike here, and I'd bet most others, too. You can now accomplish that, but only if you share this tech."

"You'd give it away," Williams said.

Nina overcame her instincts and ran a fingertip along the top of an alien dome. It felt smooth and tingly.

"This tech can give us the stars, but only if we engage the collective capabilities of our entire species. Learning the science, engineering our own equipment, building starships—you're powerful, but that's beyond your ability."

Someone in the hologrammic crowd muttered.

Nina looked out at them. "Even if we *try* to keep it all for yourselves, we won't be able to. Some military corp will seize our intellectual property 'for national defense,' or a big fish will get greedy and knock us out of the pond. Such companies don't have magnanimous leaders. Their vision is limited to stockholder profit. Going to the stars offers no guaranteed profits, so they'll grow fat off something they didn't even discover. They'll scatter your dream. The only way to reach the stars is by making sure what we learn here belongs to *everyone.*"

"I won't let competitors take this tech," Williams said.

Nina put a hand on his shoulder and looked into his eyes. "You're Don Williams," she said. She gestured to the hologrammic crowd. "Everyone here signed onto your dream. Mike's in a coma because he believes in you. Humankind will never reach the stars if you're out to win the capitalism game. Your vision requires everyone working together. Even the aliens who left us these relics—*who could create a pocket universe and live there for thousands of years*—needed help to get free. Collectively, humankind is far more capable than one company."

"What do you propose?" Williams asked.

"Offer exactly what you did when you set up JoveCo," Nina said. "Make them *all* work for *JoveCo* to get their hands on this. They'll accept your offer."

Williams smiled and winked at her.

*The bastard knew.* She shook her head and took a long sip of the wine.

Williams turned to the crowd. "How do you feel about inviting the *entire human species* to become shareholder-employees?" he asked.

Muttering, then a cheer. Pretty soon everyone was talking at once.

Williams turned to Nina. "Looks like we need to get busy hiring people," he said. "But first we have a lot of patents to file."

Through the porthole beneath her feet, Jupiter reached full day. Down among those gigantic storms, billions of creatures floated, minds linked into a vast radio choir. A tiny fraction of the light that erupted from the Sun 40 minutes ago reflected off those clouds, and a tiny fraction of that found its way through windows into a little vessel at humankind's remotest frontier. Three artifacts forged from pure information shone in that starlight, but not nearly so bright as the eyes of the men and women who gazed upon them.

More than ever, Nina could hardly wait for Mike to wake.

((•((•((• ◎ •))•))•))

**Chris McKitterick's** work has appeared in *Analog, Artemis, Captain Proton, E-Scape, Extrapolation, Foundation, Aftermaths, Ad Astra, Locus, Mythic Circle, NOTA, Ruins: Extraterrestrial, Sentinels, Synergy: New Science Fiction, Tomorrow,* various *TSR* publications,

*Visual Journeys, Westward Weird,* a bowling poem anthology, and elsewhere.

His debut novel, published by Hadley Rille Books, is *Transcendence,* and he recently finished another, *Empire Ship.* Current projects include *The Galactic Adventures of Jack and Stella* and a memoir, *Stories from a Perilous Youth.*

Chris teaches writing and Science Fiction at the University of Kansas and succeeded James Gunn as Director of the Center for the Study of Science Fiction. He also serves as juror for the John W. Campbell Memorial Award for best SF novel. He can be found online at Twitter, Facebook, and his Web site: www.christopher-mckitterick.com.

*And now we return to our own planet's orbit as high school physics teacher Jay Werkheiser's tale explores a race to be the first to visit a Near Earth Object . . .*

# AROUND THE NEO IN 80 DAYS

## by Jay Werkheiser

Dark Sky Station floated lazily over the equator like a hydrogen-filled silver starfish. It drifted through the mesosphere, as high as its buoyancy could lift it, where the sky above was the color of space and the hazy glow of the troposphere hugged the curvature of the Earth below. A habitat tube ran along the keel, tracing the mile-long inflated arms. Within, Felix awaited his prey.

He sipped a bulb of coffee, intently watching through a porthole as a puffy v-shaped airship drifted closer. It kissed the base of DSS's arm, a perfect soft docking. The clanging of airlock doors and a jumble of voices sounded from the pressure hatch a few yards away.

*Soon.*

He tried to focus on the incident report on his tablet—some newb on the construction crew forgot to depressurize before suiting up and got the bends—but his mind was on the hunt. And the money it would bring.

The first man through the hatch was one of the most recognizable people on Earth—handlebar mustache, mutton chops, and unruly salt-and-pepper hair contrasting with a three-piece suit and white gloves. Phil Foggerty. Rich, eccentric, famous for being famous. "Be a good man and see to our arrangements," Foggerty said in his faux haughty voice. "I'll find my own way to my chamber."

The man following him said, "Of course, sir." As soon as Foggerty disappeared through the hatch, the man collapsed into a chair across the aisle from Felix.

Felix caught his eye. "First ascender flight?"

The man nodded. "Wasn't bad. A little rocking, but no worse than being at sea. It's the next flight that has me worried." He glanced up, as though he could see the black sky through the station's skin.

Felix suppressed a smile. "Oh, I didn't know an orbital ascender was headed out tomorrow." He always smiled when he lied.

The man nodded, then stretched out a hand. "John Keyes."

"Detective Felix."

"Detective?"

"Station this size, they need someone to keep an eye on things."

Keyes grunted. "I suppose so."

"So your boss is some kind of space tourist? Rich guy who wants to make a few orbits around the Earth?"

"Not quite."

Felix could see that the story was itching to burst through Keyes's lips, so he prodded it. "Oh? Where to, then?"

"We're going to be the first to go to a NEO."

"NEO?"

"Near Earth object. Some tiny asteroid making a close approach soon."

"You're going to land on it?"

Keyes waved his hands, erasing the thought. "Oh, no. That's much too difficult. We're just going to swing around it, get some close-up pictures, and return home."

"Unmanned mission could do that faster and cheaper."

"Where's your sense of adventure?"

Felix knew there was more to it than adventure. There was money on the line, big money, a fool's bet that Foggerty could be the first person to make it to a NEO and back, with a time limit that expired in less than three months. A wager that Foggerty intended to win by cheating.

And a nice chunk of change would go in Felix's pocket if Foggerty missed the deadline. "I wish you a speedy journey, then," he said with a smile.

Keyes headed to the hub, where the station's five arms converged, for the preflight briefing. He and Foggerty would be passengers, not crew or mission specialists, so there wasn't much he needed to know. He abandoned his plan to explore after the briefing; the trip to the hub had shown him that there was nothing to see but an endless tube punctuated by frequent pressure hatches.

He pressed his hand against the plastic wall. It felt like Mylar, rigid from air pressure. He ran his hand along the smooth surface, feeling the lightweight trusses supporting the tube. Same as the last compartment. And the one before that.

He slipped through the hatch to the next compartment and found three crew members sleeping in their bunks. He sealed the hatch as silently as he could and tiptoed through the compartment. There was little privacy in DSS.

Except for Foggerty, of course. The section of tube outward of his bunk stored meteorological instruments that rarely needed maintenance, affording him the closest thing to private chambers money could buy above the stratosphere.

"Everything still on schedule?" Foggerty asked.

"Indeed, sir. The ascender will be returning to DSS within the hour, then refueled and—"

"Oh? I'd assumed we'd be using the one parked outside. Save the refueling time."

"I asked, sir. That one is still under construction," Keyes said. "They only have one fully operational so far. Had to use it to get your extra fuel tank into orbit, and they're already cutting their turnaround time short for you. I get the feeling they're a bit miffed about it."

Foggerty chuckled. "Not the first time, my man."

"We'll be boarding the orbital ascender at five A.M. GMT." Keyes glanced at his phone. "That's eleven hours from now."

"Good show. Timing is going to be critical. Just a little late and our orbit won't intersect the NEO's."

"Forgive my asking, sir, but are you sure this is safe? You've had minimal training, and I've had even less. Didn't NASA used to spend months training their astronauts? Years, even?"

"NASA no longer exists, now does it?"

"But still—"

"Tut. These airships are much safer than rockets, no heavy

acceleration to deal with or fuel tanks to explode. It's like riding a balloon to space. Who trains for balloon rides?"

Keyes huffed, but knew further discussion was pointless. "Now there's something I don't understand," he said, switching gears. "How is it we can ride a balloon to space? There's no air!"

"But there is, a good way up anyway, just not much of it."

Keyes frowned. "I guess I just don't understand it."

"Look," Foggerty said, a devilish smile spreading from mutton chop to mutton chop, "buoyancy depends on the weight of air displaced, right? So if you make your airship bigger, you displace more air and get more buoyancy."

Keyes nodded slowly. "That's why they made the airship so big."

"Biggest airship ever built, by far. Over a mile long. They had to build it up here; it would never survive the winds down in the troposphere."

"Even so, you'll eventually reach a point where there's no air, and then no amount of buoyancy can help."

"True enough. Buoyancy can only lift the ascender to about two hundred thousand feet. Then they turn on thrusters, some sort of chemical/electric hybrid, and push the rest of the way to orbit."

"And all the way out to the near-Earth asteroid."

"Well, they use up most of their fuel just to reach orbit," Foggerty said. "I had to pay good money to lob that refueling tanker up there. The company's not thrilled with having to do a docking maneuver on short notice, but I spread enough money around to bring the thrill back." His grin widened.

Keyes shook his head. He knew it was pointless to ask why Foggerty would spend more on this venture than he stood to win, and pledge the winnings to space research at that. He turned and gazed through the compartment's porthole at the curve of the Earth below, mostly cloud-dotted ocean with a sliver of land rising over the horizon, all shrouded in the blue glow of the atmosphere. The question answered itself.

Felix had done his research long before Foggerty had arrived on the station. Foggerty was a deep sleeper, difficult to wake in the morning. Felix's tablet chimed, alerting him that Foggerty's phone had connected to DSS's wireless network and that Felix's software had cracked its security.

The data files were encrypted, of course, with coding that would take centuries to crack. But routine functions were not. Felix opened Foggerty's clock app and disabled its alarm function. He implanted a bit of code in the phone that would send a message to mission control an hour before launch.

The new valet, Keyes, was a wild card. He'd been hired mere days ago, so Felix didn't know his habits. He had to take some risks to keep him from foiling the plan. He lingered near the module where Keyes would spend the night, waiting for the hatch to open.

At long last, Keyes emerged.

Felix walked toward him casually and smiled. "Oh, didn't expect to see you here."

"Nature calls."

"Hah. Well, while you're out, how about a drink for the road?"

"Is that legal up here?"

"I'm a cop, right?"

Felix waited for Keyes to hit the head, then led him to a seldom-used science module. He looked to make sure no one was watching, then pulled the hatch shut behind him.

"Chilly in here," Keyes said.

"Never gets used, other than some science geek checking an instrument every now and then. They don't waste money heating more than they have to." He tossed Keyes a bulb. "This'll keep you warm."

Keyes cracked the seal and sipped. "Ugh. What's in it?"

"Whatever the engineers pulled from their still last week, with some lime juice." *And a little something extra in yours.* Felix opened his own bulb and drank.

"So tell me, how does a guy get to be a lawman on a space station?"

"DSS isn't in space," Felix said, dodging the question, "and it's not orbiting. That's why you're not weightless. We're drifting in the upper atmosphere somewhere, and the countries that we fly over feel more secure with some form of legal authority aboard."

"Yeah, but why you?"

"Long story." Cops who blew the whistle on their superiors didn't stay cops very long, unless they had friends in high places. Then they got shuffled out of the way. Far out of the way.

"Get much work?"

"If you mean paperwork, hell yeah."

Keyes chuckled. "I suppose Mr. Foggerty's little stunt kept you busy for a while."

"You have no idea."

"They don't make 'em any stranger than Foggerty, but he's a good man." Keyes took a long pull from his bulb. "Ever since they killed NASA, he's been looking for ways to reinvigorate the space program."

"This trip of his is a publicity stunt, then?"

Keyes nodded. "He stands to make a bundle, too, if he makes the deadline. Already has the money committed to R&D for more space balloons."

"Airships," Felix corrected automatically. "Don't let the company boys hear you calling them balloons."

Keyes started to speak but tripped over the words. "Woo, this stuff is wicked." He looked at his bulb accusingly.

"That it is."

He raised his bulb. "To becoming the first humans to see an ass . . . uh, heh, an asteroid up close."

"Your orbit's a cheat, you know."

"Whadda ya mean? We'll pass out the, uh, I mean, outside the NEO. It's legit."

"Barely. It'll pass just inside your apogee as you swing by. The intention of the bet was to *go* there, not skate by on a technicality."

"S'all legal." Keyes's eyes lost their focus. "Mr. Fogg checked with lawyers."

"Bad wording, then. A cheat."

"He's gon' win his bet, y'know." Keyes swayed, took a wobbly step to the side. "Show that pompous ass . . ." He leaned against the module's wall.

Felix pushed his guilt pangs down into his gut and buried them with enough bile that he could taste it. "I'm sorry."

"Fer what?" Keyes's back slid down the wall. "Gonna . . . uh . . . sit. Rest a . . ."

Felix waited for him to stop moving, then slipped out of the module and pulled the hatch shut behind him. Guilt stabbed at his conscience. Keyes seemed like a good man; he deserved better. Felix forced himself to think about the money, enough to get out of police work and set up his own business. Private investigation, maybe, or security. Somehow the vision seemed flatter than it used to.

❈   ❈   ❈

It was cold.

Keyes reached for a blanket but found only smooth floor. He wrapped his arms around himself and shivered.

He drifted back toward sleep, but the chill nudged him closer to consciousness. *Mr. Foggerty will be expecting his morning tea.*

He rubbed his eyes, shielding them from the light. His head pulsed. He peeked at the glare outside his eyelids.

*I'm on the space station!*

Not space. Dark sky.

He fumbled for his phone and stared at the time. *Jeez!*

They'd be sealing the airlock any time now, if they hadn't already. Why hadn't anyone come to wake him? *Foggerty must be furious.*

He scrambled to his feet, kicking the half-empty bulb from last night. Wicked stuff.

But he'd only had half a bulb. Nothing was that wicked. He rubbed his hazy head. Felix was long gone.

Felix.

*Did he actually drug me?*

No time to wonder. He composed himself and pushed the hatch open. He bounded down the endless tube, not stopping to close pressure hatches behind him. Someone shouted a curse after him, but he wasted no time looking back.

He reached the hub, swiveled, looking at the hatches leading to the five arms of DSS. Which one? Cold sweat stung under his arms.

"Looking for something?"

Keyes's eyes snapped to the lone crewman on duty in the hub. "Uh," he said, trying to force words past his thick tongue. Finally, he managed to get out, "Space launch?"

The crewman smirked and pointed to a hatch. "Better hurry."

Keyes stumbled through the hatch and down the tube. His hazy brain could focus on little more than opening the next hatch in line. Damn, how much further?

"Oh, it's you," a voice said. "What're you doing here?" Keyes vaguely recognized the woman from yesterday's briefing. Her silky black hair had been down then, not tucked away in a neat bun. He struggled to remember her name. Flight chief something or other.

The patch sewn to her flight suit reminded him. "Aouda."

"What?"

"Uh, nothing. Just . . ."

She arched an eyebrow at him.

"On time?" he managed to stammer.

"Barely. We're just about to close the airlock." She looked him over, frowned. "I thought you weren't coming."

"Wha—?"

"No time. If you're going, you better get in there now."

The airlock door was an open hatch on the floor, which the chief ushered him through. Keyes found himself in a long thin tube clinging to inset rungs. He glanced down into the dizzying depths below. The hatch clanged shut above him.

With nowhere else to go, he climbed down the tube. A clang sounded from below, then a voice. "Get a move on. We need to shove off if we're going to make our launch window."

He hurried his pace and soon found himself climbing through another hatch. A man in a flight suit slammed the hatch behind him. The flight engineer, but Keyes couldn't remember his name.

He looked Keyes up and down. "Thought you guys cancelled."

"What? No. Why would we do that?"

He shrugged. "Dunno. Mission control said they got a message from Foggerty an hour ago."

"Mr. Foggerty would never—"

"Whatever. Get strapped in."

He had himself almost strapped in before his foggy brain thought to ask the next question. "Isn't Mr. Foggerty on board?"

The pilot continued her preflight work, ignoring him. The flight engineer looked at him with his eyebrows raised. "You see him anywhere?"

"I have to find out where he is!"

He reached to undo his straps, but the engineer grabbed his hand. "You're not going anywhere."

A slight tug pulled Keyes forward as the attitude engines fired. On the pilot's video display, DSS lazily receded.

Flight Chief Aouda's image in Felix's tablet looked harried. "Better come over to the ascender dock, Detective. We have a situation here."

"What is it?"

"It's that Foggerty guy. He's on a rampage."

"On my way." Felix charged down the tube, slamming pressure hatches behind him. The ascender docking module wasn't very far; a good cop plans ahead.

When he arrived, Foggerty was mostly calm. "Look," he said, "I don't know where this text message came from, but I surely didn't send it. But that's water over the dam. What's important is how you're going to get me onto that ascender."

Aouda sputtered. "Get onto it? You can't."

"My good woman, where there's a will, there's a way." He turned his attention to Felix. "I'm sure you'll agree, Mister . . ."

"Detective Felix."

"You don't say." He eyed Felix appraisingly. "Are you in charge of security on this station?"

"I am."

"Then we must have some words when this is all said and done. But first I must get aboard that airship!"

"If the chief says it's impossible, sir, then it's impossible."

"Tut. You have those atmospheric airships I rode up in. Take me up in one of those."

"No, no, no," Aouda said, agitated. "If they could get to orbit themselves, we wouldn't need the orbital ascenders. DSS is at the limit of their buoyancy, and even then they need special low-pressure propellers after seventy K feet." Foggerty began to object, and the chief added pointedly, "Not that we'd risk an airship or its crew trying, even if it was possible."

Foggerty's face dropped. "Well that's it, then. I knew Stuart would try to cheat. Didn't think he'd be clever enough to pull it off though."

Felix averted his eyes from the crestfallen man and tried to focus on the money he stood to make. It would have been so much easier if he didn't have to face his victim.

Victim. The word made Felix feel like a criminal. Maybe Foggerty was bending the rules, but Stuart was outright breaking them. And I helped him, Felix thought.

Damn it.

Inexplicably, Foggerty's lips erupted into a smile beneath his handlebar. "Ah, but you have another ascender under construction!"

"Really, sir," Aouda said. "It'll be another few months before it's ready for flight."

"Well, it looks complete. What's it missing?"

"The engines," Felix said.

"Oh." Foggerty's smile collapsed and his shoulders hunched in defeat.

I have him, Felix thought. All I have to do is keep my mouth shut. "But it still has plenty of buoyancy."

"Oh ho! That it does!"

Aouda frowned. "You can't be serious. I can't authorize—"

"I can," Felix said with a smile.

"Bull," Aouda said.

"Well, I have override codes. I can release the tethers holding it in place before anyone knows what's happening."

Foggerty clapped him on the back. "Good man!"

Aouda arched her eyebrow at Felix. "I hope you know what you're doing."

*Ending my career. Giving up my dream. Doing the right thing.* "Will we be able to catch the other ascender in time?"

"We?"

"Mr. Foggerty doesn't know how to fly. I'll have to go with him."

"The good news," Aouda said, "is that without engines the ascender is a lot lighter than the fully loaded one. It'll rise faster. If you leave soon, you just might catch up to them before they reach two hundred K."

"That's when the engines kick in," Foggerty said.

"That's the bad news."

"Well then," Felix said, "let's get a move on."

Stealing a spaceship wasn't as difficult as it sounded, especially when the next closest cop was a hundred forty thousand feet below. Felix looked over the work crew rotation. Luckily, the engines were preassembled on the ground and none of them had arrived on station yet, so just a few maintenance guys were aboard the ascender at the moment.

"I need you all to evacuate the ship." Felix suppressed a smile. "Police matter."

"Let's see a badge."

"Don't be a smart ass, Charlie."

The maintenance guys laughed and filed out of the crew module and up the airlock tube.

When the last of them was gone, Foggerty grinned. "Good show. Let's shove off."

"Yes, let's," Aouda's voice said from the airlock tube.

Felix looked up just in time to see her climb down the last few rungs. "What do you think you're doing?"

"Someone's got to fly this thing."

"I put in my required time on the simulator."

"Wait," Foggerty said. "You were going to try to fly solo with only simulator training? And they say I'm crazy."

"Ha," Aouda said. "Strap in and let's get this bird moving."

Felix sat and fastened his straps. "You know you're throwing away your career," he said.

"I couldn't let you two kill yourselves trying to fly. Besides, Mr. Foggerty is rather charming when he's not badgering innocent flight chiefs." She grinned impishly.

"Oh, I must apologize," Foggerty said. "No excuse for treating a lady that way."

"Pssht," Aouda said. "He thinks I'm a lady."

The radio hissed and Aouda dialed the volume down. "I don't suppose mission control is happy with us," Felix said.

Aouda grinned. "I can't hear them. Antenna hasn't been installed yet."

"I doubt they have anything interesting to say anyway," Foggerty said. "So what's your excuse for breaking the law, detective?"

Felix met Foggerty's gaze for a moment, then dropped his eyes. "I owed it to you, Mr. Foggerty. I . . . uh, I'm the one who made you miss your flight."

"Yes, of course you were."

Felix's eyes snapped to Foggerty's. "You knew?"

"Who else could it have been? You're the fellow who best knows security."

"Why didn't you report me?"

"No need for that; the deed was done." Foggerty harrumphed. "I just wonder how much the old windbag paid you."

"Not enough to crush a man's dreams."

"Didn't take you for a philosopher."

Felix chuckled. "Neither did I."

"Uh, we have a problem." Aouda's voice was ice cold.

Felix's heart skipped. "What's wrong?"

"Our O-2 tanks are empty. The ascender must have been getting its air from the station. I opened the auxiliary O-2 supply, but . . ."

"But what?" Ice gripped Felix's throat.

"We'll be cutting it close, making it to the buoyancy ceiling. And there's no way anyone's making it back down."

"Well then I guess we're all going over to the other ascender together." Foggerty's voice betrayed no fear; he might have ordered a cup of tea with that tone. "Have you made radio contact with them?"

She tapped the radio console.

"Blast."

"I'm sure DSS mission control has been squawking since we left. Believe me, they know we're coming."


"It has to be Mr. Foggerty," Keyes said. "Who else would come after us in a stolen airship?"

The flight engineer looked at him sharply. "They still haven't responded to DSS. We have to assume hostile intent."

"Nonsense! Have you tried to contact them? I'm sure he'll talk to us."

The pilot pinned Keyes with a stern look. "I'm not taking any risks. As soon as we reach the two hundred K ceiling, we're thrusting to orbit."

"But Mr. Foggerty will—"

"Foggerty can just float his ass back down to DSS."

Keyes tried a new tactic. "But the whole point of the launch is to get him to the NEO and back."

"Mission parameters are to refuel, execute a Hohmann transfer, snap a few pics, and come home. Doesn't matter who's aboard."

Keyes huffed. "Without Foggerty's money, there wouldn't be a mission."

"We have a narrow burn window," the pilot said sternly. "We miss it and all Foggerty's money is wasted. Now shut your trap and let me do my job."

Keyes folded his arms and looked away. That Felix guy had drugged him last night. Probably made Foggerty miss the launch in the first place. What if it was him in the stolen ascender? To what lengths would he go to stop the mission?

Maybe the pilot was right after all.

Felix shivered and sucked in another breath of stale, freezing air. The chill spread through his lungs. "How much longer?"

"Soon," Aouda said. Her video screen displayed the feed from the topside camera. The ascender showed as a tiny V against a black sky. She zoomed the blurry image. "Crap."

"What is it?"

"They're maneuvering into position to begin thrust."

"Well, then, we'd better get moving," Foggerty said. "How are we getting over there? Some sort of escape pod?"

Felix's face flushed. What else had he failed to consider before running off half-cocked?

"Not a chance," Aouda said. "We're going to have to shoot a tether to them and climb over. Hope you have strong arms, because it's a long way down."

"Won't it be cold?" Foggerty asked.

"Ha! I'd be more worried about the lack of air if I were you."

Felix locked eyes with Aouda. "Please tell me we have suits aboard."

"I checked the inventory before I came aboard. Let's get suited up."

Felix blew out a breath he hadn't realized he was holding. "Thanks for saving our butts. Again."

"Don't thank me yet. There's no time to depressurize."

"Crap."

Foggerty fumbled with his suit. Felix helped him get into it and checked all the seals, then got into his own suit. At least I can do something right, he thought. Aouda double-checked everyone's suit before locking down her own helmet.

Felix savored the warm, fresh air flowing into his helmet. It smelled metallic but had none of the moisture, sweat, and carbon dioxide that permeated the crew module.

"You know how to deploy a tether?" Aouda asked over the suit radio.

Felix nodded.

"Uh, I can't hear you nod."

"Right." He felt heat in his face. "Yeah, I do."

"Good. You guys get up to the airlock. I'm going to maneuver us as close as I can, then set this thing to descend back to DSS altitude so they can recover it."

Felix climbed up the long access tube with Foggerty close behind. "I don't understand why," Foggerty groused, his voice winded, "you people built the airlock," a pause for breath, "so far away."

"The ascender's crew module is anchored to its keel, just like DSS. It docks at the bottom of the station, so the airlock has to go on top of the hydrogen cells."

"Bloody inconvenient."

The rest of the climb was silent other than Foggerty's heavy breathing. Felix stopped when he reached the hatch. "Let's take a breather."

"Shouldn't we just go through? Save some time?"

"Airlocks cycle slowly," Felix said. "If we go through now, Aouda will never get out in time."

"On my way now," Aouda said. "Get your asses in there and put your finger on the cycle button. This is going to be close."

"Engine four green," the flight engineer said. "Engine six green. All engines show good to go."

"Roger engines green," DSS control said over the radio.

"We really should wait," Keyes said.

The pilot gave him a sidelong glance. "Establishing launch attitude."

"Roger attitude adjust."

"Wait!" Keyes pointed at the video display. "There's activity on the other ascender."

The flight engineer zoomed the display. The airlock was open. As Keyes watched, a spacesuited figure crawled out and clung to the top surface of the ascender. A second figure followed, then a third. The first opened a panel and began unraveling a tether.

"I don't believe it," the pilot said. "They're going to try to board."

"It's Mr. Foggerty," Keyes said. "It has to be."

"Damn fool," the pilot said. "If we don't make this burn in a half hour, we're going to miss our window."

"They should be close enough for us to pick up their suit radios," the engineer said.

Keyes's heart leapt. "Try it!"

"Yes, tell them to get back inside."

"Ascender one to rogue ascender, please identify."

A crackle of static, then, "We're out of air. Coming aboard."

"Is Mr. Foggerty with you?" Keyes asked. The pilot withered him with her eyes.

"Is that you, Keyes?" Foggerty's voice said through static. "Good man. How the devil did you get aboard?"

"Can we save the reunion?" a new voice said. "Time is of the essence here."

"Chief Aouda?" the pilot said.

"In person. Now open your airlock and let us in."

"That's it, then," the pilot said. "Mission abort. Get up there and cycle the airlock. I'll move into position below them so they can rappel down."

"Don't you dare abort the mission," Foggerty said. "We'll be there in a jiffy."

"We'd have to burn in twenty-five minutes. The airlock takes longer than that to depressurize."

"Keyes, don't you let them cancel that burn."

"I'll do my best, Mr. Foggerty."

The engineer said, "We can pop the airlock without depressurizing."

The pilot pounded her armrest. "Damn it."

Keyes said, "What does that mean?"

"We could open the airlock without depressurizing it. Let the air inside blow out into space. Wasting good air."

"What are we waiting for? If we can rescue them and still complete our mission, let's do it."

"One more thing," Aouda said. "We didn't have time to camp out before suiting up."

"Jeez!" the pilot shouted. "That tears it, then. Get up there with some oxygen. I'll get us in position. Move!"

Felix knelt on the stiff Mylar surface of the ascender. He had expected to be buffeted by wind, but the black emptiness surrounding him was still as space. He looped his foot through the handhold—it was a long way down even if he couldn't see the ground from up here—as he worked with the tether.

"What was that about camping out?" Foggerty said.

"Something I should have thought of earlier," Felix said. "Our space suits feed us pure oxygen at low pressure. We're supposed to take time to purge nitrogen from our bloodstream before an EVA."

"I dialed back the air pressure aboard the ascender," Aouda said. "It'll help a little, but we're still probably going to get the bends."

"Bad luck, that."

Felix finished clamping his harness to the tether. "Secured," he said. "Better play the line out quickly. I'll try to keep up."

"Just be careful," Aouda said.

Felix crawled along the handholds, feeling silly because the slope was so gentle. But the Mylar was smooth, and one slip could be disastrous.

He noticed slack in the line and hurried his pace. The hull's curvature increased unexpectedly and his feet slipped beneath him. He clung to the handholds, his breath catching in his throat. As he rounded the edge of the ascender, the curved horizon appeared. His vision swirled around the dizzying landscape far below. He instinctively gripped the handholds tighter. "Jeez!"

"You okay?"

"I'm good. It's just . . . jeez. It's a long way down."

The line began to slack again. "Be careful!"

"Roger that."

Felix climbed down the side of the ascender, acutely aware of the tug of gravity toward the abyss below. His elbows and shoulders ached with the effort. He risked a quick look down and saw a Mylar mountain moving below him. The other ascender drifted cloudlike beneath his dangling feet, sliding into position below him.

He gasped at the realization that his feet were no longer in contact with the ascender. He clasped the last handhold with a death grip. The line hung loose above him.

With great force of will, he released his grip. He let out a brief yelp, but the tether arrested his fall with a quick jerk.

The ascender pilot said, "I have visual on you, detective. Hold your position while I bring the airlock around."

"Roger that," Aouda said.

The tether stopped descending, leaving Felix dangling above the drifting Mylar surface. The cramps in his arms worsened as he hung motionless. He bent his elbows to relieve the pain.

The bends! Damn it. "Better make it quick," he said.

"Problem?" Aouda's voice dripped with concern.

"Nothing a little pressurized O-2 won't fix."

"In position. Bring him down."

The tether began descending with a jar, making Felix cling to it reflexively. He scanned the surface below. "Got a visual on the airlock. It's already open."

"Good show," Foggerty said.

This close, the ascender surface looked like it was rushing up to meet Felix. Fast. He braced his legs, knees bent. Impact. A shock of pain jolted his knees, ankles, and hips.

"Contact," he said.

He scrambled across the Mylar, ignoring the ache in his arms. The open airlock hatch wavered in the distance, spinning and moving away from him as he crawled toward it. He reached to rub his eyes and his glove bumped against his faceplate.

*Focus.*

He squinted, centering the airlock in his swimming field of view. His arms and legs were throbbing agony, but he kept moving them. At last his hand closed on the rim of the airlock. He fumbled with the end of the tether. After a few tries, he managed to clamp it fast.

"Tether secured," he said. He folded his arms and legs into fetal position, trying to alleviate the pain.

"Roger. Sending Foggerty down."

"Better make it quick," the pilot said. "Launch window closes in less than ten minutes."

"Don't you dare abort," Foggerty said. He huffed, out of breath, but still managed to whoop. "Look at that view. Invigorating!"

Felix caught sight of him sliding down the tether fast. Too fast. "Slow down."

"I know what I'm—oof."

The impact sent a tsunami across the Mylar surface and Foggerty collapsed in a heap.

"Careful," the pilot said. "You're damaging the solar film."

Felix unfolded his limbs and gritted his teeth at the throbbing pain. "He's down! Get a move on, Aouda."

"Roger."

He tugged Foggerty toward the airlock. "You okay, Mr. Foggerty?"

"Still in one piece. Little worse for the wear, I must confess."

Felix wrestled him into the airlock and waited for Aouda.

The pilot's voice broke in. "Time's running out, guys."

"Almost there," Aouda said.

Her spacesuited form rounded the edge of the ascender at high speed. Felix held his breath, dreading the impact, but she braked hard at the last minute and landed next to the airlock with a whoosh and a long wavelength ripple.

"It's now or never," the pilot said.

Aouda crammed herself into the airlock, dinging her boot on Felix's helmet. She yanked the hatch shut and turned the seal. "We're in. Fire those engines!"

Thrust pushed Felix facefirst into the wall of the airlock. Someone slammed into his back, forcing the air out of his lungs. "Oof."

"Everyone okay up there?" the pilot asked.

"We'll live," Felix said. For the first time in years, his smile was honest.

"Glad to hear it. We're pressurizing the airlock now. It'll take a half hour, so get comfy."

Keyes yanked the hatch open as soon as the pressure indicator showed green. He helped the first spacesuited figure out of the airlock, handed him off to the flight engineer, and reached for the next. Thrust pushed him off balance, and he nearly tumbled down.

He helped the flight engineer remove the helmets from the spacesuits. As soon as Foggerty's helmet was off, he said, "Are you okay, sir? Do you need oxygen?"

"I'm well enough, but the good detective could use some help. Got a bit of the bends, it seems."

"Him!" Keyes said. "That man drugged me. And sabotaged you, made you miss—"

Foggerty put a hand on his shoulder. "I know. But he made up for it by getting me here, and saving my life to boot."

"You're a more forgiving man than I," Keyes said, but he turned to

Felix and strapped an oxygen mask to his face. "You have yet to earn my forgiveness."

Felix nodded and gave him a feeble thumbs-up.

Aouda said, "Get a mask on Foggerty as soon as you can, then on me. We'll both be symptomatic soon enough."

"Bah," Foggerty said, "I can take a little pain. Important thing is we're on our way. I'm going to win that wager after all. To the NEO and back! In what, no more than eighty days, Stuart and his windbag friends will be eating crow."

Keyes lowered an oxygen mask over Foggerty's face. "You may get the last word with them, but at least for today, hush and get some rest. The journey has just begun."

((•((•((• ◎ •))•))•))

**Jay Werkheiser** teaches chemistry and physics to high school students, where he often finds inspiration for stories in classroom discussions. Not surprisingly, his stories often deal with alien biochemistries, weird physics, and their effects on the people who interact with them. Many of his stories have appeared in *Analog*, with others scattered among several other science fiction magazines and anthologies. You can follow him on twitter @JayWerkheiser or read his (much neglected) blog at *http://jaywerkheiser.blogspot.com/*. The author wishes to thank John Powell from JP Aerospace for providing technical details of the ascenders and DSS used in this story.

*In Brenda Cooper's tale, a miner and her robot companion answer a distress call and wind up getting more than they bargained for, as they come face to face with a rogue robot in . . .*

# IRON PEGASUS

## by Brenda Cooper

I sprawled across the big bed with my feet tangled in star-covered sheets. Harry stroked my foot, talking of inconsequential things, a comfort that had stood me well for hundreds of days. His voice caught and his hand stopped, resting on my heel. I opened my eyes to see that he had closed his and gone slack and still. Just for a moment, but when he reengaged, his voice had switched from soft to all business and his demeanor from mostly human to mostly robotic. "Cynthia?"

He only used the long form of my name when he judged a situation to be formal. "Yes?"

"There's a mayday."

"Where?" I sat up and started detangling my legs.

"The ship is called the *Belle Amis*. It's a family mining op on a small M-type."

The starry sheets puddled on the floor. "How far away?"

"About three days."

"How old is the request?"

"Months. It's updated daily. They still need help."

Ugh. We were deep into the Belt. International law required ship-to-ship help whenever possible. Our ship's signature was now recorded as having received the mayday, so our choices were help or fork out a fine bigger than my bank account. "Must be our lucky day. Emergency level?"

"Two."

That meant a live human, not in immediate danger, but in need. Of course, anyone in immediate danger out here had a four nines' chance of dying.

"I'll get you coffee." Harry strolled to the kitchen. Even though he was companion rather than servant, he did this for me every morning. I'd ordered him thin-hipped and wide-shouldered, with warm, pliable skin in a pale brown, dark eyes, and a shock of white hair. After I brushed my teeth, I sat at the table in my PJ's, listening to the kitchen steam and rattle.

Harry brought coffee and waited patiently for me to drink.

I hadn't had human company for two years. I had become okay with that, because of Harry. Singleton asteroid miners make a lot of money, and I was halfway to cashing out. Ships and stations need our products, but they don't want to risk their citizens to get them. Fully automated systems are illegal. So it's us and the rocks, and a thousand or so tiny robots stored in our holds to do the physical work.

In the ten years or so that it takes to earn enough to vacation for the rest of your life, about a quarter of us commit suicide. It's the loneliness. Another quarter fall in love with their robots. I hadn't done that, and didn't use Harry for more than casual touch. In fact, I'd made sure he wasn't designed for more. I didn't want to jump the line and choose a machine lover.

Without Harry, I'd be loonier than the moon.

I finished the dregs while he massaged my shoulders, savoring the bitter last drop. "Tell me what you know."

"Medical emergency. There's solar power, which is why life support still works. There's a companion and a little girl, and the girl can't fly."

"The robot can't fly either?" I said.

He shook his head. "Her model number isn't approved for flight. She's a simple companion."

Harry was more; I had wanted someone to take part of the load.

"Did you tell them we accepted the signal?"

"It's your decision."

He made so many choices I sometimes forgot some were reserved for me. "We have to. Copy me on your reply to them?"

"I will." Harry flowed off to accept the mayday and explain the change to the nav system, and I headed for the shower.

Any ship certified for the Belt is by definition maneuverable, and my *Iron Pegasus* slowed and turned as fast as anything out here among the rocks.

The enormity of the task sank in with the drops of hot, recycled water. I had never rescued anyone. It might be yet another way to die. There were already a million ways, at least according to the songs. I could be hit by rocks or get sick or make a single mistake and float off into space. Or have engine trouble, set up a mayday, and wait so long for anyone to get near me that I went stark, raving mad.

Maybe the caffeine was finally settling in and I was waking up and smelling the danger.

Two days later, Harry and I sat in companionable silence and examined the first clear visual. The asteroid was no more than five kilometers or so around, vaguely an elongated sphere. Nothing much to look at. The spin had been stopped, so clearly the mining setup had started when the emergency happened. The *Belle Amis* was maybe twice the size of the *Iron Pegasus*. Six legs splayed out from the center of the craft and held the ship firmly to the sunward side of the rock. "It looks like a spider," I mused.

"We probably look more like one," Harry replied. "After all, we have eight legs. We just never see ourselves from the air."

"I suppose." White solar fabric stretched between the ship's dark struts, effectively obscuring much of anything else from view, but explaining why they had plenty of power. "Everything looks normal. Do you trust this?"

"No."

So my instincts and Harry's calculations were both yielding up worries. "What if they're raiders?"

He shrugged, one of those too-human gestures that served to remind me that Harry wasn't. "We have half a hold full of gold and other minerals."

"They have a damned good claim," I pointed out. "If we could transfer that, we'd have a full hold, and I'd be able to stop this nonsense."

He didn't answer. We both knew I'd probably sell him with the ship. I liked to pretend he cared.

I glanced at the display. "We can start hailing in about half an hour."

"See a place to land?"

"Why don't you run the calculations?" he suggested.

Practice would annoy me, but I'd encouraged his insistence on my own self-reliance. Another way to survive. "Okay."

I hunkered down and ordered the computer to run analytics across our maps of the asteroid. The smaller the surface, the harder it was to land on it. Out here you measured four times and cut once. I sent my results to Harry for double-checking just as the *Belle Amis* chose to respond to us. "Thank you for answering our call."

I looked over at Harry, confirming I'd take it with a nod of my head and clicking my mike on with my tongue. "You're welcome. I'm Cynthia Freeman. What's your situation?"

"Yes. This is a family operation. A father and a daughter. The father died in a fall and the daughter is unable to fly."

"Who am I speaking to?"

"I'm an automated companion named Audrey."

I glanced at Harry, who looked completely unsurprised. But then he usually looked unsurprised. "How is the daughter?"

"She is . . . difficult."

She had been alone with nothing but a robot for company for some time. Hard for me; harder for a child. "What's wrong with her?"

"I'd like you to come see."

I drummed my fingers on the table. Audrey must be as bright as Harry, or close. The girl could be sick, and must be traumatized after losing both parents. Nothing felt right. "Is there anything or anyone down there that will harm me or Harry?"

"It's safe to come down. I'll wait for you."

Robots didn't lie. "We'll be there soon."

Harry cut the communication link. "I finished reviewing your calculations. I'd pick your second choice."

"Why? It's further away from the *Belle*."

"It'll be easier to get away from there. Their thrusters won't have any direction they can fire that will prevent us from an easy exit."

He was thinking defensively.

Landing was the first way anything major could go wrong.

The *Pegasus*'s nav system managed the slow-motion process. Before we even touched the surface, all eight of our legs had crawled it, finding rocky protuberances to grip. Fine metallic dust obscured every camera, hanging in the air as if it were frozen in a photograph. Harry and I sat, strapped into chairs, watching the readouts and the dust.

Each leg settled itself in slow motion.

Next, the two ships used robots to string an ultra-light, thin ribbon of reflective line between them. It snaked under the canopy of solar film that fed the *Belle*. Waiting for dust to settle in microgravity took hours; we slept. Harry curled around me, his skin warm and soft like a human's skin. He threw an arm over my waist. He didn't breathe, but fluids coursed through him, creating the slightest ebb and flow to his skin, the barest illusion that what comforted me was alive.

I dreamed of lost little girls alone on asteroids.

When we woke, I drank my coffee and ate a light breakfast. "Harry?"

"Yes?"

"It doesn't feel right to be here."

He cocked his head at me, his expression between quizzical and a soft smile. A rare look for him. "This was forced on you."

Smart robot. I convinced myself to stop worrying. After I suited up and checked everything twice, I turned off the light and stood in the lock, looking out. The largely metal surface of the asteroid was coated in dust from the inevitable and ever-present small collisions, dust gathered both from itself and from all of the things that it encountered. It would be a bitch to mine, and toxic. Rich, though.

Just above us, stars. The light from the faraway sun drove our shadows to our feet like frightened dogs. A few hundred meters from the doorway, solar fabric roofed the world. The supports and struts that held it in place created lines of shadow on the regolith. I took a deep breath, stepped slowly over the threshold and away from the magnetic floor and reached up to grab the line and attach it to the loops on my suit. From there, it was a matter of hand-over-handing my almost weightless self through the still dust of our arrival. Everything was coated to resist the fine grime, so it slid off of our faceplates and joints and the tips of our toes as if we were swimming through water instead of potentially toxic fines.

I led and Harry followed. His suit looked like layered cellophane. But then, life support for a robot was as simple as providing power and protection from the elements.

As I led us under the tent of material, my faceplate lightened to show the *Amis* in the center of the vast web, looking even more spiderlike from this angle. Funny how I never thought of our setup this way. The lock door opened as we neared it, and Audrey hung just outside, offering a hand to guide me from the line and into the lock. She looked more like a girl than me, with an improbably slender waist and rounded hips. Her designers had given her brunette hair, blue eyes, and a tiny mouth. When her hand took mine, it was done gently. Yet under the gentle touch, she had the same sense of strength as Harry.

Once we were through the other side of the lock, I could stand normally again. Or almost. The mag-grav in the *Amis* was slightly higher than we kept ours. In her current situation, the *Amis* had more power than she could possibly use, at least given that I'd seen no sign of active mining on the way in.

"Hello, Cynthia." Audrey's voice sounded like whiskey and honey. She led us to a kitchen table, laid out with a teacup and a plate of crackers. No fruit or anything from the garden, just tea and crackers. "Thank you for coming."

"You're welcome." Surely she knew I hadn't had a choice. The room looked neat and sterile, and smelled of tea and cleaning solution and nothing else, not even the stale ghost of cooking oil or rehydrated soup.

One cup of tea.

"Will you take me to see the daughter?"

"Of course. But she's sleeping now."

The tea water steamed. The feeling of not-right crawled deep in my nerves. "Can I see her? Just look in?"

"She might stir. Please drink."

"I'm sure it will just take a moment." After all, while the living quarters on the *Amis* were bigger than my *Pegasus*, it wasn't by much. There couldn't be more than ten or fifteen rooms.

"Very well." Was it my imagination or had her voice warmed even more?

She turned on her heel and walked down the single hall that branched off of the big shared galley and meeting space. Four bright blue doors were the only thing of interest in the corridor itself; the walls and floor were bare and white, the roof full of pipes that gurgled with water or other fluids.

We passed a dark entertainment room. The next door hung open.

Pale yellow light illuminated a dingy garden. Planters were either empty or full of scraggly plants with drooping, yellowed leaves. A tiny maintenance bot labored to keep dead leaves from the floor. It was probably responsible for whatever green remained in there, and I imagined it growing desperate in spite of its steady, industrious whirring.

Audrey stopped in front of a third door, the one almost at the end of the hall, and opened the door with exaggerated slowness and a crook of her little finger. I peered into the door.

An almost-empty room. One chair. A screen as dead and black as the space around us on one wall. Two beds, one with a small figure on it, covered up to her chin. "See?" Audrey whispered.

I pushed the door open a little further, stepping in.

Audrey's hand clamped down on my arm. "Don't wake her."

That convinced me to cross the empty floor and kneel by the bed.

The girl was at most three or four years old. Her red-brown hair had been caught back in a ponytail, and she wore a blue jumpsuit that probably served as pajamas.

She wasn't breathing.

I turned, full of concern and questions.

The door was closing behind me. I caught the briefest glimpse of Harry's startled face just before the lock clicked.

I stared at the back of the door. After a while, my situation started to sink in, thoughts coming together coherently in spite of how betrayed I felt. And how stupid. I had, after all, known something was wrong.

I was on a strange ship, alone, and captive. An easy way to die out here, and a stupid one.

Crimes against humans meant certain destruction for robots. Not that we were near anyone with the authority to carry out a trial and issue a self-destruct order.

Harry would help me. Wouldn't he?

I sat back on the bed and looked down at the little girl, her face slack with death. Had she been killed?

My hand trembled, but I managed to touch her cheek with the back of my hand.

It felt cold.

Cold?

Well, of course. She hadn't just died five minutes ago. But if she had been thrown into a freezer, surely she would look worse. There had been a manual on what to do when people died in space. I hadn't paid attention other than to pass the test and forget most of the details. But her body had to have been deliberately prepared; raw death wasn't this pretty.

If the robot had done this to a little girl, what would she do to me? It had to have been an accident; no companion robot would hurt its person. Maybe something horrible had happened and Audrey had become confused?

Still, she had left a prepared body to trick me into this room. The unimaginable slowly sank further and further in. What could she have been thinking?

I should have drunk her damned tea.

What were they talking about without me? Why did Harry let this happen?

Why wasn't he saving me?

I peeled away the girl's clothes, gingerly. I had never touched a dead body before, never even seen one up close. It felt completely wrong, like an arm or a leg might fall off. From being frozen? Before she died, she had been healthy. Her ever-so-slightly plump face looked clean and her hair had been combed and trimmed. I searched for a cause of death, but didn't see anything except maybe the marks on her elbows and feet that could have come from needles to administer drugs or to drain fluids before she was sent off into space.

If only Harry were here. He remembered things like manuals about preparing the dead for burial in space. Harry would have been able to help me figure out what was wrong.

I dressed her again, and then covered her with the sheet on the bed, so that she looked like a lump instead of a dead child.

A million ways to die out in the Belt, but how had *she* died?

I sat in the chair, thinking. Then I moved to the bed. Then back to the chair.

Water would be really, really good.

Hours passed before the door opened. I looked up, hoping for Harry. Audrey came in and bundled up the child in a sheet. She stood and looked at me, holding the dead baby in her arms like a pile of laundry, her head cocked ever so slightly. "Tea?"

"Yes, I'd like that."

I hoped to find Harry in the kitchen waiting for me, but there was no sign of him. I watched Audrey place her bundle carefully into the freezer, her movements smooth. Then she switched effortlessly to making fresh tea.

"How long have you been alone?" I asked her.

"Eight months."

"What happened to her?"

Audrey closed the freezer door and turned to look directly at me, her baby-blue eyes fastened deeply onto mine. "Her father killed her. He smothered her. Right after we got here."

I blinked, surprised. I sipped more tea, buying myself time to think. At least *she* hadn't killed the little girl. Robot killers were the stuff of scary science fiction, but there were always rumors. "And what happened to him? To the father?"

"Richard? He died."

She was being evasive again. Even though I knew that, I asked, "Where is Harry? My companion?"

"He went back to your ship."

I glanced at the hooks by the door. My helmet hung there, but Harry's was gone. "Did he say why?"

"No. But I'm sure he'll be back soon. He seemed upset, but I told him that you needed time to think."

If there were no humans here to rescue, we could take off. That would maroon Audrey on the asteroid, perhaps forever.

Audrey herself was worth something. But her pink slip wouldn't pass to me, and I didn't trust SpaceComSec to be any more helpful than they had to be.

I sat back, resolved to escape, but also not to hurry so that I didn't disturb Audrey. Harry had to take my orders, but she did not.

"Is there any more of your story that you're willing to tell me?" I asked her.

"I'd been with Richard for a long time. I was his only companion."

She was surely a sex-bot. There were plenty of people who weren't as squeamish as me. Audrey continued. "The baby is Carline. We found her mother when she was pregnant—she sold herself to him, dumb girl—and he killed her as soon as she weaned the baby. Launched her body right out of the gravity well here."

I felt the need to clarify. "You're telling me that Carline's mother was a murdered sex slave?"

Audrey nodded. "He told me that I couldn't tell anyone. He said I had to lie about it for all the rest of my life."

A slight catch in her voice suggested she felt bothered by this request to lie. And Harry's instruction video had said he wouldn't lie. To me, or for me.

Companion robots are programmed with a deep sense of fairness.

The situation felt so strange I had no words for it. I struggled to sound casual. "Was that hard for you?"

"Yes." She took my empty cup and refilled it with fresh hot water. She set the cup down and sat down opposite me, close enough to touch me if she wanted to. "Before you came, there was no one to tell. I didn't have to lie."

"But you're telling me?"

"Someone has to know."

"Why? He won't be able to hurt anyone else."

She stopped, and if she were Harry, I would say she didn't like my answer. She wasn't, and I didn't know her well enough to be certain of nuances. She fell silent for what felt like a long time, and then seemed to come to the conclusion that she should revert to her most basic self. She cocked her head, smiled, and said, "Tell me about yourself. Why did you become a miner?"

I struggled to shift topics. "I didn't. I decided to be a dancer, but before I can open a dance company, I need money."

"How long have you been a miner?"

I had to count in my head. "Seven years."

"Do you want to mine here?"

Of course I did. "It's not my claim."

"I can see that it gets transferred to you."

"How can you do that?"

"I know where all of the documents are. I've been researching how to do this, because I don't want to be left alone. Eventually, something will happen that I need help with and there will be no one to help."

"Are you lonely?"

"Robots don't get lonely. But being alone means that I have a good chance of dying, like Carline died, like Richard died."

"How did Richard die?"

The door opened and Harry came in and sat down at the table. I stared at him, trying to understand what emotions he was projecting for me. He wore a default easy smile, but not the usual eyes that went with it. Those looked troubled, the way he looked when he had a hard question for me. I reached out to touch him.

He took my hand and squeezed it gently. "It's good to see you out of that room."

Maybe we could escape. "Can we both go back to our ship?"

"Of course we can," he said. "But wouldn't it be more polite to visit longer?"

Did he understand what she had done to me? I swallowed, thinking. Maybe not. It wasn't like he felt bad if he were locked up somewhere; that happened whenever we docked at a station. I spoke carefully. "I would like to go home for a bit. We can come back."

He and Audrey shared a glance. Once more, I wondered what they had talked about while I was locked in the room. I could order him to obey, but some fear deep inside me fluttered up when I thought about it, and caught in my throat. I looked at Audrey. "I'm curious about how Richard died."

"I can show you."

I wasn't really up to two dead bodies in one day, but I'd rather be out looking at something I needed to know than sitting through an awkward conversation with a robot I didn't trust. We suited up and began following the lines that ran between struts. Audrey's suit cinched at her waist. Harry's looked more like a plastic bag. Mine was bulky with life support and left deeper footprints. We walked slowly so the swirling dust didn't rise above our waists or thicken enough to hide our feet. We picked our way around rocks, and twice we had to hop over crevices.

"He's not far now," Audrey said, her voice amplified in my ear. "See him?"

Between the helmet and the dust, I had to look hard to spot a suited body prone on the ground. Ten more slow steps and I could tell that his leg had been caught between boulders.

It shouldn't have been a problem out here in low gravity. Richard had sprawled forward, hands splayed wide. Three boulders buried his right foot. I couldn't make out how the fall could have happened. He would have had to shove his foot into a trap. I moistened my lips and waited for Audrey not to lie to me.

"This is what happens when there is no one to help you," she said.

"Did you set the rocks on him?"

"Someone had to do it."

I was beginning to understand. "So that you wouldn't have to lie?"

She looked right at me, her eyes visible behind the shield of her helmet. Blue, guileless. "Yes."

I had started thinking of her as a victim. "Did you kill him?"

"No. He ran out of oxygen."

"Did you trap him out here?"

"I had to trap him or I had to lie. I cannot lie and I cannot kill, but he killed Carline and he wanted me to lie. So I had to make a choice."

I shivered. A million ways to die out here, and one of them was asking a robot to lie for you. Who knew?

We were all silent as we walked back.

How should I handle a robot who had killed in a circumstance where I might have done the same, if for different reasons?

Carefully.

The silent walk gave me time to think. If I abandoned Audrey here, I would have nightmares about a beautiful, lonely robot trapped on an asteroid with her charges dead around her. I would imagine her hugging the dead, frozen child from time to time. Or I might make up stories in my head about someone who landed here and needed Audrey to lie. After all, she was an expensive sex-bot as far as I could tell. Another man might be foolish enough to ask her to lie for him.

I couldn't leave her here to trap an unsuspecting and lonely miner. But I couldn't allow a robot capable of murder in my ship, either.

When we got back to the kitchen and stripped down, Harry rubbed my tight shoulders. "Audrey said something about being able to transfer the claim," I said quietly.

He spoke formally, carefully. "We can. That's what I went back to the ship for. The process will take a week."

"What about SpaceComSec and the mayday beacon?"

"I have videos of both of the dead. They will release you from your mayday obligations."

"Thank you." I sat still and silent, smelling the slightly oily tang of him, memorizing the feel of his hands, the stroke of his fingers on the long, tight muscles that connected shoulder to neck. "You can fly the *Belle Amis*, can't you?" I asked him.

His hands both stopped. I wriggled under them. "Keep going."

"Yes, I can fly her." He squeezed a little harder, and then returned to his perfect, familiar touches. After a long time, he said, "Thank you."

A tear rolled down my cheek. A million ways to die out here, but for me it wouldn't be guilt at stranding Audrey or death at her hands. It might be loneliness. "I'll miss you."

He didn't say he would miss me. He said, "You will be fine. You're stronger than Audrey."

I let so much time pass that his touch began to abrade my skin. "You will have to take the bodies. I don't want to live with their ghosts."

"We will release them."

More tears came. Harry stayed with me, wiping them away one by one.

They left the next day. I stood out on the regolith holding onto a line and staring up at the *Belle Amis* as it flew out of sight. That night, I put on some jazz music and danced in the biggest empty room, and from time to time tears fell onto my fingers like glittering stars.

((•((•((• 🌀 •))•))•))

**Brenda Cooper** is a working futurist and a technology professional as well as a published science fiction writer. She lives in the Pacific Northwest in a house with as many dogs in it as people. In addition to her several novels, her short fiction appears regularly in *Analog* and other venues. Her latest novel, *The Edge of Dark*, was released from Pyr in early 2015. Find out more at *www.brenda-cooper.com*.

*As we consider privatized space travel, one common topic is what role corporations will play. In our next tale, space-enthusiast-author Michael Capobianco imagines an astronaut caught in a bind when a corporation is in control . . .*

# AIRTIGHT

## by Michael Capobianco

I never get tired of looking at the Earth. From four light-seconds, the Earth is just a little bigger than the Moon from the Earth's surface, 37′ in diameter. From eight light-seconds, half that, but still identifiable as a substantial blue and white marble. That's about where I am right now, closing in on the extinct cometary nucleus they're calling Ondine. As I get closer every day, it grows appreciably, but it still looks much smaller than the Earth. I can blow it up on my screen until I can see a wealth of detail on the dark gray surface, but mostly I just like to watch it grow on its own.

I always get the equivalent of blank stares from the uninitiated when I explain what I'm doing and why. It's a quirk of the legal system, mostly. The 2035 International Treaty on the Ownership of Small Celestial Bodies specifies that you have to have actual human being(s) come in contact with said celestial body to take ownership. And, to make matters even more fair, said human being(s) cannot sell, license, or otherwise place encumbrances upon their ownership rights until they have taken ownership.

So I will own Ondine when I get there, assuming that I can "take possession" by putting on the single-use space suit and lighting down on the surface in Ondine's microgravity. After that . . . well, that's much more complicated.

In any case, my name is Lon Innes, and I've been bumming around

163

in earth and lunar orbit for most of my thirty-eight odd years. I was one of the first jockeys of the lunar ferry, so I logged a lot of time in space and got my résumé padded with highly complimentary references that I'm still coasting on today. And that led to me being hired for this mission, which is a doozy. Forty weeks in deep space, which is about forty times more than I care to spend exposed to solar and cosmic radiation, but they provided the appropriate medications and will potentially make it worth my while. Ondine is in a very particular orbit, you see. It's heading for a close pass by the Earth-Moon system in about three months, which, if everything is jiggered correctly, will bring it back into a lunar capture orbit in about twenty-nine years. It won't take a lot of delta-vee to get it there; in fact, Ondine's orbit so closely matches Earth's right now that it only comes by about once a half century. The rest of the time it's either slowly catching up to Earth or slowly pulling away. Hardly any eccentricity, either. It's a celestial-body owner's dream come true.

Because . . . water mainly. No one knows for sure what's inside what is almost certainly a very thin coating of organic materials left behind when the outer layer of the comet evaporated into space and put on a spectacular show. But planetary scientists know enough about comets now after exploring twenty or so that they can make fairly good guesses. And the guesses all come down to an enormous quantity of $H_2O$, which, at present prices, is worth a few billion cu's in a suitable microgravity environment that can be reached with minimal delta-vee.

There's no way to effectively orbit a body as small as Ondine. Its gravity is so low that the best you can do is maneuver into a matching heliocentric orbit close by and use the thrusters to keep your position. And so, when the time was ripe, I dropped MK212 down to within less than a kilometer of the surface, and set the autopilot. Fortunately, Ondine is a fairly regular little guy, almost spherical except for a big crater taken out of the northwestern quadrant (as arbitrarily defined by the mapping software) and a barely noticeable bulge at the South Pole. Also, luckily for me, it's not a fast rotator, spinning at a leisurely full rotation in 17 hours. I've heard some stories from the sole proprietors who've been claiming pieces of solar detritus in Earth orbit, and it's almost impossible to do if the things are irregular and spinning too fast.

I've been in full communication with Earth during this whole trip, and that has made everything go a lot faster, but as the distance grew, the time delay became more and more annoying. A three-second lag is a real conversation killer, but sixteen seconds is even worse. Of course, there's plenty of onboard memory, and I made sure it was packed with every conceivable game, movie, interactive, and simulation, so that's not been a problem. I pretty much gave up on spoken conversations and rely on audiotext messages, except when I really want to hear someone's voice in near-real time. That hasn't happened lately. In this particular case, now that I'm here, I need to report and respond to the big boss's questions, so I lock my eyes on the main screen, turn on the link, and direct the call to headquarters.

"Hello, folks. As I'm sure you can tell from the sensor relays, I'm here. Everything is, as they say, nominal. I'm going to sleep for a few hours before I stake my claim, so don't get worried if I'm not reporting."

Bezospace's Vice President in Charge of Legal, Donna Sutherland, a chunky, dark-haired woman of indeterminate age, is sitting within the camera view next to BS's CEO, smiling old silver fox Jonnie Nyvatten. I haven't seen him since shortly before launch, when he came up into NEO to wish me well and reassure me that, even though there could be no formal agreement between us, BS understood that I would be well compensated and there would be no legal shenanigans once I had succeeded in setting foot on Ondine and could begin negotiations. Neither of us would say anything until that happened, so why was Sutherland here?

Sixteen seconds pass, and I see Nyvatten's smile widen. "I just wanted to congratulate you on your accomplishments so far, Nebulon. My techies tell me that you've used much less than the predicted amount of fuel to reach the hoverpoint, and the Autonomous Unit is fully checked out and ready to go once we've reached a deal. Best of luck to you during the most hazardous part of the mission. I have every confidence in you, Neb."

"That's fine," I say. Not much more to say, actually, at this point. Yes, that's my first name, and that's why I automatically correct him. "Lon."

Sixteen seconds. Sutherland leans in a little toward the camera, dark swatch of hair slipping down over that smooth, ivory forehead, and the enhanced stereo effect makes the look in her hazel eyes deep and profound. "I'm looking forward to the signing-over ceremony, Mr. Innes. I'm sure we'll be able to get you started back to Earth in no time."

Strangely, this doesn't sound very comforting.

Did I mention that my sponsors have designed this mission to be as inexpensive as possible? That's why there's only one person aboard, if you hadn't figured that out. While all of the water and oxygen is recycled very efficiently, they did have to provide decent food for a long journey, and that takes up twice as much space if there are two. Saves on rocket fuel, too. And it makes it much easier to divvy up the proceeds.

Even after almost three months, I haven't gotten sick of the various kinds of bars that fill a good percentage of the storage space in the mid-module. If anything, it's the lack of variety in texture that gets a little wearing. And the lack of easily readable labeling. I get ready for bed by stripping off my flight suit, nestle into the coolest part of the command space, and pull out what I think will be a crunchy, fried meat roll-up and some "celery with cream cheese" sticks and unwrap them, letting the clear wrappers float up into the disposal airflow. And then it's sleepy time.

I put my head in the half-clear suit's helmet, twisting the fasteners tight and the space suit inflates with a loud hiss. I'm not going to pretend this isn't going to be dangerous. Emergency space suits are foolproof to put on and are reliable, but going out into the micro-G environment of a basically unknown cometary surface is fraught with all sorts of potential hazards, and touching down too hard or at the wrong angle could raise an opaque cloud of regolith dust that would take hours to dissipate. I've got many hours of practice with this rig, and I know the maneuvering unit's strengths and weaknesses, but . . .

It takes about nine minutes to depressurize the crew quarters. Not the most elegant system, but this is basically a second-generation Dragon capsule with an overlay of new electronics, and it doesn't have any amenities.

Every time I've done this before, I've been tethered, so it does feel strange to float away from the open hatch. I catch myself on the handgrip on the inside of the swung-wide hatch door, shrug to better situate the maneuvering unit's harness, and let myself go, executing a 180 and then dead stop.

Prepositions like above and below don't mean much to someone who's spent as much time weightless as I have. It's just *there*. A vast wall of marbled slate, filling up my vision, irregularities masked by the low phase angle. I know that it's intrinsically very dark, far darker than asphalt, but it seems bright compared to the ring of starless space around it.

It's time to start documenting this historic mission, for the sake of posterity but also because this is the only way I'll be able to prove that I conformed to the letter of the Treaty. Mounted over my shoulder is the tamper-proof evidentiary camera that must be delivered intact to the authorities before the claim can be certified. It is protected by an impregnable shell and records on a nonmagnetic substrate that can't be modified once the images have been laid down. An external laser activated from my glove turns it on. A standard helmet cam also sends an image back to Earth via MK212.

If I try, I can imagine that I'm falling, but in fact, I'm propelling myself to a point on the surface where Ondine's rotation is minimal. I find my shadow, a slightly irregular blob of real black among swirls of dark and lighter gray. Still no sign of the boulders and concavities that show on the imagemap. I'm breathing harder, and there's a faint tang of ozone.

As my trajectory takes me toward the pole, the shadows start to break out, and I get more of a sense of the approaching surface. There are certainly spots that I need to avoid, but a big, flat area is coming up that should present no problem. The last few seconds it does feel like falling, but when I touch down, there's hardly any sensation through the boots. A puff of regolith spins up and spreads out on ballistic trajectories, but it's not a problem.

And suddenly, it's mine. Whatever good sense that would make me want to just make the claim and get out of there is held off for a minute by sheer sense of wonder. In all directions, broken, crumbling ash like someone had emptied out a thousand cremation urns here. Above, and it truly feels like above, MK212 is a tiny, irregular stylus shape, Autonomous Unit mounted on the docking hatch at the forward end like a small head. Overwhelmed by the Sun, no stars are visible, no Earth-Moon, but there's still a deepness to it all.

But it is, after all, time. I remove the evidentiary camera from its holdtight and hold it at arm's length, so it can see both me and the surface. With the other hand I pull the metal ball that's encoded with my information and let it fall. It takes a full minute, but when it's down the process is complete. No need to say anything, but I do. "Thank you, Ondine. You've made me very happy."

And I'm back. Inevitably, removing the emergency space suit renders it unusable a second time, but unless something goes disastrously wrong, I won't need one, since MK212's trunk is pressurized and accessible. And if something goes disastrously wrong, I'm pretty much screwed whether I can do an EVA or not.

My lawyer is located in the Leeuwenhoek complex on the Farside, where they operate on the standard UTC day-and-night schedule, so I can give her a call and expect to find her in her office. The protocol we've developed includes a number of encryption algorithms, but, considering the fact that I'm using Bezospace software mounted in Bezospace hardware, it's likely that it won't be secure.

Xandra Rawal swims up out of the depths of the viewscreen, and then the back wall of her office crystallizes behind her. Even as a projection, she comes across as a solid mass of chutzpah. First impression comes from the chiseled strength in her cheeks and jaw, barely softened by the stylish sweeps of crimson and blue that enclose the face in parentheses. At the moment, she looks thoughtful, her dark, tattoo-shadowed eyes staring into middle space until they snap on to my image.

"Congrats, Mr. Innes. Your success has already been announced, and is dominating the collective mind for at least a few hours. I have heard from your sponsors, and that doesn't bode so well, I'm afraid."

Fuck. I did sort of anticipate this, but it still takes the edge off my elation. Is she waiting for me to say something? The lag is excruciating.

"The contract they offer is, perhaps, the worst of its kind I have ever seen. Certainly the worst aspect of it is an undefined net amount rather than the gross percentage you presumably want. The deductions are computed on the basis of future expenditures that I can only characterize as flights of fancy."

She scowls down at the audiotext function of her desk. "And they have said right out that this aspect of the contract is nonnegotiable.

Now, you and I both know that that would normally be just a negotiating tactic, but, in this case, I'm afraid they're backing it up with threats."

"Threats?" I say, knowing that the word will probably arrive in the middle of her next statement. "What kind of threats?"

And indeed, she continues to speak. "I've looked through the language of the Treaty and even into the stated intentions of the treaty parties and it's obvious that they never anticipated something like this. Even though the intent of that section is to give sole possession to any explorer who sets foot on a minor planet, there are no provisions that cover what happens afterward. In fact, Bezospace would probably be within their rights to just turn off MK212 and let you die."

"That's why you've drawn up the trust, though, right?" Which ties up the rights to Ondine and puts them in limbo practically forever if I don't make it back. "I'm ready to sign it now, by the way."

After a while, she looks back at me. "The paperwork should already be there. The threat, however, is not so severe. They indicate that unless you sign the contract as is, they will not modify Ondine's orbit and it will continue on in its Earth-crossing orbit. Your ownership would then, of course, be valueless."

"Send them the counteroffer we discussed. I give you full authority to negotiate in my stead. You know what I want, and what I won't accept."

Rawal fades and I open the trust document, read through it quickly, authorize it with full authentication, and dispatch it to the lunar cloud for safekeeping. It *should* protect me.

Exactly three hours later, there's a rude noise and the viewscreen comes back on. It's Sutherland, alone this time. That didn't take long. I climb out of the exercise cage that takes up a good portion of the command deck and push off, catching a handhold to swing myself down into the position to interact.

She pushes in against the limit of the stereo, and I can't help but compare her to my own lawyer. She's just as much of a hard-ass, but it's expressed in a totally different way. I would dearly love to watch the two of them engaged in negotiating the contract.

"Mr. Innes, Lon, it's good to see you again. It's so gratifying that the mission has progressed so smoothly. I must tell you, however, that your associate, Ms. Rawal, is not behaving very professionally. I think it would be best if we left third parties out of the discussion."

"So you *are* willing to negotiate?" There's no point in waiting for my sarcasm to register, so I continue. "Xandra Rawal is my lawyer and I have delegated full authority to negotiate to her."

I feel like this is the opening move of what will be a long chess match. At least I'll have additional time to formulate my responses because of the lag.

"That may very well be, Lon, but you will find that your ability to communicate with Ms. Rawal may become compromised by your distance. Our direct link is secure, but I can't promise that it will be able to accommodate other communications."

Hardball already. "You will find that I am just as 'unprofessional' as Ms. Rawal, Donna. My counteroffer stands. It's fair. All I want is 25% of gross profits up front, based on current value algorithms. Take it . . ." I float into the region where stereo is maximized, and sixteen seconds later am gratified to see her sink back a little. "Or leave it." I'm searching with my fingers for the viewscreen's connector to dramatically disconnect communications, when the screen goes off by itself, and with it all of the little telltales in that section of the bulkhead.

I've been disconnected.

A quick check shows that only the electronics connected with communications and entertainment have been shut off, all of which was built onto the underlying Dragon control systems. I guess this means they think that losing my ability to entertain myself and stay connected with home is a significant hardship. And, in a way, it is. For the first time, I feel really *alone*. There's a hollowness, a realization that I'm totally on my own out here. It's hard to explain. I've always been connected. My first memories are of the virtual world. Lame though they were, I could always connect with the characters in the interactive games or even experience the older noninteractives. The lag wasn't a problem, and staying in touch via audiotext was actually a relief in some ways. Now. *Nothing*. Pretty clever of them, I must admit.

The cage is basically mechanical and on its own circuit, though, and so I transfer over and strap myself in. I need to think this through, and a little monotonous movement will help.

I run through the moves I've made to secure my position. Bezospace knows by now that they can't kill me, or they lose Ondine.

They haven't even begun to negotiate, so this has to be just to let me know how much power they have over me, and maybe soften me up a bit. Loneliness out here is something I've never really worried about before, but eventually it will wear me down, and I might be susceptible to some kind of trick. How long would that take?

They don't have a whole lot of time, though. As Ondine approaches the keyhole that will take it on the desired trajectory, it will become more and more difficult to divert it. The Autonomous Unit is not infinitely powerful. Since it's a proprietary device developed during the Taweret Crisis of 2040, and actually worked in that case, I have a lot of faith in it, but I don't know exactly how it works. It's presumed to be some sort of mass driver, but the details, especially of how it gathers and projects material from the surface of the asteroid, are only known to a select few at BS.

As time passes, Ondine moves ponderously ahead, closer and closer to the point at which it will continue on past the Earth, never to be captured no matter how far into the future the orbit is calculated. Worthless to me, but worthless to them, as well. So they have to make a move soon.

Exactly twenty-four hours go by, and I'm awakened by the hum of the fans in the communications unit. The viewscreen comes on with a flash and Sutherland solidifies within the light. She looks tired, and the shadows under her eyes look like a light bruising, not a tattoo. Has she been working on this message since I saw her last? I swim over into the field of view.

"I hope the loss of communications hasn't been a problem, Lon." The concern in her voice is indistinguishable from the real thing. "We're working on it. Meanwhile, I have a new offer for you. It boils down to 15% of the gross after the basic costs of the mission have been subtracted. Fuel, consumables, that sort of thing. Give the go-ahead to Ms. Rawal and we'll let her handle the details. Considering the problems that have developed with MK212, I think it would be better to get this over with. We wouldn't want you to be marooned out there."

Not nearly enough. "Can you quote me a number?" I'm really not expecting anything definite from her, but there is a minimum number I'm looking for.

"Sorry. Not until we see what the AU does."

I wait about thirty seconds before replying. "That doesn't work for me. There's no way I'll agree to a deal like that."

Sixteen seconds later, her jaw firms up and she looks genuinely hurt. "In that case, we are withdrawing the AU and bringing it home. The mission is over. Unless you agree right now, we'll miss the keyhole. You have sixty seconds to agree."

"No deal," I say. "I think you're bluffing."

"This is not a game, Mr. Innes. Feel free to return to Earth at your convenience. Remember, MK212 must be turned over to the originating office within three months, or usage fees will start to apply. Goodbye and good luck."

Another thirty seconds or so, enough time for me to tell her I've thought about it and agree, and the screen shuts off. This time the unit doesn't go completely dead, though. The little green light on the audiotext screen stays on, basically saying, "It's not too late to change your mind."

There's a shuddering thud from up forward, the sound of the AU detaching itself from the docking mechanism. MK212's porthole is pointed toward Earth, and if I push my face up against it, I can barely make out the complicated, gold-foil enshrouded shape, rotating slowly, pulling away.

Now this is a convincing bluff. Or was she telling the truth?

A week has passed and I've put MK212 into eclipse behind Ondine to reduce the damage caused by solar radiation. I don't know why I don't just start back, but I feel like staying here is making the statement that I haven't given up, that I believe they are bluffing. Out the porthole, I watch the silhouette of Ondine against the zodiacal light, and it's about the only thing that feels real. I've gone over the details of the plan so many times that I must have engraved my brain with them. I just don't see what I could've done wrong. There's no way that BS would give up on this just because of a lousy 25%. If this is just a negotiating tactic, it's gone on way too long. I'm not going to initiate contact, though. It would be a sign of weakness. My position is airtight. It can't not work. I won't give in.

Or am I going crazy?

Another few days pass, but I'm really not counting any more. It's clear that it's too late to make a deal now. I suppose I might be able to sell my ownership of Ondine to a company with a really far-reaching future plan; if space development continues at the rate it's been going, it could be of some use. Not enough, though. Not enough.

At least they could turn the damn entertainment unit back on. What have they got to lose? I could audiotext them and tell them I give up. The green light says I can.

There's a whisper louder than the air flow that grows into the hum of fans that I've gotten used to not being there. The viewscreen comes on, a blinding light, and a person forms within. It's not Sutherland. I can hardly believe it. Xandra! And she's grinning, which looks really strange.

"You won!" she says, "Twenty-five percent of gross. A couple of caveats, but you basically got everything you wanted."

It doesn't sink in, and then it does. The AU must not have gone very far.

"Tell them I'm interested in buying MK212 if they'll sell it for a reasonable price. I'm coming back, but I won't be staying long."

((·((·((· ◎ ·))·))·))

**Michael Capobianco** has published one solo science fiction novel, *Burster* (Bantam). He is co-author, with William Barton, of the controversial hardcore sf books *Iris* (Doubleday, Bantam, reprinted by Avon Eos), *Alpha Centauri* (Avon), *Fellow Traveler* (Bantam), and *White Light* (Avon Eos), as well as several magazine articles on planetology and the exploration of the solar system. He served as President of SFWA from 1996-1998 and again in 2007-2008, and is a member of SFWA's Writer Beware and Contracts Committees. Capobianco has been SFWA's Authors Coalition liaison since the coalition's founding in 1993. His website is *http://www.michael-capobianco.com*.

*This next tale was a top finalist in the annual Jim Baen Memorial Contest. Its inclusion of Brazilian astronauts immediately caught my eyes but it was the fast pace and steady tension that sold me. Herein Venus is the setting of an accident that puts lives at risk . . .*

# WINDSHEAR

## by Angus McIntyre

Two hundred kilometers above Ishtar Terra, the aeroshell completed its last braking curve and settled into level flight, its flight control systems counting down the seconds until separation. It was still slowing as it passed over Maxwell Montes, hull cherry-red from the heat of reentry. Ionized gases crackled in its wake as it blazed like a meteor across the Venusian sky.

One hundred kilometers high now, its explosive bolts fired automatically. The aeroshell's hull split cleanly into four segments that folded back like the petals of a flower, revealing the streamlined shape of the recovery dart nestled inside. The dart's systems came alive as the thin atmosphere kissed its skin, and it slipped smoothly into the air like a diver entering water.

The aeroshell was gone now, tumbling on a high-altitude wind. In thirty minutes what remained of it would scatter itself across the surface far below, burned and crushed beyond recognition. High above, the dart spread its wings and flew free.

The dart banked left, searching for a data downlink from the command station in orbit. Diagnostics checked the state of its flight systems, registering a shallow gash in its port canard where something had slashed across it during aeroshell separation. The aircraft's bioelectronic brain assessed the damage, concluded that the integrity of the wing was unaffected and adjusted its trim to compensate for the additional drag.

Still seventy kilometers up, the dart slid downwards through the thickening atmosphere. Gusts pawed at its surfaces, weak echoes of the tempests below. Its brain sorted radar returns, filtering out the echoes of thunder cells, searching for solid objects. It registered and ignored a hovering aerostat the size of an oil tanker. At last, it found what it was looking for: seven objects shaped like stubby arrowheads, strung out in a loose V.

The dart flared its air brakes and pinged the lead aircraft with a radio pulse. The reply came back at once: come on down, we're waiting for you.

From the observation deck at the tail of the lead *merleta*, the cloud tops were a choppy froth of whites and grays stretching unbroken to the distant horizon. Even through the tinted glass of a viewport, they were painfully bright.

"Dart's on its way down," said Vinicius. "And none too soon."

Bruno Almeida shrugged. The pickup had been scheduled for two days before but a line of storms had pushed through from the east and the controller had judged conditions too rough for a dart to reach them. Now conditions were finally right and they could go home.

Vinicius chafed at the delay, but Bruno was philosophical. He was sad to be leaving. Riding the *merleta* was an adventure, as close as he or any human could come to standing on the surface of Venus. Fifty kilometers below, the surface was a baking hell, with ninety atmospheres of crushing pressure and temperatures high enough to melt aluminum. Up here above the clouds, conditions were comparatively welcoming—if you overlooked the unbreathable atmosphere, the intermittent drizzle of weak sulphuric acid, and the perpetual squalls.

The data display in his left eye told him that rendezvous was still more than twenty minutes away. He left the observation deck and started to climb the stairs leading to the dorsal passage.

"Where are you going?" asked Vinicius.

"Just going to take a last look from the bow," Bruno said. "Don't leave without me."

"Don't make me wait," Vinicius said. He already had his flight suit on, his bag of samples at his feet.

From the narrow passageway that ran along the aircraft's spine,

Bruno could look down on the sloping expanse of the wings and the fat pods of the engines. The *merleta* was approximately triangular, half lifting body and half aerostat, buoyed up by the nitrogen-oxygen atmosphere that filled its internal spaces. For all its size, it was surprisingly light. Most of its weight came from the skeleton of composites that held it together and the tanks in the thick wings, each one filled with a soup of water and photosynthetic blue-green algae. The wings themselves were transparent, allowing the algae to bask in sunlight that came from two directions: from the Sun above, and reflected from the clouds below. From a distance, the seven aircraft of the flock looked like butterflies of translucent glass skimming across the cloud tops.

The bow nacelle offered the same view as the rear observation deck, a sheet of white cloud stretching away to the curving horizon under a turquoise sky. Bruno never tired of watching the clouds scroll by underneath, an insubstantial landscape that changed and refreshed itself continuously. Even when the winds carried the *merleta* around to the night side of the planet, the view was just as enthralling. Storms at lower altitudes lit the clouds from beneath with flashes of lightning, and sometimes an eerie phosphorescence outlined the towering cloud stacks. Consensus said it was a chemical reaction, but it made him think of bioluminescent plankton in the waters off Bahia.

"Pick up in five," said Vinicius's voice in his ear. Bruno shook himself. He had not noticed the time passing. Reluctantly, he turned his back on the clouds and made his way aft.

On the observation deck, Vinicius was ready to go, suited and helmeted. He waited impatiently as Bruno took his flight suit from its locker, fumbling with the stiff fabric.

The dart was visible now, a gray delta shape against the wispy clouds overhead, wings spread out for low-speed flight. It bore down on them, growing steadily larger. By the time Bruno got his helmet on, it filled half the sky behind them.

"Here it comes," said Vinicius. "Locked on and ready to dock."

The wind shear hit almost without warning. Bruno heard the first note of the alarm and grabbed reflexively for the handrail. Through the canopy he saw the dart stagger in the air, its sharklike nose tilting up suddenly. Something dark detached from the aircraft's port side and whirled away on the wind. The dart plunged downwards.

Afterwards, he had no clear memory of the actual impact. The plastic bubble of his helmet muffled the tearing crunch as the dart smashed into the canopy. With his eyes squeezed shut, he never saw the dart's port wing tear loose, sending the aircraft cartwheeling. He only felt a muted shock through his feet as the body of the dart slammed into the *merleta* again somewhere further forward, and then everything disappeared in a white and silver explosion as the tailwind whipped fragments of the shattered canopy across the observation deck.

The *merleta* groaned and tilted, and Bruno clung desperately to his handhold as they plunged downwards.

The alarm woke Tania before the end of her allotted sleep cycle. She came awake quickly and blinked her eyes rapidly for a status update. Her field of vision filled with indicator displays. All were green; the space station's systems were still optimal.

When she reached the bridge, Tom Weatherell was seated at the engineer's console, talking in the calm voice he used for his school broadcasts.

"... happened this morning, about seven o'clock station time. Two scientists from the Euro-Brazilian mission were being picked up from what the Brazilians call a *merleta*, a self-sustaining platform that can stay airborne in Venus's atmosphere indefinitely. Something went wrong during the linkup, and the platform was damaged. That's all we know right now, but we'll bring you updates as we learn more." He paused for a moment. "Obviously, we may not do much science today, so your teachers will arrange alternative activities for you. This is Tom from Venus, wishing you good studies and signing off for now."

He cut the channel and turned to Tania.

"How bad is it?" she said.

"Very. One dead for certain." He nodded towards the microphone. "The kids didn't need to hear that from me."

"What the hell happened?"

"The dart that was supposed to lift them to the skyhook crashed into their platform."

"Jesus." She struggled not to imagine the scene. "Who was it?" she asked.

"Bruno Almeida and Vinicius Santos—do you know them?"

She shook her head. "Not well." With just fifty explorers from all nations working around Venus, everyone knew everyone else to some degree, but the separate missions still functioned mostly independently.

"I had Ivar on the comm earlier, freaking out," Tom added. Ivar was the commander of the E-B mission, sitting up in their command ship in orbit, Tania remembered. In his position, she would have been freaking out, too.

"Who died?" she asked.

"Vinicius," said Tom. "His telemetry's offline. Bruno says he's dead."

"And Bruno?"

"Hurt but alive. But—" He stopped speaking, his face grimmer than ever.

"But?"

"The platform fell. It's down at forty-eight kay, drifting with the wind."

The *merleta* swung and lurched on the wind, buffeted by fists of turbulence. In the dorsal passageway, Bruno clung to the handrail and braced his legs against the sides of the passage. Clouds swung crazily overhead and spatters of rain streaked across the clear plastic of the roof. The air outside was dim and misty, with a yellowish tinge.

The telltales on the inside of his visor said there was breathable air in the passage, so he unsealed his helmet cautiously. He smelled burning, faint but acrid, mixed with something fouler. Sulphur compounds, he guessed. It occurred to him that he was the first man in history to smell Venus.

The right arm of his suit was torn open from wrist to elbow and the exposed skin of his arm was pink and tender to the touch. He plucked a thin splinter of plastic from his flesh with clumsy gloved fingers, wincing at the pain.

When he pulled up his feeds, most of the displays flashed red. The worst damage was to the left side, where the tumbling dart had punched through five or six cells. Theory said that equivalent internal and external pressures meant that the lifting oxy-nitrogen mixture inside would bleed out slowly through any tear in the envelope. But theory didn't cover the possibility of the skin being not simply torn but shredded, or of changes to the aerodynamic profile of the hull. The *merleta* had lost a significant amount of lift.

The worst part was the fall, a nosedown plunge with crosswinds pushing the *merleta* this way and that. It had seemed to take forever and Bruno could do nothing but wait for the moment when the increasing pressure would rupture the remaining air cells and the skeletal remains of the *merleta* would drop towards the inferno below. He wondered whether it would be pressure or heat that killed him and how far above the planet's surface he would actually die. It would have been a distinction of a kind to be the first living man on Venus, even if only for a few seconds, but he doubted he would reach the surface alive.

To his surprise, the worst had not yet happened. After an hour, the *merleta*'s fall had slowed perceptibly. Eventually, it had settled into a configuration that couldn't be called stable but which was mostly level, suspended in midair with its tail and one wing tilted down, swaying painfully with every gust.

"Bruno," said the voice in his head. "You still there, man?"

"Hanging in here," Bruno said. He grinned mirthlessly at his own joke.

"Listen, Bruno, we're going to get you out of there," said Ivar.

"Great," said Bruno. He pressed his heels against the sides of the passage and pulled himself upwards with one arm. He had to do this every few minutes to stop himself sliding down towards the tail. Vinicius's body was there, just inside the airtight door. Bruno didn't want to go down there.

"I'm going to patch you over to HighPoint. They're going to coordinate everything."

"Wonderful," said Bruno. "It was their damned dart did this to us. Big confidence builder."

Ivar was silent, and Bruno regretted his outburst.

"Okay, thank you, Ivar," he said.

"No problem."

"Hey, Ivar—"

"Yes?"

"I—never mind. Nothing."

"Bruno, this is Tania Stern from HighPoint Industries. I have Tom Weatherell and Mason Cline with me."

There was no immediate response, and Tania thought for an instant that she'd forgotten to allow for the lightspeed delay, then remembered that Bruno was somewhere over the planet beneath her, not on distant Earth.

At last, the Brazilian responded. "Hello, Tania."

"Ivar has asked us to coordinate the"—She searched for the right word.—"the response." She had almost said "rescue," but it felt wrong to promise something she might not be able to deliver.

"Okay." Even through the radio, fuzzed by static, he sounded guarded.

"Can you give us access to your platform's telemetry?" Tania was glad to move on from the awkward pleasantries to exchanging practical information. "If we can see what kind of shape you're in, then we can work up a plan."

"I don't know. Maybe. The high bandwidth antenna's gone."

"Is that something you could work on?" Tania asked.

"The rest of their platforms are still flying. He could route via one of them—" Tom suggested.

"If he has line of sight, perhaps a laser—" put in Mason.

Tania silenced them both with a look.

"If you can't do it, it doesn't matter," said Tania. "Just tell us what you can about your situation."

There was a noise that she thought might have been a laugh.

"Not good," Bruno said. "I think we fell about ten klicks. Most of the systems are offline."

"How's your air supply?"

This time it was definitely a laugh.

"Infinite. I'm sitting on top of several thousand liters of tailored algae. They can make oxygen faster than I can use it." He paused. "I can even eat the little bastards if I have to."

"That's good," said Tania. "What about the platform? Do you think it's stable?"

"Not even slightly. I'm getting bounced around pretty badly. I don't know how much longer it'll hold together."

Out of the corner of her eye, Tania could see Tom signaling to her. She nodded to him.

"Okay, Bruno, this is what we'll do. Our people Earth-side are simulating the problem now and working up a plan. We're going to review, check in with the other missions and find out what resources we have in the cloud layer and here in orbit. What I need you to do is to find a way to send us as much data as you can on the status of your platform. Can you do that?"

His answer came through chopped and distorted.

". . . try."

"Good enough. Out for now, I'll get back to you when I have some news."

Bruno looked out from the access door at the base of the port wing. The damaged area of the wing was clearly visible, a tangle of twisted struts and shredded transparent paneling. The closest algae tanks were in fragments.

*Mãe de Deus*, he thought, did that thing fly all the way through the wing?

He thought about the Stern woman in the command ship up above. She had promised to do what she could, but he noticed that she hadn't said what that might be. She knew it was a bad situation, and she hadn't raised his hopes with empty promises of rescue. He appreciated her honesty. At the same time, he did not entirely trust her. She was still corporate and corporations always put the bottom line first.

Time to start saving yourself, he thought.

The problem was that the *merleta* was too deep in the atmosphere, down in the turbulent zone. It had been designed to glide above the cloud tops, not wallow around in the muck. If he wanted to live, he had to gain some height.

The first thing to do was to try to patch the damaged sections. Like other rigid and semi-rigid airships on Venus, the *merleta* leveraged the fact that ordinary air was a lifting gas in Venus's dense carbon dioxide atmosphere. If he could refill the cells, he could level the craft and maybe even start to ascend.

The *merleta* had been assembled *in situ* in the cloud layer, its skeleton covered by swatches of polymer fabric extruded from purpose-built bioreactors. It was designed to be self-repairing; an onboard synthesizer could extrude new hull panels to be sewn and sealed in place by one of the *merleta*'s four spiderlike maintenance robots. He could see one through the transparent wing, hunched motionless at the very edge of the damaged section, clinging to the wing rib.

He brought up a command interface and selected the maintenance panel. The four robots were all marked as idle. He blinked a question at the *merleta*'s AI.

Maintenance drones idle because of lack of materials, the AI responded. Bruno frowned.

Bring material synthesis online, he instructed.

Synthesizer activation failed, the AI said after a moment. Insufficient power to initiate material synthesis.

Explain.

Power generation levels 18% of normal, it answered.

Bruno started to enter another question, then stopped. He knew what the problem was.

The *merleta* was down below the cloud layer now, pitching in the yellow-tinted gloom. The solar cells that generated most of the platform's power were starved of light.

"We've run multiple simulations," said Derek Kelly. "The AIs are unanimous. This is not a survivable accident." He paused for a moment. "I'm sorry."

Tania touched her transmit button.

"Understood, Control. Please ask the AIs to identify the solutions with the highest chance of success," she said.

Mason slumped in his seat.

"Well, that's that then," he said.

"The AIs aren't infallible," said Tom.

"They're smarter than we are," Mason said. "At least at this kind of task."

They sat in silence, waiting for the response from Earth. When it came seven minutes later, it was unequivocal.

"The consensus is that there isn't any course of action that offers a significant likelihood of success," said Kelly. "The platform is too deep in the atmosphere for a dart to reach it." He hesitated for a second, then added, "The corporation will not authorize the use of any further resources for a rescue mission." His image flickered and disappeared.

"So, what now?" asked Tom.

Mason stared at him. "Didn't you hear the man? No further resources."

"Tania?"

Tania breathed out slowly.

"We need more information about the state of the platform. If Bruno can't give us a data feed, do you think we could use one of the Explorers to do a low-speed flyby?" she said, ignoring Mason.

Tom pulled up a shared virtual console.

"Difficult. In terms of temperature and pressure, it's already at the edge of the envelope for an Explorer. You'd almost certainly lose the aircraft, and you might only get a few minutes of observation time."

Mason gestured angrily, filling the shared display with data from the package that had accompanied the video message.

"Did you even look at this stuff?" he demanded. "Here. 'Platform will continue to lose altitude and will suffer structural failure once power reserves are exhausted and it can no longer maneuver to avoid local extremes.'" He called up an image of the planet, with the day and night zones marked. A tiny spot of red light marked the location of the damaged craft, creeping slowly closer to the black line of the terminator. "Look. It's going to go nightside in just a few hours."

"Then we need to act before that happens," Tania said. She waved away the display. "Are you ready to start helping, or do you have other objections to make?"

"Do you actually have a plan?" Mason asked.

Tania looked at him. "Yes," she said. "I believe I do."

Bruno crouched in the bunk room he had shared with Vinicius, bracing himself with his back against the wall. Close to the center of gravity of the *merleta*, the swings and lurches of the craft were less violent. He could grab a few moments of rest without worrying that he was likely to be battered into unconsciousness.

His earpiece pinged for attention, and he blinked up his personal feed and saw that he had new email. It was from Sandrine, the fourth member of the team. The subject line said simply "Good luck." He left it unopened in his inbox, along with a half dozen routine messages from home that he could not bring himself to read.

He died reading his email, he thought. On Venus. That would be a hell of an epitaph.

The discovery that the ship's repair systems were unusable had left him feeling numbed and helpless. He had tried to find a way to divert more power to the synthesizer but nothing had worked. It was like playing chess against an implacable and sadistic opponent. Every time you thought you had a possible move, you found yourself checkmated.

He wondered what Tania Stern and her colleagues were doing. Had they given up on him already, or were their corporate AIs formulating some ingenious plan to rescue him?

He felt an almost overwhelming desire just to stay here in the bunk room, waiting for the end in relative comfort. Maybe he could even lie down on his bunk. He imagined himself stretched out on the bed in his flight suit, the plastic bubble of his helmet resting on the starched pillow. Too bizarre.

He pushed the thought away. The planet could kill him, but he would die as an explorer and a scientist, reasoning, observing, fighting until the end. He pulled up the command interface and started to sort through the status feeds, looking for a way to pare them down to the essentials so that they could be uploaded over the narrowband interface. Data first, he thought. Then I can work on shedding some weight.

"Why now?" asked Tom. "Why send a policy update now?"

"It's simple," said Tania. "They're serious about us not using any resources."

"I can't launch any of the Explorers."

"I doubt that's all. The skyhook isn't responding either."

She paged through the systems under her control. Everything was locked down. The new policy update had ridden in on the coattails of another video message from Kelly, uploading itself to the command system and rewriting all her access permissions. The update was flagged as a temporary maintenance fix. No doubt it would be revoked once the damaged platform had fallen from the sky.

"It's as if they wanted the poor bastard dead," said Tom bitterly.

Tania said nothing. It would be convenient for HighPoint if the *merleta* fell. With the wreckage scattered across the surface of Venus, it would be hard for anyone to say exactly what had happened or how much of the blame lay with the programming of the dart. As a way to dispose of damning evidence, it would be difficult to do better.

She shook her head. Her corporate masters were not monsters, simply pragmatic. They weren't trying to murder the helpless Brazilian, just prevent her from pointlessly squandering expensive resources. It comes to the same thing though, she thought.

She freed herself from her seat restraints and floated towards the central command console. She slid her magnetic key from its pouch.

"What are you doing?" Tom asked.

"Executive override," she said. The cover of the console slid up, exposing a touchscreen. She summoned up the management application.

Mason blinked, looking worried. "Communications to Earth just dropped," he said. He stared at her. "Did you do that? Did you just firewall Mission Control?"

She nodded. "Just making sure that they can't send us any more updates."

"Tania, we are offline. Do you know how serious that is?"

"Calm down," she told him. "It's just a temporary maintenance fix." Out of the corner of her eye she saw Tom grinning.

"But you're still shut out," Mason said. "You haven't changed anything."

"No?" She tapped her way through the message log until she found the record for the update package. She marked the update as corrupt. The screens in the command center flickered for an instant as the system rebooted.

"This is . . . irresponsible," said Mason. "I protest."

"Your protest has been noted." She looked at him. "Relax, Mason. If this doesn't work, I'll take the blame. And if it does, corporate can take the credit."

"I've got the Explorers back," said Tom. "Do you want me to launch one?"

She shook her head. "No," she said. "Forget the drones. We're going to use the *Landis*."

Draining the algae tanks was exhausting work. The interior of each wing was divided into multiple cells in order to minimize potential losses in the event of a puncture. To move from one cell to another, Bruno had to use a utility knife to slash through the tough plastic that separated each one from its neighbors. The damage he was doing would make the *merleta* unsafe in the long run, but he doubted that this particular vehicle would last long enough for anyone to care.

There were vent valves on the underside of the wings, but the *merleta*'s AI had reverted to some sulky emergency mode in which it refused to carry out routine operations. Whoever had trained it must have classified draining the tanks as a maintenance task. Nothing Bruno could do would convince the AI that it might also be part of a strategy for saving the vehicle.

He needed to rebalance the *merleta*. It was currently drifting with one wing high, pummeled by every gust of wind, twisting this way and that. If he could drain some tanks in the undamaged wing to counterbalance the ones lost in the collision, it might be possible to get it back onto an even keel. Then it could go back to doing what it did best, gliding with the wind. It might even start to climb.

Pulling himself along the struts that gave the wings their shape, he reached the first tank. Even stripped down to shorts and T-shirt he was sweating freely. The wings were not climate-controlled and conditions inside were little short of infernal. When he tried to turn the stiff wheel that operated the valve, his sweat-covered fingers slipped on the smooth plastic.

At last, the valve clunked open and he felt the pipe vibrate under his fingertips. A flushing mechanism kicked in—Bruno said a silent prayer of thanks to the designer who had realized that it might one day be necessary to drain the tanks under more than one bar of pressure—and a hundred liters of water and blue-green algae gurgled through the pipe and spewed out into the Venusian atmosphere. The *merleta* lurched.

Bruno stuck his knife between his teeth, gripped the strut, and started to crawl deeper into the wing.

"Your bosses are trying to route a message to you through us," said Ivar. "Do you want me to pass it on?"

"No, Ivar, that's okay," Tania told him.

"We wouldn't normally filter anything marked urgent, but the firewall blocks anything above a certain size automatically, so—"

"I understand. Listen, Ivar, you can just keep filtering that stuff. We've taken ourselves out of the loop for the moment so that we can focus on Bruno." She frowned at the options on the communications console. She would need to block indirect as well as direct messaging.

"Got it," said Ivar, sounding doubtful. "But are you sure—"

Tania cut him off with a gesture. I'm trying to save your guy, she thought. Don't second-guess me.

"Telemetry from the platform shows it in level flight," said Mason. Once it became clear that Tania could not be swayed, he had stopped working against her and started being helpful.

"And the *Landis*?" Tania asked.

This time it was Tom who sounded doubtful. "Holding for now, but it's going to get bad the further down we go. It's not built to cope with that kind of turbulence."

I must be mad, thought Tania. I'm about to wreck a billion-dollar airship trying to save the life of one man. They won't be able to find a book big enough to throw at me.

The simulations she had run locally were no more encouraging than the ones that Mission Control had sent over. The huge aerostat was the only piece she had on the chessboard, the only aircraft close enough to reach the stricken *merleta*, and the only one with enough reserves of gas and ballast to allow it to maneuver up and down through the cloud layers. Tom had sent it wallowing after the Brazilian platform, like a whale chasing a swallow through a tempest. But she was acutely aware that they had only one chance to get it right. Even if wind shear didn't pull the airship apart, its maneuverability was painfully limited. Squander too much lift and she'd never be able to bring it back up. If that happened, all she would have accomplished was to give Bruno a larger space to die in.

She came to a decision.

"Mason, call Bruno. He has to find a way to gain some height."

It was getting dark outside, and the interior of the wing was lit only dimly by lights strung along the spars. They glowed like faint stars in the semi-dark. The real stars were invisible, hidden by layer upon layer of dense cloud overhead.

He knelt at the base of the wing, gathering strength for another attempt. He tried to calculate how many journeys he would need to make. He would have to alternate between wings, crawling out to drain one tank, then dragging himself back to work on its counterpart on the opposite side. Only that way could he keep the *merleta* balanced.

"—need you to do what you can—"

That was one of the men on the command station, his voice was squeezed to the point of unrecognizability on the congested narrowband channel. Yeah, yeah, thought Bruno. Let's change places, and you can see how easy this is. He wiped sweat from his eyes.

Tania had explained the plan to him. They had diverted one of their aerostats, an unmanned airship the size of a small town. But the aerostat couldn't survive in the shear zone, where fast-moving air masses generated ferocious turbulence. He needed to find a way to climb to meet it. That meant shedding more weight.

On an impulse, he pulled up the command interface again. To his surprise, there was more green than before. Evidently the return to level flight had convinced the *merleta*'s AI that conditions were less critical than before.

Hardly daring to hope, he called up the maintenance subsystem. Options that had not been available before were now illuminated. He flipped through screen after screen until he found the page with the controls for the algae tanks. The overlay lit up with a schematic of the *merleta*'s internal plumbing, a tangled network of lines like the subway map of a small city. The tiny icons representing the vent valves glowed green: responsive to commands.

He sat back on his heels, forcing himself to remain calm. He needed to plan his next moves carefully.

"That's great, Bruno," said Tania.

"I can dump pretty much everything," the Brazilian said. He sounded as if he was smiling. "The only problem is that some of the tanks outboard of the damaged section aren't responding. The pipes must have self-sealed."

"It may not be critical," Mason observed. "It looks like he can still drain better than eighty percent."

"I think I can get those too, though," Bruno said. "I'm sending the maintenance robots out onto the wings to open the valves manually."

Tania closed her eyes. Thank you, she thought. It's about time we caught a break.

"How far away is your airship?"

"It's still a long way behind you, but it's picked up a tailwind. You need to start climbing soon."

"I'm on it," said Bruno. "Out for now."

Tania looked around and saw Tom and Mason exchanging high-fives. She frowned.

"Let's not get ahead of ourselves," she said. "The hard part is still to come."

They nodded and turned back to their instruments.

With much of its load gone, the *merleta* was unstable, jolting violently as it climbed. The airframe flexed and moaned in protest. Bruno sat strapped into the command chair, tensing as each impact slammed the craft sideways. It felt like being shaken in a giant's fist.

Radar showed the airship creeping closer, a bright dot against a backdrop of swollen thunderclouds. The storms behind the *Landis* were dissipating now but there were new convection cells boiling up from below, exploding up from the lower atmosphere with frightening speed. He ran the simulations again. The most optimistic projection gave them no more than an hour before the new storm hit, right about the point where the two craft were predicted to come together.

He resisted the impulse to divert more power to the maneuvering engines. He had to trust the AI to have chosen the best option, balancing speed against the load on the airframe. He closed his eyes and focused on his breathing.

When the radar showed the airship less than five kilometers away, he freed himself from the chair and started to pull on his flight suit. His hand caught in the torn sleeve and he frowned. That was something else he needed to fix.

He found tape and some plastic sheeting in the supply closet and used it to improvise a patch, wrapping the tape tightly around his arm. The plastic would not survive the corrosive rain of Venus for long, but it might last long enough to spare him any more acid burns. Satisfied, he pulled on his helmet and checked the oxygen levels in the miniature airpack.

"How the hell is that thing still flying?" said Mason.

Seen through the cameras on the underside of the *Landis*, the *merleta* was a sorry sight. Fragments of paneling trailed behind the damaged wing and the cluster of antennae on top were little more than tangled wreckage. The faceted canopy of the observation deck had been torn away, only a few shards of clear plastic still clinging to the twisted remains of the frame. Two of the engines were stopped, propellers turning idly in the wind.

"Buoyancy, baby," said Tom. "And Brazilian engineering."

The image on the screen was the ghostly green of night vision, but it was remarkably sharp. Tania could make out a tiny figure on the rear deck, the plastic bubble of his helmet reflecting the lights of the airship.

"We see you, Bruno," she said into the microphone.

"I can see you, too," he said. "What do we do now?"

"Mason's lowering a cable. If you can fasten it onto something, we'll try to winch your ship in close enough that we can drop a ladder to you. Think you can do that?"

"I think so," Bruno said. "See if you can get it across one wing."

"Why the wing?" Mason asked.

"Just do what he says," Tania told him. "Tom, hold her steady."

The cable dropped into sight in the top right corner of the screen, coiling and twisting in the wind as it fell towards the other vehicle. The end plunged out of sight just ahead of the *merleta*.

"Left just a hair," Mason instructed. "Don't foul the propeller."

The cable started to slacken, draping itself across the wing. "Perfect," said Bruno. Something spider shaped scuttled across the surface of the wing, reaching for the cable with metal pincers.

"He's using a robot to grab the cable," said Mason. "Smart." The robot crawled back towards the center of the wing, dragging the cable with it.

"Got it," came Bruno's voice through the speaker. "Want to send me another?"

The rounded belly of the aerostat loomed above Bruno like a moon about to fall. Flickers of lightning reflected from the rain-wet hull. Tethered beneath the giant, the *merleta* lurched and jolted, twisting on the anchoring cables. Downdrafts from the airship's huge propellers battered at Bruno with hurricane force as he scanned the underside for the promised ladder.

"Going to bring you closer," said Tania's voice in his ear. "Can you cut your engines?"

He ordered the AI to stop the last two motors, and the *merleta* swayed, now simply deadweight dragged behind the larger vehicle. He glanced forward to check that the cables were still holding.

"Where do I look for the ladder?" he asked.

"We're going to open a hatch on the underside," Tania told him. "Should be almost directly above your head."

"Copy."

Abruptly, a square of light appeared in the gray expanse overhead.

"I see it," Bruno said. "Looks good." His heart was thumping at the thought of making the climb. He wished he had time to improvise a climbing harness, so that he could simply anchor himself to the ladder and let himself be dragged aboard.

"Fifty meters to go," said Tania.

Out of the corner of his eye, Bruno saw one of the cables suddenly go slack. A moment later, it began to fall, twisting in the air, no longer attached at the upper end. The *merleta* dropped and he fell heavily to the deck.

"What the hell just happened?" Tania demanded.

"I've lost the *Landis*," said Tom. The image on the main screen blinked out.

"They found a way back in," said Mason.

"Oh, hell no. Not now."

She called up the command interface and searched for assets still under her control. A video window popped up in the corner of her field of vision. The miniature face of Derek Kelly looked out at her.

"I'm sorry, Tania, but we have had to revoke your command," he said.

"Not now, you asshole," she screamed at him. "We were just about to save him. Give it back!"

It would be three minutes before Kelly would hear her words, another three before he could answer her. Even if he restored control, it would be too late.

She waved the video away, cutting the recorded message off in mid-sentence.

"Bruno," she said. "This is Tania, can you hear me?"

"— hear you. What's happening?"

"We've lost control of the airship," she said. "You have to get aboard now."

"— can't climb. Think . . . my arm —" A ripple of static washed out the rest of his transmission.

"Listen to me, Bruno. In a few minutes, that ship is going to rise.

We're not controlling it any more. You have to get aboard. It's your only chance."

The main screen was dark but she could see the situation clearly in her mind. The *merleta* was tethered only by a single cable now, dangling a full hundred meters below the *Landis*, rocked by the winds. No human being could make such a climb. She almost sobbed in frustration.

Bruno's voice came through with sudden clarity. "—have an idea," he said.

The sky was almost completely dark, the rising thunderclouds visible only as somber masses against the gray-black murk beneath. The wind tugged at him and the cloudscape swung sickeningly around him as he twisted in the air. Fifty meters below, the battered *merleta* was still lit brightly by the airship's spotlights. He watched it spin beneath his boots and fought the urge to throw up. Then the lights went out and the outline of the *merleta* vanished in the darkness. He caught a last glimpse of the red light at the tip of one wing before an arm of cloud swept across it and hid the aircraft from his sight forever.

He let himself dangle limply, cradling his injured arm. In the glow of his helmet light he could see the plastic patch on his arm starting to bubble and discolor where the acid rain had touched it. Water beaded on the backs of his gloves.

A flicker of lightning from below revealed something in the air nearby, like a piece of white rope. When the lightning flashed again he recognized it as a stream of water falling from above. The airship was shedding ballast, dumping water from its tanks so that it could rise.

Bruno was rising, too. The maintenance robot's rear legs gripped him under the armpits, the manipulators at the tips digging painfully into his chest. The machine's other six arms were locked to the cable. It climbed with mechanical single-mindedness, one leg at a time, indifferent to his weight, pulling him inexorably upwards. His helmet knocked against the robot's carapace as it slowly ascended the cable.

He twisted his head back and looked up. The hatchway was still open, a glowing rectangle in the darkness above, almost within reach now. He smiled to himself.

"I'm coming home," he said.

((•((•((• ◉ •))•))•))

**Angus McIntyre** is a computational linguist by training, with degrees in linguistics and intelligent knowledge-based systems from the University of Edinburgh. Born in London, he now lives in New York, where he works as a software developer. Prior to moving to the United States, he was a researcher at Sony Computer Science Laboratory in Paris, working on computational models of language evolution. He has also lived and worked in Milan, Brussels, and Bangkok. He is a graduate of the 2013 Clarion Writer's Workshop. He is an enthusiastic if not particularly-gifted amateur photographer, likes to travel, and speaks five languages with varying degrees of fluency. He lives in Manhattan with his girlfriend and the world's least friendly cat.

*Next, in Sarah Hoyt's fun twist on the time travel trope, three roommates get more than they bargained for when their quest to invent instant package delivery opens a portal in time with surprising results.*

# ON EDGE

## by Sarah A. Hoyt

It was the summer of '32 and I was living in a dilapidated Victorian in the Colorado Springs suburb of Greater Denver, with two mad geniuses, both of whom were trying to court me.

As a group we were recipients of the Bezos grant for developing a system of instant package delivery.

We weren't the only recipients of the grant, which was structured as both a stipend and a contest. Twenty teams had been given funds sufficient to live on and create a prototype for a year, and the team that created the winning system would get the prize of twenty million.

We were one of the smaller teams, and also probably the most odd.

Kenyon was tall and dark-haired, with the sort of complexion that, when exposed to sun, turns a little less pale. Since he was a theoretical physicist and mathematician, exposure to the sun rarely happened.

Xavier was a little shorter and a lot darker, with broad shoulders and huge hands, which nevertheless were very good at assembling together the tiniest components. He was an electrical engineer. Kenyon and Xavier had been friends since kindergarten and had assembled their first computer together at eleven. Sometimes, I thought they spoke a private language that only other geniuses could understand.

Me? I was the administrative assistant. Oh, that's not what they'd called me in the grant application. I believe they'd called me a, general synthesis specialist, and both of them piously believed I could take a lot of information and come up with something new.

They had no backup for this belief, beyond the fact that I'd taken degrees in math, languages, art, and biology, and I could convert their convoluted theories into smooth write-up that made it all sound sane. Was it sane? I wasn't sure. I didn't understand most of what the men said, even when they said it at length.

But I do remember at the time I thought it was all crazy.

It was late at night, in summer, and we had the windows open, leading to a slow creeping of the number of mosquitoes in the room. They wormed in through the rips in the ancient screens and clustered around the candle we'd stuck on an old, empty bottle.

By its light we were sharing a new, full bottle and a loaf of French bread, which constituted our dinner for the evening.

"You realize," I said, "what he's asking for is nothing less than teleportation? A transporter system, if you will," I said.

Kenyon nodded. "I think the Alaska University team is trying that thing. Molecular building and stuff." He waved around with a piece of French bread. "Vats of molecules and nano builder things. Like magic."

"And ours isn't like magic?" I said.

Xavier was doing something to a circuit board that involved a soldering iron and a great deal of smoke and zapping. He had it pushed right up to the light of the candle. His big hands moved swiftly and with minute precision. "Well, if we're going to talk about that," he said. "The only ones who don't seem like magic are the guys at Pacifica, who are experimenting with fast guided rockets." He made a face. "Someone should have told them the other name for that is missiles." He made a gesture with his left hand that seemed to denote the spreading tendrils of an explosion.

"Yeah, but we are working on what? Teleportation? Magic tricks?"

There was silence for a long while. Look, maybe it was because it had been so long. A long summer of watching them assemble what looked like a gigantic computer, a long summer of getting the impression both of these very intelligent men were courting me, but never having one of them actually say anything unambiguous enough to be sure, a long summer of listening to them talk in what seemed like a strange code.

The silence lengthened, so absolute that I could hear Kenyon break a piece of bread. He gestured with the bottle of wine towards my empty glass, and I covered it to indicate I'd had enough. Outside, a cricket chirped loudly and inside, across the large coffee table, Xavier zapped something with the soldering iron.

Kenyon dug into his pants pocket and took out a coin, flipped it midair. It was a quarter, and it came down, a shining, silvery streak in the candlelight. "Heads or tails?" he asked, but before I could answer, the coin fell, perfectly balanced, on edge.

He grinned at me. "There is no reason it shouldn't fall on edge," he said. "All right, given weight and gravity and surface area, it has a greater probability of falling on one side or the other, but it doesn't mean that a not-statistically-insignificant number of times it won't fall on edge."

"So, magic and tricks," I said. "I'm not complaining, exactly. They gave us a grant. We can use it, but—" I sighed. "But I'd like to have a chance at the big time." Big time, real relationships . . . something. Something beyond talking a lot and playing with circuit boards, and setting coins on edge. "Is that a trick coin?"

He shook his head. "No. There is a way of throwing it. A flick of the thumb that makes it more likely than not to land on edge."

I didn't say anything. It would be easy to say something, and get this conversation going. We'd done this before. They would speak through the night, happily spinning nebulous theories.

Apparently, the fact that I was silent wouldn't stop them. "See," Xavier said, putting down the soldering iron and reaching for a piece of bread. "In some ways, distance doesn't exist. Or time. Well, they exist, but in a mathematical way. Time is an abstraction of the human mind, and every piece of matter in existence touches every other piece. Some people have theorized that the universe is a hologram. And if you work from that hypothesis, then it should be possible to move one piece of matter from one place and time to another, without passing the space intervening. Other people have worked on this theory, for instance—"

"And your magic bullet is?" I said.

"Beg your pardon?" Kenyon said.

"If other people have worked on it, your magic bullet to get it to work for you is . . . ?"

"Oh." He grinned at me. "That is where Xavier comes in. We're building a computer that will perceive time/space in its intrinsic togetherness, so that to it the universe will be just one hologram, a flat set of coordinates, where matter can be transposed from one side to the other."

"Really," I said, aware my voice sounded sarcastic. I'd heard all this before, as they added chips and circuits and soldered and talked. "Just a trick of the thumb for the computer."

"Uh, what?" Xavier said.

"I think Cass is tired," Kenyon said, his eyes shining with something like amusement. "Maybe we should show her the test?"

"Not tonight," Xavier said. "I need to iron out the bits of code, unless we want to send a package to last Wednesday again."

"Last Wednesday?" I said.

"Next Wednesday, actually," Xavier said. "We tried to send something across the living room, yesterday, but what we did was send it to next Wednesday. At least from the energy or whatever, Kenyon calculated that it went some distance in the future, no further than next Wednesday."

"I see," I said. "That will not solve the problem of instant package delivery."

"Probably not," Kenyon said, and looked away from me, "Hey, Xav, have you considered that perhaps a person needs to go through with the package?"

"What?" Xavier dropped bread crumbs perilously close to the soldering iron he'd taken up again, as he bit into a chunk of bread.

"Perhaps a person needs to go with the package. Oh, sure, I mean, the computer can move things because it doesn't have the perception of time and space we have, but maybe some perception of time and space is needed, or—"

"Or we'll end up anywhere at all. Yah. But building a transporter portal the right size is going to take forever, and I don't think—"

"We don't need a portal. Just an area of conductivity we can attach the computer to."

"Uh."

They'd quite forgotten I was there. I should tell them that there were laws against human experimentation—and animal experimentation, should it come to that—but I didn't think they'd hear. They'd just nod, then go back to arguing over something that made no sense at all.

I left and climbed the stairs in the dark to my room. Downstairs, I heard the click of the keyboard that meant one of them had dragged his laptop in. Mostly Kenyon talked, a bright stream of words, and Xavier interrupted with monosyllables, often in a questioning tone.

Up in my room it was very quiet, save for the hum of the mosquitoes and the song of the crickets. I pulled back the sheers and stood at the window, looking down at the lights of the cityscape, and wondering, precisely, where all this was leading.

I didn't even know if I had any interest in either of them. I wasn't raised to expect a man to support me, or necessarily even to get married. But there is a madness that comes to women in their mid-twenties. Or perhaps it was just that I suffered from an unwarranted attraction for very smart men who most of the time didn't seem to notice I was around. My mother had accused me of collecting geniuses as far back as kindergarten. I thought it would have been much easier if I'd collected them like my brother used to collect butterflies, with a pin through the heart.

At any rate, I'd helped Xavier and Kenyon win a grant, and we had money through the fall, and after that, when the first snows of Colorado flew, they'd probably admit defeat and go on to do something or other with large computers and circuits and soldering irons and I'd—

I'd probably go back to college and study something else. And learn to stay away from dreamers who dreamed in calculations and science.

I closed the drapes and went back to bed. It wasn't until I was almost asleep that I thought about the package they'd sent to last—or was it next—Wednesday. Did they mean that? At least, they should have managed to make it disappear, right? Or had they just misplaced it and hoped really hard?

I woke up with the sound of banging. One of them—or maybe both—was in the kitchen and doing something.

We hadn't any dishes between us, but this house had come with full cabinets of dishes and baking ware, which we'd used to warm up pizzas, mostly.

Now, from the sound of it, the two of them were banging pans together. Perhaps they'd given up on instant teleportation and started working on a garage—or kitchen—band.

I grabbed my robe, put it on, and went downstairs on my bare feet, because if there's one thing you can be sure of is that two geniuses, together, in a kitchen, are as likely as not to make something explode.

But when I got downstairs, they'd moved the noise into the dining room, the place where they'd set up their supercomputer and all its accoutrements. On one side of the dining room, connected to the computer, there was this . . . platform built of pizza pans.

They heard me come in—a miracle, over the din they were making—as a pan fell, and grinned madly at me. "Ah, just in time for the experiment," Xavier said. "Kenyon, here, is going to be our package delivery man, and, if everything works, he's going to step on that platform there, and he's going to appear on the other side of the dining room," he said. "With the package clutched in his hands."

If I'd had the slightest notion that anything would happen beyond maybe Kenyon getting a very mild electrical shock, from those leads that connected the computer to the pizza pans, I'd have protested. But all I could think is that he was wearing boots, after all, so even the small amount of electrical current flowing onto the pizza pans would make no difference.

Xavier did something at the computer, which was really just a naked bank of chips and circuits and a spaghetti confusion of wires. He nodded to Kenyon, who put safety goggles on and grabbed a carefully wrapped box, then leapt onto the pizza pans with a resounding clang and . . . vanished.

I jumped after him.

It wasn't sane. It wasn't rational. It wasn't what any human being in the history of science should have done. It was the instinct of someone who'd just seen the impossible and wanted to unsee it. I jumped after Kenyon, because I was sure I wasn't seeing things right and that if I just got there I would see him clearly.

I landed on soft dirt, and heard something like a scream, and Kenyon was grabbing my arm and pulling me upright, and he threw the carefully wrapped package at something.

It was hard to know exactly what I was seeing. Once, when I was ten, I'd had anesthesia for an operation, and as I was coming out from it, what I saw was a jumble of colors and heard a jumble of sounds, and nothing made sense. Someone later had explained this to me by saying you have to learn to see. Babies have to learn to use their eyes and how the shapes they see translate to three dimensional objects. Until they do that, all they see is a jumble of colors and movement.

The colors and movement I saw were relatively familiar. I was sure the green things nearby were plants. I wasn't sure what the huge thing in front of me was. It might have been a parrot grown to a million times the size, with claw arms.

"T-Rex," Kenyon said, with certainty, as he tried to shove me backwards. I stepped back, but I didn't fall through the pizza platters into the dining room.

"This is not the other side of the dining room," I said indignantly, as if by saying I could make him fix it.

"I kind of noticed." he said, and stepped back again, retreating into the shadow of a plant.

The alien parrot thing that he thought was a T-Rex sniffed the air and made a sound like a bull with laryngitis, and Kenyon whispered, "We must somehow have traveled back in time."

"This is not next Wednesday," I said.

"Not unless next Wednesday is really interesting." He smiled a lopsided smile. "Right, we have to find our way back. Xavier should be calculating how to get us back right now."

"You were supposed to make sure the computer got the right coordinates. What kind of coordinates did you have in mind?"

At that moment there was a sound not quite a zap, and a kind of glowing light over a spot to the left of us. The parrot-rex turned towards it, and Kenyon pushed me upright and towards it. "There, move it."

His shove was so hard I fell through the glowing spot, and onto the floor of the dining room. Xavier jumped out of the way as I picked myself up, and we turned to look at the pizza pan, as a heavy weight crashed on it, and Xavier screamed and cut the connection.

We sat there for a long time, on the dusty floor of the dining room, absolutely quiet, looking at something about the size of a French loaf, but green and ending in a claw.

Then Xavier got up. He made a sound like a hiccup and returned to the keyboard, where his fingers moved, furiously. Again and again, he told me connection had been established, but nothing happened. The toe of the parrot-rex oozed a silvery bright liquid onto the pizza pan and nothing happened.

"I'll go," I said. "I'll look around. I can't understand how the two of you were so crazy as to try this out when you can't temporally control it at all."

"We thought"—he waved in midair—"we thought, the other side of the dining room, how dangerous can it be."

He punched keys on the keyboard again. "And you can't go. It's dangerous if you go. Clearly it's dangerous. You shouldn't have gone to begin with."

"I had to do something. He vanished."

"He was supposed to vanish. If you hadn't thrown yourself in after him, when I reestablished connection, he could easily have got back. But he saved you."

I wanted to protest, but of course he was right. Kenyon had saved me.

I went to the kitchen, got the barbecue tongs, and moved the toe claw aside. "Fine," I said. "So it's up to me to go again. Maybe the parrot creature, the . . . owner of that toe, wounded him. Maybe he's there, bleeding, and he can't get back in. I'll go in and pull him into the gateway?"

"But you can't. I'll go."

"If you go, there's no one who can operate the computer part."

"Right," he said. "Right. So . . . Try to keep very clear in your mind where you want to go."

"You mean, remember where I was and what we saw?"

"No. This is not magic. The computer understands a set of coordinates." He glared at the toe. "Okay, the computer is *supposed* to understand a set of coordinates. If you keep those in mind, you should get to the same place."

"The same coordinates that Kenyon thought of?"

"Yes." He frowned. "Thing is, you shouldn't have been able to go back and forth through the gateway, and that"—he pointed at the claw—"should never have come through. You should have to be connected to the computer to get it, and Kenyon was wearing the sensors. You and the thing must have gone through on . . . residuals or something." He made a sound like hiccupping again. "We shouldn't be doing this. The process is clearly not worked out enough."

"Yes, well, you should have thought of that before sending Kenyon to the land of the T-parrots."

His mouth made a very thin line, but he nodded. "Right. Okay. I don't like to do this."

"I'm not ecstatic, either, but we need to at least try to get him back."

So, Xavier had attached sensors to my forehead, little dots that were hidden by my hair, and told me a long string of letters and numbers to keep in mind at all times, which was rather like thinking of a pink rhinoceros in that all sorts of other thoughts kept intruding.

"Ready," he said.

I stepped on the pizza pan. And found myself . . . somewhere. There was the moment of disorientation, while my eyes tried to process what I was seeing, and then I focused on a line of distant, coral-colored mountains. There was a dry wind blowing, and the sun in the sky looked like it was enclosed in a dark ring.

I stepped backwards into the glow, and into the dining room.

Xavier glared at me, "Ready," he said again.

I stepped through into—nothing. And fell back again, taking gasping breaths of the living room air, which still smelled of candles, wine, bread, and soldering iron.

"Ready."

I tripped through and into . . . salt water. Salt water around me, above me, and something huge swimming towards me even as my lungs labored to take in a breath, and—

Back into the living room, dripping water onto the floorboards.

"Damn it," Xavier said. It was the first time I'd heard him curse. "Damn it."

"Yeah," I said. "I was underwater."

"No more," he said. "No more. Let's call for help."

"Who are we going to call for help?" I said. "Nine-one-one?"

He shook his head. The hiccup sound came again, and I realized that he was trying very hard not to cry. "Someone. Someone has to be able to help us. One of the other grant recipients, maybe. It's said the grants went out to the best minds in the world."

"Like us?"

He made a face. "Well, someone has to be able to figure it out."

"Why? I don't think anyone has done this before."

"But now we've done it," he said. "Someone should be able to figure it out."

"And by then Kenyon will be gone. He thought the creature that put that toe through was a T-Rex. Maybe Kenyon evaded him, but how long do you think he can survive in the Jurassic? We have to keep trying. Sooner or later we're going to get the right time."

"Okay," Xavier said. He sounded hoarse. "Okay."

He returned to his keyboard. He shouted, "Ready." I stepped onto the pizza pan.

Fire and ice, burning and freezing, underwater and what appeared to be floating out in space. Over and over again, and I thought, well, we were in Colorado. The mountains had changed height and it had been underwater through the geological ages. I thought of the coordinates, and I thought of Kenyon, and I thought of the landcape I'd seen. On and off the pizza pan, and deserts and mountains and seaside beaches.

Dawn was a streak of light on the horizon when Xavier croaked, "Ready," and I stepped on. And stepped back into the dining room.

"We have to stop," I said. "This is no use."

Xavier looked pale and exhausted and looked at me with that kind of look people get when they haven't slept in a long time and there's a good chance they're never going to sleep well, ever again, "Why?" he said. "You're the one who said we had to try and the next try could find him."

I sat down. I felt very tired and as though I'd lost all force in my muscles. I felt as though I couldn't communicate what I'd seen or what was so important about it.

"The last place I went to," I said. "There was a city." I paused. I could see Xavier try to shape the question of what city. Before he could, I said, "And two suns in the sky."

The rest of it is in the history books, of course, though some details never made it in. For instance, the toe was not a T-Rex, but no one knows what it was. The form of life might be terrestrial or simply have followed a parallel evolution.

When we called for help, there was an investigation by the best minds of our time. It turned out that Xavier and Kenyon had managed to create a teleporter of sorts, which could take a human being and take them through what might be best described as a fold in space and time almost instantly. But what they thought could control it, couldn't.

It took the next several decades to perfect the process, but in the end we had ships that could reach the habitable worlds on the distant stars, with ninety-five percent accuracy. The vehicles that were created with the Kenyon-Xavier process were called Schrodingers, despite Xavier's lobbying for them to be named Kenyons.

We're credited, the two of us and Kenyon, with finding the way to the stars. It turned out it was neither a great government program nor a directed private initiative that opened space to colonization, but accident and three young idiots playing with that which they did not understand.

We got married, of course, partly, I think, so we could wait together.

You see, that portal they created took him somewhere. We don't know where he is. But Xavier has updated the system and made it better as new things were discovered. And we try. Over the years we've tried again and again, without ever finding the world where Kenyon disappeared.

However, as we know, it's a matter of time. Sooner or later, the coin will fall on edge.

(((((( 🔘 ))))))

**Sarah A. Hoyt** was born in Portugal (where her birth family still lives) and English is her third language (second is French.) This possibly explains why she's on the kill list of most copy editors. To avoid them, she lives high and dry in Colorado with her husband, two sons, and a variable clowder of cats, reading and writing, with an occasional leitmotif of pastel painting, sewing, or carpentry thrown in when someone complains she's been at the keyboard too long. Her most recent books are *A Few Good Men*, *Noah's Boy,* and *Night Shifters* from Baen books, indie *Witchfinder*, a regency fantasy, and upcoming *Through Fire* and *Darkship Revenge*, also from Baen Books.

*In another diversion from the serious, Mike Resnick's most wanted man in the galaxy is just looking for a place to hide from the authorities when he stumbles into far more on . . .*

# TARTAROS

## by Mike Resnick

Tarter looked back, which didn't help much since he was in the pilot's chair of the small ship. He cursed and turned back to the computer. "Anybody on our tail yet?"

"I do not possess a tail, Jerome Tarter," replied the ship reasonably.

"Is anyone following us, and you don't have to use my name every goddamned time you speak," growled Tarter.

"No, no one has been following us since I took evasive action in Saturn's rings."

"Okay, just keep going, and let me know when we get near anything you can land on."

"We are entering the Kuiper Belt," answered the ship.

"Fine," said Tarter. "What the hell does that mean?"

"It houses hundreds, perhaps thousands, of minor planets and dwarf planets, many of them not yet identified or catalogued," said the ship.

"And beyond that?"

"Nothing I can reach in less than six human lifetimes," answered the ship. "Until faster-than-light drives are developed, the Kuiper Belt is the physical limit for human travel and exploration."

"Big whoopee," said Tarter. "I don't want to go to another star system. I don't even want to stay where we are. I just need to lay low until the cops find someone else to bother."

"You realize," said the ship, "that if they do apprehend us, I will be forced to testify that I had nothing to do with your crimes."

"Crime," Tarter corrected it. "One crime. It got a little out of hand, and I had no idea there'd be so many bystanders, but it was one crime."

"Your biographical record shows that you were convicted and sentenced for theft, extortion, murder, and crimes against humanity on Earth, Mars, Venus, Ganymede, and Triton, and that you escaped from incarceration in all five instances, leaving a trail of dead and maimed bodies behind you."

"It really says all that?"

"You're quite famous, Jerome Tarter," replied the ship. "Or perhaps infamous."

"Makes a man feel proud to know he's been all written up in song and story."

"I did not mention song, Jerome Tarter."

"Sooner or later they make up songs about everyone in my line of work," answered Tarter. "And if you insist on calling me by name, make it Jerry."

"Yes, Jerry. I will remember to do so, Jerry."

"And go easy on it."

"I do not understand you, Jerry."

Tarter signed. "Never mind." He looked ahead. "Show me where we are."

A screen appeared.

"Ain't much out here, is there?"

"There may well be tens of thousands of minor or dwarf planets, Jerry."

"I can only see one," said Tarter.

"That is not a planet, but an escaped moon from a minor planet, Jerry."

"Big difference," said Tarter. "Okay, it's time to find us a world to hole up in for a while."

"I do not understand 'hole up' or 'a while,' Jerry," responded the ship.

"Then suppose you let me worry about it." Tarter looked at the screen. "Are we the first to get this far?"

"No, Jerry. There are scientific or mining communities currently on the minor planets of Eris, Haumea, Orcus, Makemake, and Sedna."

"Makemake?" repeated Tarter, frowning.

"It is from the religious tradition of the Rapanui people of Easter Island, Jerry," answered the ship.

"Wherever *that* is," muttered Tarter.

"It's one of the few places on Earth where you have not committed a felony."

"Bully for them," said Tarter. "Now stop using my name for a while, and concentrate on finding a world—"

"A dwarf planet," the ship corrected him.

"Whatever. Just start looking."

The ship fell silent for almost fifteen minutes, then uttered two words: "That's odd."

"What's odd?" demanded Tarter,

"We are 104 astronomical units from the Sun, and—"

"Translate that into miles."

"We are approximately five billion miles from the Sun," continued the ship, "and yet I detect a world with a core that is even hotter than the sunward side of Mercury."

"And all the other worlds are as cold as you'd figure them to be when they're a hundred times as far from the Sun as Earth is?" asked Tarter.

"Precisely. That's why this is so odd."

"Take us there. At least we won't freeze to death."

"I cannot freeze," replied the ship, "and not being alive, I cannot die."

"Thanks for that information, which is doubtless vital to my survival," said Tarter sardonically. "Okay, you say the whole planet isn't that hot?"

"Just the core."

"So the surface might be livable."

"For creatures that do not require oxygen and water."

"I'm not staying there forever," said Tarter, "just long enough for the fuzz and the military to get tired of looking for me and go hunting someone else. And I'll bet none of the other worlds out here has any oxygen or water either."

"That is true."

"So let's go. What did you say the name of this world is?"

"It has no name. According to all available records, no one has ever touched down on it."

"Then I guess I'll name it after myself."

"Jerome Tarter?"

"What now?"

"Is that what you'll name it?" asked the ship.

"Sounds a little formal. Maybe just Jerry."

"Shall I enter it in my records as Just Jerry?"

"Let me think about it," answered Tarter. "You just get us there. I'll worry about naming it."

It took another five days, but finally they were close enough that Tarter could observe the world on his viewscreen.

"Doesn't look like much," he noted.

"It looks like all the other dwarf planets," said the ship.

"That's what I mean," answered Tarter. "I figured with that molten core it might, I dunno, maybe glow a little, or something."

"That's curious."

"What is?"

"The core *should* be molten, but it isn't."

"I thought you said the world was hotter than Mercury?"

"It is."

"Well, then?" demanded Tarter.

"I need more data."

"Then land and start acquiring it."

"I'll try," said the ship. "But . . ."

"But what?" replied Tarter sharply.

"But after you stole me during the massacre . . ."

"It was a bank robbery," interrupted Tarter. "The bloodletting is just what happened to a bunch of do-gooders who tried to stop me from making a living."

The ship was silent for a full minute.

"Well?" demanded Tarter.

"I am trying to equate your notion of making a living with the definition of morality that is in my data banks."

"Forget that shit and tell me why you're hesitant about learning why the core isn't molten."

"I am not hesitant about *learning*," answered the ship. "I am hesitant about acquiring the knowledge. When you stole me and the police began firing to stop me, they destroyed some of my sensing mechanisms."

"Improvise," said Tarter. "That's what *I* do."

"I know the definition, of course," said the ship, "but I have never actually improvised before. I don't know if I can."

"Work on it," said Tarter. He shrugged. "Or don't. As long as the damned planet doesn't blow up while I'm on it, I don't much give a damn about what's causing the heat."

"But if it doesn't obey the laws of the Universe . . ." began the ship.

"Then me and the planet are brothers," replied Tarter. "In case you haven't noticed, I don't obey them either."

The ship entered orbit after another two hours, searching for the best place to land.

"Uh . . . Jerry," it said suddenly.

"Yeah?"

"I hate to bother you . . ."

"I can tell," was Tarter's sarcastic reply.

"But someone on the planet has contacted me and is giving me landing coordinates."

"I thought it was supposed to be uninhabited," said Tarter, frowning.

"That's the problem," said the ship.

"*What's* the problem?"

"It *is* uninhabited. I have done a thorough scan, and my instruments confirm that there is no life form, at least not any I am programmed to recognize as such, down there."

"But it's giving you coordinates, not telling you to go away?"

"That is correct."

"Then what the hell, let's land."

"Without knowing what it is or what it wants?" asked the ship.

"There are four armies, two Solar Patrol units, and a couple of thousand cops from various worlds looking for me," responded Tarter. "I know exactly what they are and what they want. We'll take our chances with this guy."

"I do not know for a fact that it *is* a guy," said the ship. "In fact, everything I *do* know tells me that it isn't."

"Just land where he tells you to."

"Where *it* tells me to," the ship corrected him.

"And shut up until we're on the ground."

They descended in total silence, and finally the ship touched down.

"I don't see any spaceport," noted Tarter, staring at a screen.

"There isn't one," answered the ship.

"Then why the hell did you land here?"

"You ordered me to."

"*I* ordered you?"

"You told me to land at the given coordinates."

Tarter frowned. "Then where the hell *is* everybody?"

Suddenly, the ship shuddered.

"What was *that*?" demanded Tarter.

"An enclosed ramp has risen out of the surface—I hesitate to call it the ground, since it consists primarily of molten rock—and has attached itself to my hatch."

"So I'm supposed to walk out through it?"

"I presume so."

"Safe?"

"I have no idea."

"I mean is the environment within the enclosed ramp safe?" said Tarter.

"Oxygen/nitrogen ratio similar to 3,200 meters on Mt. Everest, temperature 19 degrees Celsius, gravity 97% Earth Standard."

"Sounds good," replied Tarter. He began checking his weapons. "Laser pistol, fully charged. Sonic pistol, fully charged. Bullets: 19 in the gun, 25 on the belt. Yeah, I'm ready." He walked to the hatch. "Open it, and don't move except on a direct order from me."

"Roger and aye-aye," replied the ship, wishing Tarter would simply let it say "Affirmed."

Tarter walked to the open hatch and peered ahead. The corridor, or so he thought of it, was dimly lit, and seemed to go directly down into the bowels of the dwarf world.

He paused for a moment, then withdrew his laser pistol, switched off the safety, and began walking slowly, carefully, down the gently inclined corridor.

He'd gone almost a mile, and when he had still encountered nothing but more corridor walls, he stopped.

"Come along, come along," said a hollow-sounding voice. "I've been waiting for you."

Tarter spun around, looking for the source of the voice, but found he was still alone in the corridor. "Show yourself!" he grated.

"Soon," said the voice. "You're almost here now."

"I'm almost *where*?" demanded Tarter.

"Your destination, of course," said the voice.

Tarter looked around, couldn't see any sign of life, and proceeded cautiously.

"By the way, you can take off your helmet," said the voice. "The air is quite breathable, and the temperature is an ambient 73 degrees Fahrenheit."

"Come on!" snapped Tarter. "According to my ship's readout, you're closer to a couple of thousand degrees!"

"Well, yes, part of my domain is," agreed the voice. "But that won't affect you."

"Your domain?" repeated Tarter. "You sound like you rule the place."

"Do I now?" replied the voice in amused tones.

"What do you call this world?" asked Tarter.

"Home."

Suddenly, an agonized scream pierced the air, and Tarter froze. "What the hell was *that*?" he demanded.

"Do you really not know?" asked the voice. "You've certainly heard your fair share of them."

"Answer my question."

"Someone's not very happy," replied the voice with no show of concern.

"That makes two of us," said Tarter, frowning and stopping again.

"Come along, come along," said the voice. "You're almost here."

"Where the hell is *here*?" demanded Tarter.

"Just follow the chain."

"Chain? What chain?"

But even as the words left his mouth, Tarter turned to his left and encountered a row of naked men and women, their bodies covered with welts and puncture marks, many with eyes and organs cut or gouged out, hanging in a seemingly endless row from a chain that stretched across the top of the corridor for what seemed like miles. A few of them became aware of Tarter's presence and begged for help, but in a language—a score of languages—which were incomprehensible to him.

"What's going on here?" said Tarter.

"Please do not expect me to believe you are at all shocked or dismayed by such a sight at this late date," said the voice. "Just keep walking. I assure you they cannot impede or harm you, any more than they can impede or harm me."

Tarter recommenced walking down the corridor, noting what should have been fatal wounds on still-active bodies.

"To your right now," said the voice, and suddenly there was not a doorway but an open space to Tarter's right, and he walked through it. Seated upon a golden throne was a man clearly showing some of the effects of age. His hair was gray, his face was lined, and his muscles had lost some of their tone. He wore a single-piece white outfit—Tarter identified it as a toga, but it wasn't quite—and he got stiffly to his feet to face the newcomer.

"I've been waiting a long time for you to get here," he said.

"I only landed an hour ago," replied Tarter.

"Nevertheless."

"All right, I'm here, I've walked by your handiwork in the corridor, and I'm not putting down my pistol until I know what's going on."

The older man shrugged and gestured to the corridor. "As you see."

"I see a bunch of men and women who've been tortured, and by all rights ought to be dead," replied Tarter.

The older man smiled. "And it didn't bother you at all, did it?"

"What bothers me is not knowing what's going on."

"I'm showing you my domain," replied the older man. "But this is just the outskirts of it. To see the truly remarkable part, we have to go deeper beneath the surface."

Tarter frowned. "According to my ship's instruments, it's thousands of degrees down there."

The older man looked amused. "Celsius or Fahrenheit?"

"Who gives a goddamn?"

"Oh, very well said. Not to worry, my boy, I promise you will not feel the heat at all."

"The ship was wrong?" said Tarter, frowning.

"That is not what I said."

Tarter stared at him, neither speaking nor moving.

"Come along," said the man. "If it doesn't hurt me, it won't hurt you."

He began walking, and Tarter reluctantly fell into step behind him.

"You got a name?" Tarter asked.

"Of course I do," was the answer.

"Care to share it with me?"

The man laughed.

"What the hell's so funny?"

"I admire your choice of words," said the man. He paused before a section of wall, waved a hand at it, and it vanished, leading to a ramp that plunged down into the innards of the planet.

"All right," said Tarter, coming to a stop. "Tell me your name, or I'm going back to the ship right now."

"No, you aren't," replied the man with a smile. "There are hundreds of warrants out for your arrest and capture, you are wanted dead or alive—preferably dead—on half a dozen moons and worlds, and you are standing in perhaps the only place in the solar system where you are safe from detection and apprehension. But if it will make you happy, my name is Typhoeus."

"Typhoeus?" repeated Tarter, frowning.

"That's right."

"That's a hell of name."

Typhoeus smiled. "Precisely."

They walked deeper into the planet, and came to a huge pit, filled with fire and perpetually burning and screaming bodies.

"Who are they?" asked Tarter.

"That one's King Sisyphus," answered Typhoeus, pointing to a lean man who was writhing in agony. "And this one's Ixion, and over here is King Tantalus." Another smile. "And I believe you might recognize this one."

Tarter peered at the man whose eyes had clearly been gouged out, and kept walking blindly into hotter and hotter flames, screaming in agony. "Hitler?" he asked.

"How nice to know such a monster's face hasn't been forgotten after only a couple of centuries. And this is Caligula, and this—"

"Is this hell?" interrupted Tarter.

"Certainly not," answered Typhoeus. "Hell has literally billions of inhabitants. Where would they all fit here?"

"Then what is it?"

"A very special world," replied Typhoeus. "There *is* a hell, of course.

I call it Hades, others call it other things, but it's where damned souls go to rot for all eternity." He paused. "But not all of them remain there. For example, King Sisyphus there decided to lead a revolt of the damned against Zeus, and since he was able to cross the barrier from hell to heaven, the gods decided to create a very special place for exceptionally vile and dangerous souls. And to make sure they remained there, they created a creature, a Hekatonkheir giant who was stronger and more vicious than any of them, and he became what I think I shall call 'the Keeper of the Flame.'"

"How come no one's ever heard of all this?" said Tarter.

"Don't blame your cultural illiteracy on others," said Typhoeus with a smile. "This domain was discussed in Homer, in Hesiod, in Aeschylus, in Ptolemy, even in Plato and Virgil."

"All ancient deists or atheists," said Tarter.

"It is also mentioned in Hellenistic Jewish literature, in *1 Enoch*," continued Typhoeus, "which stated that God created the pit and its guardian, which are both known as Tartaros."

"So you're Tartaros?"

Typhoeus shook his head. "I told you: my name is Typhoeus."

Tarter frowned. "Then I don't understand."

"Of course you do."

Tarter just stared at him.

"I called myself Tartaros while I served as the keeper of the pit until the *true* guardian came along," continued Typhoeus. "I have reclaimed my name of Typhoeus since the instant you landed. I have waited a long, long time for you: the one true Tartaros."

"Me?"

Typhoeus nodded his head. "A being so cruel, so lacking in compassion, so creative in his capacity for evil, that no one in his charge will ever be able to outwit him, to revolt or escape from him and his world." He extended a hand. "Welcome, my lord."

"Tartaros," said Tarter, considering the name and nodding his approval. "It's very similar to Tarter, as if someone was hinting." He stared at his companion. "You're the Hekatonkheir giant, aren't you?"

"In my true form."

Tartaros who had been Tarter looked around. "Well, let's finish the chef's tour."

"Follow me."

And when it was done, they returned to the surface.

"Wait a minute," said Tartaros, suddenly stopping. "I'll need a helmet."

Typhoeus shook his head. "No longer."

"All right," said Tartaros, emerging from the corridor and taking a deep breath of what passed for air. "The ship can be a little uppity, a little contrary. Don't let it pull any shit with you."

"I've had experience with uppity, contrary entities," replied Typhoeus.

"Then good-bye and good luck," said Tartaros. "By the way, what do gods eat?"

Typhoeus grinned. "Anything they want. And the beauty of this world is that it always grows back."

Then he was aboard the ship, and a moment later Tartaros was alone on his planet. He created a corridor—somehow he knew how to do so—and decided to give his domain a more thorough inspection before deciding which of his few thousand subjects his predecessor had ignored for too long.

((·((·((· 🔆 ·))·))·))

**Mike Resnick** is, according to *Locus*, the all-time leading award winner, living or dead, for short science fiction. He is the winner of five Hugos from a record 37 nominations, a Nebula, and other major awards in the United States, France, Spain, Japan, Croatia, Catalonia, and Poland. and has been short-listed for major awards in England, Italy and Australia. He is the author of 74 novels, over 250 stories, and 3 screenplays, and is the editor of 42 anthologies. His work has been translated into 26 languages. He was the Guest of Honor at the 2012 Worldcon and can be found online as @ResnickMike on Twitter or at www. mikeresnick.com.

*Next, in another look at the way corporations might play in space, a work-from-home sysadmin faces a crisis when the space rock he's charged with shepherding safely to Earth changes its trajectory and has a . . .*

# MALF

## by David D. Levine

*I see it*, Jamal typed in the chat window, just as Marissa shouted the same in her headset. An excited burble of talk and text followed, messages filling my right-hand screen and my ears as I peered at my main display for a glimpse of the incoming package. And then I saw it myself: a tiny streak of bright white light in the gray Atlantic sky, bobbing and weaving as the pickup boat rolled on a light swell.

The camera operator zoomed in and the streak swelled to a slash, a long band of incandescence that split the sky, its leading edge a brilliant four-pointed star. "It's so bright, mon," came Raphael's voice in my ear. "Hurts the eye." He was on the pickup boat, too; this was *his* package, the culmination of over four years of work, coming in hot and heavy, and he'd flown to Ecuador at his own expense to see it in person. Not the choice I'd have made, but I could see the appeal.

The camera zoomed out, zoomed out, but the slash of white grew too fast to follow and the view switched to a static shot from shore. A curve of black smoke cut across the gray clouds with a coruscating star at its tip, reaching down from heaven at orbital speed to touch the sea. And then, fifteen eternal seconds after it had first appeared: splashdown! A tremendous waterspout spewed from the point of contact, a foamy white geyser rising eighty stories into the air before dissipating into fog and fumes.

Pandemonium on the audio channel; the chat window a chaos of congratulatory messages, many in all caps, scrolling too fast to read. And then, audible even above the excited chatter of happy Space

Resources employees, came the rolling thunder of the package's entry and splashdown, the crawling speed of sound making it tardy in its arrival.

That package had once been an asteroid, minding its own business somewhere between here and Mars. But then Space Resources Corporation had fitted it out with rocket engines, mining robots, and an automated refinery, all supervised remotely by Raphael, who had remade it into a lifting body with a silicate ablative crust and a core of solid refined molybdenum. After settling to the continental shelf, it would be hauled to the surface by the pickup boat, brought back to shore, and turned into a big pile of glorious cash.

A distinctive *queep* announced a private message: *You're next, Jorge!* accompanied by a grinning animated emoticon. It was my boss, Amanda, reminding me that with the successful arrival of Raphael's package, mine would be the next to be welcomed home.

Not that I needed to be reminded. A constant presence in the upper right corner of my main screen was a countdown clock, superimposed over a photo taken from the balcony of my little condo in San Francisco. Of course, it wasn't "my" condo yet, but the papers were all signed, and when my package came in—three days, two hours, thirteen minutes, and eight . . . seven . . . six seconds from now—the money would pay off my Space Resources loan, buy me the condo, and still leave enough for a modestly comfortable retirement.

I glanced at my left-hand screen, where my package's orbital track still lay almost on the money line. *Looking good*, I texted back to Amanda with a thumbs-up emoticon.

But wait . . . *almost* on the money line? I frowned with concern. Three days to entry was no time for almosts. I called up a more detailed view. Yes, there was a deviation from the optimum orbital path. Not big enough to trigger an alert, but worthy of attention.

I signed off from the ongoing celebration and squirted myself a cup of coffee. There wasn't any sign of what had caused the deviation, which was worrisome, but it might just be a minor variation in the solar wind or an unexpected burst of gas from some internal cavity as the asteroid drew closer to the sun. In any case, I wanted to correct it as soon as possible; if my baby hit the atmosphere at even a slightly wrong angle, it could burn up on entry or go tumbling irretrievably away into space. No payout for anyone if that happened.

I composed a thrust sequence to fix the deviation, ran a quick simulation to verify it would have the desired effect, then queued it up on the Deep Space Network for delivery to my package. Once the sequence hit the head of the queue, it would take only twenty-five seconds to crawl at the speed of light to the incoming asteroid. Hardly anything by comparison with the day and a half of turnaround time I'd had to deal with at the beginning of this job, but it was enough time for me to sip my coffee and ponder my situation.

I'd been working for Space Resources for just a hair shy of five years, shepherding asteroid 2019 CN 1018 in its conversion from a random hunk of space rock into a sleek, profitable package. My official job title was "Asteroid Miner," which looked cool in my online profiles, but in fact I was just another work-from-home contract sysadmin—albeit one who couldn't ever touch the systems he was admin-ing.

It was tricky, tedious work. The asteroid itself was an all-natural product, rife with voids and inclusions and impurities that required constant fiddling with the mining manipulators and automated refinery. Its orbit was subject to perturbation by other asteroids, solar winds, and magnetic flux, which had to be compensated for in order to hit the half-kilometer target circle. And the thrusters, manipulators, grinders, refinery, and all the other hardware and firmware had been "tested and proven"—in other words, already five years behind the times—when they'd been bundled up and scheduled for launch over twelve years ago.

That last detail was why I'd gotten the job, actually. After my parents disowned me, aborting my college career, my fabulous uncle Roberto had found me a job doing maintenance on an ancient manufacturing control system. I enjoyed the work, but it had turned into a trap: between the eighty-hour weeks and my lack of degree, I had never been able to train up on anything more recent. As my skills grew more and more outdated, I'd found fewer and fewer job openings, so when this opportunity had appeared—just happening to require expertise in the obsolete operating system I'd been wrangling for my whole career—it had been a godsend. In effect, my baby and I were made for each other.

But obsolete hardware and software weren't my only source of pain. A licensing snafu had delayed the launch for nearly three years, during which time the equipment had sat in a hot, humid Florida warehouse with its seals decaying, lubricants deteriorating, and software undergoing whatever mysterious bit-rot causes intermittent bugs. It all added up to my job being a constant battle against nature and machine, leaving almost no time for real-world socializing. In fact, the only human being I'd seen this week was my cleaning lady. All my other interactions were handled online or by delivery drone.

My global co-workers were okay, I guess, with most of them very willing to answer a question or lend a hand at any time of day or night. Which was a good thing; like taxi drivers, we were independent contractors, each having bought into the project with our own savings—or, in my case, a hefty loan, cosigned by Uncle Roberto—and pretty much self-supporting. Space Resources Corporation was little more than a corporate shell, an investment vehicle for the owners who'd put up the big bucks to launch the hardware years ago. But though I could always ring up Jamal or Kyra or Miyuki for a chat, it wasn't the same as hanging out at the bar with friends.

Even when I managed to pry myself away from my screen long enough to socialize in the real world, which hadn't happened for months, the results were highly unsatisfying. I'd moved to Jacksonville for a boyfriend, but it hadn't worked out because I spent too much time and attention on work—an accusation I couldn't deny—and for the same reason I hadn't found the time to move elsewhere or even make any local friends. So I hit the bars, where I got hit on by crackers with less brains than a Florida alligator, and went home lonely and frustrated.

Suddenly, a descending tone interrupted my self-pitying thoughts, accompanied by a red-bordered error popup I'd never seen before. *Transmission rejected*, it read.

I looked deeper. My command sequence had been accepted by the DSN for transmission to the package at the first available opportunity, as usual. It had gone through the queue and been transmitted without apparent problems. But the asteroid's command processor had not accepted the command, returning an error code I wasn't familiar with.

I tried not to worry. It might very well be just a malf—a temporary malfunction. I sent the command sequence again.

While I awaited the result, I checked the DSN network status, the solar weather report, and anything else that could have interfered with transmission of the command sequence. No sign of any issue. The package's navigational beacon was still sending out its regular omnidirectional ping, indicating that it was still present and at least somewhat alive and giving me a fix on its location, but told me nothing about the package's attitude or the state of any of its other systems.

Then came another descending tone. *Transmission rejected.*

I pressed my lips together and tried not to panic. My baby's hardware was old and cranky, and I'd had problems before, but I'd always managed to get it back online eventually.

I looked up the error code. It supposedly indicated authentication failure—basically, lack of the correct security certificate for the encrypted command stream—but according to the notes other miners had added to the documentation over the years, it was more likely indicative of a hardware problem in the main antenna. I sent a please-reply ping via the secondary antenna to test that out.

Six minutes passed in anxious silence while the command worked its way through the DSN queue, the transmission sailed across space to my package, and the reply came back.

Descending tone. *Transmission rejected.*

I screamed a curse at the screen. The neighbor's dog barked back at me; my apartment walls were ludicrously thin.

Then the barking was joined by another, different error noise. *Orbital track parameter violation*, read the popup.

Whatever had sent my baby off its course, it was getting worse.

*Queep.* A message from Amanda: *Just spotted your track violation. What's up?*

Of course she would have seen the error on her console as well. I took a moment to calm my breathing before replying; I needed to maintain the appearance of being in control. *Looking into it*, I temporized.

Another *queep*. This message came from Stan in the Orbital Tracking Center. *Unauth orb tranf burn on 2019 CN 1018 at 13:37 UTC*, it read in his usual telegraphic style. *Pls advise.*

I swallowed and stared at the screen, where the detailed orbital track view showed my asteroid moving further and further off course. Not only was it not answering my commands, but according to Stan it had fired its main engine to move itself into a different orbit without my having alerted OTC first. This wasn't exactly a capital crime, but it was a violation of protocol and too many of those could reduce my payout.

The time stamp, 13:37 UTC, was right around the time the package had begun to deviate from its planned course.

While I was trying to figure out how best to reply, two more *queeps* sounded, both from fellow asteroid miners expressing concern.

I took out my earbuds and took a quick walk around my little office, kicking a discarded Hi-Kaf Kola can into the corner with a satisfying clatter. This was bad. Very, very bad.

*Having unknown issue,* I replied to everyone. *Investigating.*

The first thing I did was to write up and send off a new thrust sequence to put my package back on its original track, though my confidence of success was low and dropping. I also sent a command to execute a system status diagnostic scan, but didn't have much more optimism about that. While waiting for those results, I tried to figure out what the heck was going on.

Setting aside the communication problem for the moment, what could have caused my package to fire its main engine? It had been almost exactly on course, and a quick scan of the orbital tracking display confirmed that there were no natural or artificial objects anywhere nearby or ahead; the automatic collision avoidance algorithm couldn't have—or *shouldn't* have—triggered the burn.

As I worked, more and more *queeps* sounded, anxious queries from all over the company. One thing about working in space: everyone can see right away when something goes wrong. I changed my messaging status to Busy/Offline and tried to focus.

I was just reviewing the log files when the results of my commands came back: *Transmission rejected. Transmission rejected.* I swore, but not too loud, and kept looking.

Nothing stood out from the logs, at least on a first glance, up to the end of the file about forty-five minutes ago. The next hourly data dump would arrive in fourteen minutes . . . or it wouldn't.

Then the doorbell rang.

Startled, I checked my calendar to see if I should have been expecting anyone. And, indeed, I should have: it was my cleaning lady. The last few hours had been so crazy I had completely forgotten she was coming today.

Despite my jitters and concern, I unplugged my earbuds and walked downstairs to the building's front door. She was such a tiny little old lady that I hated to shout at her through the intercom. "I'm sorry, Cheryl," I told her, "I'm really, really busy right now. Could you come back tomorrow?"

She gave me the stink-eye and consulted her phone—she was so old-fashioned she still kept her calendar in her phone—before assenting. "All right," she groused, "just this once." She might be a tiny little old lady, but she could still be pretty straightforward. "Normally I wouldn't, but I can see you're really frazzled. Is everything all right?"

"I'm sure it's just a temporary glitch," I said, though I was beginning to worry that it was far worse than that. "But I really need to keep an eye on it, so if you'll excuse me . . ."

Just as I got back to my office, my watch buzzed with an incoming voice call.

*Amanda*, read the display on my wrist.

What I wanted to do was strip the thing from my arm and fling it into the corner with the Hi-Kaf Kola can, but I sighed and took the call. "Hey, boss," I said, trying to keep it light.

"What the *hell* is going on with your bird?"

"It's rejecting my commands." I slipped into my seat. No new information on the screen. "And the main engine burn . . . that wasn't me. I'm still trying to figure out what caused it."

"I don't care what caused it. Have you seen where it's *going*?"

"Uh." That was something I hadn't had a chance to look into. "Hang on."

I pulled the orbital track view back from detail level to overview.

The package was on course to enter Earth's atmosphere over the Kamchatka Peninsula, with exactly the correct angle for a successful insertion. Depending on the exact attitude of the lifting body, it might still bounce off or burn up. But even if it didn't, it would land in the mid-Pacific . . . where the water was far too deep for a profitable recovery.

"Uh," I repeated brilliantly.

"Do you realize how much money is riding on this?"

I knew *exactly* how much money was riding on it. If my package didn't pay out, not only would there be no condo in San Francisco, but it would be the end of my job, and—given my obsolete skill set—probably the end of my career. I wouldn't be able to keep up the payments on my Space Resources buy-in loan. Which meant bankruptcy not only for me, but for my fabulous octogenarian uncle Roberto.

Roberto had been so good to me. If I repaid everything he'd done for me by losing him his house . . .

Could be worse, though, I thought. Could be coming down on New York.

Suddenly the text window on my screen that showed the last few lines of the package's system log file burst into life, thousands of additional lines scrolling rapidly by. "Whoa," I said, "I just got the hourly data dump." I hit Pause and started inspecting the data. "At least it's still talking to me, even if it's not listening."

"Can you use this to get it back on course?"

"Maybe, if you leave me alone!" I snapped.

"All right. But keep me posted on your work! I want hourly updates."

"Sure," I said, not meaning it, and cut the connection.

Orbital tracking could tell us where the package was going to hit, assuming nothing else changed. Telescopes and radar could tell us if it did anything to change its trajectory. But unless we understood *why* it had fired its engines on its own authority, there was always the possibility it would do so again, throwing any plans we made out the window . . . or turning the situation worse. Much worse. I had to understand what had happened so we could figure out what was going to happen next . . . and maybe regain control before it was too late.

I settled down to read the log files.

Reading log files is tedious. Mine were incredibly voluminous, recording every system activity no matter how trivial. Some asteroid miners turned the log level down, or even off, to save bandwidth, but I kept mine all the way up because you never knew when you might need them. In this case, I was glad that I had all this data, but it still took time to sort through it.

In addition to simply skimming the text with my eyes, I used a variety of scripts I'd developed over the years to spot anomalies and trends. Every once in a while I'd notice something that might or might not be indicative of something interesting, and sometimes I'd write a new script to investigate more closely.

My first breakthrough came when a script I'd written to look for unusual numeric values spotted an unexpectedly large data upload about half an hour before the unauthorized burn. It was a standard push of doppler correction factors for Earth-based communication, but those were usually only a couple of kilobytes and this one was several megabytes. A megabyte wasn't much by modern standards, but the package's control system had been designed when DSN charged by the kilobyte, and it generally ran much leaner than that.

I looked deeper. Although the log didn't record the content of the upload, just its size, it did include the sender's network address. And that sender wasn't the same as any of the other doppler correction pushes. I didn't recognize the address block at all.

I sent off a query to the DSN administrators, including a snippet of the log file, asking if they had any idea what might be going on. Then I kept looking.

There weren't any other uploads from that same address. But there were lots of log entries mentioning addresses in the same block. Not regular, and not very frequent, but there had been as many as several per day, going back weeks.

Each one was an attempted upload of some kind of data to one of the package's many subsystems that accepted it, and every one had been rejected due to lack of appropriate authorization. In other words, they hadn't presented the appropriate security certificate.

No, wait. Not all of them had been rejected. One of the attempted uploads from the suspect addresses had gone through. It had been a doppler correction push, of only a few bytes.

The big upload had followed that one by a few hours. And half an hour after that, my package had fired its main engine.

I was getting an itch between my shoulder blades.

I'd been hacked.

"It's an old bug," I explained to Amanda. "Actually two bugs. One is a security vulnerability that allows a doppler correction push without a valid security certificate under certain circumstances. The other is what's called a 'buffer overrun,' which is a class of bug that used to be a big problem back when this operating system was originally written. Basically, it lets you put more data into a buffer than the buffer has room for. If this happens, the data goes past the end of the buffer and overwrites executable code. Usually this just crashes the system, but if you know exactly what you're doing, instead of crashing it you can make it do whatever you want." I rubbed my eyes, which burned like crazy after eighteen hours of staring at screens. I'd lost count of the number of delivery drones that had brought me Hi-Kaf Kola. "Both of these bugs were fixed years ago in the real world, but the fixes weren't in the space-certified code branch so they didn't get included in our updates."

"Why the hell not?"

"I don't know. Not high enough priority, or not tested by the right people, or maybe they just slipped through the cracks. In any case, we're pushing a patch out even as we speak. I've notified our competitors, too, in case they have the same bugs in their code, and Raphael's heading up a search for any other such vulnerabilities."

Amanda sighed with relief. "So we're back on track, then?"

"No, we aren't." I ground my teeth. "We're patching the *other* packages, but not mine. When the hacker or hackers took control of the command processor, not only did they fire the engine, they changed the certificates. We're still getting log files and a few other data downloads, but we can't send commands. We're locked out of our own package."

"Hack them back! Break in the same way they did!"

"We thought of that already, and so did they. According to the logs, closing those loopholes was the first thing they did after changing the certificates. Looks like they patched a lot of other bugs, too. One of the things Raphael is looking for is any vulnerabilities they *don't* know about, but so far it looks like they were pretty thorough."

"Why . . . why would anyone *do* such a thing?"

"Why does anyone do anything, these days? Money."

"Are they holding the package hostage?"

"Doubt it. We haven't received a ransom demand, right?"

"Not to my knowledge."

"They wouldn't be subtle about it. And if they can get the whole package for themselves, even at black market rates that's a lot more than we'd pay in ransom. No, looking at the orbital track, my guess is that they plan a last-minute retro burn to bring the package down somewhere in the Bering Sea. The hackers could have a pickup boat waiting, bring down the package right next to it, and get away with the core before we or anyone else can make it to whatever isolated location they've chosen."

"That's not what I'm thinking they have in mind."

Bad as the situation was, the despair in her voice surprised me. "Oh?"

"They could boost instead of doing a retro burn. With that orbital track, they've got enough delta-V to hit Seattle. Or Vancouver. Or San Francisco."

My eye flicked to the clock display—two days, eight hours, twenty-six minutes—and the view from my San Francisco condo . . . condo-to-be, *if* I could turn this mess around. I swallowed hard.

"Whatever they have in mind, I promise I'll do what I can to stop them."

But when I awoke the next day, bleary-eyed and jittery after a two-hour nap that no amount of coffee and Kola could stave off any longer, I was no closer to fulfilling that promise than when I'd made it.

Raphael had come up dry. Even trolling the least savory communities hadn't come up with a vulnerability the hackers hadn't already closed. And almost all of the tricks I'd learned over my years as a sysadmin for resetting or rebooting a hacked system required physical access to the machine, or at least to its network or power connection, and this system was literally a million miles away. Though it was racing closer by the minute, and would be hitting the atmosphere in less than twenty-four hours.

There hadn't been a ransom demand, nor any threats from terrorist groups. Nor had the package changed course—it was still, apparently, headed for the mid-Pacific—but if I was right about the hackers' plan they wouldn't make their retro burn until the last possible minute.

I'd tried everything I could think of to regain control. I'd asked DSN to intercept or cut off the hackers' access to the package, but they couldn't—the hackers weren't going through them. All the security certificates and passwords had been changed. Even the low-level maintenance channel had been taken offline.

I'd been reduced to guessing passwords, and even that wasn't going well. I knew nothing whatsoever about the hackers, not even what language they spoke, which gave me no basis for my guesses.

Amanda wasn't even bothering me for updates anymore. I think she had given up on me. She was probably working directly with Orbital Control to take immediate action in case the asteroid was retargeted to come down on some city.

Not that there was much action they could take, other than trying to evacuate the target city. In theory, an incoming asteroid could be destroyed or diverted with a nuclear missile, but all international, national, and private efforts to actually develop the means to do so had foundered on issues of technology, treaties, liability, and especially cost. Despite the undeniable threat posed by potential asteroid impacts, whether natural or mined, nobody had ever ponied up the trillions of dollars it would take to build a system to prevent one.

I dragged myself from the filthy, sweaty couch where I'd fallen asleep and sat down at my screen. But the windows full of code and notes, and orbital tracks of doom, and hundreds and hundreds of unanswered messages stared right back . . . and I couldn't take it.

I got back up.

I paced around my office.

Then I punched the wall so hard I put my fist right through it.

Standing there looking at the hole, sucking on knuckles that tasted of blood and drywall, I couldn't help but think that some city, maybe even San Francisco, might wind up like that . . .

This was all my fault. If only I'd taken more care with my patches, done more research on critical security updates, kept a closer eye on my logs . . . maybe I could have prevented this.

I collapsed to the floor and bawled like a baby.

And then the doorbell rang.

It took a while for the sound to penetrate my sleep-deprived, miserable brain to the point that I could understand what it was and comprehend that it was coming from outside the apartment. I hadn't even thought of the outside world in almost forty-eight hours . . . even though my concerns were out in space or halfway across the planet, my *focus* had been on the screen ten inches in front of my nose.

The bell rang again, and this time I managed to recall what it really meant.

My cleaning lady. I'd told her to come back tomorrow. And that had been yesterday.

"I'm really sorry, Cheryl . . ." I began, but she didn't let me finish.

"You look like shit," she said, setting down her bucket of rags and bottles. "Are you in trouble?"

"I . . ." I took a deep breath, ready to put on a good face, but somehow the oxygen just made everything worse, fueling my fears and anxieties and making me realize just how hopeless the situation was. "Yes!" I sobbed. "Yes, I am in deep *deep* trouble." And I told her the whole thing, with tears running down my face and my nose filling up with snot.

"That's quite a story, son," she said, and handed me a tissue from the box in her bucket. "But crying never solved anything. Come on, let's see if we can fix this." She picked up the bucket, pushed past me, and headed up the stairs.

I wiped my eyes, blew my nose, and—not knowing what else to do—followed her.

She made me tell her everything—all the technical details, all my guesses and blind alleys and failures. She asked a lot of questions; they got sharper and sharper as we went on. Then she started suggesting solutions. Nothing I hadn't already tried, but still . . . "You know this stuff already?"

"This stuff in particular? Nah." She shook her head. "But I owned a contract structural engineering firm for twenty-seven years. You get pretty good at sussing out technical issues when there's a different problem every month."

"I had no idea you were anything other than a cleaning lady."

She snorted. "I've been fighting that attitude ever since college. No matter how good my grades, how strong my evaluations, no one would take me seriously as an engineer. Later, when I started facing ageism as well as sexism, I sold out to my employees and retired. Gimme that." She took the stylus from my hand and started poking at the screen herself. "But I got bored with retirement, so I started cleaning houses. I always liked to clean things. Made me feel good to bring order out of chaos, you know?"

"I wondered why your rates were so low . . ."

She grinned at me over her shoulder. "*That* was just because I thought you were cute. Most people pay market rates, but you remind me of my second husband." She turned back to the screen. "Here's what I'm looking for." She pulled up a block diagram of the system on the big screen, started peering at it, snapped her fingers behind her back at me. "Get me a cup of coffee. Black."

I went to the kitchenette and found a clean mug, then brought it back to my office and filled it with coffee. She took it with a grunt, swigged, made a face, and kept scrolling around the diagram as though looking for something she wasn't finding. "If the roof is cracking," she muttered, "check the foundation."

"Huh?"

"There has to be some kind of foundation to this whole thing. Some kind of technical underpinning that touches every system. It's not on this chart."

"There's the power system . . ." I took the stylus from her papery fingers—it felt weird—and called up another diagram.

"Is there some way you can use this to get around the hackers?"

I tapped the stylus against my teeth, staring bleary-eyed at the diagram and thinking like mad. There was the reactor, the voltage regulator, the . . . "Whoa."

She gave me another over-the-shoulder grin. "I like the sound of that."

I tapped a line on the chart. "The reactor has its own connection to the high-band dish." Almost every other subsystem communicated only via the control processor, but the reactor had its own comm link. "We used that during start-up, before the control processor was active."

"Is it still up?"

"I have no idea."

"Find out."

To answer that question I had to pull up old documentation I hadn't consulted in nearly five years. "Hey!" I said. "The reactor has its own OS."

"Is that good?"

"It might be . . ." I copied a basic status command from the documentation, pasted it into a terminal window, tapped *Transmit*, and held my breath.

Half a minute later a reply came back, a line of hexadecimal digits. I let out my breath in a huge inarticulate yelp of joy.

"What does that mean?"

"It means I can talk to the reactor." I put my stylus between my teeth, pulled up the keyboard, and muttered semi-intelligibly, "Now let's see if that does us any good . . ."

Two hours later, after frenzied conversations with other miners, a retired power system engineer, and some anonymous programmers on a sketchy message board, I had a potential solution . . . sort of. "The reactor's firmware is version 10," I told Cheryl, "which has a command for an emergency shutdown that doesn't require a password. The fool who coded it thought it was a safety improvement, but it was actually a massive potential denial-of-service attack. They closed that loophole in version 11 . . ."

"How does this help?" She looked nearly as fuzzy as I felt.

"Sorry, I'm getting distracted. An emergency shutdown on the reactor will force the command processor into safe mode. From there I can change the root password and get control back. But I have to get in before the hackers do, or they might beat me to it."

"Is there any way to cut off their access?"

I shook my head. "I've tried, but DSN can't cut them off. They aren't going through DSN." Suddenly something occurred to me that I hadn't considered before. "Which means they must have their own dish, or dishes. Let me check something."

I wrote a quick script to check the logs for all transmissions to or from the hackers' addresses. "Aha," I said, pointing at the screen. "They *do* have their own dish . . . and just *one*." The data showed that the hackers only communicated with the package during eight or nine hours out of every twenty-four. That window was fairly consistent in length, but had moved gradually from the middle of the night to morning to midday over the past week . . . corresponding with the package's movement through the sky as it drew closer to Earth. "Looks like it's somewhere in the Western Hemisphere."

"Smart boy," Cheryl said, nodding.

I compared time stamps in the log with the current wall clock time. "If we want to do our shutdown while they aren't looking . . . the earliest we can do it is two o'clock this afternoon." I pulled up an orbital track and blew out a breath. "Which gives us less than an hour to get in, change the passwords, and fire engines to divert the package back to the original target area. Any later than that and we won't have the delta-V to change course before atmosphere entry." I tapped my front teeth with my stylus. "Tight. Very tight. But if we try it any earlier than that, they'll certainly spot the shutdown and know what it means. Then it'll be a race to see who changes the password first."

"And if we lose . . ."

"Then they'll have hours to figure out what happened and patch the hole we used. We won't get another chance."

We looked at each other. "So we wait," she said.

The hours until two o'clock were not idle—I spent them preparing procedures, scripts, and fallback contingencies. I kept Amanda and the rest of Space Resources in the loop, though at Cheryl's request I kept her name out of it. "As far as the public is concerned, I'm just your house cleaner. Don't want to have my name in the papers."

"Even as the one who saved San Francisco?"

"Never liked that town anyway." But there was a twinkle in her eye as she said it.

Finally the hour came, and another fifteen minutes to make double-sure, as I hadn't been able to nail down the hacker dish's exact longitude. A full hour would have made me more comfortable, but I didn't have an hour to spare. "Okay," I said, "here goes." I tapped *Transmit* on a prepared command sequence.

Thirty seconds later the package dropped carrier. The reactor had gone offline, as planned, putting the whole package on emergency battery power. I blew out the breath I'd been holding. "So far, so good. Now we wait." The safe mode boot sequence would take anything from ninety to three hundred seconds, depending on exactly what the system had been doing when it shut down.

We waited. Somewhere out in space a computer was rebooting.

I could only hope that nothing went wrong.

And then the carrier indicator switched from red to green. "Now!" I said, even as I tapped *Transmit*.

A series of bytes flew from my computer to the Deep Space Network control center in Colorado Springs, from which it was immediately routed to Barstow, California, and transmitted to the package by one of an array of dishes, from which it spent about three seconds crossing empty space. The result of that command would take a further three seconds to return.

I bit my lips. I held my breath.

The words *Password changed* appeared on my screen, followed by a single hash mark.

"We're in!" I screamed, and grabbed Cheryl and kissed her.

"Ow," she replied.

"Sorry, sorry." I backed off. "I don't even like girls."

"Neither did my second husband, alas. Come on, there's work to do."

The first order of business was to change all the passwords and certificates. I had a command file prepared, so that didn't take long. Next I upgraded the reactor firmware to version 12 to close the barn door I'd entered by. That took a little longer, and by the time it was done, I had the first proper telemetry from the package in days. "I've got my baby back," I crooned.

The package's attitude and trajectory were perfect for atmospheric entry over Kamchatka. "They might be evil hackers," I said, "but they know their stuff." All I needed to do now was to redirect the package to Baja California, where a Space Resources pickup boat awaited. I double-checked the thrust sequence I'd previously prepared, tweaked it to account for the latest telemetry, and tapped *Transmit*.

Six seconds later the acknowledgement arrived as expected, and I sighed with relief.

Then came an alarm tone, and the message *Equipment failure*. "What?!" I cried.

"Don't panic," Cheryl chided me.

Cursing the Space Exploitation Licensing Board who had kept my baby confined to a warehouse for three damaging years—not for the first time—I checked system status, ran diagnostics, worked through troubleshooting checklists. "It's the goddamn main hydrazine valve again," I spat at last. "Damn thing sticks half the time even when it's at proper operating temperature, but with the reactor shut down . . ." I stopped dead.

"What's wrong?"

"The valve's frozen. I usually boost reactor power to unfreeze it . . ."

Appalled comprehension dawned on Cheryl's face. "But the reactor's shut down."

"And it takes six hours to bring it back up."

We didn't have six hours. We had at most two.

I put my head in my hands. "We were so close . . ."

"No time for regrets. Look at the orbital track."

The main engine had fired for several seconds before the valve had seized, diverting the package from the mid-Pacific toward Baja California.

Most of the way . . . but not far enough.

The new projected impact site was an ellipse that included most of Los Angeles. Even a near-miss would raise a tsunami that would wipe out half the city. And there wasn't time to evacuate.

The package would burn off most of its kinetic energy, along with the silicate crust, in the atmosphere, but the molybdenum core's impact energy at the surface would still be in the vicinity of a hundred kilotons.

About six Hiroshimas.

And there was no way to stop it—no asteroid defense system. Just like climate change and the oil crisis and the ocean die-off, everyone had seen the problem coming for years but no one had ever been willing to do anything about it. And that wasn't going to change in the next two hours.

"There has to be something you can do."

"There isn't. The package has only one main engine, and the valve is a single point of failure."

"Then use the other engines!"

I shook my head. I had never felt so tired in my life. "Not enough delta-V."

"Don't give up!" Cheryl's red, tired eyes were as intense as I'd ever seen them—and in the last however-many hours we'd spent together, I'd seen them pretty intense. "It's never too late! There's always another solution!"

"I'm sorry, Cheryl. This valve problem is pretty intractable. We've worked out a lot of tweaks to get past it, over the years, but they all take time."

"Time we don't have."

"Yeah." I looked at the dot moving along the orbital track. "Yeah."

The dot represented my package. My baby. My retirement fund. My San Francisco condo. My lack of bankruptcy.

Six Hiroshimas.

"I'm sorry, baby," I said.

"What?"

"Never mind." I picked up my stylus and programmed a thrust sequence. It was so simple and basic I didn't bother simulating it. I just tapped *Transmit*.

Three seconds later, somewhere out in space, a vernier thruster fired, and the nose of the lifting body angled up by about twenty degrees.

"That's it," I said, and slumped in my chair. My stylus clattered to the floor. I didn't bother picking it up.

"What have you done?"

"I've changed the package's attitude. When it hits the atmosphere, instead of entering it'll tumble and burn up over the Pacific."

Cheryl just looked at me, comprehension darkening her face. "I'm sorry," she said, and held out her arms.

I rested my head against her shoulder and let her pat my back while I cried.

After a while she handed me a tissue and I wiped my eyes. "Still," she said, "you did save Los Angeles. I imagine they'll be rather grateful for that."

"I imagine they will."

Together we watched the dot creep toward its rendezvous with the atmosphere.

It was going to be quite a show.

((•((•((• ((◎)) •))•))•))

**David D. Levine** is the author of novel *Arabella of Mars* (Tor 2016) and over fifty SF and fantasy stories. His story "Tk'Tk'Tk" won the Hugo, and he has been shortlisted for awards including the Hugo, Nebula, Campbell, and Sturgeon. Stories have appeared in *Asimov's, Analog, F&SF*, multiple Year's Best anthologies, and his award-winning collection *Space Magic*.

*Another potential for corporate involvement are space elevators and other stations above the Earth such as the setting for our next tale. When her partner passes out, a female astronaut must work to save both of their lives in . . .*

# TEN DAYS UP

## by Curtis C. Chen

The alert sounded right after lunchtime: high temperature warning, cargo pod two.

"Your shift, lady," Nick said. He pointed to the board showing our assigned extra-vehicular activity rotations.

I suited up with minimal complaining—that Nick could hear, anyway—and went EVA to inspect the cargo pod while he ran remote diagnostics. We left the cargo bay doors open to radiate heat while hunting down the malfunction.

I had just finished tracing a coolant intake pipe down the side of the nonstandard cargo pod, and started cursing whatever third-rate South Pacific factory was responsible for its manufacture, when I felt dust impacts ringing against the thin walls of the cargo bay and vibrating through my boots.

The micrometeoroids were nothing unusual—just the disintegrated remains of some orbiting space junk. They might have circled Earth for decades before hitting anything, and wouldn't have been an issue except for the work delay. You can't expose delicate components while tiny rocks are battering your equipment.

I didn't want to go back inside and then spend another hour cleaning and reprepping my spacesuit. Most dust storms passed in just a few minutes, and damage wasn't an issue—both my suit and the cargo pod were well-armored.

"I'm going to wait this out here," I told Nick.

"Do I offend?" he replied with a sniffle.

"The hell does that mean?"

The tiny video Nick in my heads-up display shook his head. "It's a euphemism for body odor." Then another sniffle.

"I just don't want to catch your stupid virus," I said.

"I am not sick."

I scoffed. Nick had nearly coughed up a lung at Clarke's Pub the night before we left Earth, and I'd watched him buy some loose pills from a young entrepreneur in the back of the bar. "Masking the symptoms doesn't mean you're not contagious. I swear to God, if I didn't need the hours, I would have ratted you out before they loaded the train."

"I'm not sick," Nick repeated. "And what's all this about hours, anyway? Doesn't your lawyer husband make enough scratch to support you and the rugrat?"

"It's not about money." I turned to look down, past the edge of the receiver hex under the pod, at the Earth below. "It's about qualification. Now shut up, I'm enjoying the view."

"Whatever."

The radio squawked. "Sierra Zero Nine, this is Gladstone Control. Got a weather update for you."

Nick coughed, then replied, "Gladstone, Sierra, roger that. We almost done with this rock concert?"

"No idea," the Control voice said. "I'm uplinking a solar activity alert. SOHO is predicting M-class flares within the hour."

I thumbed the transmit switch on my wrist controls. "Nick, let me see that alert."

He frowned. "What, you don't trust me to read a damn screen?"

"I just want to see for myself," I said. "I'm the one who gets fried out here, right?"

"Fine." He jabbed at his controls, missed, and looked confused. "That's weird."

"You okay, partner?"

"I'm fine!" His forehead glistened with sweat. When had that happened? "Sending uplink now."

My helmet display lit up with the space weather advisory. I checked the hazard ratings. There was major gamma radiation coming our way—more than my suit was rated for.

"Okay, I'm calling it." I snapped my tether back on the work line leading to the airlock. "Prep for ingress."

The micrometeoroids were still serenading us with white noise, so it took me a few seconds to realize that Nick hadn't acknowledged my last. I looked at his video and saw a limp arm floating above the console.

"Nick?" No response. "Dammit, Nick!"

I toggled my radio from our local frequency to the control band. "Gladstone, Sierra. My partner just passed out."

"Sierra, Gladstone. What do you mean, *passed out*?"

"I mean he's unconscious!" I demagnetized my boots and pulled myself out of the cargo bay. "I'm going to need an override procedure for the airlock."

"Stand by," the controller said.

I moved in silence until he returned a minute later.

"Sierra, Gladstone," the controller said, "we have an update on those solar flares. The one-hour estimate was inaccurate."

"Thank God," I said.

"You've only got twenty minutes."

I've always wanted to fly. Into the black, slip the surly bonds, all that buzz. And when Haley Wu became the first human being to set foot on the Red Planet—that was *it*. I've still got my "Comet Hits Mars" T-shirt from fifth grade, threadbare and nearly unreadable now, but I'll never throw it out.

The day of the Mars landing changed my life. I was ten years old and watching a *woman* make history fifteen light-minutes away. At that moment, I knew I could do anything I wanted. It didn't matter if I was a girl; there was no such thing as "just a girl" anymore. And I wanted to be an astronaut.

The punchline is, gender aside, I wasn't elite enough to break into the big leagues. That's the real deal: working for a national space agency, doing hard science, unraveling the mysteries of the universe. But there's no profit in pure research, and a very limited number of governments still put humans into space. These days it's all robots and telepresence, and not everybody likes math that much.

Of course, private firms are always looking for outer space technicians. Satellites and stations don't fix themselves—not yet, anyway—and there's plenty of room in Earth orbit for workers who can handle the high-wire act. They can't legally call us "astronauts," but who cares what's on the dox when you get to see the curve of the planet and the stars beyond?

I ended up on the space elevator—sorry, the "McCormick-Dewey ground-to-orbit lifting conduit." That's the official name. Everyone on the job just calls it "the EL." I work an on-call service rotation, riding up and down one train every month. It's not exactly rocket science, but ostechs get paid well, and like HR says, we have a fantastic view.

"I've tried three times, Gladstone," I said, doing my best to stay calm. "Airlock is jammed. Outer door is not, repeat, *not* opening. Please advise."

"Copy that, Sierra, stand by. Is your Ops still not responding?"

I leaned over the top edge of the crew compartment and banged my multitool against one of the raised observation bubbles. Nick's unconscious body had drifted out of view on the video feed, but there was no way he wouldn't hear that noise.

"Negative, Gladstone." I started to put away the multitool, then had a thought. "Hey, how about this? I can smash through the airlock window. I'll seal the breach with my helmet after I get inside."

"Negative, Sierra," the controller said. "You can't hold your breath that long."

"You don't know that. I need to minimize my radiation exposure." I raised the multitool with both hands.

"Sierra, be advised your airlock is *not* adequately shielded for M-flares."

I lowered the multitool. "Are we on speaker, Gladstone?" I didn't want the entire control room to hear what I wanted to say next.

After a pause, the controller said, "You're on headset, Sierra. What's up?"

"I've got less than twelve fucking minutes until a wave of lethal radiation destroys my immune system." I was starting to reconsider putting that countdown timer in my HUD. "You get me some fucking options or I'm smashing my way into the cabin. I can get a helmet onto Nick before he suffocates—"

"Okay, two things, Sierra," the controller said. "One, please watch your language. This conversation is being recorded for training purposes. Two, this is *not* your decision. Unless you completed a medical degree in the last week, you don't know that your Ops will survive the exposure."

I looked around the hexagonal ascender vehicle. "Then you tell me what the hell I can cannibalize from this train to make a radiation shield—" My eyes stopped on the open cargo bay doors. I had an idea.

"Did not copy your last. Say again, Sierra?"

"Stop calling me 'Sierra.' I had an aunt named Sierra. I hated her." I began moving toward the cargo bay. "My name's Kenna. And I need you to look up the cargo manifest for our pod number two."

Sometimes, when I tell people a round trip on the space elevator takes twenty days, they're shocked that the travel time is so long. But ten days up is a bargain.

An EL train moves at a hundred and sixty kilometers per hour. You launch from "Anchor," the company's equatorial deep-sea platform, right after breakfast. By lunchtime, you've passed low Earth orbit, where the old International Space Station used to fly. Your destination is the McCormick-Dewey Geostationary Orbital Transfer Station— "GEO"—orbiting more than thirty-six thousand kilometers above the planet.

That's a tenth of the way to the Moon. Yes, it takes a week and a half to get there, but the EL doesn't require hundred-meter-tall rockets, millions of kilograms of specialized fuel, or multiple integral calculus to operate. For the cost of two hundred hours of microwave-beamed electricity, you can buy your very own ascent to an altitude where Earth is the size of a basketball held at arm's length.

But we don't get many passengers on the EL. A ten-day-long elevator ride is not hugely interesting for anyone. Most space tourists opt for a Kármán-line rubber-stamp flight, or a private rocket to one of many low-Earth-orbit sightseeing platforms. GEO is not a vacation spot; it's where the commerce of the Solar System begins.

Most of the bays on an EL train carry cargo, which is why the bay walls don't protect against hazardous radiation. Clients shipping fragile or perishable goods must provide their own shielded cargo storage pods.

"Seriously? Your name is *Roger*?"

"Hey, you asked," the controller said. "My parents didn't know I would pick this career."

Confession: I'm terrible at small talk. Especially if you're a flight controller and your first name happens to be a voice procedure keyword.

"Okay, Roger—no, dammit, I can't do it," I said, already giggling. "Sorry. I'm just going to call you 'Gladstone.' Or would you prefer 'Control'?"

"I'm indifferent," Roger said flatly.

"I guess your parents weren't British, either."

"Polynesian."

I finally managed to stop laughing. "Okay. Any word on that manifest, Gladstone?"

"Still waiting to clear Legal."

"I'm a little short on time here." SOHO showed less than nine minutes before the first solar flare.

"We're doing our best." I heard a muffled voice—someone off-mic in the control room. "Wait one."

He clicked off the line. I stared at the sealed cargo pod in bay two: a long, white, rectangular shape, nearly as big as the cabin which Nick and I inhabited during transit. The only markings on the pod's surface were encrypted bar codes, but this was the cooling rig that had malfunctioned. If the cargo inside was sensitive enough to require precise temperature regulation, it probably needed radiation shielding, too.

Roger's voice came back. "Sorry, Kenna, we're still trying to contact the shipper."

"Look, Gladstone, I don't recognize this make, but if I pop the clamps, there should be a serial number on the bottom panel. Will that be enough for you to find an override procedure?"

"That's not the problem," Roger said. "Legal says we need the shipper's express permission to access their cargo in transit. It's a . . . contractual issue."

I counted to ten before responding. "Are you still recording this conversation? For training purposes?"

"Affirmative."

"Gladstone Control," I said, enunciating clearly, "this is Outer Space Technician Kenna Belecky, work code Sierra Zero Niner, requesting clarification: are you telling me that McCormick-Dewey International considers the contents of a *single* cargo pod to be more valuable than the *life* of one of their employees?"

Static hissed at me. "Sierra, Gladstone, please stand by."

I didn't wait. Whatever the company wanted to do to me after this—dismissal, lawsuit, blacklisting—I'd worry about that later. I wasn't going to die up here. I wasn't going to succumb to radiation poisoning before my son graduated high school. That wasn't going to happen.

I fired up my plasma cutter and carved into the pod's lockout panel.

The cargo turned out to be medical blister trays of little green pills, sealed in thin cardboard boxes and packed inside translucent polymer crates. All the text was in Hindi, which I'd never learned to read, but pharmaceuticals were definitely perishable and radiation-sensitive. Each shelf of crates had its own cooling apparatus. The walls of the pod were as thick as the width of my palm. Maybe not the best shielding ever, but still better than my spacesuit.

The clock in my helmet pinged. Seven minutes until the flares hit.

No time for finesse. Everything I threw out of the pod would burn up on reentry anyway. I ripped crates off the shelves nearest the door to make room for my spacesuited body, then turned down the power on my cutter and softened each metal shelf until I could bend it out of the way.

That was the most nerve-wracking part: I had to work quickly, but avoid burning through the cooling tubes lining the shelves. A leak would mean balls of thick eutectic gel floating everywhere and obscuring my vision. I finished with less than a minute to spare, unreeled my suit's auxiliary antenna, and stuck the far end to the outside of the pod, hoping the door seal wouldn't crush it completely.

My clock pinged again. I pulled the door shut, sealing myself in total darkness except for my HUDs. The SOHO feed showed radiation surging around Earth's magnetosphere. My medical monitors all glowed green. I was safe. Now I just had to wait out the solar activity— an hour, maybe two—and hope Ground Control had things sorted out by then.

I was actually dozing off when the entire pod lurched, banged against something, and started tumbling.

✵   ✵   ✵

"What the hell do you mean, *separated*?"

I was yelling. I couldn't help it. I was on the verge of completely losing it, and Roger was not helping.

"You broke the seal on the cargo pod," he said. "It was programmed to release docking clamps upon reaching its destination, and opening the door is a signal indicating end of transport."

"I didn't unlock the door," I said. "I *cut through* the damned lock, because you people wouldn't tell me—"

"I didn't say 'unlock,'" Roger snapped. "I said 'open.' You interrupted the circuit. If you had waited for us to clear Legal—"

"If I had waited, I'd be dead," I said.

The line was silent for a moment. "You know what? Let's just move on."

"Fine." I took a deep breath. "Now what?"

"We're tracking the pod." I heard keystrokes. "You're in freefall right now, with an orbital period of one hundred and thirteen minutes. The flares will subside before you complete half an orbit. I'll tell you when it's safe, and you can exit the pod. Then we need to maneuver you back to a safe docking trajectory."

"Sorry, Gladstone, I understood all the individual words there, but I'm not sure I got your meaning."

"You're going to crash into the EL ribbon and grab onto it," he said. "But first you need to burn off some velocity."

Maybe it didn't look like such a crazy plan on paper, or in Roger's computer simulations. But he could see the big picture. I was hurtling around the planet at seven kilometers per second. I wouldn't see the ribbon until I collided with it.

The tether connecting Anchor and GEO is called "the ribbon" because it's flat, so the ascender vehicle's wheels can press against it on either side, holding a train on the track by friction alone. The shape was dictated by efficiency. It takes no power for an EL train to stay clamped on, and the rolling action causes minimal wear and tear.

The carbon nanotube in the ribbon is stronger than diamond, but it's flexible—it has to bend, in order to survive the normal swaying that occurs as trains move up and down its length. Any change in altitude causes a change in angular momentum: a rising EL train pulls the ribbon westward; a descending train yanks the ribbon eastward. Coriolis effect. We compensate by scheduling only one transit at a time, limiting our vertical speed, and using thrusters on the train and at both endpoints—Anchor and GEO—to null out excessive motion.

Anchor had survived several tropical storms in the past, so I knew the EL could handle pretty severe vibrations. I just didn't know how the ribbon would react to a one-hundred-kilogram mass hitting it dead on. Or whether the one-hundred-kilogram mass would still be alive after impact.

"Coming up on final course correction," Roger said.

I had been clinging to the outside of the cargo pod for nineteen minutes. This was my ninth course correction.

The pod had started tumbling end over end when it fell off the train. I needed to stop that rotation before attempting any other maneuvers. After the solar flares passed, I had crawled outside, flattened myself against one end of the pod, and used the reaction control system in my spacesuit to counteract our spinning.

After stabilizing the pod, I lined up its long axis with our direction of travel, so the door was facing "forward." I had to work the RCS manually, with Roger directing me, and any mistake—too much or too little thrust, too long or too short a burst, not quite the right angle—was magnified as my orbit brought me closer and closer to the EL.

Roger was kind enough to not tell me when I had over- or undercorrected. He just gave me a new vector each time, in a calm and steady voice.

"I feel like I'm wasting a lot of reaction mass," I said. "RCS fuel's down by half."

"You're still good," Roger said. "You needed the pod's extra mass to dampen your acceleration. Hohmann transfers at this scale are finicky, and your suit thrusters aren't precision instruments."

"I am going to pretend I understood all that," I said, "and then just push whatever buttons you tell me."

Roger read off a thrust vector, and I programmed it into my suit jets. I had no idea how far off course I still was. My suit didn't include a radar unit. Even if I could find visual references, like known satellites or orbital stations, I couldn't accurately judge distances by eye. I was depending entirely on Roger's math to get me home.

"Good to go," I said.

"Thrust on my mark," he said, and counted me down from five.

When he said "zero," I started the program. I felt and heard the jets firing, a gentle pressure against my back and a soft hissing noise that came in pulses—a safety feature, to prevent an operator from building up too much velocity while spacewalking. I'd have to un-safe the RCS later.

*One thing at a time, Kenna.*

A few seconds later, the suit jets cut out, leaving me in silence again.

"Talk to me, Gladstone," I said.

"Stand by, Sierra."

I waited for Roger's ground computer to plot my new trajectory. I turned my head and saw the Earth below. Heavy cloud cover obscured land masses and oceans, so I couldn't tell which continent I was looking at. I turned my head the other way and saw an endless black void.

"You know why I was working this shift in the first place?" I heard myself saying. "Because I wanted the hours. I wanted to qualify for unaided spaceflight. I wanted to get promoted off the EL and into free transport.

"Which is stupid, right? Because I'd be working just as much, away from my family for just as long, and I wouldn't even have this view. I'd be stuck in a tin can for weeks on end, with nothing but black out the window. Why the hell do I want that? Why am I going to die for something so stupid?"

I stopped to keep myself from crying. I couldn't have a nervous breakdown now.

"You're not going to die," Roger said, the slightest tinge of anger coloring his voice. "And it's not stupid to want more—to want to fly."

A laugh choked its way out of my throat. "I guess I'm flying now."

"You're doing fine, Kenna," Roger said, in a softer voice. "We're going to get you home. Just don't wig out, okay?"

"Thanks for the sage advice."

"Okay, I've got the numbers back. You are on course, repeat, on course." Roger's voice brightened. "Intercept in twelve minutes, that's seven-two-zero seconds. Go for braking maneuver."

"Copy that," I said. "Setting up retro burn now."

The course corrections had been the easy part. I was definitely going to collide with the EL now. This next bit would determine whether I survived the impact.

An hour ago, when I had tested the flammability of the coolant gel inside the pitch-black cargo pod, the flaring brightness and positive sensor readouts in my HUD had been a flash of hope. Now, as I prepared to detonate my improvised explosive, I wondered if that fire would burn me to death before the crash into the EL could. I wasn't sure which one would be more unpleasant.

It was ironic, really: the same shoddy safety standards that had caused this cargo pod to fail, putting me outside the train at just the wrong time, were also going to be responsible for my rescue. Shipping companies aren't required to use non-flammable coolants unless they're for life support or installed within a certain distance of manned crew compartments. The blue gel flowing through cargo pod two's cooling tubes had burned clean and hot when I ignited it with my cutter. It had a ridiculously high combustion temperature, it needed an oxidizer to burn, and it wouldn't be half as efficient as my suit thrusters—but there was a lot more coolant gel in the pod than fuel left in my RCS.

Siphoning the coolant out of the tubes had been easy. Hacking together a complete retro rocket from parts never intended for propulsion service had been much trickier. First I cut a hole in the pod door, then removed one of my RCS thruster nozzles and welded it onto that opening, measuring and remeasuring to make sure everything was lined up precisely. Next I packed all the coolant into one plastic crate, cannibalized one of my spacesuit's oxygen tanks plus its valve assembly, rigged all that to the inside of the door nozzle, and attached my plasma cutter as an ignition charge.

If this didn't work, I wouldn't have enough air to make another orbit. My hands trembled while I rewired my backup hand radio into a remote detonator. I willed myself not to hyperventilate as I crawled to the far end of the pod.

*Don't wig out. Don't wig out. Don't wig out . . .*

"Gladstone, I am in position," I said at last. "How's my trajectory looking?"

"Looking good," Roger said. "Any time you're ready."

I placed my spacesuited self as flat as I could against the pod, clanking the back of my helmet against the hard surface. "I'd feel better about this if I had some padding."

"You've only got one rescue kit. You're going to need that for the ribbon." The retro burn would slow my approach speed from several thousand meters per second to only a few hundred meters per second, which was still suicidal, but we were hoping that my rescue gear would absorb most of that remaining velocity.

"If this explosion doesn't kill me first."

"It's a controlled blast," Roger said. "It's going to work. Trust me, I did the math."

I gritted my teeth. "Retro burn in three, two, one, zero."

Before getting this job on the EL, I had spent six months in the asteroid belt between Mars and Jupiter, running exploratory demolitions for mining concerns. I'd blown up a lot of big rocks, but I was never on the ground during a blast. Even in training, we used remotes. The closest I ever got to an explosion was when Travis wanted to see what would happen if he microwaved one of his air scooter's spent battery packs.

I didn't expect the burn to be so *loud*. Outer space is hard vacuum, dead quiet. When my cutter ignited the mixture of coolant gel and pure oxygen, it was a firebomb going off inside a sealed metal box with one tiny opening. The blast only had one place to go—out through the nozzle in the door—and the kinetic energy of that plume of flame kicked back against the pod's orbital velocity. The coolant burned unevenly, sputtering in an irregular ska-jazz rhythm and rattling the pod's exterior hull against the back of my helmet. I hoped my welds would hold.

"This is really how we used to get into space?" I asked nobody in particular. "Strap yourself to a tube full of explosives, and then set it on fire?"

"Hey, rockets got us to the Moon," Roger said. The radio sounded fuzzy over the noise.

"The Moon's a dump," I said. "Total junkyard. Even the museum's crap."

"I'd just like to see it with my own eyes, you know? Stand in Armstrong's footprints, cover the Earth with my thumb."

"Oh God, you're a tourist," I groaned. "Trust me. Luna's not worth it. You want to see a real moon, go to Titan."

"Someday," Roger said. "You're at twenty-five hundred mips and—"

Something inside the pod exploded with a muffled *boom*, smacking the hull backward into my helmet. I spat out a long string of curses, then waited, expecting Roger to comment on my unladylike language. Nothing came.

"Gladstone, what's my delta-vee? Gladstone, do you read?" I shouted into the radio. The noise behind my skull seemed louder, as if combustion inside the pod had suddenly accelerated.

Another stream of expletives escaped my lips as the Earth crept up into my field of view.

I knew what the explosion had been. It was my cutter, bursting open when the surrounding heat passed the melting point of its exterior casing. We had expected that, and it was a good thing. A hotter burn meant I would slow down even more. The bad news: the second blast must have deformed the exhaust nozzle, and now the pod was no longer thrusting true.

It was pushing me down toward Earth.

"Gladstone, I am tilting forward! I need a reverse vector!" The hazy curve of the planet continued moving upward. "Gladstone, please respond!"

An alert popped up in my helmet display: EXTERIOR TEMPERATURE WARNING. The pod wasn't insulated against this much direct heat. The fuel inside my plasma cutter must have acted as an accelerant—

"Plasma!" I said out loud, followed by more cursing.

The fuel in my cutter was designed to combust in a very specific way. My jerry-rigged rocket was no longer just burning; it was now expelling a superheated, high-velocity stream of ionized particles. The entire metal exterior of the cargo pod had become a giant electromagnet, interfering with radio communications.

I wouldn't be talking to Roger again until my rotgut rocket fuel ran out. If I wanted to stop this new rotation from pushing me off course, I had to do it myself.

*Think, dammit, think!* The Earth grew bigger, a giant ball coming up to meet me. That image triggered a thought. *Ball. Sphere. Rotating!*

The planet had been just out of view earlier, when the pod-rocket was braking directly opposite its own orbital velocity. My helmet was still pressed against the pod, so to get back on course, all I had to do was get Earth down out of my view. I didn't need to know the numbers; I could use the giant visual reference below me.

*Positive pitch. Upward rotation along lateral transverse axis.* I remembered my flight school terminology. *You always wanted to be a pilot, right? Now's your chance. FLY.*

I switched my wrist controls over to the forward-facing suit thrusters, vectored them forty-five degrees down, and pulsed them once. The Earth began setting, barely fast enough to see, then stopped as the pod-rocket continued pushing. I pulsed my jets again and again, watching each time to make sure I didn't overcompensate.

"Nice and easy, Kenna," I muttered. What was it Travis always said, when he was running circles around me in one of his video games? *Small moves, Mom.*

It wasn't easy. The rocket was still firing unevenly, so I had to nudge myself backward a little bit at a time, hoping the fuel in my forward RCS wouldn't run out.

More alerts popped up in my HUD. The pod exterior temperature had reached one hundred twenty-five percent of my suit's rated tolerance. My pulse was pushing one eighty. I took a moment to silence all the alarms so I could concentrate on maneuvering. My fingertips felt wet inside my gloves; I was sweating faster than the material could wick away the moisture.

I watched the curve of the Earth slide up, down, and just enough from side to side to make me nervous. I could deal with one axis of rotation and a little wobble, but too much more and I wouldn't be able to eyeball it.

And so I passed the longest twenty-three seconds of my life, tapping my thruster controls while a plasma fire roared behind me and the Earth bobbed up and down in front of me. The view might have been beautiful. I didn't notice.

All I could think was, *I will never again tell my son he plays too many video games.*

When the burn stopped, it was so abrupt—from noise to silence, without any sputtering or fading—and I was so focused that it took me a second to realize what had happened. Then the radio came back, and I nearly wept.

"—are you there?" Roger's voice was tight and flat, as if he'd been repeating himself over and over. "Kenna, this is Gladstone, please respond—"

"I'm here!" I said, blinking away tears. "I'm still here."

I heard him exhale. "We lost you for a minute," he said. "What happened?"

I told him about the plasma fire, the EM interference, and my seat-of-the-pants maneuvering against the misfiring rocket. "Am I still on course?" I asked.

"Affirmative," Roger said after a long pause.

"Would you tell me if I wasn't?"

"Absolutely," he said, too quickly this time.

I decided I didn't really want to know. "Okay. I'm moving to the other end of the pod now."

"Copy that."

I stood up on the cargo pod, walked across its length, and leaned over the door to inspect my rocket nozzle. Amazingly, despite a large crack down one side and charring all around, the bell was still intact. I took a picture and resolved to only buy space equipment from that manufacturer for as long as I lived.

I pulled myself upright again and bent my knees. Then I demagnetized my boots and kicked off as hard as I could, jettisoning my used pod-rocket stage.

I had one final maneuver left. Only one more thing that could possibly go wrong—or so I thought.

"You're sure the train's holding position?" I asked Roger.

"We issued the remote command as soon as your pod separated," he said. "It took some distance for the emergency brakes to decelerate the vehicle to a complete stop, but it shouldn't be more than a few kilometers above where you're going to hit the ribbon. Within range of your suit jets, in any case. Your Ops must still be unconscious; he hasn't responded to any radio hails."

"And what happens if he wakes up and decides he needs to continue the ascent?"

"We overrode the drive controls and added a password lock. The vehicle's not going anywhere until you get back aboard."

"How'd you clear *that* with Legal?"

There was a pause. "We . . . haven't exactly told them what we're doing. It'll take them a couple of hours to figure it out, and longer than that to get a security team out here."

I felt a lump in my throat. "Thank you, Roger."

"Don't thank me yet," he said. "Let's see if this crazy stunt works first. Two hundred seconds."

I cleared my throat. "Thank you for trying."

"Hey," Roger said, "I've been on this control desk for four years. You're the first ostech who's ever asked me what my name is. That's something."

"My husband's a lawyer," I said. "Whatever the company does to you and your team after this, he'll represent you."

"Aw, hell, you're married?" Roger said. "*Now* you tell me."

I smiled. "Yeah, I'm a wrinkled old lady. Did I not mention that?"

Roger chuckled. "You got kids?"

"We have a son." I saw Travis' face in my mind: smiling, crying, sleeping.

"Well, you'll have one heck of a bedtime story to tell him in a couple weeks," Roger said.

"Yeah." I swallowed the lump in my throat. "Listen, if I don't make it, I want you to tell my family something."

"Your signal's breaking up, Kenna," Roger said.

"I said, if I don't make it, I want you to give a message to my family."

"Do not copy, Kenna," Roger said, "and if you keep talking that way, I'm not going to listen."

I laughed in spite of myself. "Don't be a dick, Gladstone."

"No, ma'am, I'm not feeling sick at all," he said. "One hundred seconds to target. Are you ready?"

I checked, double-checked, and triple-checked my equipment. My right glove held a coiled work cable with my multitool tied to one end and the other end secured around my waist. My left glove rested on my suit's rescue paddle. "Good to go."

"Target in thirty seconds," Roger said, his voice cool and calm again. "Prepare for capture on your starboard, repeat, starboard side."

"Copy that," I said. "Thirty seconds, starboard side." Timing was going to be everything here. I could barely see the silver line that was the EL ribbon, twinkling ahead of me like a single strand of a spider's web.

Roger counted me down from fifteen.

When he reached "zero," I swung my right arm as hard as I could and threw out the cable. At the same time, I squeezed the rescue paddle to deploy my suit's crash gear. A series of airbags inflated all around me, and tiny reservoirs at the edges of my backpack burst open and sprayed quick-setting polyfoam to fill the gaps between the airbags.

Everything after that was, as they say, in Sir Isaac Newton's hands.

The EL was a momentary grey blur as I flew past. But I had flung my cable across to the far side of the ribbon, and when those perpendicular lines collided, the weights on either side of the work cable—my spacesuited self and my heavy multitool—swung out of their forward trajectories and into rapidly decaying orbits around the ribbon.

I had played out the entire length of my work cable, but my relative speed was so great that the whole cable wrapped around the ribbon in a matter of seconds. I didn't even have time to become nauseated. I felt three things in rapid succession: a gentle tug when the cable first hit the ribbon; a sharp lurch when the multitool ballast smacked into the ribbon, anchoring that end; and a skull-jarring crash when I collided with the ribbon, transferring all my velocity into it.

My ears were still ringing when I regained my senses, and it took me a moment to orient myself. All but two of my airbags had burst, and most of the polyfoam had been smashed into a white haze all around me. I waved away the debris until I could look up and down the EL.

It's mind-boggling to witness something that big actually *moving*. I saw waves traveling along the ribbon, moving downward and making the carbon nanotube shimmer in the lower atmosphere, then racing upward to shake the stopped train. I wondered if that would finally wake up Nick. I also wondered how many alarms were going off in all the various EL control centers right now.

*Yeah*, I thought, watching the ripples propagate and interfere with each other, *that's definitely coming out of your paycheck.*

I popped my ears and realized the buzzing noise I'd been hearing was actually Roger talking to me.

"Sierra, Gladstone, please respond, over." He sounded more than a little frantic. "Sierra, this is Gladstone, come in, over. Dammit!"

"I'm here!" I said, hardly believing it. "Gladstone, Sierra, I am going to get you an ancient bottle of single malt and the best legal defense in the Solar System!"

"That's great," Roger said. I heard shuffling noises in the background. "Listen, we've got some visitors here, but you are go for ascent. If you need help, ask your favorite aunt. I repeat, if you need help—"

The line went dead. I checked to make sure my suit radio was working, but I suspected I knew what had happened.

It hadn't taken Legal quite as long as Roger had hoped to get wise to his shenanigans, and they'd sent a team to shut down Gladstone Control. Security wasn't going to listen to a bunch of flight engineers explain why they needed to crash a human being into the EL. They were going to lock down that tiny tracking station in the wilds of Oregon and make sure they didn't have some kind of terrorist cell going on there.

Six different disasters in one day. I briefly wondered if that was some kind of record, then got back to work.

As my un-safed RCS thrusters pushed me upward, rattling my teeth, I wondered what Roger had meant by asking my favorite aunt for help.

It took me the better part of an hour to fly back up the ribbon to the train. My retro burn had cost me a lot of altitude. Then it took another fifteen minutes to climb around the power receiver panels to the crew compartment.

Miraculously, Nick was awake by then, and he opened the airlock for me. Stale recycled air had never smelled so sweet.

A moaning sound greeted me when I pulled off my helmet inside the cabin. Nick was slumped over the control station, head against his arms. I tapped him on the shoulder. He jerked upright, sending drops of sweat flying backward off his pale skin. His eyes were bloodshot but alert.

"Where the hell you been?" he slurred. "Shit. You get sick, too?"

"What? No." I glanced at a nearby mirror and saw that perspiration had plastered my hair to my head in an unflattering mess. "Oh, that. Funny story."

"Could use a laugh," he grumbled. An alert sounded, and he smacked the console to silence it. "Shut up."

"You know that was the radio, right?" I prepared to wrestle him down if he became delirious.

"Yeah, yeah, it's Ground Control again." Nick waved at the sea of blinking red lights on the neighboring drive station. "Computer called emergency stop while we were both out. Oh, we also lost pod two. You know anything about that?"

"Later," I said. "What's the problem with drive control?"

"Locked out!" Nick said. "Ground says they're locked out too, and we need to do a local override. But stupid computer won't accept my password."

*Thank you, Roger.* "Let me take a look."

"Whatever." Nick put his head down and resumed moaning.

I pulled myself over to the drive station. Our instruments still showed some sway in the ribbon, but within normal tolerances. GEO was thrusting upward and had already dampened most of the vibration from my impact. Status reports showed only minor equipment damage at both ends. Of course, someone would need to go EVA to remove the mess of cable I'd left behind, and probably rebond that section of the ribbon. Later.

I brought up the drive controls and smiled. The computer wanted the password to login a user named NEEDHELP.

I typed in SIERRA. That didn't work. AUNTSIERRA did.

The console indicators changed from red to green, and our drive controls came back online with a flurry of electronic chimes.

*Thank you, Roger.*

"What?" Nick raised his head and squinted at the console. "The fuck? How'd you do that?"

I set the controls to resume our ascent. The cabin shuddered as we began moving again. "It's a long story."

Nick wheezed. "We've got a few days to kill."

He pointed at the clock above his head, which showed our remaining mission time: five days, eleven hours, and forty-two minutes.

Five days up, then ten days down. Another two weeks of routine maintenance duty.

That wasn't long at all, compared to the rest of my life.

"Sure," I said, grinning like an idiot. "Just let me get out of this stinking spacesuit first."

((·((·((· 🔆 ·))·))·))

**Curtis C. Chen** writes speculative fiction, puzzle games, and freelance non-fiction near Portland, Oregon. His short fiction has appeared in *Daily Science Fiction*, *Leading Edge* magazine, and *SNAFU: An Anthology of Military Horror*. He is a graduate of the Clarion West and Viable Paradise writers' workshops. Curtis is not an aardvark. His debut novel, *Waypoint Kangaroo*, is forthcoming Summer 2016 from Thomas Dunne Books.

For a complete bibliography, visit his Web site: *www.curtiscchen.com/stories*.

*In the following story, Grand Master James Gunn takes us on a journey where no one has gone before, at least in reality, as a team of travelers pass through a wormhole, going down . . .*

# THE RABBIT HOLE

## by James Gunn

"Curiouser and curiouser!" cried Alice.
—Lewis Carroll

They existed inside an explosion of light. It filled their waking moments and their dreams. They heard it as a background of white noise; they smelled it underlying a stench of human and machine effluvia; they felt it like the warp of their world; they ate it with their breakfast cereal.

The external viewscreens were blank. They had been turned off; nobody remembered who had done it or when. But they knew the glare was out there just beyond the walls of the ship. It was the only thing they knew for certain since they had entered the wormhole.

"No one knows what happens inside a wormhole," Adrian Mast said, turning in the swivel chair that faced the useless controls.

"Except us," Frances Farmstead replied.

They were inside the control room of the spaceship they had helped build. Although there was nothing to control, they found themselves meeting there as if by prearrangement. But that was impossible.

"If we really knew what was happening," Adrian said. "Or remembered from one encounter to the next."

"We should make notes."

"I've tried that," Adrian said. He wrote a note to himself on a pad of paper. He showed it to Frances. It read: *make notes*. "But I've never come across any record of anything I've written, on the computer or by hand."

"That's strange," Frances said, leaning back. "I'll have to try it."

"It's as if there is no before and after," Adrian said.

"It's a mystery," Frances said. She was seated in the swivel chair next to him. She was wearing loose-fitting khaki coveralls. Moments earlier, he thought, she had been wearing a kind of body stocking. No, that had been Jessica, and it wasn't moments earlier. It had been before they entered the wormhole.

"We've got to solve it like a mystery," Frances said. "Like Ellery Queen or Nero Wolfe. Putting together clues."

"There's something wrong with that," Adrian said, "but I can't remember what. Maybe that's the trouble. We can't remember."

"We should make notes," Frances said.

"I'll try that," Adrian said. "What's the last thing you remember?"

"We had been accelerating for a long time, and then—and then—"

The crew had built the ship from alien plans. That was strange enough, but what was stranger was that the plans had been decoded from a message communicated in energetic cosmic rays picked up by SETI, decoded by a computer genius, and then smuggled to an incurious world disguised as a UFO cult book titled *Gift from the Stars*. Adrian had discovered it on a remainder table and recognized that the designs might work, and Frances had helped him track down the author, Peter Cavendish, only to find that he was in a mental institution. Just because he was psychotic, however, didn't mean that all his ideas were crazy. The ultimate bureaucrat, William Makepeace, took Cavendish's notions seriously, and, even though Makepeace tried to stop them, Adrian and Frances released the information to the world.

It didn't work out the way Makepeace feared, but it didn't work out the way Adrian and Frances had hoped, either. Rather than building a spaceship, the world used the aliens' antimatter collection process and engine designs to solve the energy problems of Earth, and once those were taken care of, most other human problems seemed to melt away. With Earth becoming utopia, nobody wanted to go into space any more, except for a few troublemakers. The Energy Board took ten years to see the wisdom of letting the malcontents depart, and the malcontents took five years more to build the ship. Then, when they started the engines, the ship began a headlong plunge into space controlled by a Trojan-horse program within the computer, inserted perhaps by aliens, certainly by Peter Cavendish. But Cavendish wasn't with them. He had been torn between his need for answers to the questions that once had driven him over the edge and the fear that the test flight would fail—or that it might succeed. In that paralysis of choice, he had stayed behind.

The immediate question was whether they should try to reprogram the computer to take back control of the ship. But where else would they go? If they continued toward an alien-chosen destination they might find the answers to the other questions that had plagued them from the beginning: Why had the aliens sent the spaceship designs? What did they want from humans? What would humans find at the end of their journey, and what would happen when they arrived? If they arrived.

The ship had worked. Unlike most human designs, even though fallible humans had put the ship together, often from salvage, it worked the way machines and creatures in space had to work if they were to survive, that is, without a glitch. That nothing malfunctioned was due, as well, to Adrian's obsession with perfection, with his insistence on checking and rechecking everything. The ship had accelerated at one gravity past the orbits of Mars, of Jupiter, of Saturn, of Uranus, of Neptune, and finally of Pluto, and they had left the Solar System.

That took thirteen days. Moving beyond the Oort cloud consumed another four hundred days. After a hundred days more of plunging into the abyss—a year and a half of living in enforced proximity to 200 other people, smelling their body odors, hearing their familiar anecdotes, speech patterns, and throat clearings, and eating recycled food—their tempers shortened and their anxieties grew. By that time Jessica Buhler had isolated Cavendish's program, and they had to fight the temptation to push the button that would put the ship back under their control and maybe cut them off forever from what had started them on this journey.

"I remember all that," Adrian said, rubbing his temples. "But what happened then?"

Behind them the Sun had dwindled into just another star, and although the stars were everywhere all the time, they could not escape the feeling of being far from everything that mattered. Then the blankness of space opened a blazing eye and glared at them.

"It was like a white hole," Frances said, "suddenly in front of us . . ."

Conflicting gravities tugged at their bodies, as if all their loose parts wanted to go in different directions, as if their internal organs were changing places. . . . The glare was blinding. Jessica reached out with a hand that seemed to know what it was doing and slapped off the external viewscreens. The relative darkness was blessed, but the wrenchings continued. If time had existed, the sensations would have seemed to go on forever, but then the twistings and displacements stopped as if they had never been.

The odor of fear filled the control room.

"I think we're in a wormhole," Adrian said, as if that explained everything.

"What's that?" Frances asked. She was seated in one of the chairs in front of a panel that had been useless for control since the ship began moving. Now its readouts were gyrating wildly.

"Some kind of distortion in space. Physicists have said they could exist, in theory, but nobody has ever seen one."

"What good is a wormhole?" Frances asked.

"It's supposed to take us somewhere else," Adrian said. "We entered one mouth; presumably there's another somewhere and the two are connected through hyperspace. Physicists thought they would look like black holes but without horizons."

"It looks more like a white hole," Frances said.

"Some scientists speculated that the relative motion of the wormhole mouths would boost the energy of the cosmic microwave background into visible light and create a kind of intense glare."

"Too bad they'll never know they were right," Jessica said. She was standing between Adrian and Frances with a hand on the back of each chair.

"These things, these wormholes, they're everywhere?" Frances said.

Adrian shook his head. "Natural wormholes ought to be small and ephemeral. This one was created."

"Why would somebody create a wormhole?" Frances asked. She didn't like anything that she couldn't connect with something that she had read or seen.

"To get from one part of the universe to another in a hurry. It may explain why Peter got a message in energetic cosmic rays. Sending a message over interstellar distances would have taken centuries, or millennia if the distances were really great. But if they were emitted from the end of the wormhole near the Solar System, the message would have arrived in less than a year. And whoever is at the other end could have used it to know we were here, maybe even keep track of us."

"Surely they couldn't see anything from here," Jessica said. "Even the sun looked like just another star."

"They might be able to pick up energy transmissions, radio, television, " Adrian said. "Maybe that's why they created it in the first place—because we started broadcasting back in the 1920s."

"This is so weird," Frances said. "Who could do something like this?"

"We couldn't," Adrian said. "Creatures far beyond our technical capabilities, maybe. What a physicist named Kip Thorne called 'an infinitely advanced civilization.' Damn! There's no 'maybe' about it. They did it, so they could do it."

"You said wormholes ought to be ephemeral," Jessica said. "This one seems to be persisting."

"So they not only had to create it," Adrian said, "they had to keep it from collapsing. Scientists think that would take something they call 'exotic matter,' something with negative average energy density, one of whose characteristics would be that it would push the wormhole walls apart rather than letting them collapse."

"Like antigravity," Jessica said.

"So what does it all mean?" Frances asked.

"We're inside something that doesn't belong to our reality," Jessica, "and it is going to take us, if we're lucky, somewhere so far from Earth and our sun that we won't even be able to identify them in the night sky."

"And if we're not lucky?" Frances asked.

"We could spend our lives in here," Jessica said, "or have it collapse with us inside it, which might strand us in hyperspace, if we survived. I think that would be pretty bad."

"That's about it," Adrian said absently. He was looking at a pad of paper.

"What's wrong?" Frances asked. "Besides being lost."

Adrian showed them the pad. On it someone had written: *make notes.*

"Seems like a good idea," Frances said.

"Sure," Adrian said. "But I didn't write it. That is, I don't remember writing it. I remember that I will write it." He looked confused.

"I remember that," Frances said. Her voice was excited. "But it won't happen—"

"What's going on?" Jessica asked.

Adrian drew a square around the words on his note pad and then constructed a square on each side. "Space is different inside a wormhole. Maybe time is, too. Space and time are part of the same continuum. We may be in for some strange effects. At some point, for instance, I'm going to say 'It's as if there is no before and after.' But that's wrong. The before may come after the after."

"Like remembering what hasn't happened yet?" Frances said as if she were making a joke.

"And maybe not remembering what has already happened," Jessica said.

"'It's a poor sort of memory,'" Frances said, "'that only works backward.'"

"Why does it sound like you're quoting from something?" Jessica asked. "Aside from the fact that you're always quoting from something."

"It's from *Alice in Wonderland*," Frances said. "Or rather from the sequel, *Through the Looking Glass*, and the reason it comes to mind is that, like Alice, we've fallen into a rabbit hole, and in Wonderland everything is topsy-turvy."

"I don't think we're going to find any answers in children's stories," Jessica said.

"I've always found Frances's fictional precedents helpful," Adrian said.

"The point is," Frances said, "that we're going to experience something that is likely to make us crazy unless we have something to cling to."

"Like what?" Jessica asked skeptically.

"When Alice fell down the rabbit hole, she encountered talking rabbits and caterpillars that smoked and cats that disappeared and who knows what all. Maybe we're going to run into the same sorts of things. If we can treat it like a kind of wonderland experience, meeting the strange but not surrendering to it, we can cope."

A patter of feet came from beyond the hatchway that led to the rest of the ship. Frances and Jessica looked at each other and then at Adrian.

"That sounded like children," Jessica said.

"'Curiouser and curiouser,'" Frances said.

In the middle of the night, Adrian heard a rustling sound and something that sounded like a sigh. He pushed the switch beside his bunk, and overhead light flooded the tiny room. Jessica was standing just inside the open door, one arm out of the body stocking that was all she wore and the other arm halfway removed.

"What's going on?" Adrian asked, sitting up so suddenly the room spun around him.

"I didn't want to wake you," Jessica said.

"I mean, what are you doing in my room?"

Jessica looked around, as if the question that Adrian had asked was being processed. "I don't know. It seemed—natural," she said. "But now I can't remember why."

Adrian looked at the portions of Jessica's body that had been revealed: the smoothness of her skin and the curvature of what seemed, under most circumstances, athletic and slender. It was as if he was seeing her for the first time as a woman instead of a member of the crew.

"It's this damned wormhole," Jessica said, shrugging her arms back into the body stocking and closing the top with one stroke of her right hand.

But it wasn't the same as it had been before. Maybe it was because he had no imagination, Adrian thought, or maybe because his imagination was focused on distant goals, but now that he had seen Jessica as a woman it was difficult to see her as anything else. But he would, he knew; the wormhole would see to that.

"What's going on in here?" another voice asked from the doorway. It was Frances, solid and square in her pajamas, almost filling the space. The room was so small that she was standing next to Jessica.

"That's hard to say," Adrian replied.

Frances looked from Adrian to Jessica and back again. "Doesn't look that difficult to me. If this were a romantic film, the next scene would show lovers springing apart guiltily, or waking up together. If this were a suspense film, they would be plotting some kind of caper. If it were a mystery, one would be planning to kill the other."

"It's a farce," Adrian said.

"People wandering into each other's rooms without any reason and finding themselves in embarrassing circumstances," Jessica said.

None of this eased Frances's air of suspicion. "Oh, there's a reason. There's always a reason."

"You forget our wormhole inversions," Adrian said. He had his feet planted firmly on the deck.

"Whatever the problems we're having with cause and effect," Frances said, "a midnight meeting doesn't happen by accident." She frowned at Jessica as if they were in a contest and Jessica had broken the rules.

"I admit it looks suspicious," Jessica said, "but I wasn't trying to seduce Adrian."

Adrian flinched. The deck didn't seem so firm.

"It just seemed natural," Jessica said.

"Of course it did," Frances said.

"You know what I mean. Not something that was planned. God knows we can't do that inside this damned hole. Just something that seemed as if it had happened before."

"I'm not surprised," Frances said.

"If it did," Jessica said.

"And it didn't," Adrian said.

"You keep out of this," Frances and Jessica said almost simultaneously.

Adrian looked from one to the other. Frances started laughing. "You look like Cary Grant in *The Awful Truth*." Then her expression sobered. "We really need to come to an understanding."

"I know," Jessica said. "If we get out of this place, we're going to need children."

"They don't have to be his," Frances said. "There's lots of other men."

"We can't afford to waste any genetic material," Jessica said. "Chances are we'll never get back. Or if we get back, it may be in the remote past or the distant future. We may be all that's left of the human species. All of space-going humanity anyway."

"That's as may be," Frances says. "But what's to say I couldn't have children."

"No reason you couldn't," Jessica said. She put her arm around Frances's shoulder. "We've got doctors, and we downloaded to our computers all the medical information available. Your uterus might not be up to the pregnancy bit, but your ova may well be harvestable."

"Thanks," Frances said. "But there's the emotion part."

Jessica hugged Frances harder. "We're going to have to get over that part. There's too much at stake."

Frances smiled and put her hand over Jessica's. "That's settled then. I'm glad we had this talk."

Jessica smiled back. "Me, too. I just wish we could remember it later."

Adrian looked from one to the other. "Wait a minute! What's going on here?"

"None of your business," Jessica and Frances said together.

"Come on, now," Adrian said, feeling confused and maybe frightened. "You're disposing of me like a prize cow—"

"Bull," Frances said.

"And you say it's none of my business?"

Frances reached over and patted Adrian's hand. "Don't worry! It will all work out. You take care of getting us out of here. We'll take care of the social arrangements."

Adrian looked from one woman to the other. "How are we going to get out of here?"

"You'll figure something out," Jessica said.

From outside the tiny captain's quarters came the sound of children's voices raised in some kind of game, but when Frances turned and Adrian reached the door, the corridor outside was empty.

When Adrian entered the control room, someone was seated in the chair that faced the prime computer station. That wasn't unusual—or at least it wouldn't have been unusual if the usual had existed as a comparison. What was unusual was that the head was familiar, and it should have been back in Earth orbit or, by now, back on Earth. But everything operated by different rules inside the wormhole, and the key to sanity was not trying to apply rules appropriate to normal existence. The person wasn't computing; it seemed to be reading a book.

"Peter," Adrian said. "What are you doing here?"

The chair turned. The person was Cavendish without a doubt, looking as real as Adrian, as solid as Adrian. "Same thing you're doing," Cavendish said. "Trying to find a way out of here."

"We left you back in Earth orbit," Adrian said reasonably.

"I remember that, too," Cavendish said. "Yet here I am."

"I don't think so," Adrian said. "I think you're some kind of illusion." He took a step toward Cavendish as if to confirm the existence of the other man by touching his shoulder.

"I wouldn't do that," Cavendish said.

"Why not?"

"If your hand passes through me, you're going to think your mind is going. If you find out I'm solid, that I'm really here, you're going to question your grasp on reality."

"You're the one who's supposed to be paranoid."

"And I'm not worried?" Cavendish shrugged. "Maybe that means I'm not really here. Or that what's here isn't really me."

Adrian went to the captain's chair, sat down, and swung around to face Cavendish. "Why are you here?"

"Things haven't worked out, have they?"

"That depends on what things you're talking about. The ship took us to this wormhole. That worked out. I gather that you programmed that into the computer."

"I just downloaded that part of the message."

"The part you didn't tell us about."

Cavendish shrugged. "It wasn't something I could share without creating crises of decision."

"So you made the decision for us."

"I didn't know that it would take the ship here. All I knew was that this was what the aliens wanted."

"They could have wanted to blow us up," Adrian said.

"If they didn't want us out here in spaceships, they wouldn't have sent the designs. It would have been a sorry joke to send the designs, with the anti-matter technologies and everything, and have a few humans spend years building a ship just to destroy us."

"Then why didn't you come along?" Adrian asked.

Cavendish shivered. "You see? I am paranoid after all. I was afraid to go and afraid not to go. I was afraid not to have answers and afraid of the answers I might get. But I had to get some answers, even if only by proxy, and the only way any answers would emerge—although I would never know what they were—was by sending you to get them."

"Thanks," Adrian said.

"They were your answers, too," Cavendish said.

"Okay," Adrian said. "What hasn't worked out, then?"

"The wormhole. Passage should be instantaneous. But the ship is still inside."

"If we knew what 'still' meant. Time doesn't exist as we know it, in the wormhole. We've found that out, though it's hard to remember. So whatever is happening, in whatever order, or no order at all, may be happening in the instant we went into the wormhole and the following instant we emerge from it."

"On the other hand," Cavendish said, "this may be a test."

"What kind of test?"

"A test of sapience. Like we test rats in mazes. Maybe picking up the alien message was a test, and deciphering it was another, and getting to build the ship was a third, and building it so that it worked was another. This wormhole may be our maze, and if we don't do anything we may never get out."

"And if we get out," Adrian said, "what's our prize?"

"That's the big question, isn't it? That's what drove me into the protection of psychosis in the first place. Maybe the prize is a bit of cheese—or what cheese represents to a rat."

"More gifts like the antimatter technologies?"

"Or maybe aliens hungry for a different delicacy."

"Welcome to the galactic civilization?"

"Or insanity as we try to cope with the truly alien."

"Whatever it is," Adrian said, "we aren't going to know until we get out of here. Do we do nothing and hope that eternity comes to an end? Or do we do something—anything in the hope that it's the right thing?"

Cavendish looked uncertain and a bit fuzzy around the edges. "I don't think it would be a good idea to do anything until you have a good idea it will work."

"That's the trouble in here," Adrian said. "Not only is it difficult to make plans—it's difficult to figure out causes and effects, when the effects come first and the causes later."

"'Sentence first, verdict afterwards,'" Cavendish said.

"You sound like Frances."

"There's a bit of Frances in me," Cavendish said. He was beginning to look transparent. "Just as there's a bit of you and of Jessica and maybe a tiny bit of me."

"I'd make a note of all this if I knew what you were talking about," Adrian said.

"And if you could find it after you wrote it."

"How do you know about that?" Adrian asked. He watched Cavendish's wispy form waver in the slight breeze from the air vents. Gradually the various parts of him began to disappear, first the feet and the hands, then the legs and the arms, and finally the torso, beginning at the hips.

"I'm not really here, you know," the ghost of Cavendish said. "You're really talking to yourself." His body had faded completely, and now only his head hung unsupported in the air.

"Some things you've said I didn't know," Adrian said.

"Nothing you haven't guessed or speculated about," Cavendish said. Now there was only a mouth. But it wasn't smiling. The corners were turned down in Cavendish's typical paranoid grimace.

Then he was gone. Adrian told himself that he would ask Frances what it all meant—if he could remember.

He looked down at the computer table. Cavendish had been reading *Gift from the Stars*.

The knock came on the door of the captain's cabin as Adrian was going over the computer readouts once more, searching for an answer that he would forget if he found it. Adrian had not wanted to occupy the captain's cabin—more of a cubbyhole, really, like the ultracompact quarters on a submarine. He preferred to bunk with the others in the unmarried men's dormitory, leaving the only private accommodation on the ship for the privacy of conjugal visits, but the crew had insisted. Partly, he thought, out of their own sense of propriety.

"Come in," he said, putting the book he was reading on the surface that passed for a desk when it was pulled down, and turning on the stool that passed for a desk chair when it was not folded into the wall.

The airtight door slid aside. Jessica was standing in the narrow corridor, fidgeting from one foot to the other, looking concerned. That was nothing different. They all were.

"Do you have a moment?" Jessica asked.

Adrian gestured at the readout. "That's all any of us have."

Jessica sidled into the room and sat on the edge of the bunk. Her knees were only a few inches from Adrian's and that was uncomfortably close. "We've got a problem."

"I know. Not only are we in a reality where the normal rules don't apply, where even the laws of physics seem to be different, we can't make plans because we don't remember anything from one series of related events to the next."

"As long as events have some continuity," Jessica said, "they seem to hang together, pretty much, one following the other in before-and-after sequence. It's when the continuity is broken that causality is suspended."

"Or reversed," Adrian said. "We do remember things that haven't happened yet. So maybe what we have to do is to lay the groundwork for what we will remember earlier. At that point, maybe, we will know what to do and be able to do it."

"Which, of course, would get us out of this place before we had a chance to lay the groundwork necessary for the proper decision."

Jessica was sharp and a hard worker—in fact, she was his most reliable assistant. He knew this voyage would never have started without her, and it was likely that it wouldn't continue without her either. "I know," he said. "It's crazy. But what we have to remember is that what makes sense is probably worthless and only the right kind of nonsense will work."

She leaned forward to put a hand on his knee. "But that isn't why I'm here."

Adrian shivered. It wasn't that he didn't like to be touched. Frances put her arm around his shoulder and hugged him. Other crew members patted him on the back and shook his hand. This was different. He didn't want to think about what made it different.

"We haven't had any time for personal matters," Jessica said. "We've been too busy with building the ship. Now we've got nothing but time until we find a way to get out of the wormhole."

"Yes, time," Adrian said. He couldn't think of anything else, anything that would stave off what he feared was coming. He could make decisions about life and death, but he wasn't good at what came between.

"We're a band of humans split off from the rest of the species, and there's little chance we'll ever get back."

Adrian nodded.

"So," Jessica said, "we've got to think about survival."

"That's all I think about."

"Not just us. The little band. What we stand for. The human species in space."

Adrian cleared his throat. The room was getting stuffy. "Yes?"

"We must make arrangements."

"Arrangements," Adrian said.

"We've got to pair off. We need to think about having babies and the gene pool and everything else."

"Everything," Adrian repeated.

"I know you don't like to talk about things like this, or think about them either," Jessica said. "So we women have to think about it for you, make plans, arrange things."

"You mean you've discussed this?" Adrian said huskily. "You and the other women?" He realized that he sounded incredulous, but he couldn't help himself.

"Of course not," Jessica said. "But we know. And I wanted you to know that I've always admired you, as a leader and as a man. Not only that, I like you." She leaned forward and kissed him.

For a moment, surprised, he responded. Her lips felt soft and sensual. Then he drew away, shocked at the way his body had responded.

Jessica stood up. Suddenly he was aware of the fact that underneath the one-piece garment she was wearing, only a foot from his face, was the body of a woman, and it was the body of a desirable woman, and if he understood what was going on, it was his if he wanted it.

"I'm glad that's settled," she said, leaned down to kiss him on the cheek, and went through the doorway and down the hall.

"Settled?" he said, too late to be heard. "Settled?" He had one saving thought: at least all this would be forgotten like everything else.

He thought he heard laughter somewhere down the hall, but it came from voices he had never heard before.

❈　❈　❈

Adrian wasn't good at talking to groups, but Frances had said it was necessary and he knew that was true. He would have been as traumatized as the crew if he had experienced over the past few hours the time reversals and the gravity wrenchings of the wormhole transition, even though they had been forgotten, and was depending on someone else to solve the problems. Adrian was as puzzled about what was going on as the crew, but he was in charge. That meant whatever was done would be done by him, and, moreover, he couldn't appear to the crew the way he really felt—helpless.

He had gathered the crew twice before, the first time before the test flight, when he had offered the opportunity to depart, unobserved, to anyone who wanted to sit out the test flight. The second meeting had discussed the computer program that was guiding the ship out of the Solar System, and the reasons for allowing the course to continue toward what they assumed to be an alien-selected destination.

After that the crew divided itself into groups—work groups and social groups, which were not always the same. The crew had been assembled from volunteers to build a ship; once that was done it had to discover new skills and new interests. At first that shakedown was enough to fill the hours. Later, squabbles arose about social arrangements and romantic pairings that had to be settled by counseling from Frances or, failing that, a ship's court, and if that was not acceptable an appeal to the captain's final review. Now, however, he had to face them all and explain the inexplicable.

They were gathered in the couples' dormitory, which had been the unmarried men's dormitory before the inevitable pairings had led to the switch. As in the two times before, men and women were seated on bunks or stools, or stood wherever they could see Adrian. Frances stood behind Adrian and to his left, providing the support of her solid presence. Jessica, on the other hand, stood by the door as if guarding the avenue of their escape. The climate in the room had been transformed from the intense boredom of space flight broken periodically by personal successes, disappointments, and disputes to a communal unease broken by moments of panic.

"We knew we would encounter some strange phenomena out here," Adrian said.

"But we didn't know it would be this strange!" The crew responded with a nervous chuckle.

"We have been through an experience that defies explanation," Adrian continued. "It is connected to our entering a wormhole. We know that much. We must have felt some gravity fluctuations."

"Why do you say 'must have'?" a man's voice asked from several bunks back.

"That's what we would expect from a wormhole, George," Adrian said, "but we're still here, so we survived them. If you're like us, however, you don't remember."

"I don't remember anything that happened after we entered whatever it was," another man said. "And that scares me!"

"It's enough to scare anybody, Kevin," Adrian said.

"There's something else," a woman said. "I'm remembering things that never happened, like an argument Bill and I had—are going to have."

"And I remember the way we are going to make up," a man answered. He laughed as if he were pleased with himself.

"We've got a theory about that," Adrian said. "You're remembering things that haven't happened yet, because time is mixed up in here. But we can't let the unusual get to us if we're going to figure out what's going on, and get out of this place."

"When's that going to be?" a woman asked.

"We don't know a lot, yet, Sally," Adrian said, "but we know this much: 'when' is a word that doesn't mean much where we are. A wormhole is an out-of-this-world means of getting from one place in the universe to another, like folding space so that distant points touch, and then crossing there. The wormhole exists in some kind of hyperspace where space and time get mixed up. We think—"

"Why do you keeping saying, 'we think'?" a woman asked nervously.

"This all is new and different, for us as well as you, Joan," Adrian said. "Give us a chance to figure this out, how this new kind of time operates and how we can function within it, and, I assure you, we'll get out of here and on our way."

Frances spoke up. "You might think about *Alice in Wonderland* and *Through the Looking Glass*. Alice was in a place where nothing made sense, but she stayed calm and eventually she got back to her safe, sane home."

"This ain't a children's book!" a man said. "And this ain't fiction."

"Sam, I hope we can be as capable of handling the unknown as a Victorian child," Frances said. "Maybe even get some answers."

"We ain't never going to get back, are we?" a woman said.

"We can't be sure of that yet, Lui," Adrian said.

Jessica spoke up for the first time. "But we've got to behave as if that's true, or we've got no chance at all."

"What I want to know," a woman said, "is where 'on our way' is going to take us."

"We don't know, Yasmine," Adrian said. "But we all signed on to have our questions answered, and we're going to have to follow the yellow brick road wherever it leads us until we get the answers."

A man said, "What's 'the yellow brick road'?"

Adrian smiled. "Frances has me doing it now."

"That's another children's book," Frances said.

"I'd rather come up with my own answers," another man said.

"If you come up with any, let me know," Adrian said. He folded his arms across his chest. "Meanwhile, we're going to have to live with uncertainty and forgetfulness and not let it make us crazy. But there's a way out of here. The wormhole was a confirmation that we are headed in the right direction. What we can be sure of is that we weren't directed here simply to strand us in Wonderland. This is a pathway. We just have to figure out how to move along it."

"Moving along it reminds me," Frances said, "of what the chess queen said to Alice in *Through the Looking Glass*: 'Now here, you see, it takes all the running you can do, to keep in the same place. If you want to get to somewhere else, you must run at least twice as fast as that.'"

"What's the good of that?" a man asked gruffly.

"We don't know, do we, Fred?" Frances said. "But I have a memory that it's going to matter. Oh, dear! That doesn't make sense, does it?"

"Frances, you're always finding a moral somewhere," a woman said.

"'Everything's got a moral, if you can only find it,'" Frances quoted triumphantly.

Shortly after that the meeting ended, with the crew informed but not relieved. For the moment, at least, they were not rebellious. Adrian had the uneasy feeling, however, that something about the meeting wasn't right: the room was more crowded than it had ever been before.

But he promptly forgot.

✵   ✵   ✵

Adrian was alone in the control room when the deputation arrived. Three were men; two were women. All of them were young and all about the same age, late teens, maybe, or early twenties. In their youth and energy, they all looked a lot alike. One of the men and one of the women were blond; two of the men were dark-haired and one of them was dark-skinned; the second woman had dark hair. Adrian had never seen them before.

The dark-haired woman reminded Adrian of Jessica. One of the men looked familiar, too, but Adrian couldn't quite decide whom he looked like.

"We're here to present our demands," that young man said. His voice sounded familiar, too.

Adrian tried to keep from flinching. "Who are you?" he asked.

"You know who we are," the blond girl said.

Adrian shook his head. "You're all strangers. And the strangest part is that we're in a wormhole inside a ship that nobody can leave and nobody can enter."

"We're the next generation," the woman said.

Adrian was seated in the captain's chair. The five newcomers formed a semicircle around him, lithe, athletic, and leaning slightly forward as if they were poised to take him apart. "We've been here that long?" Adrian asked.

"Duration is a word that has no meaning," the first young man said.

"It's hard to break old habits," Adrian said.

"We don't have any to break," the other dark-haired young man said. He sounded bitter.

"We agreed to keep this civil," the first young man said. He looked back toward Adrian. "We're here to present our demands."

"You've got to let me get used to the idea that the crew has had children who have grown up while we have been stranded in a wormhole that was supposed to provide instantaneous passage. I don't feel twenty years older."

"That's old-fashioned thinking!" the other blond young man said contemptuously.

"He can't help it," said the young man who appeared to be the spokesman for the group, if not, indeed, its leader. "He's system-bound."

"He's got to help it," the blond young man said. "He's the captain."

"How many of you are there?" Adrian asked.

"Many," the blond young woman said.

"Enumeration is as difficult as duration," said the spokesman.

"Are you all the same age?" Adrian asked.

"You see?" the young man asked. "He'll never learn."

"Sometimes yes, sometimes no," the spokesman said patiently. "None of these questions you're asking has any meaning unless we get into normal space. And that's what we've come about."

"To present our demands," the blond young woman said.

Adrian folded his hands across his lap. "I don't know what you can ask for that we can provide, but go ahead."

"We want you to stop trying to get out of the wormhole," the spokesman said.

"We can't do that!" Adrian said.

"Why not?" the young man said.

"We're in never-never land," Adrian said. "Nowhere. No memory. No continuity. Virtual nonexistence. And then, you see, we committed ourselves to finding out why the aliens sent us the plans for this ship and brought us here." He gestured at the book lying in front of him; it was *Gift from the Stars*. Often he found himself reading it as if he could find there a way out.

"We didn't," the bitter young man said.

"Didn't what?" Adrian asked.

"Sign up for this trip."

"But—" Adrian began.

"You've got no right," the spokesman said, "to take us somewhere against our will."

"And against our right to exist," the dark-haired young woman said.

"What's that?" Adrian asked.

"What do you think will happen to us if you get out of this wormhole?" the spokesman asked.

Adrian was silent.

"We won't exist."

"What kind of existence is that?" Adrian asked finally. "What is life without memory? What is existence without cause and effect?"

"The only kind we know," the bitter young man said.

"We are your children," the spokesman said. "You brought us into this world, crazy as it seems to you. But it's our world, and you owe us."

"He also owes the rest of us," a woman said from the door. It was Frances. "And the species. If you're more than illusions, you'll be born at the right time in the right place. But now—be gone. You're nothing but a pack of possibilities."

The five turned toward her, frightened and uncertain, and disappeared like snowflakes evaporating before they hit the ground, leaving their potentials etched into the air.

Adrian rubbed his forehead. "They were so—real. So like the children the crew might have had—might have. Our language wasn't meant for in here."

"One of them looked like Jessica," Frances said.

"And another one—" Adrian began and stopped.

"What?"

Adrian looked into one of the darkened vision screens. There were no mirrors in the control room, but he could see his reflection. He knew who the spokesman for the group looked like.

He looked like Adrian.

A familiar figure with a familiar walk and a familiar look to the back of the head turned at the far end of the corridor and, before Adrian could speak, disappeared down the side corridor that led toward the mess hall. It was a man. Adrian was sure of that. "Hey!" he called out, but by the time he reached the corridor it was empty. Only Frances was in the mess hall, cleaning the table that doubled for conferences, and she looked puzzled when he asked if anyone had just come in or passed.

But when Adrian returned to the corridor leading back toward the control room, he saw the same figure in front of him. He ran toward it, but it got farther away the faster he ran. By the time he got to the control room, it was empty. He went back down the corridor, trying to figure out what it meant. When he turned to look behind, he saw the back of the figure again, still moving away. This time Adrian turned and went the other direction, and came face to face with the man just outside the mess hall.

"Adrian!" they each said. Then, "I don't believe it!"

"We'd better speak one at a time," Adrian said.

"I agree," Adrian said.

"We've got to decide, first, who's the real Adrian and who is the doppelganger," Adrian said.

"I'm real," they said together.

"Look," Adrian said, "this isn't getting us anywhere. I'll tell you what. As Frances would say, 'If you'll believe in me, I'll believe in you.'"

"That sounds reasonable," Adrian said. "Maybe this is the opportunity we've been looking for—to find a way out of this place. Let's go in here and talk about it."

Adrian nodded. "We can put our heads together."

And Adrian added, "Two heads are better than one."

When they entered the tiny mess hall, Frances was gone. Adrian didn't think enough time had passed for Frances to have completed her cleanup and departed. He didn't know whether that meant he was in his doppelganger's reality or whether it was another example of the wormhole's vagaries.

"Obviously," Adrian said, seating himself on a stool at the table, "the time variables have us tied up."

"Obviously," Adrian said, leaning back against one of the microwaves, not wanting to put himself in a mirror-image position. "But what isn't obvious is what we're going to do about the fact that we only remember what happens later."

"That's true," Adrian said. "So the secret is to prepare later for what we need to know earlier."

Adrian nodded. "I've thought of that. At least, I think I've thought of that. The difficult part is remembering that we have to store information for earlier use."

"We have to come to that realization independently, every time. We have to learn to think differently, just as we have to learn to think differently about Jessica and Frances."

"What do you mean?" Adrian asked.

"It's clear to me, and it should be clear to you, that both Jessica and Frances are fond of us."

"And I'm fond of them," Adrian said.

"One, or maybe both, are going to want that relationship to get even closer."

Adrian nodded. "That's an uncomfortable thought, but if it happens I will have to handle it."

"When we 'handle it,' as you say, we will have to think in unaccustomed ways."

"I know," Adrian said.

"I don't mean just the business of allowing emotional involvement, even intimacy, but the possibility of sharing, or being shared."

Adrian took a deep breath. "I understand you. What am I saying? I am you."

"In the same way," Adrian said, "we are going to have to think about our physical predicament in unconventional ways. Logic doesn't work."

"We'll have to try illogic," Adrian said. "As a matter of fact, I've already tried it. I caught up with you by going the other way."

"I was the one who caught up with you," Adrian said and then waved his hand. "No matter. We'll have to think impossible things."

"As Frances would say, 'I can't believe impossible things.'"

"'I daresay you haven't had much practice,'" Adrian continued. "'When I was your age, I always did it for half an hour a day. Why, sometimes I've believed as many as six impossible things before breakfast.'"

Adrian moved from in front of the microwaves. "I'm glad we had this meeting, even though it was a bit of a shock." He didn't offer to shake hands with the other Adrian. That would have been too much. "But I hope it doesn't happen again."

He went through the doorway into the corridor. This time he didn't look back.


They all knew it was time to act. Jessica looked at Adrian, Adrian looked at Frances, Frances looked at Jessica. They had been in the wormhole too long. None of them knew how long it had been: days, weeks, maybe even years. But they knew that if they didn't do something soon, they would never get out.

Jessica looked at the gyrating readouts on the control panel. "We have to know what is going on outside," she said.

"None of our instruments work," Adrian said. "Or if they work, they aren't recording."

"We could turn on the viewscreens," Frances said.

"We've tried that. All we see is glare," Jessica said.

"That's the cosmic microwave background boosted into visible light," Adrian said.

"I think the viewscreens are as unreliable as the readouts," Jessica said. "We try to cut back on the light, and the screens go black. Somebody has to go outside and report."

Adrian nodded. "I agree. And I'm the only one who is capable of making sense of what is happening. I'll get ready."

"You can't be spared," Frances said. Her face had that "there's no use arguing with me" look.

"Frances is right," Jessica said. "I'm the most experienced in working on the outside, the youngest, the most athletic, the steadiest—"

"You can't be spared either," Frances said. "You're young, all right, and you have a life ahead of you if we ever get to a place where you can live it. That leaves me."

"There's radiation out there," Adrian said. "God knows what. Even if it isn't fatal, whoever goes out there is going to take a lot of damage."

"Besides," Jessica said, "you get sick just turning your head quickly."

"I can do this," Frances said. "I can do whatever I have to do. And you've got a young body and young ova—all that needs to be preserved if we're going to have a future." She stood in front of them both, in the control room, square and ready.

"I'm not going to talk you out of this, am I?" Jessica asked.

Frances shook her head. "In a movie you'd hit me on the head and take my place, but this isn't a movie, and it isn't going to happen."

"I'm glad you know the difference," Adrian said. "No heroism."

"Just common sense," Frances said. "Now I need some help in getting into a suit." She smiled at her admission of inadequacy.

Spacesuits had not been built for someone as short and wide as Frances, but a man's suit had been adapted by removing sections of the leg and welding the remaining pieces together. That didn't help Frances's agility, but then she hadn't used the suit much. Now she struggled into it, and Jessica checked all the closures twice.

"Don't stay out there more than a minute or two," Jessica said, "and don't try to do more than a simple survey. Be sure to snap yourself to the interior hook and make certain your magnet is firmly attached to the outer hull before you—"

"Hush," Frances said. "You're only making me nervous."

She turned and hit the large button beside the inner hatch. It cycled open as Frances turned, patted Jessica's shoulder with her glove, and touched Adrian's hand. She adjusted her helmet and stepped over the sill into the airlock.

Jessica spoke into her head-held microphone. "Can you hear me? Be sure you keep your mike open all the time. I'm going to suit up so that I can come out and get you if you're in trouble."

Frances shook her head inside the helmet as she pushed the inner button and the door began to close. "We don't want to lose two of us," she said. "Don't worry. If I don't get back, it's been a great run." But her face looked pale before the door completely closed. "I'm opening the outer hatch. God, it's bright out here!"

Jessica looked at Adrian, and Adrian looked back, but their thoughts were outside. "What's going on?" Adrian asked.

"I'm darkening my face plate. There, that's better."

"What can you see?" Jessica asked.

"Wait a minute. I feel a little sick. There's nothing to look at."

"Frances!" Jessica said. "Look at the airlock. Look down at your feet. Then look at the ship. Orient yourself to the ship!"

"Got it!" Frances said. "The ship seems to be moving. I can see some kind of disturbance in the glare that might be exhaust, so the engine is still operating, but we knew that, since we've had gravity."

"Which way are we going?" Adrian asked.

"Hard to say," Frances said. "There seems to be a dark place in the glare."

"Which direction?" Adrian asked.

"Toward the rear of the ship," Frances said triumphantly. "Where the anti-matter stuff comes out."

"That must be the mouth of the wormhole where we entered," Adrian said.

"That's enough," Jessica said. "Come in."

"Not yet," Frances said. "I'm looking around while I'm here."

"Don't look around!" Jessica said.

"Funny stuff out here," Frances said. "A weird-looking contraption just went by. All twisted pipes and girders. Speak of ships that pass in the night!"

"You're not doing us any good out there," Adrian said.

"There's another ship, or vehicle, or something," Frances said. "Only it's like a stack of waffles with a flagpole through the middle."

"Frances!" Jessica said. "You're making us nervous."

"Goodness knows, you've made me nervous often enough," Frances said. "There's an alien, I think. A creature of some sort with tentacles. And one shaped like a cone with eyes. And another, and another!"

"You're losing touch!" Adrian said. "Come back! Now!"

"There's the Mad Hatter!" Frances shouted. "And Humpty Dumpty. And the caterpillar smoking the water pipe. And the Queen!"

"Come back!" Jessica said softly. "Come back, Frances!"

"Off with their heads!" Frances said.

Adrian looked at Jessica. She turned and began climbing into her spacesuit.

"Remember," Frances said, "you have to run twice as fast as that!"

Something clanged from outside the ship, like a magnet being freed and metal-shod feet pushing against the hull.

Jessica stopped halfway into her suit. "I knew I should have gone," she said.

Adrian shook his head. "There's no way we can go faster," he said. "But maybe we can make Frances's sacrifice meaningful." He didn't know how that was going to happen, but, as unshed tears burned his eyes, he knew he would make it happen.

Jessica slapped the viewscreens back on and let the glare fill the control room. "We've got to do something. Frances has—is going to—oh, I don't know what the right tense is. But she has given us all the information we're likely to get, and she's dead—surely she's dead."

"There's not much doubt about that," Adrian said. "We're remembering things that have yet to happen, including things that might happen, and we've got all the memories of what has yet to happen that we're likely ever to get."

"Even though we've just entered the wormhole," Jessica said.

Adrian nodded. "That's the funny way time works in here. Now we know but later on we'll forget. So we've got to do it now."

"Frances said we had to run twice as fast," Jessica said.

"And I said there was no way to do that," Adrian said, "or any reason to think going twice as fast would get us anywhere." He looked around at the control room. In spite of the glare, for the first time he was seeing things clearly: Frances, Jessica, the aliens and their plans. "We've been trying to reconcile the unreconcilables, the time anomalies, or own inability to adjust to inversions and potentials."

Jessica looked at him hopefully, the way an apprentice looked at her master, anticipating wisdom.

"We've got to turn the ship around," Adrian said. He turned to the controls. "Go back the way we came. If we were in real space, we'd have to decelerate for as long as we've accelerated, but this is hyperspace and we haven't moved far from where we entered."

"Let me do it," Jessica said. She began punching instructions into the computer. "But isn't that just giving up?"

"Maybe," Adrian said. He tried to isolate a cold feeling in the pit of his stomach. Maybe it was giving up. "Logically we should come out the way we came in, and then everything will have been for nothing— all our psychological torment, the felt years of experience, Frances's sacrifice—"

"But maybe not?" Jessica said.

Adrian could feel the ship swinging even though there was nothing to see, no way to get information from gauges, nothing but glare. . . .

Something surged.

Conflicting gravities tugged at their bodies, as if all their loose parts wanted to go in different directions, as if their internal organs were changing places. . . . Then the glare and the gravity fluctuations stopped suddenly. Adrian and Jessica looked at each other, remembering everything that had happened or might have happened inside the wormhole. They turned to look at the viewscreens. The glare was gone. Outside was the blackness of space with here and there the pinpoint hole of a star. It could have been anywhere in the galaxy including back near the spot from which they had been drawn into the wormhole.

Jessica adjusted the controls and new arenas of space swam into view. The stars were few and distant. A single star loomed closest, but it was old and faint.

"That isn't our Solar System," Jessica said. "That isn't our sun."

Adrian shook his head. "Wherever we were going, we've arrived."

"How did you figure it out?" Jessica asked.

"If time was inverted," Adrian said, "maybe space was, too. In order to get out, we had to reverse our course. But then, I had some help." He thought about the other Adrian, who now would never exist, except maybe in the never-never world of the wormhole, and how he had caught up with him only when he went the other way. But maybe that never-never existence, like that of the children and maybe even of Cavendish, was as real as any other. "Maybe I'll tell you some time.

"Meanwhile," he continued, "I think we have managed our rite of passage and have a rendezvous with destiny."

"Whatever that means," Jessica said.

Adrian smiled at her. There would be great moments ahead, he thought, and moments of tenderness and fulfillment and maybe distress and regret and pain. But it would be living.

He heard a noise behind him and turned toward the entrance.

"Frances?" he said. "Frances?"

((•((•((• ◉ •))•))•))

**James Gunn** has had a career divided between writing and teaching, typified by his service as president of the Science Fiction and Fantasy Writers of America and as president of the Science Fiction Research Association, as well as having been presented the Grand Master Award of SFWA and the Pilgrim Award of SFRA. He now is Emeritus Professor of English at the University of Kansas and continues to write.

He has published more than 100 short stories and has written or edited 42 books, including *The Immortals, The Listeners, The Dreamers, Alternate Worlds: The Illustrated History of Science Ficton, The Road to Science Fiction,* and, most recently, *Transcendental* and its sequel, *Transgalactic*. "The Rabbit Hole" was originally published in *Analog* and is the central portion of the novel *Gift from the Stars*.

*Next, a Chinese taikonaut encounters a strange vessel and finds herself dealing with Ben Bova's irascible scoundrel, Sam Gunn, in . . .*

# RARE (OFF) EARTH ELEMENTS
## (A SAM GUNN TALE)

## by Ben Bova

You must understand that it all happened many years ago, when I was very young and inexperienced in the ways of the world.

Oh, I was not completely naïve. After all, to be trained as a taikonaut was a demanding discipline, especially for a young woman. To be first in my class was a fine accomplishment that I am still proud of. And to be chosen to claim the asteroid was not only a great honor, it was a heavy responsibility.

The People's Republic of China was expanding into space in those days. While the Americans and Europeans restricted their efforts to space stations in low orbits, China built its base on the Moon. When the Russians sent an automated probe to scout the near-Earth asteroids, the great ones in Beijing decided to send taikonauts to claim some of them for China.

One of the taikonauts they sent was me: Song-li Chunxi.

My mission was to reach asteroid 94-12, an undistinguished chunk of rock that was hardly more than three kilometers long, at its greatest axis.

Romantics dreamed of finding gold and silver among the asteroids, platinum and high-quality nickel-iron. I was sent to asteroid 94-12 because spectroscopic studies of the rock showed it contained many tons of rare-earth elements.

You seem puzzled. Rare-earth elements such as neodymium, lanthanum, cerium, and the others were very important in the manufacture of computer memories, rechargeable batteries, cell phones, magnets, and the whole panoply of modern electronics devices. What copper was to Morse's telegraph and Bell's telephone, rare-earth elements are to today's digital world.

The American capitalists had formed several private companies to mine the asteroids. So China led the movement in the United Nations to require that a human being personally claim an asteroid for his (or her) nation's utilization. Otherwise the greedy capitalists could have sent out fleets of robotic vehicles and claimed the rights to everything in sight!

International law was quite specific. No nation may claim sovereignty over any natural object in space. No nation may claim the Moon, for example, or any asteroid, as part of its national territory. But a nation—or even a private corporation—may claim *use* of the natural resources of a body in space, so long as the claim is made by a human being actually present on that body.

So China sent me to asteroid 94-12. It was one of the near-Earth asteroids: hundreds of them orbited within a few million miles of Earth. The so-called Asteroid Belt was much farther away, of course; millions of asteroids were in that region, out beyond the orbit of Mars, too far for economically profitable mining operations.

My mission was a simple one: fly from our launch center in Sinkiang to asteroid 94-12, claim it for the PRC, and then fly home. I would be alone for the three months it would take to reach the asteroid, claim it, and then fly home again.

That was before Sam Gunn entered the picture.

Even as a little girl, long before I entered taikonaut training, I had heard of Sam Gunn, of course. He was a legend: a scheming, devilishly clever entrepreneur who had made several fortunes on various space endeavors, and then managed to lose everything and had to start all over again.

He was known as a conniver, a fast-talking pitchman who would bend or even break any rules that stood in his way. And also an oversexed libertine who pursued women—any and all women—relentlessly. Although no one would admit it officially, I had heard several times that the great ones in Beijing would not mind at all if Sam Gunn got himself killed while pursuing one of his wild schemes.

For more than six weeks I coasted through space toward a

rendezvous with 94-12. To the scientists I was living in microgravity, but it was effectively zero-gee. It might have been enjoyable, if only I'd had enough room in my tiny cabin to actually float free. But I didn't. My spacecraft was officially described as "compact." After the first week of my mission, I thought of it as cramped, confined.

And it was lonely, with no one even to talk with except the disembodied voices from mission control, back in Sinkiang. After two weeks, I began to take EVA jaunts outside merely to relieve the feelings of claustrophobia that were pressing in on me.

After all, I was expected to work, eat, sleep, attend to my hygiene, all in a compartment little larger than a coffin. My world was no bigger than two meters across: everything from the panel displaying my spacecraft's systems' status to the zero-gravity toilet I had to strap myself onto was within arm's reach.

Even with the regular messages from the mission controllers in Sinkiang, I felt alone, abandoned, so very far from home, far from warmth and the touch of another person.

So I would suit up and go outside. The huge, vast universe was all around me out there: the distant blue sphere of Earth and myriads of bright unbinking stars, the endless infinity of eternity. It soothed me, it kept me sane. I would float at the end of my safety tether and stare at the star-flecked darkness for hours. Somehow the loneliness I felt inside my cabin was dispelled by the grandeur of the universe. I even composed poetry in my head out there in the emptiness.

At last I approached the asteroid and made ready for the rendezvous maneuver. The spacecraft's automated guidance and propulsion systems were programmed for the landing, of course, but I sat in my contour chair with both hands hovering above the control yokes, ready to take command of the ship if the automated systems faltered.

The mission controllers in Sinkiang were of no help: I was nearly three light-minutes away from Earth; it would take them six minutes or more to respond to my requests. I was on my own.

The automated systems worked flawlessly, almost. The asteroid grew bigger and bigger in my observation port, until it blotted out everything else and all I could see was its lumpy, pitted surface rushing up to meet me.

And a spacecraft sitting in the middle of an irregular, lopsided crater!

A spacecraft? How could that be? There was no record of another spacecraft mission to 94-12, no communications from such a spacecraft.

Glancing at my panel readouts, I saw that I would be touching down on the asteroid in less than four minutes. No time to ask Sinkiang for orders. I had to make my own decision.

Feeling excited, happy even, I grasped the control yokes firmly and jinked my spacecraft with a spurt from the attitude control jets to land softly in the same crater beside the unexpected craft already there.

I touched down feather light, but still kicked up a cloud of dust. As I waited for it to dissipate, I realized that the other craft was much bigger than my own. Very much bigger. It was huge, actually: a trio of bulbous spherical shapes studded with antennas, thruster jets, solar panels and what looked like airlock hatches, with a quartet of rocket nozzles at its far end. My spacecraft looked like a pitiful child's model beside it.

As I shut down my propulsion systems, I felt a sudden wave of anxiety. The stranger had obviously landed on 94-12 before I had. He had probably already sent his claim to the asteroid back to whoever had sent him here. My mission was ruined and I was a failure.

But when I tried to send a message back to Sinkiang, I found that all the communications wavelengths were being jammed.

Jammed? By whom? Why?

For several long minutes I sat in my contour chair wondering what I should do. The other spacecraft loomed in my observation port, silent, seemingly inert. Perhaps it was uncrewed, I thought. No, that couldn't be. A robotic vehicle would not need to be so big.

Could it be an alien spacecraft? A visitor from another star?

I fought down the thrill of excitement that surged through me. Occam's razor, I told myself. The simplest explanation is usually the correct one. Don't go inventing extraterrestrial visitors; that's the wildest possible explanation.

And yet . . .

My spacecraft had a pair of telescopes mounted outside on its skin, for visual observation of the asteroid during my approach phase. I could feel my heart throbbing excitedly beneath my ribs as I worked the control panel and turned the smaller of the telescopes onto one of the hatches along the other craft's hull. Focusing it, I saw that there were operating instructions printed next to the hatch—in English.

No extraterrestrials.

I tried the radio again, this time attempting to contact that spacecraft. No go. The signals were still being jammed, up and down the frequency range.

Well, I thought, if I can't get a signal through to it, it can't get a signal through to me. Whoever it is might not even know I've landed alongside him.

Then a new thought struck me. Perhaps whoever is in that craft is dead. Obviously the ship is too big for just one person. Maybe the entire crew has died.

Of what? The craft did not appear to be damaged. Some malfunction of their life support system? Some virus or a leaking gas line that poisoned them all?

There was only one way to find out, I finally decided. So I suited up and prepared to leave my spacecraft. The space suit should protect me from any virus or poisonous agent inside the other ship, I reasoned. The suit is a self-contained little ecology. If I can get inside their ship, I can see what's happened to them. If it's some sort of disease I can skip out quickly and get back to my own ship. Any disease organisms that might attach themselves to the outside of my suit will be quickly killed by exposure to vacuum and the high-intensity radiation out in the open between our two ships.

Wishing I could contact Sinkiang for approval of my decision or even advice, I wriggled into my space suit and touched the control stud that pumped the air out of my compartment. When the panel light showed the compartment was in vacuum, I opened the hatch then floated halfway out. The asteroid's gravity was so minuscule that I was just about weightless.

The other ship was too far away for my EVA tether to reach, so I strapped the maneuvering jet pack to my shoulders before pushing myself completely out of my cabin.

Slowly, carefully, I picked my way between the rocks strewing the dusty ground. With each cautious step I floated almost a meter above the ground. It wouldn't have taken much effort to jump completely free of the asteroid and go into orbit around it.

Once I got to the airlock hatch, I read the instructions printed alongside it, then pressed the stud beneath the printing. The hatch popped open a few centimeters. I pulled it all the way open and hauled myself inside.

The airlock chamber was lit by a single red light on its control panel. Using my helmet lamp, I peered at the instructions and worked the keypads in the proper sequence. The outer hatch closed and locked, the airlock filled with air, and the panel light turned from red to green. I stepped to the inner hatch and opened it.

On the other side of the hatch a passageway stretched in either direction, fully lighted. Which way should I go?

Then I heard a voice shouting in the distance. At least someone was alive in the ship!

I cracked open the visor of my helmet and took a quick, testing sniff of air. Perfectly good. Sliding the visor all the way up, I heard the voice much better. A man's voice. Swearing with profound, profane, infuriated vehemence. In English. American English.

Tingling with a mixture of apprehension and excitement, I made my way slowly along the passageway.

". . . no good, mother-humping, brain-dead, backstabbing pustule of a control circuit . . ." the male voice was raging in a sharp, slightly nasal tenor.

The passageway ended at an open hatch. On the other side of it was a small compartment bearing dials and viewscreens and gauges on its walls, with a command chair in their midst, its arms studded with switches and pushbuttons. The man doing all the yelling was in that chair, his back to me.

"Hello," I said. In English, since that was the language he was using so fluently.

No response. He simply kept on yowling and banging his fists on the armrest controls, like an infuriated little child.

"Hello," I repeated, louder.

He whirled his chair around. "Yipes!" His eyes went round and he bounded out of the chair. In the low gravity he soared across the compartment and banged into me. We staggered backwards, arms and legs entangled, and toppled to the deck.

"Who the hell are you?" he demanded, his face bare centimeters above my own.

A little breathless from the fall, I replied, "Song-li Chunxi."

"You're Chinese," he said, scrambling off me and to his feet.

"Yes." I started to get up from the deck. He grabbed my arms and hauled me erect.

And he stared at me. "Lord, you're beautiful!"

I knew that I was very plain and ordinary. But he was gaping at me as if I were a goddess.

I asked, "And you are?"

He made a little bow. "Sam Gunn, at your service."

That's how I met Sam Gunn.

He was not much taller than I: not more than a hundred sixty centimeters, I judged. Wiry as an elf, with a thatch of rust-red hair and freckles sprinkling his stub of a nose. His eyes were greenish blue, or perhaps bluish green. His round face was far from handsome, but somehow when he broke into his lopsided, gap-toothed smile, he seemed almost attractive.

"What are you doing here?" Sam demanded. "How'd you get here? Where'd you come from?"

"The People's Republic of China has sent me to claim this asteroid," I replied. "But apparently you have already done so."

"I would've if I could've."

I felt my brows knit in puzzlement. "You mean you haven't registered a claim?"

"Not yet. All my comm systems are down."

"You're being jammed, too?"

Sam shook his head. "It's not jamming. It's the lousy, overpriced, underperforming fusion propulsion system on this ship."

"Fusion?" I gasped. "Your ship is propelled by a nuclear fusion system?"

"When it works," he said, his words dripping with disgust.

Before I could ask another question, Sam explained that he had bought a prototype fusion rocket from the university professors who had invented it, with the intent of prospecting for valuable asteroids among the near-Earth objects.

"A prototype," I echoed.

"Yep. Far as they were concerned, they thought they had hired me to test the system on a run to the Moon and back. I made them go through the legalities of selling the crate to my company, Sam Gunn, Unlimited. Told them it would relieve them of any legal responsibilities if something went wrong. They signed on the dotted line." Sam grinned evilly. "Academics."

"And your test flight?"

"I never intended to just waltz out to the Moon. Been there, done that. I figured a fusion-powered ship could get me to the NEAs in a jiffy. I'd claim a nice, fat asteroid, and that would pay for the damned fusion bucket plus making me a sizeable profit."

I was stunned by his audacity. "You took their ship out here."

"My ship," Sam corrected. "I own this bucket. Not that it's worth much."

"Your crew—"

"What crew? I couldn't ask anybody to risk their butts on this flight. It's one thing to put my own ass on the line, it's something else altogether to drag others along with me."

"You came out here alone?"

"Alone, alone, all, all alone, Alone on a wide, wide sea," Sam quoted. I knew it was from some old British poem, but I couldn't remember which one.

Before I could say anything, Sam added, "Besides, if I brought some crew with me and anything happened to them, the goddamned lawyers would be all over me."

"But you didn't register your flight with the International Astronautical Authority. You kept radio silence all the way out here."

He grinned again. "What they don't know can't hurt me."

"And now you're marooned here on this asteroid."

With a nod, Sam admitted, "Looks that way, unless and until I can get the fusion reactor working again. All it's doing now is putting out a loud squawk up and down the radio spectrum."

"The jamming."

"Yeah. Sorry it's screwed up your communications."

"Can't be helped, I suppose."

Spreading his arms in a gesture that might have indicated welcome, or helplessness, Sam said, "Long as you're here, why don't you stay for dinner? I've got a fully stocked wardroom, complete with a small but select wine list."

I realized that, like many capitalists, Sam was a hedonist. Imagine bringing wines along on a mission to the asteroids! On the other hand, though, I hadn't eaten anything but prepackaged frozen meals since launching from Sinkiang. Nourishing but hardly a treat for my taste buds.

Sam coaxed, "Just take off that suit of armor you're wearing and come on down to the galley with me."

Something in those blue-green (or green-blue) eyes of his sent a warning spark along my nerves. Yet I reasoned that I was fully dressed beneath my space suit. But would it give Sam lecherous ideas if I disrobed, even partially? From what I had heard of Sam Gunn, he most likely already had lecherous ideas in mind.

Then he said, "I'll go up to the galley and get dinner started. You can go to the lavatory, get out of your suit, and wash up."

I allowed him to lead me to the lavatory, which turned out to be bigger than the entire compartment in my spacecraft. I locked the door, though, before I began to clamber out of my space suit. And looked around for hidden cameras.

Dinner was spectacular: ham and melon for appetizer, then roast duck, rice, a salad and real strawberries for dessert. Sam talked nonstop through the whole meal.

". . . so I figured that if I could claim a couple of asteroids rich enough to mine profitably, I could recoup what I'd lost on the orbital hotel deal and go on to bigger and better things."

He told me about his magnetic "garbage remover" device for clearing orbiting debris from low Earth orbits, his zero-gravity "honeymoon hotel," his hopes for building a tourist entertainment center on the Moon.

"There's plenty of money to be made in space," he said as he scooped up the last of the strawberries. "Mucho dinero."

I finally managed to get in a word. "I suppose so."

Then he said, "So I guess you're going to have to rescue me. I mean, with my ship crippled I can't get off this rock. I might have enough supplies to last another month or so, but I really need to be rescued."

I actually blushed with shame. "I . . . I can't, Sam. My spacecraft isn't big enough to carry two people."

He broke into a lopsided pout. "Really?"

"Really. I can call the IAA, once I get out of range of your jamming—"

"It's not intentional!"

"I know. But once I'm away from this asteroid I can call the IAA. They'll send a rescue mission."

"Maybe."

"Of course they will! They'd have to!"

Sam didn't look convinced of that. But then he said, "You know, you've got to be on the body you're claiming when you send your claim in to the IAA."

"Oh!" I hadn't thought of that. I couldn't claim the asteroid unless I was physically on it when I made the claim. And as long as Sam's fusion reactor was blocking all the comm frequencies, I couldn't get a message back to Earth while I was still on the asteroid.

He saw the crestfallen expression on my face. Getting up from the table—slowly, carefully, in the light gravity—Sam said, "I'll try to fix the damned reactor."

I expected him to act like a male chauvinist and leave me to clear the table. Instead, he picked up everything and tossed them all—dishes, glasses, dinnerware—into what looked like a dishwasher.

"Come on," he said, "let's have another whack at that goddamned fusion reactor."

As we shuffled along the passageway, Sam asked, "So China wants to start mining asteroids for rare-Earth metals."

"Oh no," I corrected. "China is already the world's leading producer of rare-Earth metals. We have no intention of mining more of them from asteroids. Why should we go to such expense? An increase in their supply would only bring down their prices."

He shot me a perplexed look. "You don't intend to mine this asteroid? Then why claim it?"

"To prevent others from mining it. We have a near monopoly of rare-Earth metals on Earth. Why should we allow others to compete against us by mining asteroids?"

Understanding dawned in Sam's hazel eyes. "Cutting the competition's throat," he muttered.

"It is a legitimate business tactic," I said.

"Uh-huh." We had reached the compartment where the fusion reactor's controls were housed. Sam turned to me and said, "But there are zillions of asteroids. You can't claim them all. Others will get to at least some of them."

I smiled with the knowledge of superior wisdom, "Sam, you're thinking of the Asteroid Belt, which is four times father from the Sun than the Earth is."

"Out beyond the orbit of Mars," he said.

"That's much too far for commercial operations. The cost of transportation would be too much to make mining asteroids in the Belt profitable."

"I guess."

"But the near-Earth asteroids are reasonably accessible. Our astronomers have studied the NEAs very carefully. Although there are hundreds of them sizeable enough to be considered for mining, only a handful have amounts of rare-Earth metals that might be possible competition for the People's Republic of China."

"And you're sending people out to claim each and every one of them."

"Of course. I am only the first. There will be others. Our only fear is that private companies such as yours will claim a few of them."

"That could cause you trouble, eh?"

"Competition," I said.

"Well, for what it's worth, I'm 'way ahead of those other companies. I'm the first guy out here among the NEAs; *my* competition is still making paper studies and trying to raise capital."

"We are well aware of that. In fact, Sam, our planners in Beijing didn't even consider you as a possible threat. You were too small to alarm them."

Sam grunted. "But I got here first."

"True."

"Lot of good it's going to do me," he muttered, "unless I can get this tin can working again."

He went to the chair in the middle of all the reactor controls. I stood behind him, resting my arms on the chair's high back. Sam looked like a little boy sitting in an adult's chair; his feet barely reached the deck. He began poking and tapping the keypads and switches set into the armrests, grumbling so low I could not understand his words.

I realized I had a moral dilemma on my hands. I could leave Sam here and return to China, of course. Once I was beyond the inadvertent jamming, if I called the IAA and told them of Sam's plight, they would send a mission to rescue him, I felt certain. But if I did that, Sam would claim the asteroid and my own mission would be a failure. I would return home in disgrace. The great ones in Beijing would not be pleased with me. Not at all.

On the other hand, I could leave the asteroid and not say a word about Sam being there. I could bring a few pebbles and samples of dust to prove that I had been on the asteroid, and perhaps the IAA would accept that as proof and award China the rights to utilize its resources. Then my mission would be a success.

But Sam would die. And I would have killed him.

Sam seemed to sense my feelings.

"Listen, Song, you do what you have to do. Get off this rock, take some samples with you, and don't tell the IAA or anybody else about me. You make your claim, don't worry about me."

All the while he was fingering the controls on his seat's armrests like a pianist playing a Bach fugue. But I didn't see any of the graphs or gauges on the status screens change by a millimeter.

"But, Sam," I said, "you'll die on this rock."

He looked up at me with that lopsided grin of his. "'Under the wide and starry sky, dig the grave and let me lie.' This isn't such a bad place to go." His grin turned wistful. "I've seen worse."

Well, his self-sacrifice literally overwhelmed me. That, and the fact that he kept telling me he thought I was beautiful. We ended up in his bed—a real bed, in a handsomely-fitted bedroom that was twice the size of my entire spacecraft. Somewhat to my surprise, Sam was a gentle lover, tender and very affectionate.

But when I woke up—after a long, luxurious sleep—I saw that I was alone. Sam was nowhere in sight.

I showered (hot water!) and dressed quickly, then went past the galley and down to the control center. No sign of him. And no sound of him, either.

A terrible flash of realization hit me. The scoundrel has left me here and gone to my spacecraft! He's taken some samples from the asteroid and he's going to fly back to Earth in my spacecraft and make his claim, leaving me here to starve to death!

The scoundrel! The seductive, scheming, selfish scoundrel!

"Good morning."

I nearly jumped out of my skin. Sam had come up behind me while

I was fuming silently. I whirled to face him, and in the low gravity swung myself completely off my feet and into his arms.

"Hey, whoa, take it easy," he said, laughing as he held me safely in his arms. I grabbed both his ears and kissed him soundly.

"Wow," he said. "You're really glad to see me, huh?"

"I thought . . ." My breath caught in my throat. I couldn't tell Sam that I thought he'd left and marooned me.

"Let's have some breakfast," Sam said. And he started down the passageway toward the galley, whistling horribly off-tune.

I followed him to the galley. Sam seemed happily upbeat, as if he hadn't a care in the world. Was it our love-making that made him so cheerful? After all, one of us was going to leave for Earth while the other waited for a rescue that might never come.

He busied himself frying eggs while I put a pot of water in the microwave to boil for tea.

"You're very cheery," I said, as I impatiently waited for the microwave to chime.

He gave me a delighted smile. "Why not? I got the reactor working."

Again I felt my heart leap. "You did?"

Nodding vigorously, he said, "Got it all cleared up. You can call in your claim."

"But, Sam, you were here first."

He flipped the eggs in his frying pan like an expert chef. "Yeah, but you've got your higher-ups to answer to. I'm my own boss."

"But you're entitled to claim this asteroid."

"And what happens to you if I do?"

"But you'll have come all this way for nothing. You'll be broke."

He shrugged as he slid the eggs onto two dishes. "I've been broke before. Besides, I've got this ship. The first fusion-powered spacecraft to go beyond the Earth-Moon system. That's something."

I stared at him. He seemed honestly pleased at the situation we were in.

"Sam, China will claim all the rare-Earth asteroids among the near-Earth objects. The PRC intends to keep as tight a monopoly on rare-Earth metals as it possibly can."

"So I'll look for a metallic asteroid that contains a few thousand tons of gold."

"I can't let you do it," I said.

He countered, "I can't let *you* do it."

We argued all through breakfast, then settled our differences in bed.

So I went back to my spacecraft and called the International Astronautical Authority to claim asteroid 94-12 for the People's Republic of China. Then I returned to Sam and we spent our last hours together. I had to start back for Earth; my supplies would barely see me through the return mission.

"What's going to happen to you, Sam?" I asked him, with tears in my eyes.

He grinned that lopsided, gap-toothed grin of his at me. "Don't worry about me, Song. I'll make out all right. Maybe I'll find an asteroid made of pure gold."

"Be serious."

He kissed me, gently, sweetly, and said, "You'd better get back to your own ship, kid, before I lose all my good intentions."

We were never destined to be together for long, I know. Sam was not the kind of man a woman could expect to hold onto for more than a fleeting encounter.

I returned to China with a heavy heart, although I was feted and honored and even invited to a special reception in the Forbidden City. Sam disappeared. No trace of him was found among the near-Earth asteroids. I feared he had died out there, alone, unloved, his dreams of wealth vanished forever. Because of me.

It was almost a year later that Sam electrified the world by claiming an asteroid in the Asteroid Belt, far beyond the orbit of Mars. He had flown his fusion-powered spacecraft farther than any human had gone before. Over the next ten months he claimed ten asteroids, including two that were rich in rare-Earth elements.

Fusion propulsion had changed the economics of space flight, as Sam knew—or rather, as Sam hoped—it would. Singlehandedly, he broke China's near-monopoly on rare-Earth metals, and made himself a sizeable fortune in the process.

I hated him for that. Yet I still loved him. And I still do, even though I never saw Sam Gunn again.

But I heard about him, from time to time. About the transportation company he founded for hauling ores from the Asteroid Belt to the

Earth-Moon system. And the entertainment city he eventually built on the Moon. And his lawsuit against the Pope. And . . .

But those are other stories.

((•((•((• 《◎》 •))•))•))

For more than fifty years, **Dr. Ben Bova** has been writing about humankind's future in space. His first novel, *The Star Conquerors*, was published in 1959. Since then he has written more than 130 futuristic novels and nonfiction books about science and high technology. His 2006 novel, *Titan*, won the John W. Campbell Memorial Award for best science fiction novel of the year. He received the Lifetime Achievement Award of the Arthur C. Clarke Foundation in 2005, "for fueling mankind's imagination regarding the wonders of outer space."

He was editor of *Analog Science Fiction* and *Omni* magazines and won six Hugo Awards for Best Professional Editor. Ben is also a past president of Science Fiction and Fantasy Writers of America (SFWA) and president emeritus of the National Space Society (NSS). His latest novel is *New Earth*.

*In the final leg of our journey together, the sister of a dead astronaut determines to honor his legacy and settle on Mars as a . . .*

# Tribute

## by Jack Skillingstead

NASA died two hundred and three nautical miles above the planet Mars. It died when Daniel Chen, the last surviving crew member of *Pilgrim 2*, ran out of breathable atmosphere. At that point, Chen pulled himself close to the nearest camera lens. Even though NASA was not sharing the feed, hackers inevitably populated it across the internet. Millions witnessed Chen's death. He was a beloved figure, a brilliant scientist as well as a twenty-first century Will Rogers dispensing wisdom and humor on the talk show and lecture circuit, in books and web TV specials.

Chen's face contorted in gasping agony, veins standing out on his forehead, eyes popping, red with burst blood vessels. He spoke three words on his dying breath: *A stupid waste*, after which he rolled away from the lens. Five dead astronauts drifted in fisheye perspective. It was the latest in a string of catastrophic failures.

*A stupid waste.*

Millions heard Chen, but his words were aimed at one person: his sister. Nevertheless, *a stupid waste* became a popular catchphrase, often heard in Congress and the Senate chamber. Most notably it was invoked by the senior senator from Ohio when he exhorted his colleagues to defund the ninety-year-old space agency, declaring it nothing more than a fiscal black hole into which a substantial portion of the nation's treasure (at that point less than one quarter of one percent of the budget) was annually dumped without any reasonable expectation of a return on the investment. In short, NASA itself had become *a stupid waste*.

The Agency continued to operate, if only on the margins of relevancy: paid consultants to private industry, managing historical archives. Even data retrieval for existing satellites and robotic missions was contracted out. For America, except in the private sector, manned space flight was as dead as the crew of *Pilgrim 2*.

*Karie.*

Getting there was the best part of the Nova Branson Orbital Resort. That's what Karie Chen thought. The orbital provided one-percenters with breathtaking views and nude zero-G "tumble bays," among other attractions. Everyone loved it, even the ninety-nine percent of the population who would never visit the thing. Maybe they enjoyed the idea of movie stars nude free-falling against the real stars.

Karie rode a Nova Branson shuttle launched from a facility in the middle of Ohio farm country. The senior Senator deemed the commercial space port a great boon to the state economy and an invaluable asset to the ever expanding space tourism industry: in short, the exact dead opposite of *a stupid waste*. It was all of that, Karie supposed, but for her it was mostly a great ride. From inside the launch facility she couldn't see the giant advertising displays that placarded the perimeter fence. Nike, Wal-Mart, Time Warner Direct Holo Vision, Amazon's Everything Experience—whoever had the money. Rocket launches still drew the Earth-bound. They paid for bleacher seats and bought cheap souvenir trinkets mass-produced in China— the last country on Earth with an active manned space program not driven by commercial interests.

Three million pounds of thrust lifted Karie and half a dozen millionaires into a cornflower blue sky. The roar scattered grazing cows in surrounding fields. Three minutes in, the boosters kicked them past seventeen thousand miles per hour, crushing Karie into her seat, flattening her eyeballs—*the price of paradise*, according to Nova Branson's literature. Karie's once-shattered and badly healed knee throbbed in perfect agony. It didn't matter. Lips skinned back in a fierce grin, she inhabited the pure joy of vertical acceleration. It had been too long.

※    ※    ※

After hard dock everyone unstrapped. Released from gravity, movers and shakers became floaters and drifters. Karie was a stranger among them. Aside from cordial greetings back at the launch facility and a couple of don't-you-look-familiar glances, the other passengers had mostly ignored her—the expected tribalism of the rich. The chip on Karie's shoulder turned it into classism—that's what Danny would have said. But then, Danny had gotten along with everyone.

Last to leave the shuttle, she pulled herself through the tunnel into Nova Branson's visitor processing bay. A resort agent in a pale green jumpsuit greeted her with a winning smile. "Welcome to Nova Branson Orbital."

"Thanks."

The agent accepted Karie's pass card and performed the required retinal identity verification. She'd already gotten the hell verified out of her before lift-off.

"You're all checked in," the agent said.

"What a relief."

"I'm sorry?"

"Never mind. Look, I thought somebody was going to meet me."

"Would you like to talk to customer service?"

"Naw. I think I'll have a look around."

Karie pushed off—and almost butted heads with a man gliding recklessly in by the same passage. "Hey—" The man caught her, which changed both of their trajectories. Karie banged her knee on the bulkhead, yelped, bit her lip hard enough to break the skin. A tiny crimson drop drifted by her face.

"Sorry about that," the man said. "I'm Jonah Brennerman. Alistair's my father. Are you all right?"

Jonah offered his hand and Karie shook it. He was about forty years old, ten years her junior. He had one of those man-boy faces.

"I'm fine. Can I have my hand back?"

"Of course. Father's waiting. I'll take you there. Afterwards, meet me in the rotation lounge. The spin maintains a one-third Earth gravity simulation. Called Forward View. Ask anybody how to find it. You'll love Nova Branson, at least that's what Dad is hoping."

Jonah pushed into the passage. She followed him to what he called the conference room.

"Word of advice? Let Dad do the talking."

"Sure."

"He likes to be in charge, is all I'm saying. If you want this to happen as much as I do, you need to be ready to compromise."

"Got it."

Jonah smiled. "Good luck. See you at Forward View. I can't wait to get this thing started."

Hand straps festooned the padded walls. The northern hemisphere of Earth appeared in a circular view port.

"Hello?" Karie said.

A holographic projector flickered on. A man, aged sixty, appeared. Athletically fit, virile streaks of gray. In reality, the head of Nova Branson Corporation was pushing ninety and had been out of view for decades. Karie checked her temper. A little seeped out anyway.

"Mr. Brennerman, you insisted on a face-to-face meeting."

"And here we are."

"Actually, here *I* am."

"Alas, my physical limitations preclude me from space travel. But I wanted you to enjoy my orbital firsthand, encourage a change in perspective.

"I've been in space before."

"Perspective in the sense of attitude, Ms. Chen."

Karie tried to make her smile look natural. She was here for something only a man like Alistair Brennerman could afford to give. "Of course I'm grateful. Getting into space isn't easy these days—not without a funded mission."

The projection wobbled. For a moment Brennerman's voice fell out of sync with his lips. "Tell me why, exactly, you want to go to Mars."

"To fix what my brother helped break."

"A morbid contest of sibling rivalry?"

"It has nothing to do with sibling rivalry. The *Pilgrim 1* habitat is still on the surface, waiting for someone to unpack it. The crew of *Pilgrim 2* is dead, but that shouldn't invalidate the mission goal: a self-sustaining beachhead on Mars. Mr. Brennerman, America is squandering its potential by playing around in Earth orbit. Until the Chinese last year, no one had even stepped foot on the Moon since 1972—eighty years, for God's sake."

"Nova Branson is not America."

"It is, actually. Along with every other global corporation with roots in the United States. You run *everything*. I'm just asking you to invest in the pioneering spirit that used to define us. You can push the frontier." She was talking too much. Worse, she sounded like a used-car salesman. Karie's pitch lacked the sincerity she genuinely felt.

She tried again: "Listen. After the *Pilgrim* disaster and congressional defunding, NASA mothballed *Pilgrim 3* and *4*. But they are viable spacecraft. You could get one at a fire-sale price and cut expenses further by reducing the crew."

"Are you quite sure you'd be up to the rigors, Ms. Chen, in light of your injury and, excuse me, your age?"

"I'm perfectly fit for the mission."

"Of course. And Jonah insists on you. I think he's star-struck by your celebrity. Hero of the *Phoenix* debacle."

"Jonah? I don't understand."

The holo wobbled out of sync again. "You are not in the least bit impressed by my resort, are you?"

Karie sighed. "It's an impressive technological achievement."

"But?"

"But it doesn't accomplish anything." Okay, Karie thought, stop talking. "Earth orbit used to be the frontier. You don't even do any science here. We have to keep pushing outward."

"Yes, as I've often heard you say. I think you must wake each morning with the words already on your lips. Have you ever, for a moment even, considered you might be mistaken? Because you're wrong about the frontier. This is the greatest business frontier in history."

"Not my field."

"Can you conceive of any circumstance under which you might modify your obvious disdain for Nova Branson and the profitable future of orbital recreation?"

"I'm not disdainful. I'm *impatient*." Karie had drifted too close to Brennerman's holo. Her shoulder interrupted the projection, fracturing organized light. She looped her wrist into a hand strap, pulled back, and the holo resumed its integrity.

"For a round-trip ticket to Mars," Brennerman said, "will you be capable of recanting your impatience?"

"Recanting how?"

"Renounce your current and often-stated opinion about orbitals. Lend your unqualified endorsement of orbital recreation, Nova Branson in particular. Participate in a public campaign which will include interviews, public forums, ghost-written books, and so on."

Karie stared. "I thought not," the holo said.

"Mr. Brennerman—"

"My son wishes to go to Mars. He wishes to go to Mars with the hero of the *Phoenix*. He admires you. Which suggests a lack of admiration for his own inheritance, since you and I are very much at odds. So this is my price for a trip to Mars. You vigorously and publicly embrace what I've accomplished, and intend to go on accomplishing, with Nova Branson. Do so and you may orbit the Red Planet as a tribute to your brother. That's how you will put it. A tribute to your brother. And that will be the end of it. If the Chinese want Mars, let them have it."

Karie was quiet, then said, "You know what it is, Mr. Brennerman?"

"Eh?"

"This kind of wasteful development of Earth orbit. It's like the prairie towns that sprang up after the frontier moved west. Those towns were mostly saloons and bordellos, places to get drunk and get laid while pretending you were in the midst of something wild. The difference between then and now is the wealth of the customers."

"Nova Branson has been in business a very long time, Ms. Chen. My grandfather started it, my father developed it, and I have been a loyal steward of the legacy. We did not succeed by indulging romantic notions such as your 'pushing the frontier' mantra."

"So you brought me up here just to slap me back down."

The Brennerman projection smiled. "I'll tell Jonah you weren't interested."

She worked the lecture circuit. People still paid to hear her talk about *Phoenix*. She had been in command. Mission: to rendezvous with a robotic vehicle that had successfully captured a small asteroid and established itself in lunar orbit. One of *Phoenix*'s fuel cells ruptured. The explosion crippled the ship and killed Karie's pilot. Despite her shattered knee, Karie babied the spacecraft back to Earth, saving herself and the three scientists on board. Her knee never healed properly. NASA declared her unfit to fly, even as they praised her heroism. That was ten years ago. *Pilgrim 2* should have been *Karie's* mission. Instead they selected Danny, the public relations star with no flying experience, two fully functioning knees, and a popular following in the millions. Privately, Danny told Karie he was glad she was grounded. Watching her almost die on *Phoenix* had been unbearable. When he saw the hurt look on her face, he immediately took it back. "Hey, I didn't mean it that way." But it stung. Sibling rivalry, Alistair had suggested. But it wasn't that simple.

Now, during a Q & A session at Wyoming State University, an old guy in the second row stood up and the usher handed him the microphone. Karie pegged him right away. Leather jacket, cap with "US NAVY Ret." blazoned across it: aging space buff. Mostly that's what she got these days.

"I have a comment and a question," he said. "The comment is: We need NASA back. The *real* NASA!" Applause rippled through an audience who wouldn't be there if they weren't already in the same nostalgia camp. They always wanted to hear about Karie's heroic save of the stranded *Phoenix* scientists. She complied, then switched to her message about the future of exploration. At that point she usually took a few jabs at Nova Branson, among others. Tonight she skipped the jabs. Karie had been thinking a lot since her return from the orbital resort.

"And the question is," the old space buff continued, "how do we *get* it back?"

More applause. Karie's anger surged—more at herself than anyone else. The applause wound down. She raised the microphone. "NASA isn't coming back." Microphone feedback whined through the hall. Karie winced, held the mic farther from her lips. "The agency that took us to the moon is dead. You should get over the idea that NASA can— or needs to—happen again. Because it won't." She paused and let them grumble. "And we don't need it to come back. The future of manned space flight exists right now, the technology, the infrastructure. The privatization of space flight is here. What our entrepreneurs lack is a *vision* without dollar signs."

She talked a while longer, departing from her usual lecture notes, but she had lost some of the audience. People began standing, gathering their coats. Later, when she stepped out into the evening air, Jonah Brennerman was waiting for her.

"Mr. Brennerman."

"Can we talk?"

"Go ahead."

"I meant over dinner."

"I'm headed straight to the airport to catch the red-eye."

"Then let me drive you. You stood me up, you know." He smiled.

"On the orbital? After talking to your father there didn't seem to be any point."

"Let me try to convince you otherwise. Please."

She hesitated then said, "The university provided a driver. I'll have to tell her."

In the backseat of the limo, Jonah offered her a drink.

"No, thanks."

"My father was pushing you."

"Yeah, I got that."

"You understand, it's about me. You represent a threat."

"A threat! He's Alistair Brennerman. I can barely fill a lecture hall."

"That's not the point. I'm in your camp. I believe we need to extend the frontier. Dad interprets that as almost traitorous. We've locked horns on this since I was a kid. Now he's old and he wants to groom me to take over Nova Branson. The corporation means everything to him. Instead, I want to fly to Mars with you."

"I'm a bad influence."

Jonah laughed. "In his eyes, absolutely."

"So why are you here?"

"This is the good part. Dad's changed his mind, or I changed it for him, or I'm not even sure what." Frowning, Jonah scratched his head. "To be honest, I'm a little baffled myself."

"Wait a minute. He's agreed to fund the mission, his *tribute* mission?"

"Yes, provided I can persuade you to his terms."

"Let me save you the trouble of trying: you can't."

"Hear me out. He's agreed to back off on the more extreme elements. No ghost-written paeans to orbital resorts, no public lectures recanting your position. We're talking about a one-time public statement of support, a willingness to play nice with the press, and passive participation in a program of advertising revenue. And, Karie, he's agreed to a landing, not just a bullshit tribute orbit."

Karie held back her elation. A Mars landing! A real chance at exploration. "I can live with those terms. But why is he doing this? I don't get it."

"I pledged my loyalty to the status quo, promised when I took over I would adhere absolutely to Dad's vision, without, as he put it, romantic deviations. Look, our relationship has always been rocky." His face made an ugly grimace, an unintended glimpse of just how hard "rocky" had been. "Now time's running out. He wants us to reconcile, he wants his legacy carried forward. We're compromising around Mars."

"He didn't strike me as the compromising type."

"Maybe in this case we're both wrong about him."

"Maybe. Are you really willing to come back and spend the rest of your life pampering rich tourists?"

"Of course not."

Karie gave him a skeptical look. "But Alistair believes you?"

"He believed me after I signed a legal document binding me to the terms." Jonah poured himself a scotch. "Of course, there's no such thing as a contract that can't be broken."

The driver spoke. "Coming into the airport now, sir."

"There's something off about all this," Karie said.

"The point is," Jonah said, "do you want to go to Mars or not?"

Seventeen months later, at a prelaunch photo op, Karie turned to Jonah and said, "We look like NASCAR drivers."

"*You* look great," Jonah said.

Joining them were James Krueger and Treva Hilgar, NASA-trained astronauts and early defecters to Nova Branson. They wanted to fly. Krueger was six feet of lean muscle mass and smiling optimism. Hilgar was compact, emotionally self-contained, and fiercely competent. She wore a small gold cross around her neck. Karie was happy to have them along. All their flight suits were emblazoned with advertising patches. Especially annoying was the wearable GIF touting Nova Branson Orbital Resort, winking and shifting like Vegas casino signage.

"Put on your smile," Krueger said. "We're going to Mars."

Later, riding the elevator up the gantry, Karie said, "The last few months, it's like launching a circus, not an interplanetary mission."

"Apollo wasn't about exploration, either."

"I know. It was about beating the Russians."

"But exploration was a byproduct of that competition. And this mission isn't about the NASCAR suits or your endorsement. So cheer up."

Jonah laughed. "I can't believe you two are even debating about something that's already a done deal. Enjoy yourselves, for God's sake."

Treva Hilgar, as always, kept her thoughts to herself and watched the booster slip by.

Mars rolled out beneath them. After seven months in space, it was time. Karie opened the hatch between the main body of *Pilgrim 3* and the landing module attached to its belly. "Go ahead, Jonah," she said.

Smiling, bearded, excited, Jonah moved toward the hatch. They had really done it. In a few hours, they would be examining the *Pilgrim 1* habitat, reporting on its readiness for future missions to occupy. If there ever *were* any future missions. Karie wished what they were doing felt more like a beginning and less like a swan song—or, worse, a *tribute*.

She followed Jonah into the LM. Krueger had already begun the power-up procedures. Treva would remain in orbit.

"Here we go, huh?" Jonah said.

"Here we go."

They were all grinning like kids.

Karie separated the LM from the main body of *Pilgrim 3*. This is where trouble had struck her brother's mission. *Pilgrim 2*'s separation maneuver had failed, trapping the entire crew in a landing module that couldn't land. *Pilgrim 3*'s separation was flawless. A short burn took them to the edge of the atmosphere. Their speed increased exponentially. Seven miles up, the supersonic chute deployed. Karie and Jim Krueger watched their instruments. A mile from touchdown, the chute separated and the retro rockets fired. Then it began to go wrong. The retros fired too hot, sapping fuel reserves. Still thousands of feet above the surface, the LM doggedly hovered.

"Damn it," Karie said. "Switch me to full manual."

"I'm on it."

Seconds ticked by, then minutes.

"Jim?"

"Problem. Hold on."

Karie watched the fuel gauges drop. They were already depleted below what was necessary to achieve orbit and rendezvous. Being marooned a given, soon they wouldn't be able to land at all.

"Jim, come on."

"*There*. The damn thing wouldn't let go."

Karie took them down, radically angling the descent, going for a hard landing while she could still control it. But it was too late. Sixty feet above the surface the fuel gauges flashed red, the engines quit, and they dropped like a stone.

"Brace!"

The desert plain came up like a wall and swatted them.

Karie dragged Jonah from the wreckage. Her knee collapsed and she fell over, cursing. The landing module loomed against the butterscotch sky, a mangle of abstract junk. Krueger's severed arm hung from a gash in the bulkhead. There was no need to pull him out. Adrenaline, fear and pain routed Karie's rational response. Gasping, she fumbled at her helmet. Then made herself stop. The readouts on her sleeve display indicated all was in order. She bore down, forcing calm, taking deep, slow breaths, then put her attention on Jonah. Behind his faceplate, his eyes fluttered. Blood crept from his hairline.

"Jonah."

He groaned.

She shook him. "Jonah, can you stand?"

"I don't know."

"You're going to stand."

"I'm sorry," he said.

"Don't be sorry, just stand up. If I can do it, you can do it."

They both stood up, leaning on each other. A wave of dizziness swelled through Karie. She swayed, almost fainted, but held on. The *Pilgrim 1* habitat was a mile away. Packed inside was everything they needed to survive—if they could reach it.

Except for the lighter gravity, Karie would never have made it. By the time they came upon the habitat, her knee was screaming and her body was drenched in sweat. Jonah, who had recovered quickly, all but carried her the last hundred yards. The habitat was roughly the size of a shipping container. They passed through the airlock, initiated life support. Kari, stripped off her helmet and gloves. She powered up the communications rig and sent a message to *Pilgrim 3*. Treva did not reply. She tried again. Still no response.

"What's wrong with that thing?" Jonah said.

"I don't know."

"Does Treva even know we crashed?"

"She tracked our descent. She knows."

Karie slipped the headphones on and tried again.

"Anything?"

"Quiet."

Karie thought she heard something—a voice, so faint and submerged in static she couldn't be sure it was real. She adjusted the radio, fine tuning, but the voice was gone.

"What?" Jonah said.

"I thought I heard a voice."

"What did she say?"

"I don't know. I'm not even sure it *was* a voice."

"Let me." Jonah took the headphones and began broadcasting, listening intently for a reply, broadcasting again. Then his expression changed. He closed his eyes, appearing almost in pain as he listened. After a while, looking disappointed, he removed the headphones. "I thought I heard something."

For the next hour they traded off on the radio, trying to contact both Treva in orbit and Mission Operations back on Earth, sometimes with the headphones on, sometimes allowing the wash of hopeless static to pour out of the speakers.

"We both heard the voice," Jonah said.

"We heard something." Karie's mind was moving off the radio. There was so much to do.


Day three.


A dust storm came howling out of the desert. They huddled inside the habitat. Dust and grit hissed against the shell. Karie had been working on a protective shield for the life support unit's loader. Attached to the outside of *Pilgrim 2*, the loader shipped Martian soil into a chamber, where it was heated and the evaporated water captured. LS apparatus then divided the water into hydrogen and oxygen, adding nitrogen directly from the atmosphere. It produced drinking water and breathable air and was designed to support five people. But the equipment proved balky, in need of constant attention. And then the dust storm drove them back inside before she could fix the shielding in place. What would be left after the storm? Feeling her optimism fray, Karie said, "I'm beginning to think people like your father are right."

Jonah scooped fruit paste out of a ration cup and sucked the spoon clean. "Dad's always right about everything. Just ask him."

"*Phoenix* was a disaster—my pilot killed, the mission aborted. *Pilgrim 2* up there right now with five dead, including my brother. And now Jim Krueger. You want to talk about a stupid waste, there it is."

"Karie."

"You know, when Danny said that stupid waste thing, he was talking directly to me. He was saying, I know you're going to try to find a way to come out here. Don't do it."

"Well, you did it anyway."

They stood by the loader. Dust and grit had wind-blasted through the mechanism, tearing rubber seals, clogging the armatures and servos.

"We're going to have to break it down, clean everything, replace the seals, and put it together again. Otherwise we can manually ship the soil, which is more labor than we want." Karie's knee throbbed. She ignored it. In the direction of the crashed landing module, something moved. She paused, holding her wrench. A dust devil tracked across the desert, like a fleeing ghost.

Day nine.

By now Treva had left orbit, headed back to Earth. Karie had tried everything she could think of to make the radio work, to no avail. There didn't seem to be anything *wrong* with it. Possibly their outgoing messages were being heard. There was simply no way to tell. She turned to the hydroponics and other matters demanding attention. Jonah, meanwhile, spent too much time monitoring the useless radio. One morning he shouted, "There's somebody! I heard somebody."

Karie, already suited up, was about to enter the airlock. Dust accumulated on the solar panel array if they didn't keep it wiped off. "Are you sure?"

"Yes, yes. I was broadcasting to Earth, and then there was a voice. I couldn't hear what it said, but it was real. I heard it. This time I'm positive."

Karie switched to speaker. She cleared her throat and spoke into the microphone, "*Pilgrim 1* habitat, this is *Pilgrim 1* habitat. Please respond."

Jonah leaned in eagerly.

"Relax," Karie said. They both knew it would be at least twenty-eight minutes before they received a reply. She was about to stand up when, faintly, a voice spoke through the static. Karie tweaked the noise reduction filter. The voice became slightly clearer. *Pilgrim 1 Habitat, this is Pilgrim 1 habitat. Please respond. . .*

An echo.

Like calling into the mouth of a deep, black, empty cave. Jonah looked stricken. After that, he rarely wasted time with the radio.


Day seventy.


Karie lay on her thin mattress. Many nights she and Jonah shared a bunk, but Karie had been sleeping poorly for weeks and wanted her own space tonight. An amber panel near the airlock provided minimal illumination. Tired as she was, she couldn't let go, her mind constantly worrying at the myriad of tasks. The hydroponics required constant attention. In nightmares, Karie awakened to discover the plants withered and dead. In reality the radishes, lettuce, and green onions were thriving under carefully controlled conditions. Still, they were a long way from a bioregenerative life support system.

From where he lay in his own bunk, Jonah said: "We're never leaving this planet."

"What are you talking about?"

"My father's not sending a rescue ship."

"And you know this how?"

"Somebody reprogrammed the LM computer. Reprogrammed it to burn all our fuel, making sure we'd crash. If Jim hadn't managed to override it and if you hadn't been at the controls, we would have all died."

"I didn't exactly execute a soft landing."

"We survived, didn't we?"

"Two of us did."

"Dad knew I would find a way to wiggle out of the agreement I signed. I thought it was odd when he suddenly conceded the point and agreed to a landing. I should have trusted my instincts, but I wanted this so bad."

"What are you saying?"

"Dad saw an opportunity, and he seized it. Think of it. Yet another fatal disaster confirms that manned spaceflight pushing the frontier is too dangerous and pointless. A stupid waste, right?"

"Jonah, it's his corporation. He didn't have to *kill* you to keep you from taking control after his death."

"That's exactly what he had to do." Jonah's voice contained bitterness like acid. "My ascension was out of his hands. *Grandfather* liked me. It was in his will that the family line not be broken. Barring death or some kind of certifiable mental derangement, I was next to take charge of Nova Branson. Period. Dad had to sign off on that before the reins of power passed into his hands."

"You're being a little paranoid."

"He's capable of anything when it comes to getting his way." Jonah shook his head. "I'm a fool. Look. The retros fail, then the communications fail. That's pretty coincidental, isn't it? You've said yourself there's nothing wrong with the radio. That means it has to be the satellite relays. Guess who NASA contracted with to upgrade and facilitate satellite data retrieval? Nova Branson has held those contracts for over a decade. They can facilitate data retrieval from Mars satellites—or subvert it, or filter out what they don't want seen. We're dead, Karie, as far as anyone back home knows. Ship crashed, no communication from possible survivors. Done. It's not paranoia. It's brilliant. Cold-blooded but brilliant. You see it now, don't you?"

"Jonah, I stopped counting on rescue as soon as we established the impossibility of communication."

Jonah was quiet for a minute. "In the old days, didn't the rovers use high-gain microwave transmissions for direct-to-Earth communication?"

"Find a rover and cannibalize it? Forget it."

"Why?"

"Because we have no idea where any of them are, and we're not equipped to go searching."

"*Damn* it."

"There's another possibility. The landing module. The locator beacon, it transmits directly on high frequency."

"Can we adapt *that* antenna?"

"No. But we can move the beacon."

"How does that help?"

"All it does now is identify the crash site. Well, crash sites don't move."

"But survivors can move the beacon! We have to go get this thing tomorrow."

"Jonah, I'm exhausted. We'll talk about it in the morning, okay? Two miles on my knee is going to be a stretch, even if I'm rested."

"I'll go alone."

"Don't. It's too dangerous to separate. I really have to sleep now, okay? We can figure out a plan in the morning."

Karie got up and found her way to the head. With the door shut, she turned on the light, opened the medicine kit, and took a couple of sleeping pills. God bless NASA for deciding the pilgrims might need artificially orchestrated rest.

She woke up groggy, her head like something stuffed with wet cotton. Dust and grit hissed against the habitat's shell. Karie checked her chronometer. It had been more than ten hours since she took the sleeping pills. Jesus. Dimly, she remembered Jonah shaking her, trying to wake her up. She had brushed him off, rolling onto her side. Now she reached for the lights. They came on in sections, flickering at first. Jonah was gone.

She checked the outside conditions. Wind speed was variable, between twenty and thirty knots, the direction changeable. She tried to raise Jonah on his helmet com but the storm shredded the signal. She needed line-of-sight. After a couple of hours, the dust storm began to subside. Jonah was running out of time. Karie loaded up with extra oxygen and headed out.

She came to the wreckage of the LM. Her knee hurt but it was tolerable. The return hike would be worse. She had tried to raise Jonah repeatedly on the helmet com, but no luck.

She climbed into the LM. Krueger's body lay frozen in place, attached at the ragged shoulder to a great dark sheen of frozen blood. His face stared at the twisted bulkhead, unmarred, fixed in a blank expression. Karie observed no inkling of the living man. Krueger's body was like another piece of the inanimate wreckage.

A tool bag from the habitat sat near a partially removed floor panel. Jonah, going after the damn transponder. Karie picked up the pry bar and ratcheting wrench. The crash had twisted the deck out of alignment. She worked on it for a half hour, finally wrenching the panel aside. The transponder, the size of a shoebox, appeared intact. She detached it from its nest of cables and braces, stowed it in the tool bag, and started back.

The wind buffeted her. Dust churned all around. The bag was heavy. She shifted it from shoulder to shoulder. Her knee and back hurt. She stopped at the midway point and sat on the gritty hardpan, her head down. Jonah was out here. By now his oxygen was depleted and he had suffocated, another piece of human wreckage. Another catastrophic failure.

She got up and went on. By the time the habitat came into view, Karie could barely walk. How would she do this, how would she go on alone, day after day, week after week, year after year? The arid future lay before her. She staggered forward. Inside the airlock she closed the outer door, equalized the pressure, entered the habitat—and found Jonah preparing dinner.

"I was getting worried about you," he said.

"Jonah."

"What's wrong—hey, is that the transponder?"

"What happened to you?"

"Dust storm caught me. I tried to make it back before it got bad, but it got bad too fast. Wound up digging in behind a hillock. After the storm backed off, I couldn't figure out where I was for a while. Beyond stupid. My air was pretty low. When I finally got here you were gone.

At that point it seemed dumb to go out again, so I've been waiting. Are you sure you're all right?"

"I'm fine. I'm just glad you're here. I'm so glad."


Day five hundred.


Karie woke before Jonah. She turned on a section of light panels, and Jonah's face emerged out of the dark beside her. He had taken to trimming his beard, after first threatening to shave it off altogether. She was glad he hadn't done that. She liked the beard, the way it transformed his man-boy features. In repose, Jonah looked like someone Karie might even love. She placed her hand on his bare shoulder and shook him gently.

"Jonah."

His eyes opened. "Hey."

"It's time," she said.

"All right."

They suited up.

The dawn was so cold Karie could feel it even through the insulating coils of her suit. They hiked away from the habitat, Karie limping, and climbed to the top of the ridge. Their feet skidded in the loose scree. Karie had to hold on to Jonah's arm until they reached the top.

"Okay," he said, "where do we look?"

She pointed to the horizon, where the sky had turned the color of burnished steel. "There. About thirty degrees above the plain,"

They waited. After a while Karie had to sit down. He helped her and then joined her, and they leaned against each other. They had both lost weight, and they tired too easily, but almost two years in, they were still alive—and not merely surviving. The habitat was designed for expansion. They had deployed the diggers, which tunneled out from *Pilgrim 1*, allowing them to construct a long underground "greenhouse," where they planted and nurtured a greater variety of vegetables and fruits. They still supplemented their diets with the supplies brought from Earth, but they were far less dependent than they had been in the beginning. The habitat was nearly a closed system, self-sustaining. Nearly. And if they had to get there, Karie was optimistic that they would. Jonah, an amateur geologist, was even doing some science. *Pilgrim 1* was a viable foothold. Now they were looking at the dawn sky. When it happened, it was so brief they almost missed it: A brilliant flash described an arc—and then *Pilgrim 2* was gone.

"Goodbye, Danny."

"You okay?"

"Yeah."

"Hey, Karie? You're my favorite Martian."

She laughed. "So we're Martians?"

"We both know my father isn't sending a rescue ship."

"It doesn't have to be Alistair, you know."

"Sure. Someday there'll be a knock on the door."

"What would happen if everyone thought you were dead and then you weren't?"

"I don't follow."

"Nova Branson is still your birthright. You told me Alistair *can't* disown you corporately, not according to the terms of your grandfather's will. I believe it will be worth it to someone to come up here looking for you. You know, there's gold in them Martian hills. Maybe that transponder trick worked."

"Karie, I wouldn't count on it. Hey, we're doing all right, aren't we? I mean as Martians."

They helped each other back to their feet.

"We're doing great," Karie said. "Come on, let's go home."

(((((((( ((◎)) )))))))

In 2001, **Jack Skillingstead** won Stephen King's ON WRITING contest. Not long afterward, Jack began selling regularly to major science fiction and fantasy markets. To date he has published more than thirty stories in various magazines, Year's Best volumes, and original anthologies. Much of his short work has been collected in *Are You There And Other Stories* (Golden Gryphon Press, 2009 and reprinted 2014 by Fairwood Press). Jack's novel, *Life On The Preservation* (Solaris 2013), was a finalist for the Philip K. Dick Award. He has also been a finalist for the Theodore Sturgeon Award. Jack lives in Seattle with his wife, writer Nancy Kress.

# EDITOR'S BIOGRAPHY

Bryan Thomas Schmidt is an author and Hugo-nominated editor of adult and children's science fiction and fantasy novels and anthologies. His debut novel, *The Worker Prince*, received Honorable Mention on Barnes & Noble's Year's Best Science Fiction Releases of 2011, and was followed by two sequels. As editor, his anthologies include *Shattered Shields* (Baen, 2014), *Beyond The Sun* (Fairwood, 2013), *Raygun Chronicles* (Every Day Publishing, 2013) and *Space Battles* (Flying Pen Press, 2012) with two more forthcoming from Baen Books and St. Martin's Griffin in 2015 and 2016. He hosts *Science Fiction and Fantasy Writer's Chat* the first Wednesday of every month at 9 P.M. ET on Twitter under the hashtag #sffwrtcht and is a frequent guest and panelist at World Cons and other conventions. His website is *www.bryanthomasschmidt.net* and his Twitter handles is @BryanThomasS.

# ACKNOWLEDGEMENTS

Thanks to all the writers for trusting me with their work, even those whose work doesn't appear in these pages. All of their contributions helped shape this anthology into the book it is—one I'm very proud of.

Thanks as always to Toni Weisskopf, Tony Daniel, and the Baen Family for giving me yet another opportunity.

Thanks to Beth Morris Tanner and Alex Shvartsman for extra eyes when they were sorely needed.

To my parents, Ramon and Glenda, and my editing partner and best friend, Valerie Hatfield, for support, encouragement, and understanding.

To Louie and Amelie, my babies, for unconditional love and snuggling.

And to God for making me a Creator in His image and opening doors for me to create.